D0880838

JUNGSOON

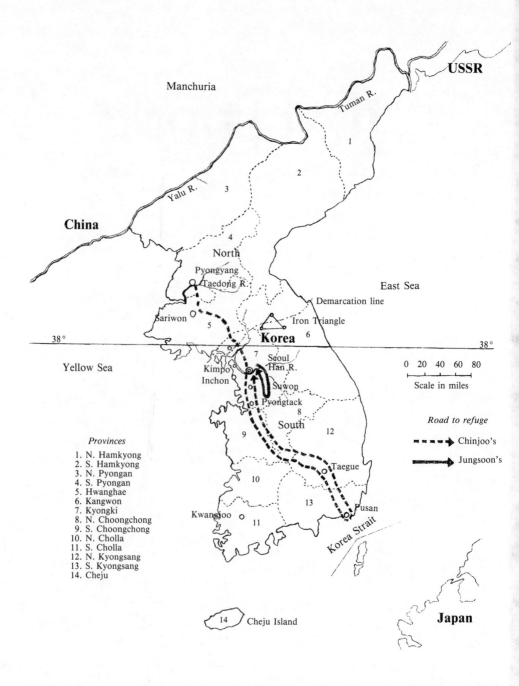

Manchuria

USSR

Tuman R.

1

2

Yalu R.

3

China

4

North

Pyongyang

Taedong R.

East Sea

Sariwon

5

38°

Demarcation line

Iron Triangle

Korea

6

38°

Yellow Sea

Seoul

Han R.

Kimpo

Inchon

Suwon

Pyongtack

8

South

12

Scale in miles

0 20 40 60 80

9

Road to refuge

Chinjoo's

Jungsoon's

Provinces

1. N. Hamkyong
2. S. Hamkyong
3. N. Pyongan
4. S. Pyongan
5. Hwanghae
6. Kangwon
7. Kyongki
8. N. Choongchong
9. S. Choongchong
10. N. Cholla
11. S. Cholla
12. N. Kyongsang
13. S. Kyongsang
14. Cheju

Taegue

10

13

Pusan

Kwangjoo

11

Korea Strait

14 Cheju Island

Japan

JUNGSOON

a novel

by

Myosik Park

M.P. Publications
Oxford, Ohio

The author is grateful to:

George Allen & Unwin (Publishers) Ltd., London, England, for the permission to reprint poems from POEMS FROM KOREA, compiled and translated by Peter H. Lee;

University of California Press for the permission to reprint poems from THE BAMBOO GROVE, edited and translated by Richard Rutt.

Library of Congress Catalog Card Number 84-90581

Printed in the United States of America

To my mother

To my husband

Acknowledgement

My sincere appreciation to:

Elizabeth Mills and Anne Long

and

Editor Robert A. Wilkin

without whose help and suggestions
the publication of this book would not have been possible.

Prologue

Legend first pierced the mists of Korean time in the 2300's B.C. Folklore credits Tangun, the son of a mythical divine being who had descended from heaven upon the Land of Morning Calm, with founding Korean civilization. A thousand years or so later, the peninsula received its first injection of Chinese culture when Kija, an exile from the sprawling giant to the north, arrived with some five-thousand followers.

Korea's recorded history began in 57 B.C. with the Period of Three Kingdoms: Koguryo, Paekche, and Silla, which dominated Southern Manchuria down to the tip of the peninsula. Buddhism and Confucianism were introduced as well as other facets of Chinese culture.

In 668 A.D., the southern nation, Silla, unified all three kingdoms with the help of Tang China. The Silla dynasty brought about a cultural renaissance whose remnants can still be seen around Kyongju, capital city of the ancient Kingdom.

In 918, Koryo replaced weakened Silla. The Western term "Korea" was adopted from the name of this dynasty. Koryo was continuously harassed by northern invaders. In the 1200's, the Mongol hoards of Genghis Khan and Kublai Khan invaded the capital city of Koryo demanding the overlordship of the Mongol Khan. After a peace treaty, Mongols eventually withdrew but continued to influence the Korean court. Despite these tumultuous times Koryo made high cultural accomplishments: civil examination system started; schools were established for education; Buddhist-inspired art and pottery flourished.

With a resurgence of nationalism in 1392, Yi Song-gye founded a ruling family which controlled Korea for hundreds of years before the coming of the Japanese. Known as the Yi dynasty, this new age spawned brilliant cultural advances leading to many scientific and technical inventions and cultural innovations. The invention of the first movable type which anticipated Gutenberg by a half century and the development of the Korean alphabet are examples. Jungsoon's mother-in-law haughtily traced her husband's ancestry back through time to a place of importance during the Yi dynasty. His was a family named Yoon, descendants of the Lord of Haepyong and holders of vast tracts of land.

In 1592, the established order was again shattered. Enter the Japanese. Hideyoshi, a cruel regent leading a sizable army, landed at Pusan in southern Korea to ultimately invade China. For six years, allied Korean and Chinese forces battled across the hills and lowlands and drove the invaders out. The final Japanese defeat was possible due to the great national hero, Adm. Yi Sun-sin, who devised ironclad warships and wiped out the enemy fleet in Chinhae bay. For the next three-hundred years, no foreigners were welcome. Korea adopted an isolation policy and was known as the Hermit Kingdom.

Eventually, the moat was bridged. Japan, in 1876, forced Korea to open several ports to trade. The United States worked out a commercial treaty with the government of Korea in 1892. Other nations quickly followed suit. When China lost a war to Japan in 1895, Japanese influence increased in Korea. By defeating Russia in the Russo-Japanese War of 1904-1905, which ended in the Treaty of Portsmouth, Japan gained control of Korea's foreign affairs. Annexing Korea in 1910, Japan developed a pro-Japanese economy throughout the peninsula. And, in 1917, the family of Jungsoon's father-in-law lost most of its land holdings to the Japanese.

1919 marked a major political upheaval. The March 1 Independence Movement, a peaceful event, spread rapidly over the nation. But after two months, the Japanese ruthlessly cracked down. Thousands of unarmed civilians were killed, wounded, imprisoned and tortured.

By 1942, Japan had tightened its grip over the land by abolishing Korean newspapers, banning the Korean language and rationing grain. It was at this juncture that Jungsoon, a daughter of a fine family, carried on her duty as a housewife and a daughter-in-law in a household where four generations lived together.

Contents

CHARACTERS

JUNGSOON's family (in the south)
Grandfather-in-law
Grandmother-in-law
Father-in-law
Mother-in-law
Daeyoung (Husband)
Chayoung (Brother-in-law)

Kangsup (First son)
Hyonsup (Second son)
Wonsup (Third son)
Jisup (Fourth son)

CHINJOO's family (in the north)
Mother-in-law
Kim Insoo (Husband)

Tongja (First daughter)
Kwangja (Second daughter)
Sunhee (Third daughter)

I. The trip

The land is no longer our own.
Does spring come just the same
to the stolen fields?
On the narrow path between the rice fields
where blue sky and green fields meet and touch,
winds whisper to me, urging me forward.
A lark trills in the clouds
like a young girl singing behind the hedge.
O ripening barley fields, your long hair
is heavy after the night's rain.

Yi Sang-hwa [1900-1943]

Fall 1942. Southern Korea.

All morning they had traveled through the solitary rural area. Dawn still lingered between the overcast sky and the bare brown earth. The small village they had just passed was trailing far behind, and was soon engulfed by the mountain ridge as they trod down the wet hill. In about two miles, the winding path would lead them to a road on which clustered a handful of concrete buildings. Oh Jungsoon turned around and called to her son.

"Let's hurry. We are almost there!"

Nine-year-old Hyonsup glanced at his mother's swollen tummy, came running and followed close at her heels.

Her dark hair parted in the middle was meticulously combed into a chignon. Her pleated, long skirt flowed down to the tips of her turquoise rubber shoes. Though her middle was bloated and heavy, the tall, graceful woman moved lithely along the winding path with a step bespeaking ancestral gentrice.

Harvest season was over. Stubbled paddy-fields, lay at the foot of the mountains, deserted and mute. "Have a safe trip." Her brother, his face weather-beaten and more haggard than ever, had wished her luck.

As she saw the contour of a country railroad depot hulking behind the cluster of buildings, her heart throbbed. Inside the station, a sparse

11

crowd formed a straggling line at the boarding gate.

"One and a half for Seoul, please." Jungsoon pushed a crumpled bill and some coins through the ticket window.

Mother and son moved to the boarding line and waited in silence. At last the gate opened and the line started to move forward. Clutching her bundles with one hand she handed over the tickets with the other. The young station man glanced at her as he punched the tickets.

"Thank you very much." She took the tickets back and rushed toward the platform beckoning to her son to hurry.

Soon the locomotive roared into the station dragging a dozen passenger cars behind. As the giant steel wheels came rolling past her, Jungsoon felt herself almost toppling over by the suction. A small group of people got off the train. She pushed her son ahead and lifted her weight up the high steps. Jungsoon scanned the interior for a seat for her son. It was packed. Many were standing in the aisle. Having released the bundles at the foot of an occupied seat, she brushed a hair strand back to its place motioning her son closer to her side.

As the train started with a loud whistle she quickly grabbed the back of the seat. The train began picking up speed, and the country station and the signal man were disappearing in the distance. A relaxing moment after the long, tiring walk from the farm. "Why don't you stay for lunch?" her sister-in-law had asked. Perhaps she should have. It might have lasted her until dinner and she would have saved a little more food for the family. But she had to leave before the Japanese soldiers came with a truck to collect the rice.

"Ma'am, have this seat here, please!" she heard a voice. It came from a man in the next seat who was looking at her round abdomen and at the little boy through the opening of the packed people.

"Oh, that's all right. This is just fine!" Jungsoon smiled shyly as she politely declined.

"Please. I've been sitting here all morning." The man stood up and came out of the seat making room for her to go through.

"Thank you." She accepted but wanted her son to take it. Hyonsup made a move toward the seat.

"Wait!" the man barred the boy and gently nudged the mother into the empty seat.

"Thank you." Jungsoon murmured as she helplessly sat down. The weight on her abdomen and knees were almost unbearable and it seemed even worse than when she was standing.

"You are a big boy, aren't you? You can stand right here with me, can't you?"

He was a young man, roughly her age but not as tall. He had a pair of impressive eyebrows. Thick, dark lines drawn distinctively parallel to his somewhat large eyes indicated a strong determination. Serene and kindly, his eyes smiled as he spoke to Jungsoon.

"It must be a very tiring trip for you, ma'am."

"Just a little, sir." Jungsoon blushed. It sounded like 'You look very tired.'

He beamed down on Hyonsup with a paternal smile.

"Still sleepy?"

Hyonsup lowered his eyes, embarrassed.

"Going to Seoul?"

"Yes, sir."

"So am I. You must be a school boy—first grade? Second grade?"

"Third."

"Third! My, my!" The man studied Jungsoon for a while, then turned to Hyonsup. "I will tell you what. You get in there and sit on that bundle by the window, all right? I am going to go out to the front and get some air." He gave him a pat on his shoulder and sent the child to his mother. Oh Jungsoon thanked him again. He nodded and made his way through the packed aisle.

Jungsoon blankly stared out the window. The denuded mountains and the country scenery swirled by. She gave herself away to the rocking of the car. She thought of her husband who wasn't feeling well. Poor man! Lately he seemed more depressed. He took cold medicine and continued going to work, but what he needed was good nutrition. And Kangsup, was he making it to school on time? And Wonsup, full of energy, and the weak baby Jisup, how were they getting along without her! Thinking and listening to the clacking sound under her feet, she watched the rugged terrain, the paddy fields and the villages with straw thatched houses.

People started gathering their things. They must be approaching the capital city. Jungsoon and her son picked up their bundles and were ready too. The train roared into the huge station terminal and freed the exhausted throng. She walked with the crowd down the steps and through the tunnel and up to the platform. As she neared the rows of ticket gates, her heart began to beat quickly. The station employees and the Japanese

13

policemen were at the incoming gates. She turned in the tickets and handed over her belongings to be examined. The hands of the station man went over the bundles feeling the contents. They passed. She thankfully started off but felt someone blocking her way. A dark uniformed policeman, wearing a sabre at his side, stood firmly in front of her.

"You, come with me to the office!" the policeman commanded and walked ahead. Oh Jungsoon's heart sank. She followed the tip of the dangling sabre with Hyonsup uneasily hanging close to her. The policeman strode into the empty stationmaster's office. A young clerk, hunched over a desk in the adjacent room, sent her a sympathetic glance. The stout Japanese policeman with his hands at his back, started to walk around haughtily examining her. The side of the scabbard tapped against his corpulent thigh.

"What is that?" His fierce stare rested on her swollen belly. She began to black out. She couldn't answer. "Bring the truncheon from over there!" roared the policeman. The young clerk reluctantly edged toward them, eyed the policeman, got the signal and carefully pressed the tip of the bat into her abdomen. He repeated it several times. "What is it?"

"I don't know, sir."

The policeman's eyes gleamed cruelly. His hand flew to its hilt and the sabre was freed from its scabbard. When the curved blade slashed toward her she almost fainted. Its tip pierced the weight under her clothes. A trickle of rice fell to the floor.

"Should I tear the rest apart, or will you take it off?"

Jungsoon gave up. She turned around, lifted her long chima (Korean skirt), untied the sack of rice from her waist and placed it on the stationmaster's desk.

"Is that all?"

"Yes," her answer was shaky.

"Search her!"

The young clerk came close and felt down her body. Hyonsup stood at a distance with his face turned blue. Finally the clerk stood up.

"Nothing, sir."

The policeman glared contemptuously.

"Our Japanese army is fighting day and night, with their lives at stake, fighting for the country. And what do you do? You're selfish, sneaking in rice like this. That is shameless, unpatriotic behavior!"

The meaning was strong enough in spite of her poor knowledge of

14

Japanese.

"I understand," she bent her head in terror and shame. Hyonsup stood by his mother dreading what would happen next. His eyes, wide with fright, traveled from the policeman to the station clerk, to his mother and back to the policeman.

"I could send you to prison. You could be severely punished. Do you understand?" The policeman angrily returned the weapon back to its place. A moment of dreadful silence. Then

"You may go!"

"Oh, thank you," she bowed. Picking up her bundles, she cast a last glance at the sack of rice lying on the stationmaster's desk. Her brother had been overly generous in selling her the rice. How she wished she could take it along with her!

Dimly lighted, the waiting room was crowded with people streaming in and out. Some were at the ticket windows, some crouched on the bench awaiting the train that was delayed many hours, and others were forming lines at the ticket gates. Through the speaker up somewhere in the dirt-stained dome droned the constant voice, reverberating and indistinct. A tiny Japanese woman with a smile on her smooth face stuck a long piece of cloth and a needle under her nose.

"Could you please make a stitch here?" she asked. "My son is joining the army. I am sure this will give him good luck and help him bring us the great victory."

Jungsoon had done this before. It was to be used as a sash for the Japanese young man. If one thousand people added one stitch each to the cloth, good fortune would dog the wearer. Jungsoon carefully took the material and the needle attached to it. The woman had a long way to go to secure the one thousand stitches. With the red thread she made a French knot for her.

"Thank you. Thank you very much." The Japanese woman bowed several times and went away to ask others.

Finally Seoul. She left it only two days ago, but the jingling street-cars, crawling taxies, buildings mingled with old palaces and gates seemed to give her a hearty welcome. After many familiar turns and a transfer, Jungsoon and her son got off the streetcar and hurried along the long stone fence.

Boonee, greeted her boisterously, opening the large gate of a prosperous-looking house with a roof of blue tile. "Oh, it's you, Auntie!"

The servant girl took the bundles from her. "Oh, Auntie, I missed you so much," then, sensing Jungsoon's mother-in-law was out on the hall room in the main house, she stopped short.

Jungsoon's mother-in-law was disappointed to see her daughter-in-law's slim figure as Jungsoon crossed the courtyard toward her.

"Just what I was afraid of. You have been caught!"

"Yes, Mother. But not all of it." Jungsoon lifted her long chima and showed the heavily sagging pockets on each side of her underpants.

"Well, it's not much, is it! You should have thought of some other way instead of carrying it so obviously around your waist. We just blew money in the air for nothing, didn't we!" The mother-in-law stood high on the edge of the hall room above the stone step like a reigning queen. Jungsoon kept silent letting her chima fall. She had taken a relative's advice. But it had failed. She stood there and felt a weighty responsibility.

"Mother, I—my ring—perhaps I can sell my ring and make another trip."

"Did I ever ask you to sell your belongings? All these years I've been supplying this household with my valuables but I've never asked any other members of this family to sell theirs!" the mother-in-law fumed.

In the somewhat strangely changed kitchen, she unwrapped one of her bundles and arranged pieces of the millet cakes on a dish for her mother-in-law.

"Put that thing away! I am not hungry," the mother-in-law said eying the millet cake with disgust. On the way to her room the mother-in-law stopped and turned around. "Now, I cleaned all those cupboards and the kitchen corners while you were gone. The way things were there, I could hardly find anything in its place."

The door to the detached room slid open and the grandmother-in-law's wrinkled face stuck out.

"What's all the commotion there? Is Hyonsup's mom back yet?"

"Yes, she is, Mother. But she didn't bring much rice. She was caught on the way," the mother-in-law explained.

"Well, that isn't her fault, is it? The Japanese police, they seem to be getting worse these days."

"That's not what I am talking about, Mother. The way she keeps things in the kitchen—"

"Leave the things the way they are. It's her kitchen."

Displeased at her own mother-in-law's interference, the mother-in-

16

law rushed off to her room.

Jungsoon started for the kitchen feeling grateful toward her grandmother-in-law.

"How are your brother and his wife?" came the voice from the wrinkled lady.

"Oh, they are fine, Grandmother. Since the harvest is over, they seem to be relaxing. They send you their best regards, Grandmother."

"It is awfully nice of them. Well, you must be very tired after the trip. Get some rest."

"That's all right, Grandmother. It was such a short trip. Would you like me to steam an apple for you?"

"No, I don't need anything. Save them for men. Apples seem as expensive as gold these days." She muttered, coughed several times and slid the door closed. The eighty year old lady maintained good health except for an occasional hearing problem. Her hair was darker than that of her seventy-eight year old husband. Relatives said the ginseng and antler she had used in better days had something to do with it. At fourteen, the skill of her brush-writing was said to have been so renowned that Queen Min praised her skill in person and had two of her works displayed in the palace rooms. Then followed the years of complicated political upheavals and the intrigue in the court. Poor Queen, she had been killed mercilessly by the Japanese soldiers who invaded the palace! After the Japanese annexation, which the grandmother-in-law detested and lamented so much, her calligraphic art had been confined to home and for pleasure, but now even that had become an effort and her daily activity was limited to reading.

In the large hall room stood a grain bin. It had an inch high rationed pressed barley, and Jungsoon stretched her arm down to reach and scoop it up. Back in the kitchen, she put the things away. Gourd scoops, dried edible mountain vegetables, radish leaves and some chestnuts and apples that her sister-in-law had packed for her. And rice! She ran the grain through her fingers. A long forgotten feeling. It was silk compared to the pressed barley from the hall room. Carefully she blended the barley with rice. A sharp cry from inside signaled her one-year-old boy, Jisup, woke up. She hurried back into the master room and noticed her mother-in-law dropping an armful of laundry on the hall room floor, a habit when she was angry.

"Here are some of the things to be washed. And don't forget to sew your father-in-law's clothes. They've been lying there for days."

17

"Yes, Mother."

"Oh, that spoiled child! A boy past his first birthday acts like a newborn baby. Don't keep on feeding him every time he opens his mouth. Oh, I had such a hard time to baby-sit!" The mother-in-law stared at the laundry pile with contempt and went into her room.

"I will take care of the baby, Auntie." Agile Boonee came for the baby and fastened him on her back. Relieved, Jungsoon collected the laundry in a large tin pail. It was too late to start the laundry, so she put it aside for the next morning and began to prepare dinner.

The eldest, Kangsup, came home from school, tossing a hello to his mother, while she was preparing cabbage soup, salad with the dried mountain herbs, broiled dried fish and grilled dried seaweeds.

The front gate was flung open and her brother-in-law peeked through the inner gate.

"I am home!" he called and disappeared into his room.

It was the beginning of the men's homecoming. Jungsoon's grandfather-in-law strode in, clearing his throat, which was a means of announcing his presence. His long white beard covered half of his chest. On his head, his ever-present horse hair hat provided a badge of past aristocracy.

"Yoon of Haepyong. Ours is the first-class yangban," Jungsoon's mother-in-law always said, although a wife didn't carry a husband's last name. When she said "ours," the mother-in-law undoubtedly included her own ancestors, the Kim clan of Andong, which had wielded power for generations. The Yoon clan had been a landlord family for some four-hundred years. Its royal connection dated back to the 16th century when a forefather Yoon married a daughter of King Sonjo. Many daughters of the Yoon clan married kings and enjoyed power and influence throughout the Yi dynasty.

With the coming of the Japanese, the Yi dynasty was shattered. And with it, the end of prosperity for the landed gentry including the Yoon and Kim clans. The only symbol of aristocracy in the household in 1942 were a celadon bowl handed down from generation to generation, and an embroidered ten-fold screen. This heirloom was bestowed by Queen Yoon, to whom the grandfather-in-law was related as second cousins, and to whom they ceased to pay their respects years ago.

As a result of the Japanese land survey 25 years ago, an out-and-out land grab, most of their properties had been turned over to the Japanese

18

government. The rest was eaten away over the years for education and the family subsistence. Hatred for the Japanese was somewhat abated in the young progressive-minded son, Jungsoon's father-in-law, who graduated from a Japanese university. He pondered reform and the system that brings prosperity for all people under such circumstance. But the ever-oppressing Japanese and March 1st Independence Movement made him think again. When Jungsoon's father-in-law refused to work further with the Japanese and resigned a minor administrative post, the family had even less income. In 1942, family fortune and social standing was to be found only in fading memories.

The sun had managed to come out of the thick clouds and sent its lukewarm rays into the courtyard where the children were busy at their play. Kangsup, eleven, the eldest child, always occupied himself with something, making gliders with paper and sticks, and seemed to get along fine with his uncle.

"I will be a pilot when I grow up."

"Wow, listen to this chap! Don't be too ambitious, young fellow! What you need to do first is to do your home work tonight, understand?" Chayoung gave his nephew a tap on his back, as he sent the boy's glider flying above the jar stand and almost over the roof, and down again. Kangsup ran after it, while younger brothers, Hyonsup and Wonsup watched it enchanted. He didn't want to go with his mother on the trip, so she had taken the second one along.

The father-in-law returned at the same time as her husband did, either from a visit to his friend's or from one of those ever speculating business meetings.

Dinner was a feast. Silver spoons and silver chopsticks clinked against the shiny brassware. Even the mother-in-law finished her rice, who always maintained finishing up everything in the bowl was a commoner's manner. Father-in-law enjoyed the meal too. He even tried a bit of millet cake which he never had dreamed of eating a few years ago. Jungsoon's husband had his meal in silence, occupying the seat between his parents and across from his brother. Her grandparents-in-law had their dinner in their room. Away from them, in the master room Boonee waited for Jungsoon, feeding three-year-old Wonsup. She glanced at Jungsoon's bowl half filled with pure pressed barley collected from the bottom of the pan.

"Auntie, I don't see a grain of rice in your bowl. Here, let me have it." Boonee switched the bowls. Jungsoon grabbed hers back from her.

19

"It's all right. I like barley. Besides yours is no different. Go on, have your dinner before it gets cold."

"Oh, these fernbrakes are delicious!" Scooping up the food with her brass spoon, Boonee reacted happily to having the auntie back home.

"Is Boonee there?" Grandmother-in-law's voice crackled from across the courtyard.

"Yes, Great-grandma," Boonee answered and rushed out.

The wrinkled lady handed over her half finished bowl to the maid.

"That's for your auntie. I don't think it went around to get to hers."

Boonee came in with the bowl.

"Oh, poor grandmother!" Jungsoon was overwhelmed, knowing that the elderly lady had particular affection toward her. Jungsoon scooped half of the rice over Boonee's bowl and spooned the rest up feeling guilty eating so much rice herself.

Boonee continued to be chatty washing the dishes with Jungsoon.

"Look, Auntie, the dust in the cupboard is still there. And Grandma says she cleaned it."

"Hush. Don't talk like that about Grandma behind her back."

"But that's true. When you were gone, I took care of the baby. She just held him once. And she left him crying so long Great-grandma had to take care of him while I fixed meals."

"I said hush."

Boonee had grown since she came four years ago. She was from a small village in Choongchong Province. Her parents had at least ten children, and she was one of the several whom her parents had given away because they simply couldn't afford to feed another mouth. She was ten years old then, shy and tanned in clothes that didn't fit her. She could hardly replace the fortyish seamstress and the fifteen year old maid who had to go back home to farm. But now she had grown tall, her face color turned fair and her bosom hidden under the chogori (Korean shirt) gave her a feminine look. She shared a considerable part of the housework with Jungsoon and was a friend when they cooked meals, did the laundry, fulled sheets, and ironed the clothes.

"Jisup is crying. Must be sleepy!" the mother-in-law called.

"I am coming, Mother." Jungsoon dried her hands on her apron and went inside. Her husband was reading the evening newspaper. She picked up her son who was slow in walking. Although her breasts had been dry for quite some time she let him have them because that was the only way she could make him go to sleep. It was a relaxing moment, luxurious and rare. Jungsoon glanced at her husband, whom she hadn't seen for two days, and who didn't seem to notice when she was present.

"Yobo, is your cold any better?" she asked.

"Uh?" Her husband lowered the newspaper to see her.

"How are you feeling? Your cold—"

"A little better," he went back to his reading.

Jungsoon waited a few minutes, then asked,

"Would you like some ginger tea?"

A minute later came the answer,

"All right."

When she put the sleeping child down on his bed, he woke up crying. Boonee who just finished doing the dishes came in to take over the baby.

From her brother-in-law's room in the front premises came the loud sounds of the gramophone playing a Japanese popular song. A doleful female voice leaked through the inner gate and filled the dusky courtyard. Jungsoon collected bits of charcoal in the fuel hole and started a fire in a small portable range. She prepared a portion of ginger root and dropped it into a kettle of boiling water. Meanwhile, she tended the heat in the fuel hole attached to the room of the grandparents-in-law.

"Grandmother, is the room warm enough for you?"

"It is warm enough. We should save wood for the severe winter. By the way, tell Boonee to bring the child over here and sleep in my room. Your grandfather-in-law wishes to retire in the front premises tonight."

"Yes, Grandmother."

That meant the guest parlor had to be warmed for the elderly. The front premises, originally the men's living and the servant's quarters, many of its rooms now deserted, stood in the dark. Only the notes of the Japanese popular song hinted that someone was dwelling there.

Boonee, who was joggling the baby to sleep on her back, didn't like the idea. She would rather sleep in her room near the children and Auntie. Sulkily and with an armful of mattresses and coverlets she went to the detached room. Jungsoon supplied the rooms of the grandparents-in-law and parents-in-law with fresh night water jugs and bowls.

"During the naval battles of Cape Esperance and of the Santa Cruz Islands, the Japanese Navy sank one enemy carrier, two enemy destroyers and damaged six other ships. . .the Governor-General issued an emergency decree. . .''

The radio droned on. Her father-in-law made a deep grimace.

"Turn that thing off, will you?"

Jungsoon obeyed. As she was cautiously retiring, the mother-in-law stopped arranging the chest drawers and lifted her chin.

"What is this I smell? Is something cooking in the kitchen?"

"Yes, Mother, ginger tea for Hyonsup's dad. He is still having the cold—"

"I wonder why he gets sick so easily," the older woman muttered and went back to her arranging.

In the adjoining room children in their nighties were roughhousing. The light bulb hanging from the ceiling in the middle of the room swung like the bob of a wall clock. Jungsoon quickly grabbed it still.

"Wonsup did it!" Hyonsup giggled pointing at his younger brother.

"No! I can't even reach that high!"

"Quiet, you two!" Kangsup shouted at his two younger brothers.

"Shh. Go to sleep." Jungsoon tucked them under quilts and turned out the light.

Daeyoung was alone in the master room sipping his ginger tea while reading the newspaper.

"That lazy bum! It's a sheer waste sending that kid to a college!" Angrily he shoved off his tea cup and the newspaper. The doleful female voice of his brother Chayoung's gramophone continued to seep into the room.

Jungsoon, devoted to sewing, wanted to say something to ease his wrath.

"I think he is just relaxing after all the hard school work."

"Relaxing? Do you call that relaxing? Loafing away twenty-four hours a day like that?" He glared at his wife as if she were defending her own brother. She kept silent and went on with her work.

Daeyoung's fury now turned to something else: there's nothing to read there anyway, since all the Korean language newspapers are suppressed and gone. Humph! 'Assimilation'! to forge Koreans into Japanese? They must be out of their mind. 'The Greater East Asia Co-prosperity'! And they've swallowed Korea, and eaten Manchuria. The Philippines fell into their hands like a piece of crumpled newspaper. They've conquered the Indies and seem to have gained absolute control in the Pacific. It's their world all over. Four-thousand and two-hundred-seventy-five years of

Korean history down the drain!

"Dogs!"

Startled, Jungsoon eyed her husband cautiously and asked, "Shall I get your washing water ready?"

"What? All right!" he growled, his fury unabated.

Jungsoon had a wash pan of water and a soap dish ready for him in the hall room. While Daeyoung was going through his routine washing and brushing in the hall room, she prepared his bed with mattresses and a quilt. When she came back after disposing of the pan of water and the soap dish, her husband had gone to sleep. With relief she resumed her work at the far end of the room under the light covered with a dark cloth.

All seemed so quiet. The children were sound asleep in the adjoining room and she just heard her grandfather-in-law coughing as he crossed the courtyard to spend the night in the front parlor.

"What are you doing up there?" The voice of her husband.

"Sewing. I have to finish this before Father's birthday."

"Why don't you turn out the light. It might attract an air raid."

Jungsoon put the things away, turned out the light and went out to wash herself.

Finally she settled on her mattress next to her husband's.

"Come here!"

She heard it half asleep. Her husband's hand was feeling around her waist, untying the strings on her underpants and her underwear.

"What are you all bundled up like this for? Take that thing off."

Against the grayish light from the window, the dark body loomed over her. With her eyes closed she went along with him. It didn't take long. He turned his back and fell asleep.

Oh Jungsoon took a moment, and quietly slipped out of her bed to go to the toilet shed. She seldom used the chamber pot when her husband was around. She remembered the story of a Chinese emperor who was very particular about beautiful girls. He finally had found the most beautiful maiden, had her, and when he found out that she too had to urinate like everybody else, ordered her to be beheaded.

In the backyard, plum trees stretched out their crooked branches over the shrubs, as if to ward off the chilly night air. Under the aged weeping willow was the abandoned dry pond that once flourished with goldfish and lotus. When Jungsoon passed it she could smell the moss-clad dirt. She still remembered the seamstress stooping over and counting the

23

goldfish. All were gone now. In the cleared sky the moon traveled fast through the lingering clouds. The lunar 15th would be here soon. The sound of some night-watcher's clappers came very near, then slowly diminished in the distance.

Jungsoon returned to her bed and joined the rest of the family in sleep. Finally, finally, it was the end of the day.

II.   Childhood

When Father begot me, Mother reared me,
When they took pains to bring me up,
They dreamed, not of a duchess or marchioness,
But at least of a bride fit for a gentleman.

Ho Nansorhon [1563-1589]

Oh Jungsoon dreamed of her home back in Kyongki Province. A tile-roofed house, attractive even from a far distance. In the backyard stood the chestnut, apricot and persimmon trees. In front, the forsythias, azaleas, cosmos, peonies, China asters, and chrysanthemums, that bloomed from early spring till frost. On summer evenings she would gather with friends, and enjoy mincing garden balsam flowers. They would wrap the strips of cloth with the minced flowers around their finger tips. The next morning they would uncover their fingernails to see how they had turned out. Her friends always envied her dark red fingernails that had come out just right. Relatives came on Father's birthdays and New Year's days. Their eyes sweeping down her newly matured figure, they would say:

"Oh, just look at her! I bet she will become the first daughter-in-law of a rich family!" Mother used to smile with content. "First daughter-in-law of a rich family" with responsibility to run the mansion with twelve gates and many servants! But the phrase actually referred to a plain girl when people had to say something nice and couldn't find anything obvious such as 'pretty', 'attractive', or even 'cute'. Friends got married off one by one. As the days went by, her parents, as well as herself, were worried about her passing marriageable age.

Then came the opportunity at twenty, at which girls were considered old maids. Her parents were excited. Mother hastening the teaching of sewing and cooking. Father bringing home materials to be sewn and articles for trousseaux. She remembered those last evenings with her mother, sewing under the dull lamplight, listening to her mother, and the crickets in chorus.

"You should be well prepared to get married. Once you go off to your husband's house, there's nobody who can teach you. They will only see your failures and talk about them," her mother went on. "It's not easy to lead a life with in-laws. There's a saying that the life with in-laws is hotter than hot pepper sauce. But try hard, as hard as you can. Absolute obedience to your parents-in-law. Do not talk back to them. Whatever they ask you to do, you do it. Even if they ask you to die, try to appear dying." Mother went on sewing, pressing down the seams with a small iron heated in the brazier. "Once you are married, you belong to your husband's family. Even after you die, you become the spirit of his family, not ours." Taking out the hot iron and pressing down on the seam, Mother continued. "Back in the old days, women sent back from their husbands' house were put to death because of the disgrace brought upon their families. I remember this one woman in our neighborhood when I was a little girl. People said she was cast out of her in-law's house. After she returned home, her brother took her into the deepest part of the mountain and people never saw her again."

Jungsoon woke, her heart pounding violently. Seeing her husband sound asleep next to her she felt relieved, went back to sleep and continued dreaming.

Her husband was there, who came to see her at the very first arranged meeting. She sat with her head low, dressed in a yellow chogori and a long red chima. Although she wasn't supposed to, she stole a glimpse at him. He was handsome. Probably more than one glance. The matchmaker's advertisement and her own parents insisted he was a son of a wealthy yangban, that he went to the First Public High School where only bright young men had to compete in order to enter. The groom-to-be and his father went home. Then it was such a long wait for the matchmaker's return. Finally the old woman, a distant relative, came. She heard her mother's low voice and her father's furious bellow. "Too old? Too tall? Why that pale, no-good smart aleck! She's only two years older than he— just as any wife would be." An upper-class scholar, mild tempered—but this time his expectation had been great. He had almost tasted the near happiness coming to his daughter. "Humph! Who's afraid of Yoon of Haepyong! Why, we, the Ohs of Haejoo are no less yangbans than any Yoon of Haepyong." But the class-conscious old fashioned father felt his pride hurt, knowing that his lineage was indeed a little less yangban than that of Yoon. There had been a queen Oh, and some of his forefathers had served in the government as ministers, but never had the Oh family been the center of power and rank like Yoon of Haepyong. Plus their fortune had shrunken to several dozen majigis of paddy-fields and those even were in danger of being transferred to tenants' hands. They had had but one elderly couple as servants who, even long after slavery had been abolished, were loyal enough to stay with them until the end of their days. About the time when Jungsoon was born.

"Doesn't matter! He is not the only fish in the sea, I will tell you!" Father's still angry bluster.

Mother came quietly into Jungsoon's room with a sigh. "Let's start dinner."

Jungsoon struggled to wake up. She knew she had married him. The people on the groom's side were anxious. There wasn't enough time to prolong his marriage by going through more candidates. His grandparents wanted to have their granddaughter-in-law before they died. So, Jungsoon finally stepped into the declining Yoon household. The first baby, Kangsup, was born. Then came two more sons, Hyonsup and Wonsup. Those were the joys. Her mother-in-law's reaction was a studied aloofness, but her parents in Kyongki Province exalted. "Three sons! You have earned a proud place in the Yoon household." And still another, Jisup. She dreamed many other short dreams—of the man in the train, giving up his seat for her, his eyes smiling softly under the thick eyebrows.

Jungsoon heard a cough from the opposite room. Dawn became bright on the door. She had overslept. The kitchen was as cold as the courtyard. Jungsoon struggled to start the fire in the fuel holes. The ball of crumpled newspaper burnt out without igniting the wood bits. She struck another match. A part of the wood caught fire and then died out. Smoke poured out and stung her eyes. Her brother-in-law strode in and peeked into the kitchen through the smoke.

"Sister, do you have some warm water? It's cold."

"Here, use this, Master." Jungsoon poured in the wash pan the water which was intended for cooking.

Soon all family members came out in the courtyard to wash. Boonee, yawning, went around to fetch the warm water. The cabbage soup started boiling and the barley began to simmer. Her brother-in-law, in his college uniform and the square hat, paced up and down the courtyard. The parents-in-law talked quietly in their room. Her husband seemed ready for work. The children stirred lazily. Since she arose this morning she had been suffering a stomachache. It gradually turned into a twitching pain.

27

"I hear the child crying," called the mother-in-law.

"Yes, Mother."

But she let the baby cry a while. Her brother-in-law sat on the edge of the hall room glancing at his wristwatch, ready to leave any minute. Just as she was coming out of the kitchen with his tray table he abruptly stood up and walked away.

"Please, Master, take a few more minutes."

"I don't have the time," he tossed the words over his shoulder as he went out of the gate. Disappointed, she took the tray table back into the kitchen. The pain in her abdomen became unbearable.

"Fetch the table for Uncle and children," Jungsoon said breathlessly and rushed into the closet room. She had missed her period in the past month. Something was happening. Clutching the ring of the dresser drawer, she bore the unbearable pain. A lump escaped from her body.

"Did you hear me out there? The child is crying!"

"Yes, Mother, I am coming!"

Her face, pale and distorted with the frightening experience, Jungsoon came out of the room to get the crying baby from Boonee.

"Something wrong, Auntie?"

"No, nothing."

Although Jungsoon refused to comment, Boonee knew her auntie was not feeling well.

Jungsoon's husband left for work and the children went to school. The morning rush slackened now. Boonee slowly took the tables to Grandmother's and Great-grandmother's rooms. The worst seemed over. Jungsoon found a moment to breathe as she fed the baby, Jisup. Her eyes roamed about the room crowded with mattresses, quilts and night clothes. The opposite door slid open and her mother-in-law raised her voice.

"This is a farmhand's bowl. Don't you know the amount I take each meal?"

Jungsoon put the child down and went to her mother-in-law who had the brother-in-law's bowl which Boonee had taken in by mistake.

"Oh, that was Master's."

"You mean he went to school without food?"

"Yes, I was running behind."

"It is always happening. I don't think he will be able to concentrate on his study with an empty stomach."

The mother-in-law's bowl was left on the kitchen counter and was cold. Jungsoon put the bowl in the cooking pot to make it warm.

"What's taking so long there?"

"I am coming, Mother."

Her mother-in-law examined the bowl and started to eat sulkily.

"Auntie, you look awfully pale, you need to lie down," Boonee suggested.

"I am all right. You go ahead and eat with Wonsup. I have to wash myself first." But she started to fold away the mattresses and quilts to make room.

Her mother-in-law came out to the hall room and glanced at her daughter-in-law freshening herself up in front of her dresser mirror.

"Well, sun is way up high now. And I see the laundry hasn't been touched yet. The day isn't going to stretch itself and wait for things to be done. Get to the laundry first and work on your father-in-law's clothes." She made a grimace and was about to go back to her room.

"She hasn't had her breakfast yet!" Boonee cried.

The mother-in-law hesitated and turned around.

"Why, that little brat! Now, talking back to Grandmother?"

Startled, Jungsoon glanced at Boonee, whose head was bent with regret for the momentary mistake, then at her mother-in-law who was blue with indignation.

"Why, that little no good brat! Nobody told her not to eat! Now, teaching the servant how to talk back!"

Jungsoon was not dull, nor incapable of talking back. But reverence to elders, complaisance on the part of the young even under false accusations to create harmony and unity within the household—those were the values and virtues she embraced. Jungsoon turned to Boonee.

"Apologize to Grandma."

"I am sorry, Grandma!" mumbled Boonee, her head low.

"You! Bad girl!" The mother-in-law stamped her foot." If I hear you talk like that once more, I will send you right back to the mud hut in that hilly valley where you came from!"

Boonee stood there with her hands gathered in front, tear drops sliding down her cheeks. The mother-in-law went into her room banging the door after her.

"Come on, let's eat." Jungsoon put her hand on Boonee's shoulder which was now shaking violently.

* * *

29

Jungsoon, feeling weak, did the laundry by the pump. She could hear Boonee sweeping and mopping the rooms, still sullen from the morning incident. Piece by piece Jungsoon soaked, applied the soap and rubbed and rubbed against the washboard in the tin pail, remembering a dream she had had last night. It's that man in the train. Funny. Why would she dream about a strange man like that?

"Is that you, Hyonsup's Mom?" her grandmother-in-law called, peering out through the small door in the detached room. Jungsoon hurriedly arose and went to her.

"Yes, Grandmother. Would you like me to do anything for you?"

"No. I was just looking at you. You don't seem to be feeling well. Are you sick?"

"No, Grandmother." Jungsoon blushed. "I am just fine." She wanted to talk to this kind old lady. 'I just had a miscarriage, Grandmother.' But it wasn't polite. There was no need to burden the aged mind with such a trivial thing of a young woman.

"Well, at a distance, you didn't look well. Take care of yourself."

"Thank you, Grandmother, I will." Jungsoon's heart was filled with gratitude.

The mother-in-law crossed the courtyard to make a visit to her relatives.

"Lunch will be ready soon, Mother."

"I don't have any appetite for anything," she spat and rustled toward the gate, the legs of a fox fur piece dangling over her shoulder. Jungsoon followed to see her off and to shut the gate after her. With relief she went into the kitchen to set the tray table for her grandparents-in-law. When it was all ready, there was a call at the gate. Boonee answered it and announced company for Grandfather-in-law. He came out of his room, greeted his friend heartily and ordered lunch for his guest, leading him to the guest parlor. Jungsoon rearranged the table and rushed a couple of more side dishes with dried fish and vegetables that were saved for dinner. Setting another table for her grandmother-in-law and her son Wonsup, she knew another long day was not yet half over.

The mother-in-law returned without her fox fur piece and with a little money from its sale. She had come from a rich family, and had brought chest after chest filled with trousseaux. She had become too old to wear colorful outfits, some of which she had never had the time to try on. Since the beginning of the household's decline, they were taken out one after the other and sold. With the father-in-law's sixtieth birthday coming around she had sold the fox fur piece.

Dusk crept quickly into the courtyard. Dinner was long over and the dishes done, but the brother-in-law had not returned. In the father-in-law's study, he was teaching three-year-old Wonsup the Korean alphabet.

"Kiuk, niun!"

"Kiuk, niun."

"Digood, riul!"

"Digood, riul."

Wonsup's feeble voice followed the father-in-law's forceful recitation.

"There was this king, Sejong the Great. He wanted to invent something very easy for everyone to learn and write. He thought long and hard. His scholars thought long and hard, too. One day, he sat in his room still thinking. And then he noticed the door on which the sun was brightly shining. For a while he stared at the paper door and the dark grills crisscrossing one another. They looked like some kind of letters. 'Aha!' he exclaimed, slapping his knee with his palm. 'That is going to be our alphabet!' And that's where our alphabet came from." The father-in-law loved the third grandchild. Jungsoon could picture her little boy, attentively listening to the long story.

A tapping at the front gate.

"Master?"

Louder taps served as an answer.

"Who's there?"

"Is this the lady who made a train trip yesterday?"

"Yes," Jungsoon answered, wondering.

"Don't worry, ma'am. I have just brought something that belongs to you."

She opened the gate. There, like the dream last night, she saw a man standing on the other side of the threshold.

"Ma'am, this—the rice. It is yours."

Jungsoon's eyes grew large as he handed the rice to her.

"Oh, you are the gentleman who rode with me," she answered softly, recognizing him.

"Yes. This is the rice you left at the stationmaster's desk yesterday morning."

She couldn't believe it. Her lips parted, and clutching the sack, she searched for words.

"Thank you, but how—"

"You are welcome. I just happened to know a Japanese policeman."
He turned and walked away.

"Why, thank you. May I ask who you are?" Jungsoon mumbled
the words hurriedly at the retreating man. But the man had gone out of
the alley.

"Oh, Mother, guess what happened!" She rushed inside to share the
good news. "Someone who saw me in the train and at the Seoul station
brought this back."

Jungsoon happily showed the rice sack to her mother-in-law. The
older woman glanced up, and smarted,

"Put that thing away. Now, where can Chayoung be?"

"Is Chayoung home yet?" came the inquiry over and over again.

"No, not yet, Mother."

"I wonder what's keeping him this late."

The mother-in-law had born her children late. She had lost a daughter
and two sons. Bearing her youngest at forty, to the chagrin of the family
at the time, she still babied Chayoung. The mother-in-law came out into
the hall room. She felt somehow his absence had to do with her first son
and his wife.

"Where can he be until this late!" she sighed.

"He will be home soon, don't worry, Mother," Daeyoung responded
bluntly from his room.

"Well, I wish you would show some brotherly concern toward
Chayoung." The mother-in-law paced up and down the hall room, staring out into the dark courtyard.

The children went to bed, and the mother-in-law fretted through the
evening and dozed off. The night watchman's clapping sound went the
second round. It must be well past midnight. Jungsoon put down her sewing in the children's room and went out to the front premises.

"Is Master home yet?" Jungsoon whispered, standing close to her
brother-in-law's room. The dark room sent out no answer. She opened
the door and turned on the light. The room was messy, with books and
records piled on top of one another, the gramophone still left open, and
the used needles scattered around. Her brother-in-law hadn't come home.

32

III. Chinjoo

A mountain in spring catches fire.
Unopened flowers burn.
Yet there is water there
To put out the flames.
Where is the stream that can kill
The fire that burns deep within me?

> *Kim Tong-nyong [1567-1596]*

Fall 1942. Northern Korea.

Sunset in Pyongyang, a city north of Seoul by a hundred and fifty miles. Several women emerged from the municipal market and scurried away to prepare their evening meals. A pair of mounted Japanese policemen cantered arrogantly through the broad street. A man pulling a rickshaw strained courageously to reach his customer's destination in a hurry. Yi Chinjoo, a brisk, young woman of medium height, hastened home with her market bag. A ragged, foul-smelling drunkard sprawled against a garbage bin. He tried to wave his hand and to get up, failing in both.

"Oh, it's you again. What's the matter with you, uh? Getting drunk in broad daylight like this? Shame on you!" Chinjoo chided in her strong Pyongan Province accent. Behind the dirt and rags, she could see a healthy young face.

"Don't be so hard—hard—on me—" Draggie grumbled. People called the derelict "Draggie" because of his sodden filthiness.

"By the way, where do you get all the money for your drinking?"

"Ah, they give it to me. Ha, ha!"

Chinjoo clacked her tongue and gave him a piece of advice.

"A healthy young one like you shouldn't waste time like this." Chinjoo slipped her hand into her mesh bag, grabbed a couple of cookies and handed them to him. "Here, have these. And tomorrow, you find work, you hear me?"

"You are right, Auntie. Work—that seems to be a good idea. I—"

I—will find wo—rk—to—morrow." Draggie waved his free hand.

Chinjoo clacked her tongue again and hurried off. A harmless creature, but what a waste! Cold wind blew through her turumagi (coat) collar, shaking her scarf. On either side of the road, buildings of many sizes hunched against the crimson sunset. Under the row of multicolored store signs, a tiny figure in a dark-brown striped kimono walked toward Chinjoo with mincing steps. She bowed to Chinjoo.

"Ahhh, it's you, Kaneyama san."

"Yes, Akisawa san." Chinjoo returned the bow.

"Why, you've already gone to market, haven't you?" Then showing her broken uneven teeth she smiled. "You are a very industrious person, aren't you?"

"Yes, Akisawa san," Chinjoo agreed, not sure she had understood Akisawa's Japanese.

"Don't forget the unit meeting tonight."

"Yes, no forgetting, Akisawa san." Chinjoo assured the wife number-two of the neighborhood unit chieftain.

"I will see you, Kaneyama san." Akisawa's wife minced away, her wooden sandals clattering. Akisawa's wife number-one lived elsewhere. He had given his authority to his wife number-two to act in his place. According to rumor, the cross-eyed Akisawa was violent with his wife number-two.

In the courtyard of her home, Chinjoo's three daughters crowded around her taking the mesh bag away.

"Ma, what did you buy? Something good?"

"Wow, cookies, may we have some?"

"Now, just a minute, you girls. Don't you eat them all. Pa has to have some, too," Chinjoo chided her children.

"Oh, Ma, you know Pa doesn't like sweet stuff."

"You naughty girls! Still Pa has to see them before he gives them away to you!"

The girls raced into the master room, the oldest, ten, the second, nine, followed by the youngest, three. Chinjoo peeked into her mother-in-law's room.

"Did you have something to eat, Mother? I had left your lunch inside the middle pot in the kitchen."

"I know," the arthritic old lady answered almost inaudibly, as she turned the pages of a Japanese magazine.

"Dinner will be ready in a little while, Mother. You should go out and visit the uncles. That's the only way you can get some exercise," Chinjoo said closing the door. She felt sorry for the old woman. She had to live either with the first son, who lived eight miles northwest of Pyongyang, or she had to take turns staying with each of her three sons including the middle one who had moved to Sariwon in Hwanghae Province. But instead, the mother-in-law remained at the home of the youngest, Insoo. Chinjoo knew the old lady was deeply attached to the youngest, and as long as the mother-in-law didn't become a real burden, it was all right with her, too.

Kim Insoo stepped into the courtyard with a plump sack. Without looking Chinjoo could tell the presence of her husband, the malt-smelling rugged man. He stuck his head into the kitchen.

"What are you cooking? I got some buckwheat noodles and some pork down at the butcher's. Fix it, will you?"

"Pork?" Chinjoo glanced at her elated husband. "But what about the pressed barley I am cooking?"

"Let's have it for breakfast tomorrow. But today let's have something different. Fix it, will you?"

Chinjoo knew it was his favorite dish. She took the lump of meat and the noodles from him.

"Oh, Pa, what is it?" The daughters shouted as they rushed out to greet him.

"Look for yourselves." He tossed the sack of small gifts to them.

"Hey, fellows, don't tear them apart. Wow, these wild horses!"

Kim Insoo always called them "fellows" as if they were boys. He really had wished to have a boy. Each girl was a disappointment. Now, after three girls he had stopped hoping for a son. At times he wondered what it would be like to have a son, to take a little boy places, to show him his business. Well, it didn't matter anyway. All the girls were healthy and he loved to watch them grow. Today he had had a pretty good sale at his general store and had bought some china dolls for them. He crossed the hall room and opened the door.

"How are you, Mother?"

"All right," the weak voice answered.

Chinjoo called to her eldest daughter.

"Tongja, where are you? Take these tray tables in!"

The dinner was served in the master room.

35

Kim Insoo seemed to have a good appetite as he noisily sucked up the noodles.

"Someday I will open a fabric store. The silks. Even Western wools. The tightwad Chinese go underground from house to house. The sly Japanese, they'd never let me get to their wholesalers. It's not the time now. But someday, I will have a huge store hung wall to wall with silks that even an emperor would envy."

Chinjoo sniffed at her husband.

"You've been drinking on the way home!"

Kim Insoo stopped eating and lifted his eyes to his wife.

"Yes, woman! You are right, I have!"

"Don't spread your money around just because you made a few yen more."

"Look here, woman! I spent only a few coins on me. Is that a lot, a few coins?"

"A few coins, and often, make a heap in time."

"You seem to know everything, don't you, uh?" he growled although he wasn't really angry. He resumed his eating. He was content knowing he was a good provider. Few husbands could bring home meat these days.

"I wonder if they will give the right size rubber shoes this time."

"Is there another meeting?" Kim Insoo asked.

"Yes, I think they will talk about collecting more metals. I hear they've collected a lot down in Seoul. Or some other new plans, I don't know."

Akisawa's wife number-two passed the circulars around. A small crowd sat on their knees on a cold dirty tatami stained with cigarette burns. Chinjoo sat down by the wife of Choi, her next-door neighbor. Akisawa himself was there, his short legs folded away from his knees on a cushion. His large eyes peered through thick lenses at the gathering, his wife and the floor in front of him. Smoking a cigarette, he sat slightly behind his wife like a tamed watchdog. Nobody could see in him the rumored temper. Akisawa's wife number-two cleared her throat and began to speak in a tone very different from her usual voice.

"I see tonight's attendance is very poor. Some people are ignorant about our country's emergency. We ought to give everything we have. We are very grateful to His Imperial Majesty and his soldiers for everything we have. The least we can do is to give to help win this war. So, we urge you to donate all your brassware that you can certainly live without."

"On a voluntary basis, that is!" Akisawa interrupted.

"Anything will do. Bowls, spoons, pans. Other units have contributed a lot and we are running far behind. I am sure this is just an emergency measure. After the victory, when we are at peace, you will all be richly compensated."

People looked at one another. Chinjoo didn't follow every word but understood what had been said.

"What is she saying?" Choi's wife murmured turning to Chinjoo.

"Please! No talking in Korean!" Akisawa's wife number-two cautioned.

"She's only asking a question. She doesn't understand Japanese," Chinjoo explained.

"Well, then, next time, send your husband or someone who does," replied Akisawa's wife number-two coldly.

"As you have read in the circular, we are to dress according to our emergency decree. Women have to wear mompei and men leggings with their defense uniforms."

She passed around the sample clothing.

"Now, Kaneyama san."

"It's Kim. Kim." Chinjoo corrected.

The chieftain's wife glared at her. "You mean you haven't changed your last name into Japanese yet?"

"We did. But Kim is still my right name."

"Why, Kaneyama san. You sound very unpatriotic. Nevertheless, I want you to be in charge of getting the people in our unit ready to wear those clothes by the end of this month." Then, stiffly, as if she were giving her own fortune away, she distributed the weekly ration tickets.

As Chinjoo was putting on her rubber shoes at the steps she felt a hand on her shoulder.

"Kaneyama san, I hear your household has the most brassware in our neighborhood. We count on you," Akisawa's wife said.

Humph! you think I've saved all those for the likes of you? Chinjoo, swallowing the urge to answer, fastened the scarf over her head.

Kim Insoo was doing the day's bookkeeping, his broad face bent over the abacus.

"Yobo, they know we have lots of brassware," Chinjoo said taking off her turumagi. "I wonder what they are collecting it for."

37

"Making cannon balls, what else! Thieves!" Kim Insoo spat out, still busy with his bookkeeping. "They sound as if they are fighting their war for our country. The barbarian brats!"

"What do we do?"

"Give them those broken ones. Just the ones we would throw away, no more."

Chinjoo crossed the hall and peeked into her mother-in-law's room.

"Are you asleep, Mother? Is everything all right with you?"

"It is," the mother-in-law answered weakly, awakened from her sleep.

Chinjoo put the children to bed.

"Let's get some sleep too. You have to wake up early, don't you— to go to wholesalers?"

"That's right." He yawned, finished counting the money and put it in the safe.

Chinjoo clicked off the light. The darkened room seemed empty. The heat of the ondol floor soaked into the mattress and warmed her back. That felt good. The smell of sool still lingering around him, Kim Insoo rested his hands on her breasts.

"Why, these things are withering away. They feel like an old man's saggy belly."

"What do you expect after feeding those girls? Even iron breasts would have withered."

"Well, all you gave out are nothings. How about trying for another one? This time for one with something in his paji (pants)?"

"Don't be silly. At our age we should be a grandpa and a grandma."

"Then I will get myself a pretty young one who can give me a dozen sons."

"You just do that! I don't think you will ever find anyone as pretty as me. I am from Kangge, remember? There's nothing like Kangge beauty, you know!"

"There you go again! I am sure you will be, when all the Kangge beauties are dead and gone!"

"When I was born, my father named me Chinjoo because I was as pretty as a pearl!"

"A pearl, indeed!" The Wonjangni sister-in-law had once snorted "She looks more like a yumjoo to me!" A yumjoo, meaning a bead.

Chinjoo, the pearl, in her late 20's, was not pretty. Nor could it be said that she came from Kangge. Her parents left the wooded mountain

38

area long before she was born. But she continued to allude to Kangge whenever she had the chance. Her waist expanded a few inches in the course of giving birth to three daughters. She had double eyelids, a minus quality of a beauty at the time. Her nose was round at the tip, as if an unsuccessful sculptor, at the last minute, had decided to stub his unused ball of clay there. It was, however, 'a nose of good fortune' as they said, that had proved to be true so far: a faithful husband who didn't mind that she had produced only daughters, and a quiet mother-in-law. Her daughters were all pretty. People wondered how an ordinary looking woman like Chinjoo and a rugged husband like Kim Insoo could have such attractive children. She had abundant energy to tackle house chores, while helping in her husband's store. Her erect, solid frame looked as if she had never known sickness.

"Talking about getting yourself a young woman. You just do that! But remember, when you run out of your money and the young one kicks you off like a pair of worn-out straw shoes, don't come crawling back to me on hands and knees: I don't know you."

Kim Insoo didn't answer. He was asleep. Chinjoo clacked her tongue. Listening to the rise and fall of his heavy breathing, she, too, slowly followed him into slumber.

IV. Sixtieth birthday

Sticks in one hand,
Branches in another:
I try to block old age with bushes,
And frosty hair with sticks:
But white hair came by a short cut,
Having seen through my devices.

U Tak [1262-1342]

1942. Seoul, Southern Korea.

"Chayoung must have gone to Japan." The father-in-law informed the family as he settled down after his visit with the dean of the college.

"Japan!" Jungsoon's mother-in-law sat aghast at the news. "Why Japan?" She came a knee closer to her husband. Her eyes red, her cheeks hollow from fretting over the younger son's disappearance.

"Evidently, they have been planning this for quite some time—he and a friend of his." The elderly man's handsome face was troubled. He thought of the many things that could happen.

"But what for?" came the mother-in-law's impatient inquiry.

"Dean tells me his academic standing has dropped below his usual in the last two semesters. He suspects that he might have been involved in some underground student movement. I said no. We would have known if he had been. The dean contacted the parents of the other missing student. His father thought he might be going to Japan because he had asked for money for the next semester registration, which doesn't start until March. And he left a note."

"But Chayoung didn't have any money."

"I hope it's just to avoid this conscription," the father-in-law said as if talking to himself.

Her tightened nerves relaxing, the mother-in-law thought: at least her son was alive. The worst fear was gone.

"He is not involved with a woman, is he?" the mother-in-law blurted out.

"Now, let's worry about one thing at a time. He has gone to Japan, or at least he said he was going to, with a friend, not a woman." The father-in-law answered with mild irritation. "Anyway it's an improvement since last week."

"Oh, he should have told us. I could have given him some money. What can he do without any money!"

"There you go again. He will let us know if he needs money. He is not a child. Let's stop worrying."

"Oh, he should have told us!"

The mother-in-law heaved sigh after sigh.

As the days went by she slowly recovered from the shock and the loss, and decided to go ahead with the celebration of her husband's sixtieth birthday, one of two major occasions in one's life, the other being his first birthday.

In the dim kitchen filled with steam, two pairs of hands busily worked over sweet rice cakes in a large wooden tray.

"Oh, Auntie, I am so glad. It's always nice to have a party, isn't it? We've never had any party like this down where I came from. I hope I can always live with you folks!" Boonee, more festive than anybody else, fondled a sweet rice cake while coating it with mashed red beans. Jungsoon's hands moved fast dusting the delicacies with toasted soy bean flour.

"When you grow up to be marriageable, I don't think you will feel the same way."

"I am not going to marry. Besides there isn't anybody for me except those poor farm hands."

"I am sure there are many others. When the proper time comes, we will look for a good man, not so poor, strong enough to support his wife and family, and we will marry you to him."

"Oh, would you really?" Then Boonee shrank at her own impudence.

"Why, you naughty girl, talking about getting married already?" chuckled Jungsoon.

"I wasn't," Boonee protested with a blush.

"Well, you don't have to worry about it now. Let's get busy with the cakes."

Tomorrow would be her father-in-law's sixtieth birthday. Food was scarce. On the eve of the festivity, it seemed unlikely the feast would be as fine as the ones she remembered. Relatives would have come and stayed

41

many nights to help. There would have been a dozen cake steamers of all sizes scattered over the courtyard, to make a variety of cakes. Two years ago, they had celebrated the mother-in-law's sixtieth birthday. It wasn't grand according to Yoon standards, and they had hoped that, in two years, at the father-in-law's sixtieth birthday, things would get better. Instead things got worse. The mother-in-law had made several trips to her relatives to barter the remainder of her silks, and brought grains, fruits, and nuts.

"Grandpa looks a lot younger than his age, doesn't he?"

"He does."

"Grandpa is nice. I wish Grandma were as nice as grandpa."

"Hush, don't say such a thing! After all she is the one who made all this party possible."

"Well, I know that, but—"

"What's all that talking in the kitchen? We haven't done much yet!" came the mother-in-law's voice from the opposite room. She was making candy with sesame seeds, pine-flower flour and honey. The steamy kitchen was hushed. Under the dim light, two pairs of hands moved faster. Jungsoon and Boonee hoped there would be enough food for everybody tomorrow.

Invited relatives came from all over the city. A couple of cousins had arrived early in the morning and helped in the kitchen. The father-in-law, dressed in the silk clothes Jungsoon had sewn earlier, ushered his own parents to the birthday table placed in the center of the hall room.

"It's your day. We don't have a place there. Oh, I am only glad to live to see your sixtieth birthday." The grandmother-in-law patted her eyelids to dry her tears.

"Come, come, what are you crying for?" the grandfather-in-law laughed, and took a wine bowl from his son.

Proudly, the guest of honor man sat behind the table against the embroidered screen, his wife at his side. Glowing with pleasure, the edges of his eyes wrinkled with smiles. He was graying at the front and at the temples. Although the stacks of the goodies on the large rectangular table were a lot lower than those on his wife's birthday two years ago, he didn't seem to mind it at all. Relatives surrounded them and cheered the elderly couples as the ceremony went on. Men and women lined up in the hall room to pay their personal respect. They bowed to the father-in-law. Some, peeping from the kitchen, awaited their turn.

"Father, we wish you a long, healthy life!" Starting with Daeyoung down to grandsons and cousins, men knelt with hands at their foreheads as they touched the floor. Women slowly, very slowly, made a gracious curtsy from a seated position. When the new daughter-in-law in the second father-in-law's household made her curtsy, she sank down so fast that she bumped the floor. Women folks, whispering among themselves, laughed. The young woman blushed. Elderly friends lifted their wine bowls wishing the father-in-law a good health and long life.

As the ceremony ended people scattered into various rooms: the father-in-law and elderly friends had their dinner table in the guest parlor; the grandfather-in-law and his friends in Chayoung's room, and Jungsoon's husband and his friends in the detached room. Women and children used the master room and the children's with the dividing door open between them. In the kitchen, younger women supplied food and delivered dishes and bowls. Men's laughter echoed from room to room.

"Did you see the youngest daughter-in-law of the second father-in-law's household?" One of Jungsoon's cousins asked, referring to the new daughter-in-law who had hit the floor when she had made her curtsy. The family was well off, the second father-in-law being the co-owner of a gold mine.

"You know, her mother-in-law lavishes her with jewels, and just lets her do whatever she likes. She doesn't care if she sleeps until midday. Can you imagine the daughter-in-law doesn't even know what the kitchen of her own house looks like? When the meal is ready, she is called and she just comes and eats like a guest. And when she is done she just puts down her silver spoon and chopsticks right there on the table and leaves for her room. Oh, I wish my mother-in-law would be half as generous. You know, Kangsup's mom, one thing is sure. You should be born pretty," the talkative cousin concluded.

"Is that right!" Jungsoon responded admiringly.

"Kangsup's mom, do come in and join us," cousins called from the master room.

"Now, Sis, let's go in," the cousin urged.

In the master room on the warmer part of the floor elderly ladies were at the dinner table. At the other end younger women gathered around another table. And Jungsoon could see the young daughter-in-law in silk, her dark hair combed neatly into a chignon, in which stuck a jade hair bar, a gold earpick and several bijou pins. Whenever she lifted her spoon, her hand, smooth and soft, the rings on her fingers shone. The woman's mother-in-law turned to her with a maternal tenderness.

"Try some of these." She turned to other women and said in a concerned tone. "She doesn't seem to be having much appetite these days. I guess she isn't feeling very well."

Jungsoon's grandmother-in-law had her meal in silence, chewing with her dentures, spitting out some of the tough portion of a piece of meat. The meal was over. Tables were removed. Children engaged in their games in the adjoining room, every so often coming and interrupting their mothers' conversation. Ladies were admiring the grandmother-in-law's health. Her gray hair meticulously combed into a chignon, and in white silk chogori and chima, she sat by her daughter-in-law listening and responding in a low voice. The mother-in-law, still concerned over her son's disappearance, couldn't keep it to herself.

"Oh, I wish Chayoung were here. I wonder where he could be! Probably he is sleeping on a cold tatami without any heat." Then she patted her eyes with the tip of her chogori tie.

"Oh, Aunt, don't you worry. He is young and healthy. He will get along fine anywhere. Besides, in Japan things should be better. They take all the rice from here, don't they? They should be eating much better there."

Cousins cheered her up chatting about their children and husbands. They admired the pretty young lady's clothes, and the young lady's proud mother-in-law sat near her all smiles. Jungsoon's grandmother-in-law's eyes traveled from one person to another, and then stared ahead for a moment. Then, like a falling leaf, she fell on her daughter-in-law's lap.

"Goodness gracious! Mother!" the mother-in-law cried. Everybody turned to her. "Someone, go tell the men. Hurry!" the mother-in-law commanded holding her mother-in-law.

"Oh, what shall we do!" One of the women ran out in panic. "Great-grandmother has fainted!"

All the doors slid open almost at the same time, and men rushed out one after another.

"Somebody fetch the doctor!"

Yoon Daeyoung and one of his cousins dashed out the gate.

"Somebody carry Mother to her room!" At the mother-in-law's order the detached room was evacuated and the grandmother's unconscious body was carried there. The birthday man sat on his knees at his mother's side, feeling her pulse and examining her eyes. His father sat next to his son, watching his wife's pale face, expecting to hear better news from his son.

"I still feel her pulse, Father."

The pulse was weak, almost indiscernible. Men waited in the courtyard and the ladies whispered among themselves. At last, the family physician arrived. He examined the patient and said,

"The Lady won't live through the night."

Guests lowered their faces. Here and there cousins were overwhelmed with pity. The feast had turned into sad anticipation. It would be any hour or any minute. But the old lady hung on for many days, breathing heavily. Grandfather-in-law ordered one final treatment with Chinese medicine. Although the woman's malady was simply 'old age', the father-in-law carried out his father's wish. Some cousins stayed and sewed the mourning outfits for the family.

"It's the wild ginseng," sighed a cousin, "which makes it so difficult for Grandma to pass away."

"But for the health she's had all these years we can't complain," another responded.

The smell of boiling herbs lingered in the darkening courtyard. Men paced about in front of the detached room like messengers sent by Death, waiting. Then, at the week's end, toward the evening, the old lady finally gave in. Cousins and the members of the family came down to the courtyard. They could see Grandfather-in-law closing his wife's eyes with his bony hand. His face drooped, and as if it were a signal, men in the courtyard lowered their heads, and women wailed. The children stood in silence, hushed and wondering.

As the sun tilted toward the west, a chill wind blew into the courtyard and up people's sleeves. Oh Jungsoon wept. The only lady who displayed authority and understanding was gone forever. Soft and wise, the voice that used to come out through the small door on the detached room in time of need would no longer be heard.

V. The unlucky

I scorn the world's madness,
The overweening men who seek to use me.
My love (brave children)—that is given
Only to those who come to me with love.
Come, children, let me kiss you and embrace you.

Choe Nam-son [1890-1957]

In a concrete building of an elementary school located in the heart of the city, classes began. Children were hushed. The flag of Japan, a bright red circle on a white background, hung at the front of the room. Accompanying it, was the portrait of the Japanese emperor. The framed broadsheet carrying the oath of imperial Japanese subjects created the triad of intimidation.

Kangsup stared at the young teacher's pretty face with its cute buck tooth. Pointing her spanking rod at the map hung over the blackboard, Teacher Toyota began her usual lecture.

"Now, the Japanese soldiers are bravely fighting at Guadalcanal. Here are the Solomon Islands. This is Guadalcanal. Our air force and navy sank many enemy cruisers and destroyers and battleships." But Teacher Toyota wasn't so high spirited as she used to be earlier in the year. "Our Japanese soldiers are determined to fight and die for His Imperial Majesty. The Americans, they are lazy. They move slowly. They have stiff legs and they cannot bend their knees. So when our Japanese airplanes swoop down on them, they just get hit and die, afraid. We are very grateful to our soldiers."

"Ah—m, sleepy." Kangsup yawned and at the end of it a word escaped from his lips in spite of himself.

"What was that?" Teacher Toyota turned to him. "You! Stand up!"

Kangsup wished it were a dream. He stood up.

"Go out in the hall. Put your hands above your head and stay there until I tell you otherwise."

Feeling the stare of the whole class, his face down, and his neck red, he marched out of the room into the hall. The hall was empty. Pictures of battleships in flames with columns of dark smoke shooting into the pitch black sky, hung along the wall.

It was a long, long while. The blood seemed to have drained from his aching arms. How he wanted to put them down! Through the window he could see the heads of the students turned toward the blackboard. They were listening attentively to the teacher who seemed to have changed the subject to the Japanese language. It was a disgrace to be left out in the hall alone. He should have been careful. But how could he help it? It had been a hectic week at home. People bustled in and out, a constant stream of visitors paying respect to the deceased. Each time there was a new arrival, a new wail ensued. Then came the funeral procession in which he, too, was included. Draped in hemp clothes and mourning cap the lady cousins had sewn in a hurry, Kangsup followed the lines of family all the way to the family graveyard in Suwon. And Great-grandma—until a few years ago she had cuddled him on her lap and stroked his hair. He could almost see the door sliding open and hear her voice coming from the detached room. But that was only memory. He was sad and frightened. The white coffin which several men had carried out of the room was vivid in his memory. The wailing, true and artificial alike—the earth spilling mercilessly into the deep where his great-grandma lay. Would she be alive somewhere as a spirit? Perhaps watching him right now? If she were, she would scold him for getting into trouble at school. The school bell rang and he jumped. The class was over, but the teacher continued talking. When she finally came out, she spoke sternly to the boy.

"Put your hands way up above your head!" Teacher Toyota walked off to the teachers' room. Children rushed out from all classrooms.

"Hey, look over there! He is being punished."

"What happened?"

"He must have done something very bad."

"Maybe he forgot to bring his books."

"Maybe he didn't finish his homework."

Children whispered as they passed by, hushed and glad they weren't the one in the situation. Kangsup wished he were dead. If only he were a mouse and could crawl into a hole! Children returned to their classes. Teacher Toyota stood behind the lectern and received the bow of the class. Another class period had begun. Alone in the hall, Kangsup rested his aching arms against the window pane. Recitations droned on in unison.

47

At intervals he could hear Teacher Toyota's solo voice. Twisting his body, he let his arms lower to his waist. Whenever the teacher's head turned toward the hall window, he hurriedly put his hands back up. When the teacher turned away to write on the blackboard, he leaned against the pane and thought about home, his great-grandma and her spirit. Suddenly, pain stung his right arm. Teacher Toyota was standing by him with the spanking stick.

"Attention!" She slapped his left arm. "Put that one straight up too!"

Another school bell chimed and the children came out, played, and returned to their classroom.

Lunch hour started. Teacher Toyota and children folded their hands. "Soldiers, thank you for food!"

Tin lunch boxes opened. They all started eating. Kangsup's ache overshadowed his hunger. He seemed to have stood there forever. For a short while he felt pain in his empty stomach. Soon that was gone too. Children came out of the classroom, went to the bathroom and returned. He wanted to go to the bathroom very badly. Several times when the teacher was going in and out the door he attempted to ask permission, but the stern face of Teacher Toyota stopped him. As the urge became stronger he twisted his legs, and his face turned red. He wished to run down the hall. The voice of Teacher Toyota and the children's loud responses—he hopped, twisted, his face swelling, his teeth clenched—-the picture of the battleships exploding on the wall. He held and held, until he lost control. Lowering his head, he watched the small lake on the floor in despair. Shadows lengthened across on the opposite wall. The school day approached its end.

Teacher Toyota walked toward him.

"Put your hands down now!" she said and strode down the hall.

Hot blood coursed through his arms. They burned. At the end of the hall, he saw a lady in hemp clothes. Her face as pale as the white mourning ribbon braided into her chignon, his mother hurried toward him. Her face twisted with pity, she placed her hand on his shoulder. Hot tears ran down his cheek. Her eyes swept down the wretched figure and saw the wet floor.

Kangsup walked down the hall with his mother. His legs felt stiff and funny. Although it was a smooth surface he felt as though he were walking up and down a rugged hill. He wanted to say something but his lips felt frozen.

48

"Oh, you must be cold and hungry. Next time, dear, just be a little more careful," Jungsoon softly said when they were out of the building.

"Oh, that ugly teacher. I hate her!" Kangsup blurted out.

"Hush, don't say such a thing."

Dark and cold, the evening descended. Passing cars switched on their headlights. His legs feeling better, yet cold and uncomfortable, his cheeks blown dry, he held his mother's hand and walked down the street vowing he would never again yawn.

That night, Jungsoon stooped over her sick son, placing a wet towel over his forehead. Kangsup dreamed, talking in delirium. He was climbing up the steps that lead to Namsan Shinto shrine. The breathless, endless climbing up the hundreds of steps and Teacher Toyota's stern face. Finally he got there, up on the mountain top, washed his hands and mouth at the ablution basin and approached the oratory with other children. He bowed. He clapped hands as he was told, casting a glance inside the dark sanctuary fearing whatever was hidden in there. Then someone grabbed him from behind. A samurai in a Japanese monk's robe. 'Reverently! Reverently! More! More!' He had done just as others had, but the samurai demanded more. He tried to run away, tripped, and slid down the endless steps on the side of the mountain. Jungsoon called to him, gently rocking her son.

"Kangsup, Kangsup, you are having a bad dream!"

By the pump, Jungsoon polished the silver spoons and chopsticks. She heard a rustle at the front premises. A letter was thrown in through the gate. Wiping her hands on her apron, she picked it up carefully. It was addressed to her mother-in-law and carried no return address. In a short while, an excited voice sounded from her mother-in-law's room.

"Oh, it's from Japan, it's from Chayoung. He is there, safe!"

"Is he well, Mother?" Jungsoon was delighted and relieved to hear about the missing brother-in-law.

All night the household was alive with the mother-in-law's reaction. The next morning, Jungsoon was summoned to her mother-in-law's room.

"Sit down, there!"

Jungsoon sat at a distance with deference. The mother-in-law sat across from her staring at the corner of the room, hesitating for a while.

"You—know how it is in this house. I have been selling my belongings to keep up with our expenses. Now I can't think of anything else

49

that can bring a sum of money, when Chayoung needs it very badly. I— didn't want to do this, but it seems there's no other way." The mother-in-law faced her. "You still have your wedding ring, don't you?"

"Yes, Mother."

"I've talked with your husband. And your father-in-law. Of course we hope things will get better and you will get it back." Her mother-in-law's voice was soft, inducing. It had been always so ever since the grandmother-in-law passed away. As if she were trying to fill that position. "It's not going to be pawned. We wouldn't get much money. There's a potential buyer, at a good price. You don't mind, do you?" she searched her daughter-in-law's downcast face.

"No, not at all," Jungsoon answered but not altogether unshaken. She had been expecting it, but for a different purpose.

"All right, then bring it to me. I will—take care of it."

Deep inside the chest drawer in an embroidered purse she kept the five-don ring of pure gold, the only jewel she had ever had. It wasn't as luxurious as those of some of the relatives. It was all the household could afford when it was presented to her at the time of her marriage. She cherished it, wearing it only occasionally to parties and on visits to her parents. Jungsoon took it out and tried it on her finger as if it were a borrowed ring. Then putting aside sentiment, she took it off and brought it to her mother-in-law. Her hands trembled slightly. Feeling somewhat empty she returned to her work.

Yoon Daeyoung was sitting at his usual place reading the newspaper.

"I gave the ring to Mother," Jungsoon said softly.

"Uh?" Daeyoung lifted his eyes above his newspaper. Then "All right," and returned to his paper.

VI. Brassware

Beaten by the bitter season's whip,
at last I am driven to this north.
I stand upon the sword-blade frost,
Where numb sky and plateau merge.
I do not know where to bend my knees,
Nor where to lay my vexed steps.
I cannot but close my eyes and think—
Winter, O winter is a steel rainbow.

Yi Yuksa [1905-1944]

Northern Korea.

On a sunny hall room floor Chinjoo, the pearl, started to sort the brassware, which she had collected during the past twelve years. They were not only good to keep food warm in winter, they were a proud addition to the wealth of the family. She had taken a sack to Akisawa already, but the Japanese might stop in any time for more. Policemen just barged into houses and took whatever they saw, people said. Carefully, Chinjoo wrapped the shiny brassware in pieces of cloth, put them into a sack and stored them in the empty kimchee barrel for her husband to bury in the backyard.

As she finished, someone rattled the gate. It was Akisawa's wife accompanied by a policeman.

"May we come in and take a look? You may not know what you have in your own house."

Before Chinjoo could answer, they strode in and stalked around, looking, circling the well against which leaned a washpan which she had forgotten to put away. The policeman went to the backyard and Akisawa's wife peeked into the kitchen. As she was passing by the kimchee barrel, Chinjoo felt her heart throbbing. They looked and circled around two more times.

"Surely, I thought you would have more," said Akisawa's wife with a wry smile, as she left with the policeman.

51

Through the mini-door in the dividing fence neighbor Choi's wife emerged with a pair of finished mompei.

"Can you imagine? They've even taken the chamber pot. I left it out there after I cleaned it. Were they here, too?"

"They were here, all right. But they couldn't find anything more. We've given enough already. They should be ashamed of themselves wanting more from us."

"Oh, I should have put the chamber pot right away. I should have replaced it with china long before. That was the last polished brassware we had."

"Cheer up, Friend! If they took the last one, they can't come back again. The time will come soon when we can enjoy life without any fear or worry."

"Do you really think that time will ever come?" Choi's wife heaved a sigh sitting on the edge of the hall floor. "Well, it seems to me we will all starve before we get bombed. Now, rationing the soybean screenings! The refuse after extracting the soybean oil. Have you cooked them yet?"

"Not yet. I will go get them this afternoon."

"I didn't know how to cook those. So I made gruel out of them. It makes me so hungry, even a bushel of them won't fill my stomach. You know, grownups can stand some, but it's a pity to see children swallowing down the animal feed."

Chinjoo, the pearl, was quick in giving.

"I've cooked some barley cake," she handed her neighbor a dish of barley cakes and bowlful of millet. "Here, cook this for dinner for your children. It will be better than the soybean screenings."

"Thanks, Tongja's mom. But what about you? You need it too."

"O, we've got some, too. We share what we have today and we'll worry with what we've got tomorrow." Chinjoo's voice with strong Pyongan Province accent rumbled with confidence.

Kim Insoo brought home some more millet and potatoes. He had gone to the farmer to trade some of his store items.

"We were lucky. The policeman and the chieftain went around and took things from neighborhood houses. That was just after I put things away. They didn't even see the washpan by the well. Now, let's start digging. The kimchee barrel's right there."

Kim Insoo dug up the hard ground and, with his wife's help, lowered the barrel down and covered it with dirt and smoothed the surface.

"That means we can't use those for quite some time," he chuckled as he scattered leaves and twigs over the newly turned earth.

Kim Insoo started his bookkeeping in the master room and Chinjoo was sewing the youngest Sunhee's little dress.

"Darn! I can't concentrate." Kim Insoo shook off the abacus. Then again his big fingers worked on the counters. He yawned. "Well, I should be going to bed early. Being a head of the family isn't that easy you know," he joked. After helping the children to bed, he himself changed into his night clothes. He was about to fall asleep when there was a loud bang at the gate.

"Who can that be at this time of night?" Chinjoo wondered.

The banging grew louder. Kim Insoo stood at the edge of the hall room and poked his head out toward the gate.

"Who's there?"

"Open the door, or we'll break in!"

"I am coming." Troubled, Kim Insoo hurried toward the front. "Who's there?" He wanted to make sure.

"Shut up and open it. Police," came the gruff answer in Japanese. Kim Insoo took off the latch. The gate was pushed open from outside. Light from the door silhouetted two policemen, their swords shining at their sides. "Are you Kim Insoo?" One of them facing him.

"Yes, I am."

"Come with us to the station."

"Come along," hissed the other as Kim Insoo hesitated.

"What's going on out there?" Chinjoo slipped on her rubber shoes and ran toward them.

"Just a minute, I have to change my clothes." Kim Insoo was about to turn when the two men stopped him.

"No time for that, you fool. Let's go." They wrestled his hands behind his back, handcuffed him, and pushed him out the gate. Chinjoo rushed outside with his turumagi.

"Here, you put this on," when she tried to cover his shoulder, one of the men threw it down on the ground. She picked it up and followed.

"Go home!" Her husband cautioned her.

With her husband's turumagi hung over her arm, Chinjoo followed them all the way to the police station. In a room cramped with desks and partitions two policemen lounged around a stove.

"Ahh, is this the one?"

53

"That's the one."

Kim Insoo stood in front of them, shivering.

"Attention, you fool!" one of the policemen who had come with him yelled, his eyes ablaze. A signal passed among them. And the policeman with eyelids which looked as if an extra pound of flesh had been stuffed in them, pushed Kim Insoo toward the basement stairs. Chinjoo was quickly barred as she attempted to follow.

"Mr. Policemen, where are you taking him? What has he done wrong?"

"You, noisy! Go over there!"

Chinjoo retreated to a corner hoping her obedience would ease the matter. Cries came from the basement. Then a succession of lashings. In shock, Chinjoo dashed down the stairs. Kim Insoo was on his knees on the concrete floor. Many people involved in the underground independence movement were said to have been tortured in this building. The cellar reeked with unpleasant smells. Stains besmirched the walls. In one corner a long water hose lay in a coil, still wet from the previous torture. In the dimness, Chinjoo took a moment to recognize the creatures there. A policeman stepped out of the shadows. His rubber truncheon rained blows upon her husband: head, shoulders, ears, face. Kim Insoo closed his eyes, his nose and lips bleeding heavily. If only his hands were free! Then he would dash to the beast and tear him apart! Through his clenched teeth came a groan. It must be that Nakamoto who, it was rumored, had beaten people, broken jaws and fractured ribs. Out of her mind, Chinjoo jumped on the man.

"Why are you hitting him? He did nothing wrong. I did. I hid all of them. Lot's of thieves around. So I hid them and forgot!" Chinjoo screamed in broken Japanese gesturing insanely.

The policeman stared at her. Contemptuously, he picked a sack from a bench and flung it at her.

"Fill the sack and bring it back here!"

"I will, Oh, I will." Chinjoo rushed to her husband. Feeling his pain, she lifted the end of her chima and wiped the blood from his battered face.

Kim Insoo, limped as his wife helped him upstairs and out of the police station. The streets and houses were dark. Chill air attacked his swollen face.

"Sons of dogs!" Kim Insoo shouted into the cold starry sky. The murky sky hung up there mutely witnessing the scene below.

"Don't worry, you will be all right. Remember the saying 'Those who get hit can get a sound sleep but those who hit can't.'? You will be all right. The day will come when we will see the bright sunshine," Chinjoo soothed him in spite of her own indignation. "Be careful. It's so dark. Watch your step."

The next morning Chinjoo dug up the ground and took the brassware to the police station, hating herself for having caused her husband senseless pain and humiliation. On the way she met Akisawa's wife. Akisawa gave her a meaningful smile.

"I told you, you might have some more." She hurried away, her wooden sandals clattering.

Yi Chinjoo tended the store while her husband recuperated. For several days, Kim Insoo lay in his bed, staring at the ceiling.

"How are you feeling, Yobo? Did you have something to eat?" It was painful to see a healthy man like her husband lying in there useless, his mind torn worse than his body. "You need to get up and move around. You will feel much better."

"Look, woman, leave me alone, will you?" Her concern only provoked him.

Japanese policemen visited the store asking questions and trying to find fault. Kim Insoo went back to work but acted like someone who had lost a member of his family. He spoke little. He didn't care if one of the door handles had come off or the girls raced. Weeks passed. The notorious policeman, Nakamoto, and his colleagues had beaten up more residents.

Then Kim Insoo abruptly announced.

"I am going to Manchuria!"

"Manchuria, did you say? Why? Why Manchuria?"

"I've got to get out of here. I loathe the sight of those island barbarians!"

"But there are Japanese police over there, too. They are everywhere."

"I will join the underground force. If I can't locate them there, I am going to go as far as Chungking. I hear there are separate Korean units among the Chinese army fighting against the Japanese. If that's just a rumor, I will start a unit myself. I will fight them until the last drop of my blood is shed. I can't stand it any more. My stomach turns. My blood boils. I am about to explode."

"Can we go with you?"

"Are you out of your mind? It's no place for a woman and children.

55

We may all die on the way. Don't you worry, I will be in touch. You just play dead here. It won't be long. Everything is meant to have an end."

Realizing he was determined, Chinjoo began to sniffle.

"Come, come, you stop being silly. I am just going away for a short while, you hear me?"

Chinjoo's glance fell sadly on the youngest girl asleep at the far side of the room. Blotting her eyes with the tip of her chima, she sniffled again.

"When is this going to be?"

"Tomorrow morning." Kim Insoo pulled some money from his safe, pocketed some, and pushed the rest toward her. "Here, this will keep you and the children going for a while. I will let you know as soon as I get settled."

Packing for him and pausing many times, she didn't forget to give him some advice.

"Clean your clothes often. Don't wear your shirts until they get too soiled. You may be needing some pans and pots too, don't you? Have the water just about up to your wrist, otherwise, the rice will cook too watery. Get to sleep early. Don't worry about your spending money. Stay in decent inns. And ride the train whenever you can. Don't walk just to save your money. And—"

"I know, I know. Noisy woman."

Chinjoo's shoulders shook violently with a sudden realization that her man was leaving her with no definite destination or date of return. Kim Insoo tapped his wife on her shoulder.

"Listen, there's nothing to cry about. Nobody is dead or anything. I said I would be gone only a short while, you hear me?"

Kim Insoo held her in his arms during the night. Early in the morning he departed, leaving a worried Chinjoo and children behind. The snow that had fallen overnight crunched under his feet as he threw the sack over his shoulder and walked away. To passers-by, he looked as though he were going to the wholesalers as usual.

VII. The maid has gone home.

Misery! They deceived me!
  Autumn moon and spring breeze,
  they deceived me!
Each season returned in time
  and I believed they were faithful.
But they left me with my greying hair
  and chased away to find more youngsters.

Anonymous

1944. Southern Korea.

Birthdays came and went, each one less festive than the one preceding. The celadon porcelain had been sold to a private collector. Gone, too, the ten-fold embroidered screen. In the detached room, Grandfather-in-law coughed and answered to Jungsoon's gentle inquiry "Is your room warm enough, Grandfather?" "Huh? No! It's chilly." Then Jungsoon would scrape wood bits and build up the fire to heat the room. He seldom came out except at meal time. Often, he took his meal in his room with a solitary table. Visiting his friend across the street had long ceased: His old friend had died. He heard without listening and looked at things without seeing them.

Sunshine streamed into the hall room. Boonee went to visit a neighbor with Wonsup, and Jungsoon fulled at a fulling-block. With a pair of slender oak clubs, she pounded on the starched sheets folded and stacked on the stone block. In a little while, the sheets became compact and pressed, ready to be sewn to the mattresses and quilt of her parents-in-law. The soybean screenings she had at breakfast had been digested long before she did the breakfast dishes. Now she was accustomed to skipping lunches. Her stomach was so flat that the string of her chima tied around her chest kept falling down to her waist. She stopped pounding and listened. Jisup crying? No, it couldn't be. The child had been dead for a year. Measles. Red bumps all over his weak body and the fever that had taken the last breath of the feeble child. She still could hear his crying and see the little legs that started walking when he was two. He always looked as though he were falling down, and when he did, he exposed his four front teeth and tried to smile. Whenever she heard a baby crying in the neighborhood, she would stop working and listen as if it were him. Poor child! Sometimes she heard her mother-in-law calling 'Jisup is crying!' The vision became hazy and she saw Boonee quietly sitting down to take over.

"Auntie, Grandma is calling."

"Did you call me, Mother?"

"Can I see you for a minute?" came her mother-in-law's voice from the opposite room. Jungsoon opened the door and quietly stepped into her mother-in-law's room.

"Sit down there." The mother-in-law searched her. "Why are you crying?"

"Oh, it's nothing, Mother. I must have thought of Jisup again," Jungsoon explained gently.

"Well, I think it was all the better for him. The way it is now, we couldn't have fed him well anyway." The mother-in-law paused for a moment.

"I wrote to Boonee's parents. I think you can get along without her, can't you? Boonee's father will be here any minute. Fix something for him, will you?"

In the hall room Boonee stared blankly at the fulling-block.

"Boonee, your father is coming."

"I heard."

The mother-in-law had written to Boonee's father asking him to take her back: her service was no longer needed. Due to the circumstances, the mother-in-law's desire to marry Boonee off when such a time arrived could not be realized. Thus, it was best she join her family.

When Jungsoon returned from the municipal market, Boonee greeted her with drooping head. On the stone step in the front premises were a pair of muddy straw shoes, a sign that a country guest was present.

"I believe your father is here?"

Boonee followed Jungsoon to the kitchen with a long face.

"Auntie, I don't want to go home. Please don't send me back. I don't have to eat anything. I will just stay and work. There are lots of things to do and you need me, don't you? You don't have to feed me at all. I will survive somehow. Please let me stay."

Jungsoon's heart ached. She had seen Boonee grow up, had shared the kitchen, had gone through many difficult times with her, yet she couldn't do a thing to help her stay.

"You are not going away for good. You can come back in a month or in a year, when things get better. Perhaps you might like your home after all. It's just that you've been away from it for so long." But both of them knew things weren't going to get better. It would get worse, never better.

Jungsoon packed Boonee's things for her. She washed and folded all her clothes as she would do for her own child going for a short trip.

A ruddy, rugged bearded man with his dry muddy hand had scraped up his meal fast.

"Let's go. Get your bundle," Boonee's father ordered gruffly. Reluctantly Boonee picked up her bundle. She eyed the grandmother, hoping the matriarch might have changed her mind.

"Good bye, Boonee. Write to us, you understand?" the grandmother said, standing at the edge of the hall room. Boonee crossed the courtyard.

"Aren't you going to say 'good bye' to Great-grandfather?" The mother-in-law called to Boonee.

Jungsoon led Boonee to the door of the detached room. "Grandfather, Boonee is leaving!" Jungsoon said at the door.

"Huh?" At last the door slid open. "Oh, all right." Grandfather-in-law's eyes and mind remained unfocused. He didn't comprehend what was going on.

"Good bye, Great-grandpa." Boonee turned her face away and walked through the front premises and out the gate. Jungsoon followed. She squeezed a couple of yen into Boonee's hand.

"Buy something to eat on the way."

"Good bye, Auntie." Boonee didn't look back. Clutching her bundle to her side, she followed silently at the heels of her father's straw shoes.

It was so empty. In the kitchen, by the water pump, in her room, when she did laundry and ironing, waiting on her parents-in-law, Boonee's absence was felt everywhere. And the sudden memory of her lost child added to it, Jungsoon cried quietly while doing the dishes and fulling the sheets.

Several weeks passed. Her sorrow gradually faded under the burden of work and worry about the source of the daily meal. Chilly weather continued. There was no fuel. Jungsoon made a hot water bottle and wrapped it in a towel.

"Grandfather, here is your hot water bottle."

No answer.

"Grandfather, here's your hot water bottle," she called a little louder. Still no answer, not even coughing. "Grandfather?" Jungsoon brought her ear closer to the door. She felt a chilly silence. Frightened, she slid the door open. She sucked in her breath. The old man was dead. His bearded chin was lifted upward, his lips apart, his eyes the way he looked at Boonee when she was leaving. His horse hair hat had fallen off.

"Father, Mother, Oh, please do come and look!"

Doors opened. Even her husband put down his newspaper and came in.

"Finally he has joined Mother," the father-in-law murmured bending his head beside his deceased father.

It was a simple funeral. The body was cremated and men took the ashes to the Yoon family graveyard for burial.

Although the family was rapidly becoming smaller, Jungsoon's work load seemed ever increasing. The mother-in-law visited relatives. Father-in-law came and went, meeting with friends, speculating on business possibilities, which eventually generated more debts. Jungsoon had to supply them with laundered and newly sewed clothes.

A gentleman came to visit the father-in-law and Jungsoon could hear them talking in the guest palor.

"Sir, I wish you would dispose of your headstrong point of view. Take the job. It's a small job, but at least you won't be starving. And, of course, you will relieve some of the burden on the younger members of this family."

"I came this far without taking any job they were offering. I don't wish to play their scarecrow in any manner, small or big," retorted the father-in-law.

"There you go again. Why, look at yourself. In debt. And without food. Avoiding your duns. This is not your life."

"Well, Sir, I will stand as long as I can."

A week later, Yoon Daeyoung was summoned to his parent's room. After a long while he came back.

"Father and Mother decided to sell the house. We have to look for a small rental house. Father has taken a job as a town chief about forty miles from here."

60

VIII. Liberation

Huge beams and rooftree timbers
  are rejected and thrown away;
While the house is falling down
  they argue with one another.
Carpenters, when will you stop
  running around with your ink-cups and rules?
                    Chong Chol (1536-1593)

1945. Southern Korea.

It had been a year since they rented the two-bedroom house in the northwestern section of Seoul. Another room in the front premises had been rented to a younger couple from a southern city. The house in Myongyoon-dong was sold. Jungsoon had not realized her parents-in-law had been so deeply in debt. A portion of the sales income went into their rent. Some underwrote the parents-in-law's move to the new post in the rural area. And a portion was saved for the son who had disappeared. Even though Jungsoon's family had become so small it made her feel strange, her husband's salary hardly met the food and fuel expenses. Necessary items were scarce and unavailable even if the family had adequate funds. Jungsoon darned children's socks again and again, and made their clothes out of her husband's old shirts and pants.

Everyone was affected by the desperate fighting of the war. Neighborhood unit meetings continued. Circulars were passed out concerning the emergencies. There were air-defense drills. Every morning women in mompei and scarf were summoned to practice defense drills. Women lined up and passed water buckets to put out hypothetical fires caused by hypothetical raids. Men dug raid shelters.

"An air-raid warning!"

"All clear!" The chieftain's shrill voice was unnerving.

"An air-raid alarm!" The sixth-grade teacher's voice and the loud siren warned that danger was imminent. Hyonsup and other children ran out of the concrete building as the siren howled. This time it was real. He ran home as fast as he could. Streets emptied. People scurried to their homes. Some peeked out of their gates to watch American B-29s which were supposedly flying over. Hyonsup searched the sky too.

"See, the thin white smoke lines up there?" one of them said.

"Where? I don't see any," answered another.

Hyonsup tripped over a stone and fell. He got up and walked home fast, a burning pain in his knees. His mother ran toward the gate.

"Goodness! You are hurt!"

Hyonsup looked down. Blood was trickling down his leg and into his sneaker.

"Come, let me wash you." Then Jungsoon explained while drying her son's knees and applying an antiseptic. "You may have to go to your grandparent's house in the country. They have asked you to come. Seoul has to be evacuated. They say it might be bombed any day."

"Are they really going to?"

"I am afraid so."

After Jungsoon sent the children to the home of her parents-in-law, she often found time to chat with Chung's wife, an amiable young woman from a southern city and the tenant in the front part of the house.

"Oh, this house looks so empty without the children," noted Chung's wife who had been good to the boys.

"My mother-in-law must be having a hard time to look after the children. I have to go and help as soon as vacation starts."

"I'm going to have a lot of children. Grown up as the only child, I've always envied households bustling with children."

"You will have your own child running around soon enough."

"My husband and I will be out of town soon, too. My parents ask us to join them."

"I will miss you."

School vacation time. The small town with a post office, police station, administration building, train depot and a few shops was like other towns Jungsoon used to know. The house in which her parents-in-law were living was provided by the government and was not far from the country's main road. A distant niece of her mother-in-law's had come to live with them and help. Her mother-in-law greeted Jungsoon with her usual coolness.

"Oh, these boys are so wild. Sometimes I wish you had had a girl for a change."

"Hyonsup and Wonsup should have stayed with us, Mother. Seoul seems all right, even though air raid warnings and the defense drills continue," Jungsoon responded meekly.

"Still, Seoul is more dangerous than the countryside. What I meant was I wish they had their mother to take care of them. But with Kangsup's father still working there, I can't ask you to come and stay with them, can I?" the mother-in-law concluded and instructed her niece to start dinner. Jungsoon put on her apron and excused herself to help in the kitchen.

"Sister, you've had a long trip. You should rest." The sixteen-year-old girl, her face round and docile, smiled timidly as she entered.

"That's all right. I am quite used to those short trips. Thank you for taking care of the children. Your hands must have been very full."

"Oh, it's nothing, Sister. I come from a very large family. I've grown up with six brothers and four sisters. Your boys seem to be well behaved children."

"Thank you. Oh, aren't those dried fernbrakes?"

"Yes, Sister. Aunt and I went to the mountain and picked them in the spring and dried them."

"You mean my mother-in-law picked those?"

"Yes, Sister. See all those dried vegetables? Radish, peas and spring cabbage? She managed to get some seeds from farmers and planted them in the garden. And after picking them she dried them all for winter. It's a little late this evening, but tomorrow I will show you where the vegetable patch is. We've planted some potatoes, sweet potatoes, and corn too. They will be ready to eat in a few weeks."

"I wonder how she managed to do that. As far as I know she has never seen a field in her life." Jungsoon could not help being amazed.

"I had to show her in the beginning, but now she is such an expert she doesn't seem to need my help."

Dinner included rice mixed with other cereal. Jungsoon was glad to serve the dinner table for the parents-in-law. It was an almost forgotten duty. At some distance, Jungsoon sat at another table with her cousin and her younger sons.

"Use your spoon! Chopsticks are for the side dishes."

The mother-in-law's hands had become rough. Whenever she lifted her hand to watch her grandchildren's table manners, Jungsoon noticed a change of lifestyle that the elder had undergone. Her dignified father-in-law appeared as she remembered, except for a little more white hair.

"So, is Kangsup's dad coming tonight?"

"Yes, Father. He will be here by the last train if he is lucky enough to get a ticket."

At the end of the evening, Yoon Daeyoung joined his parents and his family. Munching his late dinner, he explained:

"Almost everybody seems to have gone to the countryside. The bombing is imminent. Even the Japanese company I work for seems to be in confusion. Some of my colleagues have evacuated already. Those sirens and warnings. But it seems to me the bombers just come here to reconnoiter."

"Stay here for a while. There is no sense remaining in the big city when you know it's dangerous," urged the mother-in-law sitting next to her son.

It was another bright summer morning. Jungsoon, accompanied by the cousin, went to the field not far away. Walking into the garden carrying a basket, she was overwhelmed with joy and memories. Although she had grown up more than thirty miles further south, the area was similar. Her family had tenants farming for them. Her mother planted a great variety of vegetables in the backyard, and when they were ripe she and her mother enjoyed harvesting them. Her parents had died, and her brother inherited the shrunken piece of land from which the family eked out a scanty livelihood. Would there ever be such a time of abundance and plenty again? Jungsoon walked through the corn patch looking for ripe ears. The cool breeze rustled tall stalks that seemed to be whispering among themselves.

"Look, Sister, how these potatoes have grown!" The cousin stooped down and dug out a good sized one.

"Do you think they are ready?"

"No, but we can try some at dinner."

"Oh, look at these zucchini squash, slender and shiny, just right for another side dish."

The cousin didn't respond. She was staring in another direction.

"Sister, look over there!"

A knot of farmers, waving flags, were hastening toward them.

"What are they saying?" the cousin wanted to know, watching them intently. As they approached they could hear the loud cheers.

"Liberation! Liberation!! Manseh! Manseh!! Long live Korea!" Jungsoon couldn't believe her ears. The crowd shouted in near hysteria:

"Manseh! Manseh! No more Japanese rule!" They waved the flag which did not have the red circle in the middle, the one that was all-too familiar. It was like the Taigeuk flag long hidden in a box in her parents' home. Jungsoon was shaken. Her heart pounded with excitement.

"Sister, what is it?"

"I—I am not sure. It can't be!" Jungsoon stooped down. "Let's just pick."

While they gathered their vegetables, another group of people hurried past. This time the meaning of the wild shouts was clear.

"What are you doing there? Liberation! You can talk and sing in Korean now. Manseh!"

Jungsoon could no longer suppress her excitement.

"Let's go home!"

Her legs trembled as they rushed toward the house. Out of breath, Jungsoon pushed the gate open and excitedly shared the news with the household. The mother-in-law stared at her.

"Now, control your excitement. Tell me what it was you saw."

"Young men waving Korean flags calling out 'Manseh,' Mother."

"Are you sure?" her husband pressed for reassurance.

"Sure, oh, sure," Jungsoon and the cousin said in unison.

"Ssh! We should be careful about what we are saying." The mother-in-law cautioned, but didn't wait long to rush to a neighbor. They were right. People were in the street watching one group of excited men go by. They appeared to be coming from another town.

The father-in-law came home with the news. The Japanese had surrendered! It had been broadcast in Seoul. Their hearts too full for words, tears streamed down their cheeks.

Toward the evening, the family settled down somewhat. Children played. Women sewed.

"So, finally, it has come to an end after thirty-five long years," mused the father-in-law, sitting on a silk quilt mat. He broke the silence solemnly as he squeezed the pair of walnuts in his hand: a folk remedy to relieve the stiffness in his hands. "It didn't work—Taewonkun's seclusion policy. He thought if we shut off all the foreign influence, we would be safe and

65

out of trouble. It didn't work that way, did it! Japan, under Meiji, opened its door to Western civilization. It acquired all the modern weapons and when their strength became as big as their heads, they invaded us. And here, like a frog inside a well, we couldn't do a thing but be swallowed. And we were left decades behind civilization. It didn't work, did it!'' For a while there was silence, broken only by the sound of the two walnuts scraping against each other.

"What happens next? Our country will be independent, will it not? I wonder if we will have Yi Kingdom again,'' the mother-in-law pondered.

"King Kojong ruined the country, and I don't think anybody will favor the restoration of the Imperial rule. Probably Rhee Syngman will come home from America.''

"What about Mr. Lyuh Woonhyung, Father? He was active in the underground movement for independence. And what about Mr. Kim Koo and the provisional Korean government in Chungking?''

"Eventually Kim Koo and Rhee Syngman will work something out. The problem is from now on. After defeating the common enemy, there follows a power struggle: rivalries, factions. And there will be victors and victims.''

Men went on with their conversation. Wonsup fell asleep on his mother's lap. The historic August night grew dark, just like any other night.

In the morning, excitement grew. The father-in-law was in and out visiting his friends, gathering the news. The next-door neighbor, a school teacher, stopped by with some more tidbits.

"The Americans dropped a secret new weapon called atomic bombs on Hiroshima and Nagasaki. They were so powerful that just one bomb demolished a whole city.''

"My, my! No wonder the Japanese surrendered so quickly,'' Jungsoon's mother-in-law exclaimed.

"They say Russian soldiers were actually fighting in the north with the Japanese. They have crossed the border and are moving south.''

"Will they be here soon?''

"We don't know yet.''

The women couldn't concentrate on their work.

"Let's get busy. We have to pick some more squash and dry them while there's sunshine.'' The mother-in-law gave orders but her mind was not wholly on her work. She even asked the cousin to go out and bring some more news.

The father-in-law returned from his office.

"I can't figure out what's going on. Funny, the Russians have stopped at the 38th parallel. The Japanese military headquarters seem to be still there in Seoul issuing orders. I wonder if we are really free."

"The 38th parallel?" the mother-in-law stared at her husband, wondering. Her son answered it for her.

"Mother, it's a latitude line that crosses right in the middle of our country."

"Daeyoung, bring me that atlas in the bookcase over there, will you?" The father-in-law pointed at the opposite wall.

Men studied the map. As the elder pointed out the line, a shadow crossed his face as if he envisioned his country's future trouble.

Daeyoung, full of his dreams, wanted to leave for Seoul but was advised not to. He decided to stay a few more days. The news came from Seoul that Lyuh Woonhyung had taken over the civil administrator's responsibilities.

"Isn't he Communist oriented?" Daeyoung asked.

"Apparently he's the only one available now. I hear the Americans are to be here, south of the 38th parallel."

Yoon Daeyoung decided to leave for Seoul anyway.

"But be careful. The Japanese are still here." His mother, troubled, cautioned him time and again.

People poured into the country station.

"Manseh! Manseh! Long live Korea!"

All arriving trains were packed with people. People in the freight cars, in open coal carts, and young men on top of the cars waved their flags. Some were returning from forced conscription and labor. Some were merely going back home. All seemed to be heading for Seoul. Jungsoon waited at the station with her husband and children. Crowded train after crowded train arrived and chugged away. It had been impossible to squeeze into any of them. Jungsoon's husband was determined to get aboard as another train roared into the station. Even before it wheezed to a stop, people ran attempting to get on.

"Wait! We are getting off! After we get off!" shouted some whose destination had been reached. The minute they managed to get themselves out, people on the platform crowded up the steps. Yoon Daeyoung, pushing through the crowd, managed to plant his feet on the step.

"Watch out!" Jungsoon called as Hyonsup and Kangsup were about to follow their father. Jungsoon, holding her younger son's hand and clutching the grain bundle with the other, tried to follow her husband, but was pushed aside by stronger men.

"I am going back to Grandma." Kangsup started to walk back.

A long whistle and the train started to move.

"Let's wait for the next train. Your father will be home ahead of us," Jungsoon told Hyonsup as she straightened her chogori tie. Soon the train, with people on the steps and on top of the cars, slowly picked up speed and disappeared in the distance. Jungsoon missed several more trains. At dusk, she decided to go back to her parents-in-law's house, too.

"He should have stayed. Sometimes I wish he would listen," the mother-in-law sighed.

A quiet evening. The excitement of the first week had faded. The father-in-law, deep in his own thoughts, watched the children play. The mother-in-law kept busy arranging her chest. Glad to see Jungsoon coming back to stay another night, the cousin put away dried vegetables. Jungsoon darned her mother-in-law's posuns (pointed socks). Except for the loud and noisy crickets, quiet settled over the neighborhood. Suddenly voices were heard.

"Is someone at the gate?" the mother-in-law inquired.

"No, Aunt, I don't think so. Just some people passing by," the cousin answered.

"Did you lock the gate?"

"Oh, I forgot. I will, Aunt."

The cousin went down the step from the hall room and toward the gate. She stopped. A crowd of people was moving into the dark courtyard.

"Aunt, Aunt!" The cousin jumped back on the stone step and ran into the hall room. Jungsoon saw the crowd hulking behind the cousin.

"Yoon town chief, you come on out!" they shouted. Some smelled of sool. Some carried farm tools: sickles, picks, hoes. The mother-in-law opened the door and peered out.

"What is the matter out there?"

"Come on out, you town chief! You Japanese collaborator!" the crowd shouted.

Closing the door behind her, the mother-in-law came out to the hall room. For a moment, she stared into the mass of dark faces in the courtyard.

"Look here, fellow Koreans. I don't understand why you are here. But believe me, my husband hasn't done anything wrong." The mother-in-law's voice grew passionate. "He took the job, but he tried everything to work for the good of the town people. Tell me if any of you has any grievance against my husband, or knows of any wrong he has done to our people."

The crowd was silent. Not expecting to see a woman, the men and women listened, uncomfortably. Her voice impassioned, her face flushed, the mother-in-law went on.

"He didn't even change his name into Japanese. He always spoke for your good under very difficult circumstance. Think if the position had been held by the Japanese. Would you have liked it? Now, you and I are all Koreans. We have a lot to do. So, go on home and get ready to work for the good of our country, not for the Japanese, this time. Go, all of you. Right now!" She stamped her foot at the last words.

People mumbled among themselves, and slowly shuffled out of the courtyard. Actually, the old couple were hardly known to the populace. The Yoons had been here little more than a year, and people had never heard anything bad about them. During the raucous revelry at the local tavern, some imbiber had suggested the patrons roust out the town chief.

"Go lock the gate!" the mother-in-law commanded.

Still in a state of shock, the cousin hesitated to move. Jungsoon, trembling, hurried to latch the gate. The mother-in-law returned to her room where the children wondered what was happening. The father-in-law sat, staring into space. How he despised himself for taking the job! He had not wanted to work with the Japanese. He wished only for the day that he and his country would be free. Now the day had come and he was the target of hatred.

"They've gone." The father-in-law seemed relieved at his wife's announcement. "They should know better than that. Oh, I wish all this confusion were settled and people would go to work in peace. The nerve! Why can't they just come and talk instead of barging in when they're drunk."

Still angry at everything, the mother-in-law turned to her daughter-in-law. "I wonder how Daeyoung is getting along, being home by himself. You leave early in the morning. I don't think you can take all the kids, so leave the youngest here."

"Yes, Mother."

69

A new day, but the station was even more crowded than the day before. Her two older sons, Kangsup and Hyonsup cooperated with their mother and squeezed onto the train. Hyonsup could not see his mother nor his older brother. He stood breathing uncomfortably, his face pressed against a man's chest. Hot, unpleasant odors filled the small compartment.

"Hyonsup, are you all right?" his mother's voice came from behind the man.

"I am all right," Hyonsup managed to answer.

It was a long trip: the train almost wheezed to a stop whenever the grade became too steep. In Seoul, the waiting room of the terminal was jammed. Reaching the street, Jungsoon and her sons gulped in the night air gratefully. Then there were shrieks, and in the dim light of street lamp they saw a Japanese policeman with drawn bayonet chasing a jaywalker.

"Let's hurry home." Jungsoon drew her sons close and quickened her steps. Streetcars had long since stopped running. When they arrived, it was early morning. Her husband wasn't home. There wasn't even a sign that her husband had been there, although he did have a key. The co-tenant's front premises was dark and deserted. They, too, had not returned to Seoul.

Jungsoon slept fitfully. When she woke, the tired children, still fully clothed, were deep in sleep on the mattresses. While she was washing her face and brushing her teeth in the courtyard, she heard someone at the gate. Jungsoon dried herself quickly and cautiously approached the gate.

"Is that you, Hyonsup's father?"

"Isn't this Sister?" A man's voice.

"Sister?" she stopped at the inner gate. "Who are you looking for?"

"Isn't this Yoon Daeyoung's residence?"

"Yes, it is."

"Ah, Sister! It's me, Chayoung!"

"Oh, goodness gracious! Master!" Jungsoon opened the gate for her brother-in-law. The face was familiar, but the youthful Chayoung was now a man. Looking tired, but strong and healthy, he entered the courtyard.

"How are you, Sister?"

"Master! What a surprise!"

She followed him into the courtyard. She didn't know where to begin.

"Oh, how have you been? Where have you been all these years? We just got back from Mother's in the country. Why didn't you write? Mother and Father have been worrying about you so much. Go on, step inside.''

Her brother-in-law sat at the edge of the hall room looking about the place.

"Go on, go inside.''

He took off his leather shoes and stepped up into the hall room.

"How are you all? Where's Brother?'' He sounded considerate and mature: different from the flighty college student she used to wait on.

"We were left behind after Brother managed to get on the train. He must have come home, but he isn't here. Since he must have arrived late the day before, perhaps he went to his friend's house. I hope nothing has happened to him. Now, how about yourself? Were you in Japan all these years?''

"Yes. But things weren't so good with me, and I didn't want to worry all of you. But I did write once, didn't I? I got money from Mother.'' Jungsoon nodded. "Ah, I had a hard time to find this house. I got the address from a friend of mine here and hoped it hadn't changed. Is this your house?''

"Oh, no, we just rent part of it. You know how things went downhill for us the last few years. Oh, what am I doing! You must be very hungry. I will fix something for you right away, Master.''

"Hey, isn't that Kangsup over there?'' Chayoung went into the room and gazed down at his sleeping nephews. "Wow, he sure has grown up. And this, Hyonsup?'' He lifted the boy who was just stirring at the strange voice.

Her brother-in-law had a hearty meal. She remembered that last morning in the Myongyoon-dong house, when he had left without breakfast. Now, it seemed he had come back for the meal. It was heartwarming.

"So, what have you been doing in Japan? You are not married or anything, are you?''

The brother-in-law grinned and shook his head.

"I couldn't even take care of myself. A wife would have only added to my burden.''

"Why, Mother talked about you just the other night. She wondered if you were still alive. Why don't you go to Mother's right away. They will be so surprised.''

The brother-in-law didn't seem eager to see his parents.

"I think I will go down there in a couple of days.'' And flipping through his address book he mumbled. "First I want to call on some of my friends. Hope they are still where they use to be. Meanwhile, I will look for Brother, too."

"Thanks. Master, try to come back for dinner. You can share the boy's room."

"But don't wait for me. If I don't come back by dinner, I will be having it some place else."

As Jungsoon was about to see him off, the Chung couple, the tenants of the front premises, returned. It was the first meeting since the liberation.

"Hyonsup's mom, isn't it nice to see you again, free? How have you been?" Chung's wife met her with happy smiles, her young face brightening as she stepped inside the house.

"How are you, ma'am? I thought our house had blown away or something. Well, it's still here safe," Chung chuckled.

"I should run. I will see you later." The brother-in-law left, leaving the Chung couple wondering about him.

"Who is that?" Chung's wife asked.

"Oh, that's my brother-in-law. He has been away a long time. I was so surprised when he walked in through that gate this morning. After almost four years!"

"My goodness. He is such a handsome young man." Chung's wife looked at her husband for agreement.

"Well, you must be attracted to him, yourself," Chung joked.

"Oh, I would have, if I hadn't met you first," Chung's wife laughed. They seemed to be a happy couple. The Chungs went into their room and unpacked their trunks. But in a little while Chung's wife came back to Jungsoon. "Can you believe it? The Japanese emperor did the right thing when he surrendered. He saw these atomic bombs wiping out the cities and his people. They couldn't win the war against America anyway. Technology there is so advanced they could produce planes like B-29s which can fly at such a high altitude, that the Japanese planes simply couldn't compete. They couldn't cross the Pacific to bomb the mainland of America."

Chung's wife was well informed. Jungsoon, not knowing a great deal about the subject, agreed with all she said.

Chung's wife continued.

"Well, one thing is sure. No one will ever start a war again."

IX. The convert

You have been gone such a long time—
even for a moment, could I forget you?
In the drizzling rain on the spring river,
mandarin ducks enjoy themselves;
But at night cold tears soak my lonely pillow,
and how can you know, my beloved?
                    Ho Sokkyun (19th century)

Summer 1945. Northern Korea.

"The Russian soldiers are here! The Russian soldiers are here!"

The mini-door in the dividing fence flung open and Choi's wife stuck her head out toward Chinjoo's side.

It had been a hectic August. Russia declared war against Japan. A neighbor man had picked up a leaflet signed by Molotov and dropped by an airplane. Russian 'Yak' flew across the northern sky and bombed Hamkyong Province. The Red Army, fighting against Japanese, crossed the Yalu River and were moving south rapidly. Daily, remnants of the defeated Japanese forces straggled through the country roads, groups in soiled army uniforms, guns in their tired hands. Finally, finally the end was coming.

"Ah, he will be home, too! He will be here soon!" Chinjoo was overwhelmed. Three-and-a half long hard years without him! Somehow, she had managed the store with the help of her daughters, but it hadn't been easy. Sometimes she hated his leaving her behind with the children, and checked the urge to take off to look for him. Kim Insoo had written once from somewhere in Manchuria. But that was all. "Oh, that no good father of yours. How could he possibly leave us alone here! Even if he is starving, he can write, can't he?" She burst into tears in front of the children, but a long time ago she had learned that such outbursts didn't help any. "Do you think your pa is sick somewhere? Do you think he is starving? He must be. He should have taken all the money instead of leaving half of it for us," she mumbled to herself.

"But he will be here soon. Perhaps he was one of the daring guerrilla commanders. Or he may have joined the Chinese army, or the provisional government that he had been talking about. If he is alive." Her wishful thoughts were clouded with doubt.

Many Japanese left. Some had met with revenge. Rumor had it that the policeman Nakamoto had been beaten to death. Five men had caught Nakamoto fleeing in disguise. Akisawa's wife number-two went insane. At night, she would be found sitting in the street, her hair tangled, crying like a lost cat. She would rasp in hollow soliloquy.

"Ohhh, whatever happened to those glorious years! The great Japanese empire from the continent of Manchuria down to the Netherlands Indies, to the west of Hawaii! What happened to those conquests in the Pacific! Ohhh, can anyone believe this? Did it really end?" The dismal grumbling might change into an outburst. "Ohhh, I hate—I hate whoever is responsible for this idiotic war. Ohhh, why did I ever come here? I shouldn't have come to this miserable country in the first place. I hate it. I hate it all!" At another time, she would dart out into the street and shriek, "Hurrah for His Imperial Majesty!" The Japanese losing the war was too much for her to bear. Then she disappeared. Some said she had fled with her husband. Some said they had seen her with departing Japanese.

"Russian soldiers?" As if awakened from a bad dream, Chinjoo put her work aside and joined Choi's wife.

The Red Army. Trucks filled with foreign soldiers rolled through the streets. On the sidewalks people waved flags and banners, welcoming the liberators. For a moment Chinjoo succumbed to the excitement.

"Manseh! Manseh!" She felt gratitude toward the young soldiers.

"Manseh! Manseh!" Chinjoo joined in the shouting, her eyes filled with tears. Her voice became hoarse. If only her husband were there to join in the celebration!

"I've got some work at the store," Chinjoo told her neighbor Choi's wife. "Let's go, Tongja." Leading her daughter, she went to her store. It had been closed for a while, and she thought she would open it for the afternoon. There wasn't much in stock. Some aluminum pans, jars, and household items filled only half of the shelves. One or two customers stopped by. Acquaintances visited, but mostly to have a chat. Chinjoo left her daughter in the front and went into the small office.

"Ma!"

Chinjoo rushed out. Two Russian soldiers were examining the articles in the store. Chinjoo didn't know what to do. She wished she could speak Russian.

"What can I do for you? Do you wish to buy something? Maybe a couple of washpans?" She showed them this and that and tried to be friendly. They shook their heads. Just kept on fingering the items. "You pick whatever you like. I will give it to you free."

The Russian soldiers stopped going through things and pointed at their wrists. There were several wrist watches on the hairy arms.

"Oh, you want me to buy those? No." She shook her head and showed them hers. "I already have one."

The soldier's eyes kindled. He stepped close to her. Chinjoo's face tightened with fear. The soldier grabbed her wrist and ripped the watch from it. He added it to those on his arm, grinned, and mumbled in a strange tongue. The other soldier's glance traveled from Chinjoo to Tongja. The mother felt a sudden instinctive dread.

"Run!" she cried to her daughter, and with all her might Chinjoo dashed out the store and ran frantically after Tongja. Two shots split the air. Gasping, she ran headlong through the narrow alley. They flung open the gate of their house, stumbled in, and hurriedly locked it. Chinjoo and Tongja were breathless and trembling.

"What's the matter?" The younger daughters peeked out toward the gate.

"Get inside! Don't come out!" Chinjoo shouted hysterically. Quivering, she double-checked the lock and went inside. The children, afraid to ask, obeyed. For a while she huddled in the master room with the children. They were alert like frightened animals. Her heart jolted when she heard someone pushing the mini-door in the dividing fence.

"Don't make a sound," she whispered to the children.

"Tongja's mom! It's me!" It was the voice of Choi's wife.

"What you doing here? Get in your home!"

"Oh, are you all home? I was just going to warn you about those soldiers. They might come to residential areas. Lock the door and don't let them in. Be careful. Remember, there's no police to protect you!"

"All right, all right. You lock your door, too, and stay inside!" Chinjoo answered. Choi's wife went back to her house. Left alone with the children, she felt unprotected. She should have joined her husband's brother in Wonjang-ni as her mother-in-law had.

"Tongja, you put this on. You are a boy, you hear me?" Chinjoo gave her her husband's pants and a shirt and covered her shiny dark hair with an old air defense cap. Still she didn't look like a boy. Chinjoo took a handful of ashes left in the fuel hole in the kitchen, and smeared them on her daughter's pretty face.

"Ma!" Tongja protested at first, but was hushed by her mother's urgent motions. Then Chinjoo's glance rested on the next daughter. She wasn't quite sure. Kwangja was only twelve, but she was tall.

"Here, you put this on too."

"Me?" Kwangja's eyes grew big.

"Yes, you!"

Reluctantly the child fit herself into her father's pants. "Remember, whoever comes in, you act like boys, you hear me?"

Chinjoo searched for more defensive measures. She grabbed a pair of fulling bats, giving one to Tongja,

"Here, grab this bat. Whoever tries to open the attic door, you club him, you hear me?" She sent the children to the attic.

"You stay there all night. Go to sleep. If I hear something I will call."

In the attic, the children's whispering turned to steady breathing. Chinjoo tucked the bat under her mat and soon dozed off.

Dawn and noises roused her. Choi's wife emerged through the mini-door in the dividing fence accompanied by her husband and a neighbor man.

"There was an incident down the alley last night. You know, the Russians are allowing their soldiers to do whatever they please for twenty-four hours. They say twenty-four hours, but that means nothing, so be careful." Choi's wife warned.

"What we need is a signal. We should come up with some kind of device warning folks of an invader before it's too late. So the whole neighborhood can hear it," the neighbor said.

"Auntie, this is a warning device for our neighborhood. Do you have anything that clangs and bangs? Bring everything over here," Choi said.

"Bring some more of those pans and pots. Bring bells if you have any. Anything that clangs and bangs. The second you hear a suspicious noise outside, just pull and shake this rope as hard as you can. Don't wait until he comes over the fence. This rope is connected through our house to the row of houses on this side of the alley."

76

After several tense days things quieted down. And Chinjoo, after many fitful nights, was sound asleep. She was awakened by rattling at the gate.

"Now!" Chinjoo cried out, and the children rushed up to the attic. The knocking on the gate grew louder.

"Tongja!" came a voice from the gate. Chinjoo cautiously opened the door and leaned out. "Tongja! Kwangja! It's me. It's me. Your pa!"

Then quickly it dawned on her.

"Ah, it's you! Yobo!" Chinjoo, barefoot, stepped down into the courtyard and dashed to the gate. "Is that really you, Yobo?"

"It's me!"

"Ah, Yobo!" Chinjoo hurriedly unlocked the gate. She couldn't believe this was real. In came her man. Chinjoo clutched his arm and wept. Kim Insoo, controlling his emotions, said to his wife,

"Let's go inside."

"Pa!"

"Pa!"

"Oh, Pa, Pa!"

The girls rushed out and engulfed him. At the same time the mini-door in the dividing fence was flung open and Choi and several other men stepped out.

"Did anybody come in there?"

"It's Tongja's Pa!" Chinjoo announced with emotion.

"Ah, wherever in the world have you been?" Choi strode toward Kim Insoo extending his hands. All the men shook his hand.

"Oh, I thought it was those Russian soldiers." Choi's wife came in too, greeting him and smiling.

"Now, let's leave them alone. I am glad another man is added to our forces. Now, let's go." At Choi's suggestion, the neighbors returned to their homes.

Kim Insoo stepped inside with his family. He was shabby and haggard, his beard and mustache grown. He had lost a lot of weight.

"My, you are alive!" Chinjoo's hand brushed down his shoulder, down the bare arms, as if to feel the real man, not the one in her dreams. Still struggling with his emotions, Kim Insoo closed his eyes sitting in the middle of the floor. Finally he opened his eyes.

"Now, let me see my children!" Kim Insoo peered intently at each one of his three daughters, commenting and marveling at how they had

77

grown since he had left. "Come on here. Where's Sunhee?" Kim Insoo looked about to find a three-year-old girl. Sunhee, who was now six and didn't quite remember him, sat close to her mother.

"Sunhee. Go to your pa!" Chinjoo pushed the youngest toward her husband.

"This is Sunhee? Why, you are a big girl now. Come on, let me hold you." He squeezed her, put her down, and grabbed his knapsack. "Children, I've got something for you all." Kim Insoo spread it open and distributed gifts to the children. Then he pulled out three men's jackets made of silk. "For you!"

"Magojas for me?" Chinjoo raised her eyebrows. On each jacket was a pair of gold buttons.

"Yes, but it's not the magojas. It's the gold there. They aren't much, but they can be a reserve for the rainy days."

Three-and-a-half years of hard work. Kim Insoo had saved money and came home with valuables bought from a man who needed money.

"Are these real gold?" Chinjoo felt the weight of the buttons. But there couldn't be any more rainy days. The days ahead should be bright and sunny! Forever! Kim Insoo sat at the dinner table and closed his eyes, muttering. The children and Chinjoo exchanged puzzled glances.

Kim Insoo did not return as a daring guerrilla commander, nor a prominent independence-movement figure. Instead, he returned as a converted Christian. It had been a difficult time. His money gave out as he crossed the Manchurian border. He could find no one who knew the group he wanted to contact, nor could he even mention these things openly. Chungking was far away. Unable to contact the underground, he roamed from city to city. With food shortages, there was no place for the penniless stranger. Discouraged, he had begun the long trek home when the Japanese picked him up for forced labor. While working as a railroad construction hand, he escaped, hidden in a coal cart, and found refuge at a Protestant mission. With the foreign missionary's help, he settled in a village where many other Koreans were living. He worked as a farm hand. The American missionary couple had left Pyongyang five years earlier when the persecution of the Christians had been at its height. They were delighted to see someone from Pyongyang. Kim Insoo, thankful for their help and impressed by their goodness, learned of their religion and came to believe in it. "Believe in Him. Meedusiyo!" The elderly American missionary's broken Korean always moved him deeply. As soon as the liberation news reached them, he started for home.

Kim Insoo stared intently at his wife. The dark cotton chogori and soiled chima bespoke the difficulty of her life without him.

"It doesn't matter now. Nothing matters now. We are free and we will soon be living in an independent country. That's all that matters. Thank you, God!"

Kim Insoo straightened up his store. He had long wanted to sell fabrics. People regained their spirits. Red Army behavior had improved. Walls bristled with pictures of Stalin. Korean and Russian flags flew atop the provincial government building.

"Kwangja, let's hurry. I hope they carry lean pork. I bet Pa missed cold noodles a lot." Chinjoo walked through the street with her second daughter to buy ingredients for her husband's favorite dish. A truckload of Russian soldiers clanked by. She shivered, remembering. Choi's wife came crossing the street, clutching a skimpy grain sack under her arm. Chinjoo waited for her and called,

"Oh, have you gone to the distribution station already?"

"Yes, I thought I better hurry before I lose my ration ticket. Oh, just look at them! The way they use their loaf of bread as their pillow and then break it to eat when they are hungry." Choi's wife pointed to the soldiers in the truck stopped by the street curb. Then she continued.

"Tongja's ma, we will soon move to the south. My husband and I have decided to go. We don't think we can live on this tiny ration, here. They say the south is much better off."

"We will miss you. You've been such good friends over the years." Chinjoo was disappointed.

"Why don't you come, too? We can go together. We will settle down next to each other down there and be neighbors just as we have been here."

"I don't know. We have a business here. I don't think Tongja's pa will agree. Besides he just came home after his long absence. We will have to manage to live here. Things will get better. But we will miss you a lot!"

"We too, a lot!" Choi's wife scurried away.

"Oh, look! Doesn't he look handsome?" Kwangja turned around and commented on a Russian officer walking down the road.

"Naughty girl! You come along quick!" Chinjoo shoved her daughter and hurried on their way.

Chinjoo glanced at her husband devouring nengmyun, the buckwheat

79

noodles in icy cold soup. He was a noisy eater.

"Wow, there's nothing like the nengmyun you make. Nice and cold. Children, you all eat a lot too. Eat a lot and grow fast. You just wait. You will all have good educations and a good life."

"Yobo, we must work hard even to afford a sack of buckwheat flour. These things will soon disappear. We won't be able to buy anything even if you have money." After a pause Chinjoo said, "The Chois are moving to the south. They say things are better down there."

Kim Insoo continued eating.

"South? North, south—it's all the same. Besides we've got our business here. This is the place where we were born and raised, and lived all our lives. How can we just pack up and leave like the Chois? They can go because they don't have anything to lose. But we can't. Besides I hear Russian troops are guarding the 38th parallel and keeping people from crossing. When they leave, it will get better. You will see. Factories are beginning to be rebuilt and some, I hear, are working. I have made some contacts with several suppliers and they said I would get some goods for the store before long. Soon, consumer goods will pour into the market. We can't go south. That's out of the question."

Chingoo agreed.

X. Brother-in-law

Did I hear those boats have gone
that late were bobbing in the waves?
As soon as the clouds gathered
were they forced to disappear?
All of you whose boats are leaky
heed the warning and take care.

Chong Chol (1536-1593)

Seoul, Korea.

Yoon Daeyoung went directly to his colleague's home after he had gotten off the train. His hopes for a meaningful position in the company became dim as their conversation went on.

"They are still working as before. Only the high-ranking Japanese and those who feared revenge fled." Shin explained.

"So, there's no immediate chance of our taking over."

"I am afraid that's the fact."

They had a few drinks, listened to the radio, and played go throughout the night. And in the morning, he went to work with Shin.

Ishikawa was there.

"Ahhh, how are you, Mr. Yoon?" Ishikawa greeted him with unusual meekness.

"Fine. And you, Mr. Ishikawa?"

"Fine, Mr. Yoon. It is awfully stuffy in here, isn't it?" Ishikawa adjusted the window. None of them mentioned the Japanese surrender, or Korea's liberation. It was like touching a wound after the scab had fallen off. Ishikawa opened the window. Dusting off his hands, Ishikawa returned. "So, finally the war is over," he commented with his hands at his back, avoiding Daeyoung's glance.

"Yes, it's over, isn't it!" Yoon Daeyoung didn't know what else to say. 'Gather up your wooden sandals, and get your ass back where it came from!' That's exactly what he wanted to say. But he didn't see any point kicking a man who was already down. The man was as good as dead,

81

even though his protectors were still on guard in the streets.

Customers were mostly Japanese. They were eager to take their money out, while the trust company was still in operation. At midday, Ishikawa called Daeyoung to his desk and handed him the receiver.

"Hello?"

"Brother? This is Chayoung."

"Who?" He couldn't get the name first. Then "Oh, it's you!" he said with amazement. "Where are you? What are you doing?"

"I am at a friend's house. Sister is waiting for you. She and two of the boys are home. I will see you in the evening."

Daeyoung put the receiver down. Ishikawa grinned, not understanding a word, and Daeyoung realized he had just talked in Korean. Feeling giddy with freedom, he walked back to his desk.

Toward the end of the day, Ishikawa called Daeyoung and Shin to his office. He asked them to have seats, then slowly explained his plan of turning the company over to the Koreans.

"All of us are going home by the end of the month. Although many have withdrawn their money, a considerable amount is still invested in stocks. I am not sure if you can recover those funds, but when you are on your own, you would probably issue new shares soon and finance a new company. At least this building and its contents will amount to something. I don't know. Eventually, this property will go to your government, but until then you are on your own and I wish you all the luck there is." Ishikawa opened his cigarette case, offered them one and lit one himself. "And there are our company houses, which you can move into if you like."

There was a long silence. Cigarette smoke curled lazily to the ceiling. Ishikawa inhaled deeply. Nervously, he snuffed the cigarette out in the tin ash tray.

"How many children do you have, Mr. Yoon?" Ishikawa asked, trying to make conversation.

"Three. The last one died of measles."

"Ahhh, I am sorry to hear that. Yes, of course, I remember you told me that once. I have three children, too. They are quite grown up now. That means we are growing old, ha, ha." Ishikawa's mouth, slit in laughter, showed a row of stained uneven teeth. Although the mirth was forced, it showed a human aspect in the hated man the Koreans kept at a distance for so long. He almost looked like a nice old grandfather.

Yoon Daeyoung came home at dusk, agitated. In all their life together, Jungsoon had never seen him so excited and emotional. He sat down on the floor, but soon got up, walked to the end of the room, came back, and sat down on the same spot. Then he got to his feet again and continued his pacing with his hands clenched behind his back. He walked down into the courtyard.

"Master has come back."

"Eh?" he turned around and stared at his wife.

"Master came home this morning. He went to visit his friends and said he would come back this evening."

"I know. He called."

"Dinner will be ready in a minute."

"All right," he nodded, and walked some more before going inside. When Jungsoon brought the dinner table in, he was still deep in thought. Seeing the tray table broke his preoccupation. "I have had dinner already with my colleague."

"You did?" Jungsoon was disappointed. She had spent considerable time preparing his favorite meat dish.

"We may be moving very soon—to a colleague's house. He is to move to the company house and I agreed to buy his and pay in several payments."

"Oh, really?" Jungsoon brightened. It was a joy to see her husband in such a rare mood.

Chayoung came home and greeted his older brother with his usual deference.

"How are you, Brother?"

"So, I can hardly recognize you."

"Why, you yourself have changed a lot. Kind of old, I guess," the younger brother grinned.

"Old? Could be. Now, what have you been doing all these years? You could have at least written to us. Mother and Father are worried about you. Go and see Mother and Father."

"I will, Brother, as soon as I know what I am doing. I'm visiting some of my college chums and catching up on the years I've missed."

"So, what have you been doing in Japan all these years?"

"I guess I was just roaming from one city to another. I went to a small technical college in Nagasaki. In fact, I could have been killed there by the bomb if I hadn't left before I finished school. Then on to Tokyo in the hope of attending the university. I ran out of money and gave up. There was nothing to report, so I didn't write. The economy there is paralyzed too. Constant bombing destroyed factories, and they were becoming as poor as we are." Chayoung played with his knuckles as he went on. The younger brother evidently had gone through a lot of things. He was more mature, his voice deeper, his speech fluent.

"So, what are your plans?"

"I don't know yet, Brother. Probably get a job some place as a textile technician. I've picked up some skill in that area while wandering. How's your job at the company?"

"We have to wait until the Japanese are all cleared out. It will take some time."

"I don't know why they are still here. In the North, the Russians have taken over and the government seems to be in the hands of Koreans. Here everything is the same as before. The Japanese are still issuing orders and threats. Below the 38th parallel, the U.S. Army is supposed to handle the Japanese surrender, but what's keeping them?"

"Well, it won't be long. Nothing can reverse the Japanese defeat."

* * *

"I will see you later, Master. Have a nice trip. Give my best regards to Mother and Father." Jungsoon watched her brother-in-law leave for the countryside to visit his parents. Chung's wife, the tenant of the front premises, eyed him in admiration as he walked out.

"Why, he is a charming young man. Is he married?"

"No, he isn't."

"Does he have girl friend somewhere?"

"I don't think so," Jungsoon grinned.

"Well, then I should be a matchmaker. Any girl would just love to be his wife."

"My parents-in-law would be glad to hear that. They are worried about him."

"They should be. Oh, what am I doing? I haven't done my morning dishes yet." Chung's wife returned to her kitchen and Jungsoon began to clean and dust. Hyonsup, who was practicing the Korean alphabet, left his desk and went out to play with neighbor children.

* * *

"Hyonsup's Mom, I've got news for you!" Chung's wife hurried in from her shopping. "The Americans are on the way. When I was down at the market, an American airplane dropped leaflets. They are going to be here soon. They haven't forgotten us." Chung's wife smiled affably and said.

"Oh, Ujeekawa's wife is selling her furniture and chinaware. Won't you come with me?"

The usually clean house was now crammed with items for sale. Several women were already there. Kneeling, Ujeekawa's young, handsome wife explained and priced the articles scattered on tatami.

"I bought this at ten yen only two years ago. I will sell it for three." Ujeekawa's wife pointed at the wardrobe.

"I will take it." It was sold to Chung.

Several other women bought other articles. Jungsoon examined the tea set. It was painted with bonsai trees in soft colors.

"Those are lovely." Chung's wife noted.

"I want to buy these," Jungsoon counted out the money. Ujeekawa's wife wrapped them carefully with newspaper. As Jungsoon handed over some coins from her grocery money, she chided herself for being so extravagant. But now it would be her very own. Her mother-in-law had taken most of the good china.

"Are you leaving soon?" Chung's wife asked when the other women had left.

"Oh, I don't know. We are planning to go in early September. But I don't know. Maybe sooner."

"I wanted to learn how to make those cute children's clothes from you."

"It's really easy, once you know how. Just follow the instructions. Here, I will give you all these magazines. They will help you." Ujeekawa pushed the pile of old magazines to Chung's wife who was counting out some coins. "Oh, those are free." Then after a pause, "We want to sell this house, but I don't think we'll be able to get the full value. But we have to sell it if there's anybody—"

Chung's wife thought for a moment.

"I would like to buy it, but we don't have that much money. Wait until I talk it over with my husband. I am sure he will be interested."

"It was nice of you to come and buy some of my things. Thank you."

* * *

85

After the Chungs had bought and moved into Ujeekawa's house, Chung's wife stopped in to see Jungsoon.

"Have you seen the American soldiers yet? I saw some passing by in jeeps."

"Americans? Let me see." Hyonsup left the desk where he had been writing the Korean alphabet fifty times. He started to go out.

"No, not here. They don't come in these residential areas. You have to go to the downtown street, around the capital building." Seeing Hyonsup's interest, Chung's wife went on. "You know, they have yellow hair, blue eyes, and skin as white as a sheet of paper. Their nose is this big and they are as tall as telephone poles."

"Oh, can they walk?" Hyonsup was excited.

"Of course they can. They are people too, you know, just like you and me," Chung's wife laughed. "There are black soldiers too. Their skin is all black."

"You mean they are black all over?"

"All over, face and hands, except the teeth and the eyes, of course." Chung's wife chattered on. "And you know what they think of us? Barbarians."

"Us, barbarians?" Hyonsup, stunned, stared at the young woman's smiling face.

Jungsoon had heard American troops had begun arriving days ago. Fearful of revenges and wild celebration, the Japanese tightened its final police grip, issued orders to Koreans to stay home, and vowed to shoot if they came out. When a group of Koreans, in spite of the orders, went into the street to welcome the liberators with wreaths and banners, the Japanese fired and some Koreans were killed. The Japanese, standing on the sidewalks, had waved the American flags that they had made in a hurry.

People moved slowly along the sidewalks. Some peered curiously at the military vehicles parked in front of the Chosun Hotel. Jeeps with white stars painted on their sides rumbled along the street carrying khaki-clad soldiers. Some were black, just as Chung's wife had said. Hyonsup stared wide-eyed, standing behind his mother and brothers. As he hoped, the Americans jumped out of the vehicle and walked toward the gate. Wow, they walked just the way he did! Teacher Toyota was wrong. His older brother had said so, too. Relieved, he stood and watched: the victor, the liberator and the new races were strange and unknown to him until then.

Gradually, the Japanese went home. Crowded makeshift stores selling underwear and ready-made clothing soon disappeared. American soldiers in their tightly fitted khaki uniforms and pointed caps striding along the street, chewing gum, became less and less of a novelty. Children went back to school.

Yoon Daeyoung's company made a new start, and he was engulfed in endless business meetings. The trust company had been reincorporated and new shares issued. Lee, a graduate of a Japanese university and a moderate, became president. Daeyoung was pleased he had been given Ishikawa's place ahead of more-senior members. And the warm friendship with Lee and Shin, who became head of the personnel section, was a good omen for his promising future. Lee moved into a company-owned residence, and Yoon Daeyoung bought his house with a nominal down payment.

Jungsoon brought the news to Chung's wife, who was making dumplings with rationed wheat flour.

"Oh, I was just going to go see you. I've got a nice girl just right for your brother-in-law."

"That's wonderful. My mother-in-law will be visiting here soon. I am sure she will be very pleased to hear it."

"She is the niece of my very good friend and very pretty. She is nineteen, a graduate of a prestigious high school in Taegu."

On a cool October evening, Jungsoon sat in the master room sewing her mother-in-law's chogori. The mother-in-law brought the remaining grandson home and stayed to visit with her own sons. Folk music, heard only in rural areas during the Japanese occupation, was now broadcast throughout the city. Nostalgia filled the people as they listened to the plucking of the kayakum strings. The mother-in-law examined the pair of finished posuns (pointed socks) and listened to Jungsoon's story of matchmaking.

"Well, the age seems right for Chayoung. They don't marry older women any more. Are they yangban? What's her family name?"

"Kim, Mother."

"Which Kim?"

"Kim of Kimhae."

The color of the elderly lady's face changed.

"That's not yangban," she snapped. "Now, you said she graduated from a prominent high school. Which one?"

"A high school in Taegu."

"Taegu? Isn't that the city in Kyongsang Province?"

"Yes, Mother."

"Why, then she must be from Kyongsang Province."

"She is." Jungsoon nodded cautiously.

"Then it's out of the question. No Yoon of Haepyong is going to marry any Kim of Kimhae from Kyongsang Province. Even in the south, Choongchong Province is as far as we can go," hissed the mother-in-law who had totally forgotten that her proud forefather had originated in Kyongsang Province. Chayoung, coming in and out and catching some of the women's conversation, was indifferent to their matchmaking.

"Well, you should get married sooner or later, don't you think, Master?" Jungsoon glanced at her brother-in-law's fair features which reminded her of her husband at the first arranged meeting.

"Well, someday," he answered, grinning.

Shortly after the mother-in-law left, Jungsoon moved into the new house. As promised, the Chung couple came with their borrowed truck and helped them move.

"What a nice place!" Chung's wife admired the new house in Donam-dong, a fashionable neighborhood. The large beam that crossed the hall ceiling was solidly supported by thick pillars. The hall's wooden floor was waxed and there were fancy sliding glass doors. Although the concrete courtyard was small, it was cozy. The house had enough rooms for her brother-in-law too. Excited, the children dashed in and out the gate.

"Why don't you stay for dinner?" Jungsoon asked but the Chungs left promising to come another time.

Jungsoon scrubbed and cleaned the house, dreaming happily. It was to be their own, not a rented house, nor the house of the parents-in-law. It was for her and her husband and children to live in for, perhaps, the rest of their lives. She would use every minute to make the house shine like silverware. She would invite the mother-in-law to have her birthday celebration here. She would have her own sixtieth birthday right there in that shining hall room.

"So, this is the house," admired the brother-in-law. "Not bad." Chayoung examined the beams and the pillars. He walked around the courtyard where the furniture was piled.

"Have a seat here, Master. I just cleaned this spot. I will clean your room first. Which one would you like?"

"Any room you can spare."

"Oh, don't talk like a stranger, Master. You know you live here."

"I am not so sure, the way Brother thinks of me. Anyway for the time being I think I will have to stay here."

"Of course, Master."

"I've got a job."

"Good for you. Where?"

"In a textile company as a printing technician."

Jungsoon didn't know what that was. But it made her glad to learn he was finally settling down with a job. Hyonsup returned after exploring the neighborhood.

"Hey, come here, chap," Chayoung called to his second nephew. "You know what? If you wait a little while, I am going to treat you to whatever you like. Have you heard of the Charlie Chaplin movie? They are showing it at Whashin Department store."

"Wow, great! Can we go today?"

"Why, listen to that. Have patience. This is the first day of my work. You have to wait at least a month until I get my first pay."

"A month! I thought you meant today."

As the days went by, the house approached completion. Wall paper and ceiling paper were redone, and a new waxed floor was laid in the master room. Her husband's salary lagged behind the soaring inflation, and with food rationing, conditions were still not ideal. But when money was available, there were at least things to buy, and in her new house she saw promise for a good life. Jungsoon budgeted the money for the groceries and the firewood throughout the dreary winter.

It was a quiet evening. The boys were in their rooms doing their homework. Jungsoon darned the children's pants, listening to the brothers' conversation. Her husband, immersed in continual meetings with his colleagues, and Chayoung, coming and going as he pleased, had few opportunities to be together.

"We are still poor as can be. There is still food rationing. And the Japanese collaborators are still walking merrily around getting richer all the time." Chayoung played with a spoon laid on the saucer, as if talking to himself. Jungsoon had served ginger tea in her newly purchased tea set.

"What do you expect? After the long Japanese exploitation, the Americans didn't have anything left to start with. Besides, when the war was over, the Yanks were still fighting in Okinawa. They were trained to fight, not to take over administrative jobs," Daeyoung explained to his less-informed brother. But the younger brother had other information.

"I wonder what they are doing here. General Hodge claims the U.S. military government is the sole government. This is liberation, isn't it, Brother? Or are we simply switching our master from Japs to Yanks?"

"What can you do in all this confusion? The American government wants to remain neutral—not supporting Yo Unhyong or Rhee Syngman. Besides, almost a hundred Korean political parties have developed overnight. The Americans need time to figure out things. I am sure they are here only as an interim government."

"Well, in the north, at least the executive committee of Korean people has taken over the administrative powers. Do you know who suggested this four-power trusteeship business? The Americans!"

Sitting at a distance, Jungsoon was deep in her own thoughts. She must buy some soybeans to make blocks for making soy sauce and bean paste. She knew her husband couldn't bring in more money, but she should at least mention it when he is free. And her brother-in-law. He must be cold. She had put a hot water bottle in his bed. What he really needs is a wife who will keep him warm and happy. She was roused by her husband's loud voice.

"What? South Labor Party? That's a leftist party. You mean you are a member of—?" Daeyoung, stunned, glared at his brother.

"I don't see anything wrong with that. We are fighting for the working class and peasants. You and I have been yangban too long. You don't understand the problems of those classes. The Russians do."

"Why, you. You quit that idea right away! They are beginning to crack down on the agitators. You will get into trouble!" Daeyoung screamed. Chayoung got up without answering and strode out, banging the door behind him.

"Stupid bum! So, that's what he has been up to. I thought he was a Japanese-influenced intellectual. Now he's become a left-winger! Can you believe it!" her husband spat.

Jungsoon was careful not to provoke him further, and slowly cleared away the tea tray. Her husband's glance darted to the bonsai-tree design on the tea cup.

"Where did you get those things? Throw them away! I don't want anything in my house that reminds me of the Japanese." His eyes flashed and he reddened with indignation.

"Yes." Jungsoon picked up the tray and quietly retreated.

Jungsoon wrote her mother-in-law inviting her to have her birthday party at her son's house. She wanted to prepare things for her. It would be a joint celebration of the father-in-law's birthday which always passed with the preparation of memorial rites for his deceased mother. The mother-in-law answered: "I don't celebrate my own birthday and never have." But she finally agreed to come. When the parents-in-law arrived, a maid accompanied them. She had replaced the cousin who had gone back home to get married. While the mother-in-law visited relatives in Seoul inviting them to the party, the maid and Jungsoon worked together making cakes. It reminded her of those days in the big Myongyoon-dong house with Boonee. Whatever has happened to Boonee? Jungsoon sighed.

* * *

At midday, an American soldier visited Daeyoung.

"American soldier?" Daeyoung tilted his head when it was announced by a messenger boy. A tall blonde with blue eyes approached his desk, his cap in his hand. Daeyoung stood up and shook the hand extended to him. He couldn't understand a word the American said. Politely, Daeyoung offered him a chair next to him. The soldier sat down and pulled a letter from his pocket and handed it to Daeyoung. It was from Japan and addressed to his brother, Chayoung. Daeyoung glanced at his visitor. He was waiting.

Daeyoung opened the letter and read: "I am too exhausted to wait to hear from you any longer. I wrote to you at the address of your brother but the letter was returned to me. I remembered your telling of your brother's employment. So, as a last attempt, I am sending this letter along with my friend's fiancé, who has been here on his vacation. With all the things that have happened during the year, I know your mind has changed. I didn't want to write to you and remind you of anything you don't wish to recollect, but I thought it was my duty to let you know you have left your drop of blood here in Japan. I had her last November. She reminds me a great deal of you and the times we spent together. . ." The color of Daeyoung's face changed many times during his reading. Finally he couldn't read any more. He trembled with shock and indignation. The American soldier watched him quietly. Daeyoung was embarrassed and

91

ashamed.

"Thank you! Thank you!" Daeyoung's broken English came in a hurry. The wondering soldier stood up, said something, and left.

The party was over and the relatives left, concerned over the marriageable age of the bachelor, and volunteering to look for an appropriate candidate. When Daeyoung, in pain and rage, recounted the letter from Japan, the family sat stunned.

"Give me the letter," ordered the mother-in-law. "Let me handle this." She cautioned everyone not to provoke her younger son. The mother wanted to be alone with him in private.

After Chayoung read the letter in silence, he listened to his mother with his head slightly bent, staring at the floor in front of him.

"You know what this means? A very bad record in a yangban's family." She didn't raise her voice but the emphasis on the phrase was too strong for him not to answer. Finally he found his voice.

"Mother, how do you suppose I lived during those penniless years? The money you sent me lasted barely two months."

"Then why didn't you write to me?"

"What good would it have done? You were as poor as anybody. I did not intend to have an affair. We came to like each other and I thought I would marry her—"

"Marry! A Japanese girl! You mean you still think so?"

Chayoung didn't answer.

"Well? Are you proud of what happened?"

"No."

"Then the matter is over. Don't even bother to answer the letter. On second thought, write her. Write her that you are already married and have a family here."

The mother-in-law fretted and worried. She had brought a bundle of clothes with her for Jungsoon. They would have to be cleaned and remade before her trip back home. From the opposite room, Jungsoon heard her mother-in-law stirring and sighing much of the morning. Finally Jungsoon was summoned to the room. The mother-in-law asked in a sunken voice.

"Do you think this girl—the Kim from Kyongsang Province, is still available?"

Jungsoon was taken aback. Then she quietly answered.

"I will find out, Mother."

Chung's wife was at home polishing her fingernails.

"Oh, I am glad to see you. How have you been? Excuse me, I have to finish this."

Chung's house had undergone many changes, too. It was modernized and the interior decor was as confused as the state of the country. The Shinto shrine in the wall was disposed of. On the shelves, side by side, stood a statue of a Western lady with an urn on her shoulder and the Japanese vases bought from Ujeekawa. On one wall hung a large picture of promenading Korean women painted by a noted artist. The opposite wall featured a picture of an attractive American movie star in décolletage.

"Very nice. Everything!" Jungsoon commented.

"Do you think so? But this tatami. I can't do a thing about it. I feel as though I am sitting on a rice sack. I like our ondol floor much better. Well, we might just build one of those Western-style two-story houses and move out, who knows?" Chung's wife laughed merrily. She had become a totally different woman. Her hair was curled and she wore a fancy negligee. On its lacquered top, a low table boasted an array of 'Made in U.S.A.' cosmetic bottles and boxes. At the end of the table stood a telephone: Chung's soft drink business was booming.

"You've become more beautiful than when I saw you last," Jungsoon complimented.

"Well, it's the things that you put on and wear that make you different. Why, look at yourself. It's time you made some changes too. You still wearing that chignon? Cut it off. That makes you look at least two centuries older. Listen, I will take you to the beauty parlor. Get a permanent and have your hair set. How do I look? Younger, right? I will take you there as soon as these fingernails are dry."

"You are young. But I—I don't think I want to do that. By the way I came here to ask you about this—young lady—"

"So, finally that proud mother-in-law of yours gave in, huh? Frankly I didn't think anyone still fussed over things like yangban. I came from a respectable family myself, but what's yangban now? Worthless pride tucked in empty stomachs! Things have changed." Looking into the mirror, and being careful not to harm her polished fingernails, Chung's wife removed the hair clips and arranged the chunky waves alongside her face. "Oh, well, I don't know if she is still available. Last time I heard, suitors were pouring in. But I will find out. I am doing this just for you."

The first meeting was arranged at the home of the bride-to-be's uncle who had moved up to Seoul years before. The future father-in-law, owner of a textile company, was impressed by the young man. He liked his appearance and the fact that he worked in the same line of business.

"I will tell you, I will buy him if I have to!" he chuckled unabashedly in front of the groom-to-be's party. The mother-in-law, frowned openly at his impudence. The bride-to-be was equally attractive. She sat silently, her head bent, her hands clasped on her lap. The mother-in-law looked over the young lady carefully. Even she couldn't find any fault.

"I hope her accent isn't as terrible as her father's." The mother-in-law managed to say afterwards, but then reasoned. "Well, once she moves up here, she will catch up with our manners. It won't be too much of a problem."

Chayoung seemed satisfied with the arrangement. Although his mother said he should wait until they were officially engaged, he took the young lady out on his own, to dinners, and a walk along the Namsan trail. The father of the future bride excitedly looked forward to the bright young man becoming an executive in his company as well as his first son-in-law.

Oh Jungsoon hesitated. But as the date of her brother-in-law's engagement ceremony neared, she made a decision: she would have a permanent. She could wear some colors too. The three-year mourning period for the grandfather-in-law was over. It had been a long time since she had worn anything but simple white cotton chogoris and chimas. The conditions in her household were improving and her life would change for the better, too.

"Chung's wife fixed her hair—permanent wave they say. Looks so nice on her." Jungsoon waited for her husband's reaction. He didn't seem to be listening. "Yobo, I am going to change my hair style."

"Uh?" he turned his head from his newspaper.

"Do you think I can change my hair style?"

"What?" He glared at her so intently she wished she hadn't spoken. Then he returned to his newspaper saying, "If you wish."

In the beauty parlor smelling of chemicals, Oh Jungsoon stared at herself in the mirror with doubts, as her long black hair was cut off.

"Imagine, you have been wearing this weight on your head all this time." The beautician admired her own work.

"Look there, is this someone I know?" Chung's wife reacted boisterously. Jungsoon wasn't so sure. The short, extremely curly hair felt so strange she immediately regretted her decision. "Why, you look twenty years younger," Chung's wife said. Jungsoon rubbed down the side of the hair in the hope it would straighten a bit.

"Oh, this is too curly."

Once the ordeal was over, Jungsoon covered her head with scarf not only because of the cold but because she was embarrassed. Everyone seemed to be staring at her. She stood on the curb waiting for the streetcar, wondering what her husband would say. Glancing idly at the stores across the street, her eyes focused on a familiar overcoat. It was her husband. He went into a bakery and bought a variety of cookies. She thought of going to him but decided to go home first and try to straighten her hair a bit before he arrived. Traffic moved steadily in both directions in the street between them. Daeyoung came out with a large cookie sack, signaled to a cab and drove off. She hurriedly stepped on the streetcar and hoped she would be home before he was. She was. Relieved, she began to work on her hair using many hair pins to flatten the curls. He would be home soon and must be in a good mood. He was bringing home a surprise for the children, a rare occasion. She hurried with dinner. When the dinner was ready, there was still no sign of her husband. She fed the children first and waited for him. Hours passed. The clock indicated nine o'clock. Where could he be? A knock came at the gate.

"Is that you, Yobo?" she called, rushing out.

"Open the door, please," came a man's voice.

"Oh, who is it?"

"Police!"

Alarmed, Jungsoon opened the gate and two men came in. They were in civilian clothing.

"We are police investigators. Is Yoon Chayoung home?"

"He isn't home yet, but let me check again." With fearful intuition she led them to his room. It was dark and empty. The plainclothesmen asked several questions and left promising to come back again.

Daeyoung returned the next day for dinner. He eyed Jungsoon's change of hair with indifference and took the news about Chayoung with disgust.

"I knew it would happen. I knew it!"

She wanted to talk about the night before, that she had seen him coming out of the store with a sack of cookies. Where did you go? But she was fearful of her husband's mood. Sewing the newly washed sheet onto his mattress, Jungsoon asked meekly.

"You had meetings—last night?"

"Sort of."

Jungsoon eyed her new hair-do in the mirror and cried.

Police investigators came several times, searched and waited, then stopped coming for a long while. Chayoung didn't come home. Nor was he at work. Some said he ran away to the north, some said he was hiding locally. There was no engagement ceremony. The reason was given that he was unable to support a wife. The father of the bride-to-be was so furious, one day he rushed into Jungsoon's house and shouted at Daeyoung as if he were responsible for the breach of the promise of marriage.

"If your family didn't like her, why didn't you say so in the first place, instead of giving a bloody lie like that? I said I would make him president of my company. The way he looked I had a hunch he wasn't trustworthy and I was right!"

Jungsoon's parents-in-law were broken-hearted, sad, and angry. As the days went by, they tried to forget their younger son altogether.

Two years passed. Jungsoon's household improved more in appearance than in diet. Wardrobes and low tables were purchased. Jungsoon arranged some of her decorative articles with Chung's decoration schemes in mind. The city water system was connected and the water tap was in the courtyard. One of the rooms was converted into a bathroom next to the toilet room and they no longer had to go to a public bath house. Yoon Daeyoung eagerly modernized his household, attended to his work, and enjoyed social evenings elsewhere. He came home late smelling of wine and seemed disposed to listen. Jungsoon's hair had grown and was combed back into the old chignon. She was quite content.

"Chung's wife had a new gold bracelet made. Her husband seems to be making a lot of money. The soft drink business." Carefully Jungsoon searched her husband's mood. Then looking down on her empty finger, she breathed, "Well—I bet a gold ring would cost a lot more these days."

Her husband didn't seem to listen at first, but after a short silence: "Not that much."

A gold ring, though, Daeyoung never brought home.

96

XI. A country divided

Who says clouds do not plot treason?
Floating in mid-air, high,
Waywardly,
Idly,
For what reason do they cover
The bright light of the day?

Yi Chon-o [1341-1371]

1948. Pyongyang, North Korea.

"Tongja, are you still here? Aren't you going to school today?" Chinjoo, the pearl, called to her daughter whose door was still tightly closed.

"I don't feel good. I think I will stay home."

Angered by the answer, Chinjoo walked briskly toward the detached room. Her daughter was still in bed with a book.

"If you can read a book, why can't you go to school?"

"Oh, Ma, I feel rotten. It's my period, again. Well, it's not only that. There's this rally again tomorrow. All those shoutings, slogans, slogans. I don't learn anything. We hardly read anything except propaganda. Class meetings and constant chanting how great somebody is. All those inflammatory speeches. I just can't keep up with it."

Chinjoo clacked her tongue. "I don't know what you are talking about. But still you have to go to school unless you want to have that self-criticism session again. You can't just stay home and waste your time like that. Anyway, it's too late now, so you can rest today, but don't you make it a habit. You will get into more trouble." Her eyes with double eyelids lost the angry shine as she closed the door.

Chinjoo wrapped up the lunch boxes to join her husband in the store. She heard a tap at the gate. "Who's there?" She stopped gathering things and peered toward the front yard. A man in dark cotton pants and white shirt walked in. A familiar face, but a very different man since the time of the Japanese rule.

"Good morning, Comrade!"

Chinjoo was now accustomed to the sight of the man and his talk. He had come several times to call on Tongja to induce her to affiliate with the Women's Alliance. Women's Alliance! Then a woman should come instead.

"Has Comrade Tongja decided to join?" He sat on the edge of the hall room without being asked.

"I don't know. She is still a student. She should study now and join it later."

"Comrade, you still have a taint of bourgeois thinking."

"I don't know what that is. But whatever that Women's Alliance is working for, I will join if you need someone so badly. Tongja has to learn things at school before doing anything else." Chinjoo said looking into the eyes of the man called Draggie, the one-time town drunk.

"Why, you talk very much like a reactionary element. As a matter of fact, Comrade Tongja doesn't have that much enthusiasm in school either. Last month alone, Comrade Tongja had two absences." His eyes narrowed as he paused for breath. "Didn't you hear our Great Comrade Kim's address to the Assembly of People's Committee? We've made a good start in the course of reconstruction and rehabilitation of our industry. Think of the great progress made since the liberation. The Japanese industrial sabotage destroyed all the factories. And in less than two years, we have made a giant stride. And look at those Hungnam Chemical works, and iron and steel mills at Songjin, and Chinnampo metal processing plants. And the mines at Koksan. The machines are producing efficiently, and our peasants are working hard. A great grain harvest is expected this year. The factories and farm villages need workers. We are all obligated to take part in the great procession of achieving the goal of reconstruction."

Han Hung, by which he was now known, delivered his impassioned speech. The once-dull eyes shone with purpose. The inept buffoon had completely disappeared. Chinjoo couldn't determine whether he came for Tongja or for something else. At any rate, he seemed a man to be feared now.

Han Hung stood up. Taking several steps toward the gate and stopped.

"Remember this, Comrade. You and your husband are being closely watched. Your name is on the list of Japanese collaborators."

Shocked, Chinjoo raised her voice.

"What did you say? How could we be? My husband was taken to

the police station and beaten because we wouldn't cooperate in their cause. He had to run away to Manchuria in the hope of taking part in the independence movement. Even if you were always drunk, if you had eyes to see and ears to hear, you'd have known what was going on around this neighborhood."

Han Hung's eyes narrowed as they had when he was haranguing a few minutes ago.

"So, what did he do? Did he take part in the independence movement? Did he carry important messages across the border to the underground workers in Manchurian fields? Did he go to jail on behalf of them? Look at him now. Going to church where a bunch of superstitious people are gathered and spreading an absurd notion about this god. They are the enemies of the people!"

Chinjoo was silent.

"As a member of People's Committee, I have specially come to you many times. And you refuse to take part in this great leap forward movement. If it weren't for those lousy cookies that you gave me one evening, I would have put you on trial before the people." With these words Draggie left.

Chinjoo felt cold inside, not because of his threat but because of the way people's attitudes were changing.

She found Kim Insoo weaving a basket behind the counter, a skill acquired in the Manchurian village. The stock in the store had been practically reduced to nothing. There were a few old items and an array of wicker baskets he had made. The dream of someday owning a silk store was too remote to be considered. Since silks and all the colorful designs had long disappeared, and the cotton and man-made materials were distributed by the consumer cooperative society, Kim Insoo was reduced to weaving baskets.

"I am weaving the basket with the Apostle Paul in mind. He made tents and earned a living while spreading God's message," he mumbled. Chinjoo had gone with him to the church where he was a deacon, but she was unable to take up the faith, and was worried about the whole situation.

"Han came again. We are on the blacklist, he says."

"What for? No reason to be afraid, as long as we live in faith." Kim Insoo was undaunted.

"Perhaps we should stop going to church for a while," Chinjoo suggested.

"That will be the day I stop breathing," Kim Insoo answered firmly.

Chinjoo, stared forlornly, wondering why her husband had become so different, quietly obsessed.

On their store window communist slogans and posters were pasted.

"Slogans. Tirades. Rallies. When will they ever have time to work!" Kim Insoo glared at them, his big fingers moving nimbly at weaving.

A massive rally in the city square. The blown-up portrait of Kim Ilsung, the premier of the northern half of Korea, hung high on the wall of the municipal building, and the newly designed Red flag flew above it. Streets were deserted. A loud chanting echoed through the city which had become the capital of the northern half of the country. Chinjoo and her husband hurried along from church, lonely and uneasy.

Kim Insoo and his wife had just returned from an evening meeting where they had been subjected to many impassioned speeches similar to Han Hung's. Members of his household gathered in heavy silence. The mother-in-law, too, who had come back from the first son's house after Kim Insoo's return, was there.

"We should have gone to the south long ago," Kim Insoo confessed. "But perhaps His intention is for me to stay here to defend and spread the faith."

Chinjoo envied the Chois who had left for the south several years ago. She had experienced many hard times with them. Some neighbors didn't seem to be the same. The Wons who lived two doors away used to visit them with news to share. But they stopped coming and were working actively in the People's Committee. The neighbor across the street who used to come with a dish of cakes, no longer came to chat but to bring party propaganda. And the neighbor at the end of the block who had come to help that frightful time, avoided her, and even denounced her in an evening meeting. Even the Christian friends were afraid to greet them in the street. They could talk briefly only in the church.

Kim Insoo was thoughtful and said,

"You could have gone while you could. They let women and children go south, I told you to go ahead but you wouldn't listen."

"I wouldn't listen to anything like that. If you stay, we all stay. How can we go anywhere without you?"

"Well, now, it's too late," Kim Insoo eyed his daughters regretfully.

100

"One thing is sure. Wherever we are, I will see that you all have good educations. Women need a good education too."

"Pa, to go to a good college you have to be a party member. Otherwise I can't go to the college I want." Tongja, who was sixteen, was concerned.

"It's too late now. This has become an absolute Communist country. But let's not give up. There's always a way if we really want it. Perhaps some other opportunity may come, who knows!"

"Sh, watch what you are saying, Yobo. Nowadays it seems every wall has ears and eyes," Chinjoo cautioned.

XII. An affair

My horse neighs and strains to go
*   but you hold me and won't let me leave.*
The sun has already passed over the hill,
*   and I have a thousand leagues to cover*
Let go, love: don't try to hold me back;
*   go and stop the setting sun!*

Anonymous

1948. Seoul, Korea.

A ray of sunshine shone on the newly painted name plate on Yoon Daeyoung's desk. Now it was his own private office. With the inauguration of the South Korean government, the company underwent considerable improvement. The name was changed into the Special Commercial Bank, its capital had tripled during the last three years and a new building fund had been allocated. With the sections promoted to departments there had been a major personnel shift. Daeyoung had been promoted to the chief of the business department.

Daeyoung came out of the department heads' meeting. Brushing off his hat with his finger tips, he stood for a moment in thought, ready to leave. Walking rapidly down the marble hall, Shin, the chief of the personnel department, gave him a meaningful smile.

"Going home?"

"Yes," replied Daeyoung, walking side by side with Shin.

"How about a drink?"

"Ah, I think I'll pass it up. I have to do something I've been putting off for so long. Some other time, but I will have to excuse myself today."

"Of course. Have a good evening." Shin walked away.

Breezes gamboled through the warm September evening. Tatters of political posters fluttered on telephone poles, reminders of the election which had taken place months ago. Sidewalks were crowded with people rushing home and out for the evening grocery shopping. Daeyoung turned up the bustling street to the jewelry store. The long postponed task, he would do today. His wife. She deserved it. His eyes appraised the array of gold rings through the glass case and finally rested on one that looked like the one he had given Jungsoon at their wedding.

"Do you think it will fit a woman's finger about this size?" Daeyoung lifted his smallest finger.

"Sure, sir. If it doesn't, we will be glad to exchange it for you."

Putting the boxed ring in his pocket, he was content. A burden on his mind was lifted. Going up the street he passed the bakery. He slowed, turned back, stood in front of the bakery for a minute, but decided not to go inside. He walked on indecisively. He stopped, deep in thought, his cheek muscles working. He hurriedly bought his usual sack of cookies, and signaled for a cab.

"Hoihyun-dong, please," he instructed the driver. The car chugged up the alley and to a hilly neighborhood. He got out, paid the fare and walked to a small house next to an imposing two story house. Sung Keok greeted him matter-of-factly. No seductive smile pursed her heart-shaped lips. He gave the sack to the woman, who latched the gate and followed him into the house.

"Well, you did remember the way here!" she said sarcastically.

"Is that the way to greet a man whom you haven't seen for ten days?" Yoon Daeyoung went inside and sat down in the master room as if it were his own. "I could have come sooner. But Father and Mother visited us. Things didn't go well with Father. After he was defeated in the election, he acted as if he had nowhere to go. I asked them to come and live with us, but Mother is attached to life in the country. She refused and prefers my supporting them there."

Keok, sitting across from him, was not interested in his story.

"I didn't know you were coming. If I had, I would have cooked dinner."

"No problem, we can go out and eat."

"And hide, always afraid to be spotted by someone? I am in no mood to go out, anyway. I haven't put on any makeup, nor do I wish to do so."

"Why, you are as attractive as ever without any makeup." Daeyoung eyed his mistress and extended his hand to touch her. Keok retreated. She was pale and there were discolored spots under her eyes. She looked tired and sulky.

"We can order some noodles from that little Chinese place up the street."

"That is a good idea, indeed!" Yoon Daeyoung agreed.

"I will be right back."

"Here, here's some money."

"I've got money, too," Keok snapped.

Left alone in a tiny room, Daeyoung noted the wardrobe and low table filled with cosmetic bottles, some of which he himself had given her: Ponds cold cream and Coty powder made in U.S.A. His eyes came to rest on the silk chima hanging on the wall. He had come a long way since that fateful evening with Shin. It should not have happened. He should have begged Shin to take him home, no matter how late it was. He should have begged him to take him some place, even to one of those shabby back alley inns. Any place but here! Yet how the hell was he to know he would pass out like that! Yoon Daeyoung wasn't exactly penitent for his affair. There was no denying the thrill of a relationship with such a beauty. Yet, at times he thought of quitting. Although having a second woman was not news to his generation, it still was scandalous, and it might get in the way of his career. He could not afford that.

It had begun on a late autumn evening. He was still a section chief. But it was a step up after having been a mere clerk under Ishikawa. Through the glassed partition he viewed with content the huge lobby, the neat rows of desks manned by employees under his supervision. He arranged his desk, put on his light coat, and was ready to go home. A head appeared above the swinging door on the partition.

"Mr. Yoon, any plans this evening?" Shin queried.

"No, nothing particular."

"Well, since we got paid today, how about a little celebration?" suggested the personnel chief.

"Sounds good!"

Another Soviet-American Joint Commission had convened and failed. On the wall of a building was a leftwing slogan hastily written in India ink. The streets were littered with crumpled seditious leaflets, which the two men kicked as they walked by.

"Let me show you a new bar I've found," Shin suggested.

Despite the smell of paint, the newly decorated establishment amply welcomed any and all to its cozy intimacy. The place was full. A couple of American soldiers relaxed with their Korean friends. Shin found two empty seats. A hostess came to their table through the cigarette smoke.

"Ah, how are you, Madame!" Shin greeted her like an old friend.

Or was it just a little showing off?

"Fine, how are you, Mr. Shin?" the hostess smiled.

"Meet my colleague, Mr. Yoon, this is Madame—Well, she is simply Madame!" Shin laughed.

"How do you do?" Daeyoung nodded.

"How do you do, sir?" Her smile sent a tremor through his body. "We have some imported Western wine, gentlemen. Would you like to try it?"

"You mean smuggled, ha, ha," Shin chuckled showing a metal filling in his front tooth. "Good. Bring it to us. All right with you, Mr. Yoon?"

"Fine."

Daeyoung's eyes narrowed as he watched the hostess move toward the bar with the order. Her hair was smoothly gathered into a doughnut shape in back. The peach colored floral chogori and the movement of the long flowing chima intrigued Daeyoung.

"She is a beauty, isn't she?" Shin hinted.

"Ah, yes, I mean—yes," Daeyoung responded, embarrassed.

"She is a widow, not a regular barmaid. Her husband was killed, or something. Has one child someplace. I hear a couple of men already have a crush on her." Shin was well informed.

"Is that right!" And Daeyoung changed the subject. "The way inflation is shooting up, I don't think our salaries will ever catch up to it."

"That's a problem. Did you see the statistics put out by the Bank of Chosun? Eighteen billion yen in circulation. Can you imagine? It's an astronomical figure. Have you bought firewood for the winter yet?"

"No," Daeyoung shook his head. "I managed to buy cabbages for pickling. That's all for now."

"It's still gloomy, isn't it? Do you think the United States and the Soviet Union will ever reach an agreement on the future of this country?"

"That's hard to say. The way the joint commission has failed to agree."

Shin leaned forward with his arms crossed on the table. "I hear the leftist leaflets were distributed again at the market and the intersection of Chongro. Policemen are looking for those responsible. Seems like those wall posters are going up faster than they are taken down. Actually, I think they are wasting their time. What's the use! People don't read them anyway. They are all busy scraping to make a living. They need peace to figure out what to do." Shin stopped talking. The hostess arrived with their order. "Isn't that right, Madame?" Shin asked for her approval.

"Whatever you say, sir!" The hostess smiled, arranging the glasses in front of them.

Shin lifted the bottle, tried to read the label, gave up and eyed the hostess. "Why don't you join us?"

"Oh, I will, as soon as I take care of the guests over there." She walked away.

"Now, let's see what it tastes like. Let's see—I believe this is what they do. Well, to our future."

"To our future!" Daeyoung lifted his glass to Shin's.

Shin took a sip. "Not bad. Not bad at all. A different flavor from our sool, but not bad." Shin took another sip and went on. "As I was saying, I have a hunch this 38th parallel set-up as a military convenience between the two powers will become a permanent division. Imagine a country as big as the palm of my hand cut in two." Shin lapsed into moody silence.

"Are those agitations and the trouble in the south the doings of Yo Unhyong and his supporters?" Actually Daeyoung wasn't interested in politics, its arena still too foggy for him to see clearly. He was more involved in economy and now his goal was to keep climbing the ladder in the new expanding company. But in order to maintain the conversation with Shin he had to make a comment or two.

"Who knows? The so-called South Labor Party is suspected. Those young ones. They are vulnerable to any new ideas. Marxism, Bolshevism, what have you. But I will tell you they are the last ones you would go to for advice on how to live a good life. Ah, here comes Madame. I thought you would never return."

Shin's eyes became red and heavy. He offered her a seat next to him.

"Now, Madame, fill the glass for Mr. Yoon. That's right!"

Sitting across from Shin and the hostess, Yoon Daeyoung drank beyond his limit. Hot blood rushed to his temple as he stared unabashed at the woman across the table. She kept his glass full. Her smile. Her lovely oval face.

In his alcoholic dream, Daeyoung made love to the woman. He tried to grab the madame's naked body slipping out of his grip.

"Water, water!"

"Bring me some water," he said to his wife. But his wife wasn't there. As the ceiling came into focus, he noticed that the color and pattern were different. A peach floral chogori and chima hung on the wall underneath. Next to it were his coat and jacket. Painfully, he lifted his head and found himself under a strange quilt.

"Are you awake, Mr. Yoon?" The door slid open and the oval-faced woman stepped in quietly. "You don't have to get up, now. You can sleep some more if you like. I will bring a glass of water." She left.

He was in her house. Pushing aside the quilt he struggled to get up and put on his pants. He was weak, thirsty, almost overcome with nausea. A footstep hesitated at the door.

"May I come in, Mr. Yoon?"

"Yes."

He finished the water at a gulp. It brought on more nausea.

"I—I am sorry. I don't know what happened."

"Oh, don't feel bad," she responded casually. "Nothing happened. You just drank a bit beyond your usual, that's all. You shouldn't have had so much to drink on an empty stomach. Mr. Shin decided it was too late for you to go home. So we drove here. It's close by."

"Where is he?"

"Oh, he went home. His wife called him at the bar. As soon as he helped me bring you here, he left."

Daeyoung was furious at Shin for deserting him.

"I will get some water so that you can wash. Why don't you stay for breakfast, sir. It's late anyway." Her hair was combed neatly but she wore no makeup. He caught a glimpse of his watch. He had just enough time to make it to the office. He washed his face, brushed his teeth in the washpan that had been brought. He was almost tempted to have breakfast but excused himself, thanked her and headed for his office.

"Are you all right?" Shin greeted him, concerned. Daeyoung apologized and thanked him. "Don't mention it!" Shin said.

That was all. But it wasn't all for Daeyoung. On the pretext of thanking her, he went back alone with a sack of cookies. He stayed to dine with her and then left. He made a second visit with gifts of cosmetics. On the third visit he slept with her. It was real, not a dream. Their passion was mutual. It seemed as though they had been waiting for one another. Her lovemaking transported Daeyoung into worlds of ecstasy beyond his wildest dreams. She was a dominant, demanding teacher, an aggressive creature of the senses. He had known only the placid, subservient Jungsoon. They met at the bar as if they were strangers, but in her home they clung together and forgot everything. The time he had been spending in the enchanted land was running out fast. Black-market gifts and dinners took a considerable part of his salary.

"He will be here soon with noodles." Sung Keok brought in the tray table and sat opposite him. She had changed, too. She was simply not as alluring, her smile no longer inviting. And lately she became easily irritated. Yet it was still entertaining to watch her beautiful oval face. He wanted to say something pleasant to her.

"I was promoted to the chief of the department."

"Oh?" she said moodily.

"Is that all? Aren't you happy?"

"Me? Happy? Why should I be?"

Daeyoung extended his hand and caressed her shoulder.

"You talk like a stranger, today. What's the matter?"

"I am a stranger to you. I always am," she replied dryly.

"Come on, cheer up!" Daeyoung stuffed the noodles into his mouth feeling odd. After a while Keok banged her chopsticks down on the table and lit a cigarette. Daeyoung lifted his head. "I didn't know you smoked."

Keok puffed out the smoke with a heavy breath.

"I do. I always do when my heart aches. There are a lot of other things that you don't know about me."

Daeyoung knew whatever he said would only provoke her. They finished the meal in silence. He read the newspaper, and went to bed. In bed Keok lit another cigarette.

"Tell me what's bothering you." Daeyoung moved closer to her mattress, putting his bare arm around her waist. Keok turned, stubbed out her cigarette in the ash tray, and glared at the ceiling. The cigarette smell lingered. Daeyoung withdrew his arm. "Look, how am I supposed to know what's wrong with you if you don't tell me?" Daeyoung's voice was raised.

Keok turned to him. She sat up. "Don't you talk to me like that. I am not your wife. I am not anyone as far as you are concerned. Yes, I am pregnant, if you want to know. But what do you care? I am just a bearer of your illegitimate child, that's all."

"You, pregnant?" Daeyoung raised himself up in bed.

"Why? What's wrong? You mean you started all this without considering the consequences? Humph, why should you? You have a home, a family and a position in society. There's no law against just playing with a wretched widow like me for a while, is there?'' Keok hissed, her lips trembling.

"Calm down!'' Daeyoung shouted.

"I won't. I can't. Look, my stomach is already puffing out. In a few weeks I will be fired and I can no longer earn my living! I have a son in middle school, and my mother expects me to send his next semester tuition when I haven't paid off his entrance fee yet! I am behind two month's rent on this house and I've sent the maid to my mother because I can't afford to feed two mouths! And look, now I have an illegitimate child growing inside—''

Daeyoung slapped her across the face. Regretting it as soon as he had done it, he stood up and put on his clothes. After Keok recovered from the shock of his blow, she left the bed and followed him.

"All right! Go ahead! Hit me! There's no law against hitting me either. Go ahead, hit me some more!'' Breathing like a wild cat, she blocked his way. Furiously, Daeyoung pushed her aside. Keok lost her balance and fell, striking her head on the corner of the wardrobe. Daeyoung was frightened. Kneeling down, he helped her up. Her forehead was cut. Blood ran into her eye and down her cheek. His hand shaky, Daeyoung took out his handkerchief and wiped at the blood. Keok became hysterical. "Don't touch me! Get away! Leave me alone! At worst I will bleed to death, so what do you care! Go away!''

"Come, come, it's all right. Just a little cut,'' Daeyoung whispered, pressing his handkerchief on her forehead.

"You! I should have known. Hitting a helpless woman? Why, you are just a common hoodlum, and I thought you were a rare gentleman. I will tell the whole world loud and clear. I will tell Shin, I will tell all of the people in your bank. I will shout from street corners and rooftops. I will shout and shout that you are a common hoodlum, until I die on the spot. You will see.'' Keok burst into wild sobbing. "Oh, what will become of me!''

"Come, calm yourself and lets talk it over. There must be a way to work out these things.''

Finally Keok, exhausted, quieted a bit. Daeyoung, relieved, thought for a moment. She looked pitiful. He felt responsible. Daeyoung remembered something.

"Here, I almost forgot. Look what I bought for you today.''

Daeyoung took out the gold ring and fitted it on her finger. She looked at the ring without emotion or comment. Then she collapsed into his arms and fell into a tortured sleep.

Daeyoung shook his head. What a fool he was! He thought of Shin's nonchalance. But the devil must know about the whole thing already. The bright career he had carefully planned and the dream he had built were collapsing. No, no! Soon there would be another personnel shift, a big one in which another vice presidency would be filled. The twice-yearly event would be stepped up according to the bank's need. He had heard the directors had favored Kim, a rival, over him for the department head. But Lee had argued in Daeyoung's favor citing his impeccable record and respectable family background. And Shin would be there, too. He knew some of his colleagues had mistresses, too. Kim had openly remarked over a glass of gin: "I am heading for the small house tonight." Casual talk between Kim and Yoon, however, was a thing of the past, a sign of the growing competition between them. Any scandal would be Daeyoung's undoing. Through the dark street on the way home he bordered on panic. He thought of meek, loving Jungsoon. Always there, carrying out her duty, raising the children. With her, all he had to worry about was the winter fuel and monthly rice.

Daeyoung was harassed several more times by Keok. Now confined to home, her temper mellowed. Daeyoung sympathized with her.

"Look, I will have a telephone installed soon. I will call you often. And if there is any emergency, you know where to reach me. How does that sound?"

"Well, it's better than nothing." Keok settled down and enjoyed answering his calls, keeping her promise not to telephone him at his office unless it was absolutely necessary.

"Don't worry, he will be my child legally. I will enter the child in my census register."

"Then what becomes of me? Toss me away like a piece of used toilet paper?"

"Don't be silly. Somehow, I will provide you a place to live. Who knows, perhaps I will be able to afford a house for you."

"Then what happens? Just a perpetual mistress, tied to you, but always living in the shadows? That's all, right?"

What does the woman want? Yoon Daeyoung's stomach tightened.

Some women were content to be mistresses with a house and other provisions. But this one seemed to be an exception.

Toward winter, Sung Keok gave birth to a boy. When Keok let him hold the infant wrapped in a quilt, Daeyoung felt a strange attachment. He had many children but had never held one in his arms. He looked at his son with emotion.

"He looks like you!" Keok smiled as if she were a happily married mother, who had just given a birth to her first child.

XIII. Exile

If you weep for your dead husband
  your tears will roll down both your breasts,
Your milk will be salty and then
  your baby will be fractious.
You poor thing! Why should anybody
  have to be born a woman?

                              Chong Chol (1536-1593)

Jungsoon managed to stuff fifty cabbages during the pickling season. The soybeans were cooked and shaped into cakes to be dried to make bean paste and soy sauce. The basic food secured, the preparation finished for the long winter, she was happy to have enough money to be a good housewife.

Kangsup, who failed to pass the college entrance examinations, went to Kwangjoo in Cholla Province for an interview to be a city clerk. It meant Jungsoon would have to send her son far away, but the job market was so tight, anything would be better than nothing at all. Accustomed to her husband's late homecoming, she did the chores and prepared his favorite dishes. She was concerned. He had little appetite and was losing weight. Today she went to the store and acquired some ginseng and honey. The ginseng had been boiling for two hours. Its fragrance filled the kitchen and drifted into the dark courtyard. With Wonsup's help, Jungsoon finished ironing, and began to mend children's pants.

"Mother, Father is home," Hyonsup called from the opposite room. Jungsoon rushed out and took his coat. He didn't have any sool smell, which was unusual when he came home that late.

"It's cold, isn't it?" Jungsoon greeted him.

Her husband walked ahead, flopped down on the mat in the master room and had his dinner in silence. Shortly he put down his spoon.

"Try these fries. They are beef fries," Jungsoon suggested arranging the dish closer to him on the table.

"I am full," her husband answered without looking at her.

"But you hardly had any. Try some more of this tubu soup. I put some oysters in it."

"I've had enough."

Jungsoon gave up urging him to eat. Disappointed to see the food she had so lovingly prepared become leftovers without having been enjoyed, she washed the dishes. The kitchen was cozy with the fragrance of boiling ginseng. She took a tea bowl from the cupboard and carefully poured the steaming tea into it. She added a spoonful of honey and sprinkled it with a few grains of pine-nuts. Taking it on a serving tray, she was filled with the joy of caring for someone so dear to her.

Her husband puffed at a cigarette, a habit he had acquired a few months back, and stared at the floor. Jungsoon placed the tray near him.

"Ginseng tea. It's been cooking for a long while, so the flavor may be a little too strong for you," she murmured cautiously.

"What did you say?"

"Ginseng tea."

"I see."

It must be something that happened at his office. Lately a lot of things must be on his mind. Problems of his parents, Kangsup's failure, and many other things. Jungsoon left him alone. She took out the sewing basket and quietly began mending. Yoon Daeyoung nervously eyed his wife. His glance rested for a while on her plain countenance. An oval face erased it. His memory was bombarded by Keok's hysterical shouts. Then Keok's smile and the infant. He looked down at the floor, puffed at his bitter and choking cigarette, and stubbed it out on the tea saucer, where the ginseng tea was getting cold. He looked once at the ceiling, then at his wife, then finally back to the floor in front of him. He mustered his courage.

"I want a divorce."

Oh Jungsoon doubted what she had heard. It was like a sudden bullet out of nowhere and it hit her hard. It took sometime for her to stop her work. The pants fell on her lap as she searched her husband's face to make sure if she had heard it correctly.

"I want a divorce," her husband repeated avoiding her stare, playing at the cigarette stub that was already extinguished on the saucer. Stupefied, she stared at her husband's glossy forehead. Her hands unconsciously stroked the pants on her lap. She drooped her head. There was so much to ask, she could ask nothing.

113

"It's not that I had planned it. It just—happened. And this seems the only way." Daeyoung explained within a breath.

Jungsoon, who, never in her life with him, dared to go against her husband's wishes, nor raise a question, listened quietly. It was a long pause. She had been suspecting something. His nights away. The late homecomings. She had fantasized they were all related to his businesses. But the shock came too soon. It could have been gradual. Yet there wasn't a single thing for her to do. The man had made up his mind. There was no way she could change it.

Her husband was waiting. Her voice shaky, Jungsoon managed to breath,

"All right."

It wasn't a dream. It was real. In her dull vision she saw her husband pointing at the floor.

"I have the paper right here. All you have to do is put your seal underneath your name. I will take care of the rest." Daeyoung, having secured his wife's agreement, took from his jacket the paper he had prepared in the afternoon. For a while she looked down at the paper. Then putting aside her mending, she went to the wardrobe drawer and brought out her seal and the inkpad. Her husband lit another cigarette.

"Where—do I—I—press?" Jungsoon stumbled.

"There!" his cigarette between his teeth, he pointed with the matchbox, as if administering an ordinary paper.

On a rectangular piece of paper a simple phrase was written perpendicularly in the handwriting so familiar to her:

I, Oh Jungsoon, hearby unconditionally grant a divorce to Yoon Daeyoung. January 1949.

Her hand fumbled for her seal and she tapped it on the inkpad many times. Slowly she took it to the paper and pressed it under her name. A tiny scarlet oval surrounding three carved letters was printed, like a drop of blood from her wound. Gently she pushed the paper toward Yoon Daeyoung, then placed the lid on the inkpad and returned it. For a while Daeyoung, too, sat with his head bowed, staring at the piece of paper lying in front of him. Slowly he folded it away. Then there was silence which made her almost believe he was reading his newspaper as usual. Jungsoon's eyes caught the untouched ginseng tea which had been there for a long time.

"I will warm it up for you."

"Uh?"

"I am going to warm the tea for you."

"Never mind."

Daeyoung's head swam. Tomorrow was Sunday, the only time he could help move Keok and the baby into the house. There would be busy months later: submitting the new building plan and the detailed estimates for the directors' meetings, his own interdepartmental meetings and the training of the new employees. He wanted the matters of his own household settled quietly. He feared Keok. The unpredictable woman might well telephone him in the middle of an important meeting and cause a scene. He couldn't possibly hope her silence toward his decision would last. He wanted to get it over with. He might weaken tomorrow.

"This will help you through the month," Daeyoung pushed a bundle of money to her side. "It's not much, but that's all I can afford now."

Jungsoon picked it up. Tears welled in her eyes as she took a long look at the bills in her hand. She got up and with her back to him cleared up the clothes and the thread basket, fiercely struggling to control her emotions. Putting on her cotton turumagi and covering her head with her scarf, she trembled and could scarcely tie the end of her scarf under her chin. Daeyoung didn't utter a sound, nor did he look at her. He puffed repeatedly at the cigarette as if trying to hide behind the smoke. Having played his part, he now seemed to be waiting for Jungsoon to take care of hers. There was nothing left for her to do. The room, the furniture, the pictures on the doors to the attic—everything so familiar and dear to her was now lost to her. Hesitatingly, Jungsoon turned around.

"The children. Can I just say good-bye to them?"

Yoon Daeyoung shook his head behind the smoke.

"That will only make matters worse."

Helplessly Jungsoon slid the door open and closed it after her. A light burned in the opposite room. Hyonsup was studying for his semester finals and Wonsup was asleep. Jungsoon put on her rubber shoes and stepped down into the chilly courtyard. The detached room was dark. Its occupant, Kangsup, was away in Kwangjoo.

"Mom, where are you going?" Wonsup followed her. He must be going to the bathroom.

"Are you still up? Go to bed. Oh, I am just going out to a store. Lock the gate tight after me."

"Who will open it for you then? I will be sleeping by the time you come home.''

"Don't worry. Daddy will open the gate for me. Now, listen to your father and older brothers and don't fight, all right?''

Jungsoon gave her son a pat on his head.

"You mean you are going away?'' Wonsup's eyes shone with wonder in the dark.

Biting her lips, she hurried through the gate and heard her son closing and locking it after her. Her back against the closed gate, she stood letting the tears run down her cheeks. It was cold and dark. All the neighborhood was settled into the late evening. Around the corner, she could hear a gate opening for a husband coming home late. And farther away a dog barked in the darkness. Patting the tears dry with the tips of her scarf she walked away.

"Buckwheat curd! Buckwheat curd!'' The night peddler's high voice echoed in the alley and faded.

Dim street lights and the neon signs guided her as she trod along the sidewalk. Headlights flashed in her eyes and disappeared into the night. With her hands in her turumagi pockets she walked up the street without the faintest idea as to where she was going. A woman divorced! The phrase struck and lay heavy on her heart. Fresh tears ran down her cheeks. She didn't bother to wipe them off. Passers-by turned as they heard a sob. Others ignored her as if she had a mental disorder. Her wet cheeks began to freeze. Snow. Many times she brushed flakes from her eyes to see where she was going.

A broad street. A streetcar came and she just got on it, gave one of her tickets, and stood by the window. Streets and buildings and stores slid by. Her tears dried and she tried to think rationally. Where would she go from here? She thought of her dead parents. Those evenings sewing with her mother, and her mother's words: "In those days, a woman kicked out of her husband's home . . .'' That was exactly what she was. "Her brother took her into the deepest part of the mountain and people never saw her again.'' Her brother would never do a thing like that. Her kind aging brother and his wife would welcome her, surprised, angry with Daeyoung, and would give her a place to live. Yet she didn't want to be a burden to the already burdened family. Chung's house for a while? No. The happy family didn't have a place for her. The streetcar came to a station and the people got off. A voice called to her,

"This is the terminal, ma'am.''

116

Jungsoon gave him another ticket to start back again to the other terminal.

"This was the last car, ma'am." The conductor explained.

"I see." Jungsoon stepped down on the snow-covered curb. The streets were empty and dark, and the stores closed. She hesitated for a moment at a sign of an inn squeezed between two shabby buildings. She went on and came to a store which was open. Inside, a middle-aged woman approached her.

"What can I do for you?"

Jungsoon looked about. She bought some cookies.

"Anything else, Lady?"

"No."

"We are about to close."

"I see." She started to walk out, but mustered her courage and turned.

"Is there any inn around here? I saw one on the way, but it looked pretty bad."

The store woman's glance swept her from head to toe.

"I don't know much about inns around here. You have to go to busy streets. This is a residential area."

"Oh, I just needed a place to spend the night." Jungsoon stepped over the threshold.

"Wait a moment!" the store woman called, and shuffled into the back room. She spoke rapidly to her husband. He peeked out and saw Jungsoon. At last the man seemed to be saying "all right". The wife reappeared.

"We have a small room. My kids are visiting with their uncle now. If it's only for a night, you can use it."

"Oh, thank you! I really do thank you very much."

Her immediate problem solved, Jungsoon settled down on a little stool behind the counter while the husband and the wife closed the store. Hungry and tired, she opened the cookie sack and took one. It tasted like sand.

"Have some cookies," Jungsoon offered them to the couple.

"No, thank you. We've had enough by just smelling them," the woman declined with a smile. After one, Jungsoon set the sack aside. She thought of home. The children. They would have loved the cookies! When the store was closed, the woman came and sat by her.

"You seem like a nice lady. But you look sad. Are you visiting someone here? Can't find the place or something?"

117

Fresh emotion brought tears.

"No. I—I am trying to find a place to live. Is there any room for rent in this neighborhood?"

The woman narrowed her eyes while thinking.

"Let me see—Well, there should be lots of rooms available. There's the realtor's place across the street. You can talk to them tomorrow. For yourself?"

"Yes," Jungsoon nodded weakly.

The woman eyed Jungsoon and sympathized with her, whatever the situation might be.

"I am sure you will have no trouble finding a room. But now, come in and I will show you the place where you can spend the night. Kind of messy."

The owner of the store, Kim, and his wife were warmhearted. Over the breakfast table in the child's small room, Kim's wife listened to Jungsoon's sad story.

"Just like that?" Kim's wife was touched and angry as the story went on.

"Of course there were nights he spent elsewhere, but usually he had late parties with his colleagues and came home about midnight. So I didn't think there was any—I didn't know it would come so sudden—" Jungsoon lowered her eyes and thought of home.

"You don't say! Why, the wrath of Heaven will descend on the man who divorces a wife who has stood by him through thick and thin!" Kim's wife swore. But that wasn't what Jungsoon wanted. She wanted him, if possible, to be happy with whatever he chose to do with his life.

"Don't you think the realtor's office is open now?" Jungsoon changed the subject.

"Oh, I guess so. Let's go and see."

Following a gray-bearded man Jungsoon went up the hilly alley and stopped at a crooked gate. It was a rundown area, one with which she was unfamiliar. A young landlady led them to a dark place in the back of the house and showed a small room and tiny kitchen.

"I will take it, sir."

"It's small but it will be perhaps the best rented room for the amount of money you wanted to spend," the realtor said.

Jungsoon counted out the money to the young landlady, who gave the gray bearded man his commission, and became the tenant. The door was so low, she had to stoop to enter. The room smelled of mildew and needed sunlight as well as new flooring and wall paper. But for whom? The house in Donam-dong—Oh, how hard she had worked on it! Now, she had nothing to do with it. With a rag, she slowly started to clean the icy cold floor.

Kim's wife came back with blankets and some other things.

"Why, what kind of a man would let a wife go without even a pan or a spoon." The woman shook her head and unpacked some of the old pans and china she had brought for her.

"Thank you. It wasn't really his fault. I just came out in such a hurry."

Kim's wife glanced at her and said,

"Now, I see how he took advantage of your good nature."

Another night alone. Jungsoon tossed and turned in the blanket Kim's wife had given her. The floor sent its chill and dampness through her bones. Her turumagi pocket held the tiny amount of money. It was enough to last her for about half a month. What then? She must earn a living. But how? When she woke up from her restless sleep, she saw a single ray had found its way into her cold and sunless room. Morning? She arose fast, then realized there was nobody to cook for. Was there any reason for her to go on living? Through her mind flashed methods by which people commit suicide. No, not her. She shook her head with repulsion. Who would cook for her children, now? Who would take care of them as she had done? Her eyes swam with tears and she bit her lips to control herself. Poor Wonsup! He must be wondering why Mom didn't come back home. Will she meet them again? She will. She must. Someday, somehow she will see the children. Suddenly she found the reason. She must live to see her children grow up and be on their own.

At Kim's store another woman was chatting with Kim's wife. Kim's wife introduced Jungsoon to the woman.

"Oh, this is the lady I was talking about."

"How do you do? Oh, I am really sorry to hear about you."

Jungsoon didn't realize her story had spread so fast.

"Oh, that's all right. She is my cousin. Her husband is in the restaurant business." Kim's wife cut in partly to defend her own chatty nature. The cousin looked closely at Jungsoon.

"If you had had such a big family to take care of, you must be very

119

good at—say, cooking?''

Jungsoon, who didn't quite understand the cousin's intent, answered with her usual modesty.

"I don't know. Every housewife would be good at cooking.''

The cousin, Chang's wife, came close to her.

"No, I mean, you must have cooked a lot of dishes in those days with your fine family background and everything.''

"Yes, in my earlier days when I was with my mother-in-law, I used to prepare lots of dishes at parties. I learned it from my mother-in-law.''

"That's right. Why don't you ask her to work in your restaurant? Why don't you let her try her dishes?'' Kim's wife suggested eagerly.

"Would you?'' Chang's wife waited for Jungsoon's answer.

While it never occurred to Jungsoon that she might find a job in a restaurant, she realized she was in no position to refuse.

"Yes, I will try my best. Thank you, thank you very much.''

For two months Jungsoon worked at Chang's restaurant. Situated in the westward of the city, the restaurant was small and unpretentious, but had steady customers. The owner, the Chang couple, were kind to her and Jungsoon got over the unaccustomed feeling that she was now an employee in a restaurant, a business of low esteem in her former surroundings. The couple rushed in and out with orders. A middle-aged janitor swept the floors and occasionally eyed Jungsoon at work. She rolled the dough on the floury board. "Roll it some more! You should be able to see the light through the thinness!'' she could almost hear the mother-in-law nag. The mother-in-law. She missed her. The father-in-law too. She wondered how they were these days. Then suddenly she realized they were no longer her parents-in-law. She wasn't related to them in any way now. How could it be possible! Tears began.

"Some more mandoo. Some more mandoo!'' Chang's wife rushed in with orders. "Oh, Auntie, they love your mandoo so much, soon we'll have to turn this place into a mandoo house.''

Then she bustled around searching in the cupboard.

"We need more fillings. Darn, we ran out of meat. Here, Auntie, here are some sirloin chunks. Slice and chop them quick. Now where is that man? We need to order more bean sprouts.'' Chang's wife ran out to look for her husband. Jungsoon mixed the ingredients to make the filling. The delicious smell of the seasoning filled the kitchen.

"Auntie, can I try some?" The janitor's voice was heard over her shoulder.

"This isn't cooked yet."

"It's all right. I like it raw."

Jungsoon took a pinch from the mix and handed it to him. The janitor looked at his hands holding the broom stick.

"My hands are dirty."

Jungsoon loathingly glanced at the man's unshaven face, and quickly slipped the food into his awkwardly opened mouth. She rubbed her fingers against her apron and went on with her work.

"Now, Uncle, what are you hanging around in here for? There are lots of tables to be cleared away."

The janitor shuffled away as Chang's wife burst in.

Toward the end of the day, the Chang couple came into the kitchen, tired and pleased.

"Oh, what a day! You really are the best cook we've ever had," Chang's wife said, settling down on a stool.

"You know what, Auntie? I am thinking of adding some more dishes. How about sinsulro? Do you think you can do it?" Chang, the ordinarily quiet man, was eager. This was a party dish Jungsoon had frequently fixed in better days.

"I will try."

"Good, Auntie. Then we will need about ten sinsulro pots as a beginning. I will get them right away."

After hesitating, Jungsoon asked,

"Do you think I can take tomorrow morning off? I want to visit my children at school. I wonder how they are doing."

"Oh, sure, Auntie. We are usually slow between nine and eleven, but take your time."

Early March—the wind was cold. With a sack of cookies and notebooks and pencils she first visited the middle school which Hyonsup attended. When the familiar figure approached from a far end of the playground, Jungsoon fought against tears. Hyonsup walked toward her slowly, his shoulder tilted to one side, his head bent.

"Mother!" he gasped. His eyes were hollow and tired, his dark uniform wrinkled and shiny with dirt.

"How are you, dear?" She put her hand on his shoulder. Teardrops

121

rolled down from his eyes.

"Fine," he stood in front of his mother, blinking and biting his lips. His hair needed cutting.

"How is your older brother? Did he get the job?"

"I think so," Hyonsup said without spirit, his eyes cast on his sneakers. He looked thin.

"Are you doing all right at school?"

"Yes," he nodded and again became silent.

"Here, take this for a haircut. Why don't you stop by the barbershop on the way home."

"That's all right. You don't have to give me money. You don't have money, do you?"

"I do. I work and make some money, dear. How is your father?"

"All right," he nodded, rubbing his shoe in the dirt on the playground. Everything was beyond his explanation, seemed complicated, and he had no control over the situation. There was nothing for him to say.

"Who is taking care of you?"

"Nobody."

"Nobody? Then who cooks for the family?"

"We've got a maid. She cooks and does all the work."

She was relieved to know there was someone who worked there.

"How are your studies? You're still doing well, aren't you?"

He didn't answer immediately but in a while responded,

"I can't study. That baby cries all the time. Day and night."

"Baby?" Jungsoon stared at her son to figure out if he were in his right mind.

"Yes, the woman and the baby moved into our house."

Jungsoon felt as though she had been struck by a heavy object.

"I hate Father!" Hyonsup blurted out.

"Don't say that. You listen to whatever your father says and be obedient, all right? Don't make any trouble. It won't help a thing, do you understand?"

He nodded silently. The school bell sounded.

"You have to go in now. I am going to see Wonsup. Be a good boy and listen to your father. Wonsup is little. Take care of your younger brother, won't you? I will come back to see you again."

With the notebook bundle at his side, Hyonsup walked away.

122

"Mom!" Wonsup came running, his face brightening as he recognized his mother. She hugged her son. He was as shabby as she had imagined. His pants had holes on both knees and the sneakers were half torn. All but one of his shirt buttons had come off. Part of his underwear showed.

"Oh—" Jungsoon put her arm around her son and held him to her bosom.

"My child!" Like a little calf, Wonsup watched his mother trying hard to hide her tears.

"Here, I brought some little things you might need. Be good to your older brother. Look after each other. Take bathes often, otherwise you'll get lice. I will bring some new clothes for you at the end of this week. Pack the soiled ones, so next time I come I can take them and mend."

"You know what, Mom? The oldest brother came home and got into trouble with Daddy," Wonsup started. "He shouted at Daddy, 'Are you out of your mind?' and that's when Daddy got really mad and threw his wooden pillow at him. And Oldest Brother packed his things and left. He has never come home since."

"Oh, where can he be now!" Jungsoon whispered with a sigh.

"I thought he went to look for you, but if he is not with you, then he must be down in Kwangjoo where he got his job."

Jungsoon scribbled her address on the cookie sack. "Give this to him if you see your oldest brother. Listen to your father. Don't go against his word."

"All right, Mom," Wonsup agreed. He wanted to know more. "I thought you went to Grandma's house. But Second Brother said no. Then, where are you staying?"

"I am living in a little rented room. It's not big but it's all right."

"Can I go there with you today?" Wonsup asked.

"No, not today. You have to have your father's permission, and I don't think he will give it to you. So, don't even ask him. I will come to see you this Saturday."

"Second Brother says you are not allowed to come home, is that right?"

"Not now. But someday I will visit you at home, too, perhaps."

The cloud in his mind lifted, and he ran back into the elementary school building with his presents.

Jungsoon bought some materials and for several nights made clothing

123

for her youngest son. Those nights she felt her life was worthwhile: she was glad she still had loved ones to work for.

With the finished clothes, she went back to the elementary school, and took his old clothes to her room to wash and mend.

When she returned to school with the clean old clothes, Wonsup stood before her dejected and afraid.

"Mom, Daddy said you shouldn't visit me any more."

"How did he find out I was here?"

"The maid asked where I got new clothes and I told her, and she told him."

"All right. I will try not to visit you again. But you will be good, won't you? Study hard."

Wonsup nodded and holding his clean clothes went away. He turned around and called to her,

"Mom, try to come back again. I won't tell anybody this time!"

Kangsup came to see his mother in the restaurant. He had changed and was mature. He was disappointed to see his mother coming out of the steaming kitchen wiping her hands on her soiled apron. He had seen his mother coming out of the kitchen all his life, but not from one in a public restaurant.

"Mother, this is no place for you." He suppressed his emotions for a while, then blurted out. "One of these days, I am just going to barge in there and kick that bitch out of the house!"

Jungsoon, aghast at her son's remark, looked at him sternly.

"That isn't going to help any. It's not going to help anybody, do you understand?"

"I know, Mother."

"Now, tell me about yourself. Are you happy with your job down there? It's so far away. I wish I could come and cook for you. Where are you staying? Somebody should take care of you. You want me to come and cook?"

"Mother, I am passed that age. I can take care of you. But now the salary is too meager even to pay the rent. I will find some better job, then I can take care of you and my brothers too. We will live all together, but not now. When things get better, I will come back. Here's some money for you." Kangsup squeezed several won bills into her palm.

"No, you are the one who needs it. Come back here, you take this back!"

Kangsup had already fled out of the restaurant and waved his hand back to his mother as he turned around the corner. He had always been more independent than her other sons. It hurt her to know he was returning to Kwangjoo alone.

Yoon Daeyoung's parents learned about his divorce in the rural area where they were still living after his father's failure in the election. The mother-in-law had sent Jungsoon bundles of clothes to be washed and sewn. When the expected due date passed and the packages came back unfinished, she had sensed something was wrong. Meanwhile Kangsup had stopped by on the way to Kwangjoo. The news horrified Daeyoung's parents.

"He should have consulted us about the matter before it happened." The father expressed disgust. His mother reacted strongly. It wasn't quite for the concern of her daughter-in-law, but rather for the reputation of the family.

"How could he do such a thing! Why, we've never heard of divorce in our family. Concubines, yes, but never a divorce. And when the children are so grown!"

She wrote her son a letter summoning him to come to see her. When he didn't come, she wrote him again to come and explain, asking him to reconsider the matter and reverse the action if possible. Yoon Daeyoung didn't come, but wrote that there was no other way, that he already had a new family with a new-born son, and that the parents could join his family if they wished to do so.

"He really must have lost his mind!" she fumed angrily. "Well, we didn't have any luck with our sons, did we!"

But as time went by she gradually dismissed the whole matter. There was nothing she could do. Besides the parents had their own problems. The long-cherished dream of her husband's political career had induced him to run for a National Assemblyman. The competition was keen and the odds were against him. Apart from the damaging fact that he had served in the Japanese government, he had been born a dozen years too early. He was old. Too old to compete with the candidates in their forties and fifties with money. They had appeared on the political scene claiming the district was their birth place or any other connection they could think of. He started off with the main issue, the land reform, but so did every candidate. He traveled by bus and gave speeches to a handful of people who happened to be there without being told in advance of his coming. He hired a couple of boys in the neighborhood to carry hand-made placards, and several times a week they walked along the country road saying, "Send Mr. Yoon Sungkoo to National Assembly!" The shabby campaign was laughed at although he was supported by some who knew him well. It could not be compared with the lavish campaigns mounted by his competitors: Hired sedans, vehicles bedecked with blown-up pictures, loud speakers, vigorous young men distributing printed leaflets.

When the father lost the election, he also lost his government house. The Yoons retired to a small rented room. Their son contributed to the rent. The mother planted vegetables in the backyard during the summer and dried them for the winter. Still, life without income was difficult. By spring, their food was already gone, and without a paddy-field, the fall held no hope.

The father-in-law sat in the master room alone reciting a sijo. Among the storms and stresses of his life, he had neglected to appreciate the classic poetry which had flourished throughout the Yi dynasty. He loved to recite the sijo written by one of his forefathers in the 17th century. His low voice traveled between the pitches, the long, trailing sound, sometimes suddenly hitting the lowest chord. It was like a stream meandering through the valley in the deepest part of a mountain: a long monotonous journey, then a sudden drop like a waterfall, resting in the hollow momentarily, then climbing back upstream and repeating the course. He sang with his eyes closed. When they were opened, it was to look beyond the clay ceiling, in musing communication with the spirits of his forefathers, who had recited the sijo in a mountain villa generations ago.

Outside, a farmers' parade noised its way through town. Households rushed out to watch. Bamboo pipes, the jangkoo, cymbals and gongs stirred up the afternoon tranquility and dust of a small country town. Farmers clad in red and blue robes danced along to the beat of the instruments. A yard-long tassel twirled from their caps as they swayed.

Standing on the edge of the hall floor, the mother-in-law heard the noise pass by. Suddenly she felt lonely. She went into the room where her husband sat in silence, his sijo reciting disrupted by the farmers' parade.

"Younggam, do you think we should join Daeyoung's family?" the mother-in-law ventured.

"Do you think so?" Her husband answered meekly. He had lost

126

enthusiasm for anything. He spent his time visiting a few of his friends for a game of go. Occasionally, he was a guest speaker at local gatherings. But these invitations were becoming rare.

"We should go. He is our first son and, after all, he has his duty to support us. Perhaps it would be better for them, too, because they wouldn't have to send us money any more." The mother-in-law convinced her husband.

With their hopes high, the elderly couple visited the son. In the beginning, the new daughter-in-law greeted them with due deference. The handsome face and the soft voice were different from what they had pictured. For a while things went smoothly as any other family with in-laws. When the parents' decision to live with them was mentioned, Daeyoung listened in silence and agreed. But it was a shock to Keok, who had thought it was only a visit.

"You mean you agreed to that? First sending piles of dirty clothes and now moving in with us? Who do they think they are, a king and a queen of Yi dynasty? Do you see any servants lined up out there? I can't serve them. My hands are full now with the kids. Why, at my age, I have no intention to start all over by serving the parents-in-law. I am not used to it," Keok fumed when they were alone.

"But I am the eldest son, and the only son for the time being. They have no other place to go," Daeyoung reasoned.

"They can go back. It will be better for them, too, to be alone. Tell them so! Send them a little bit more money if that's what they need! I just—"

"Quiet!" Daeyoung raised his voice in spite of himself.

"Why, you don't have any nerve to tell them, but you have the nerve to yell at me. Nobody asked you to bring me here."

"Neither did I wish to bring you here!"

"So, now you tell me! The old saying is right: You can't change your lot by marrying again. Oh, the misfortune of mine. It's always there. You! You are the one who ruined my life!" Keok's face turned blue. Foam collected at the corners of her mouth. Daeyoung slammed out of the room.

In the beginning, the mother-in-law thought it was a typical married couple's quarrel. But when she overheard their loud voices and heard the door slam, she realized she and the father were the cause of the upheaval.

"Daeyoung! We are leaving! We cannot stay for one moment in a house where we are not welcome!" the mother-in-law called to her son in the courtyard. Daeyoung slipped into his parents' room.

"Mother, please! Calm yourself. We can talk it over and settle things in the best possible way."

"Well, I just wondered! You seem to have plucked out a paddy plant and got yourself a weed! This is the end of the Yoon family!" Then the mother-in-law moved to the gate. The father-in-law followed with his cane and without a word, his pride deeply hurt. Daeyoung went after them to the gate trying in vain to stop them.

"We will not see you again, and don't you dare set your foot on the threshold of our house either!" his mother declared. And she stepped out of her son's home with her aging, silent husband.

XIV. Outbreak of the war

Mounting a swift steed,
Well fed, groomed,
A brilliant sword in hand,
Well ground, polished,
I would repulse the invading foe,
Strong in war, brave in death.

Choi Yong [1316-1388]

Spring 1950. South Korea.

Clutching a bundle of leftovers from the restaurant, Jungsoon climbed the hilly alley through the darkness. She had been climbing the same alley now for almost a year and a half. From the time she had left the streetcar terminal she had a strange feeling someone was following her. She turned but found no one there. She hurried along. She turned again thinking she had heard footsteps. The footsteps seemed to have halted too. When she made a last turn to her house, a murky figure appeared at her side.

"Auntie," came a sool-smelling mumble. Jungsoon stared into the shadows. The janitor!

"It's you, my goodness! You scared the life out of me! What are you doing here? You should be home by now," gently Jungsoon reproved the man.

"Home? I don't have a home!" He reeled a bit.

"You left way ahead of me, didn't you? This isn't your neighborhood. Did you move?"

"No, but Auntie, I want to go with you—to your house."

She began to be frightened.

"Go home! It's very late. You might miss the last streetcar."

"I am a human being too, you know. A hu—man being." He tried to balance himself.

"Listen. You've got to go to work early tomorrow morning. If you are late, Mr. Chang will be very angry." Gentle Jungsoon tried to make it sound firm.

She went ahead and tapped at the gate, ignoring the man following closely. The landlady came out rubbing her eyes, looking suspiciously at her and the man as she opened the gate. At far end of the yard, the young landlord was practicing weight lifting. Jungsoon unabashedly approached the young landlord.

"Oh, here you are, Chayoung. Now, this is the gentleman who works with me, but it's too late for him to get on the streetcar. I want you to grab a taxi for him. Here's the money. Oh, this is my brother Chayoung." Jungsoon talked rapidly and squeezed the money into the hand of the amazed landlord. "Here, hurry before it gets too late. Grab a taxi for him, will you?"

The muscular young man got the message.

"Okay, Sis!" He hulked toward the janitor, who retreated, eying the weights lying in the courtyard and the biceps nearing him at eye level.

"No, no taxi. I mean I can grab a taxi by myself. Thanks. Good night, Auntie." The janitor stumbled off into the darkness.

"Ha, ha! Auntie, you be careful," chuckled the amiable landlord returning the crumpled bills to Jungsoon. "If he bothers you again, just let me know."

Jungsoon went into her room frightened and heavy-hearted. Now, she didn't belong to anyone. A thing thrown into the street to be picked up or kicked around. "In those days" a widow as young as nineteen or twenty was said to have slept with a sharp knife tucked under her mattress so that she could lead a chaste life. She was twice that age, but perhaps that's what she should do! In bed, Jungsoon buried her cheek in her pillow shivering in humiliation, dreading the long lone years ahead.

In June, the small kitchen was hot and humid. A square-foot wide window in a smoke-stained wall was a needle hole for ventilation. The janitor skulked in his dirty apron. He seemed ashamed, and avoided Jungsoon. Her sleeves rolled up, Jungsoon prepared a sinsulro dish. She thought of her children. She should take some time off and visit them again.

"You must be very hot too, aren't you?" a raspy voice asked. A hand touched her waist. Jungsoon wriggled away.

"You, go over there and sweep the floor as you are supposed to do!" Jungsoon shouted angrily. Unabashed, the janitor leered at her.

"I know what I am supposed to do," he responded peevishly as he turned away. In a few seconds he came back to her. "Don't play hard to get! Let's face it. You are a woman divorced. You can't remain chaste the rest of your life. Look here, an eligible widower like me is hard to come by. So, think it over.''

The man left the kitchen but his abominable presence lingered. She felt degraded and offended. She was almost through with preparing the sinsulro dish when the janitor rushed back. Jungsoon jumped.

"If you come any closer to me, I am going to smash this over your skull." Jungsoon grabbed the sinsulro pot, the hot charcoal burning red underneath. The janitor stared at her equally startled.

"Auntie, are you crazy? I just came in to tell you the North Korean Army invaded us this morning!''

Jungsoon, blinking, put down the heavy brass pot. The Changs rushed in, too.

"Auntie, the Communist army invaded us! They have crossed the 38th parallel already and are coming down toward Seoul.''

"Oh, Auntie, war has broken out." Chang's wife shivered.

"Can it be real?" customers asked in hushed voices. "You mean there's going to be a war right in this peninsula?'' They had their meal in a hurry and left.

"Oh, what shall we do?" Neither owners nor employees could concentrate on their work.

Next morning, Jungsoon went to see the children at school, but the school was closed. She tried to put her mind on cleaning the nearly-closed restaurant. Chang came into the kitchen.

"There's a schoolboy out there who wants to see you.''

Jungsoon rushed out. There stood her son. Was it a dream!

"Hyonsup!" She took her son's hands into hers. "How did you get here?'' His face was sad and his eyes drooped. He couldn't say anything for a while.

"I came to be with you. Father doesn't know.''

"Then, he will look for you. Rest a while and go back home, all right?''

Chang and the janitor went out to get some more news. And in the corner Jungsoon and her son sat in the dim light and talked.

"Now, how did you find me?''

"One of my classmates said he saw you here the other day. At first I didn't believe him." Hyonsup looked around the place and at his mother in despair.

"Mother, I don't want to go back. I want to live with you."

"Now, now, let's not talk about it yet." Jungsoon searched her younger son. His hair was bushy and he had grown since she saw him last.

"Where is Wonsup? He's home?"

"I told him I was going, but he didn't want to come with me," Hyonsup explained. "You know, he calls her 'Mom' and seems to like her. He wanted to stay there. Stupid kid!" he grumbled.

Chang's wife approached bringing some food.

"Why, look, what we've got here, a fine looking young man!" she patted Hyonsup's shoulder. "There's nobody like your own dear old mama, is there?"

Chang's wife sat down with them. Chang and the janitor came in with more news.

"They are coming down closer to Seoul. Our army is helplessly retreating. They weren't prepared for this surprise invasion. At this rate, the Communists will be here soon. It's only twenty-five miles from here."

"Mother, what shall we do?" Hyonsup, agitated, mumbled. Jungsoon didn't know. She couldn't just let him go. There was no telling what would become of him, once he left her.

"Let's go to my place," she suggested with finality.

Joy of the reunion was tempered by apprehension as they headed for Jungsoon's living quarters. People scurried in all directions, confused, worried and afraid.

Her son looked about his mother's shabby room.

"I would have put on new wallpaper if I had known you were coming. I will go out tomorrow and buy some new wallpaper if there's any store open."

"Mother, we don't need to have anything like that. That's not important. Father won't be here to see it anyway."

Hyonsup looked thoughtful. He was still in his school uniform, tall and quiet. Then he lifted his head. "Mother, why don't we go and bring Wonsup here? He is too little to know what's going on. He should be with us, too."

Jungsoon thought of her youngest son. She had decided not to think about him but couldn't dismiss him so easily. He should be eleven by now, but to her he was the baby, the one to be cared for the most.

"All right. I will go and see him first thing in the morning."

People milled around the radio shop and in front of the bulletin board near a newspaper press. Jungsoon walked past the crowds and through the alley where once she passed on her way home from grocery shoppings. The familiar gate was left ajar. A little figure sat on the threshold. He was alone. A piece of broken string dangled from his hand.

"Wonsup!" Jungsoon called. The little boy lifted his head and stared at her as though she were invisible. His cheeks crisscrossed with scratches. Jungsoon peered closer.

"Wonsup, are you all right?" she squeezed his hands, examining his face. "Goodness, dear, where did you get all those scratches?"

"Had a fight with a neighbor kid," Wonsup answered disinterestedly.

"What are you doing out here?"

"Nothing. Just my top. The string is all broken. Where is Brother Hyonsup? He said he was going to find you. Did you see him?"

"Yes. I came to get you, if I could."

Somebody was coming out from inside the house calling his name. It was the maid. The maid stared at Jungsoon and fled inside to inform her mistress. The courtyard and kitchen door were still the same as she had remembered. A handsome woman with an oval face came to the door. Her dark eyes appraised the plain, gentle woman at the gate. A strange emotion swept Jungsoon. Getting control of her voice, she asked,

"Is Mr. Yoon Daeyoung home?"

The younger woman eyed her suspiciously.

"No, he isn't home." But the younger woman didn't ask who she was.

"I am Wonsup's mom. I—came here for his father's permission to take him with me. Hyonsup is at my place."

Sung Keok froze for a minute, then she soon softened.

"Do come in. He is not home. But if you want to take Wonsup along, I don't see why you can't."

Wonsup followed them in, hoping everything would turn out all right so he wouldn't get into trouble.

"Their father was worried about him when he disappeared. I told him he would be safe some place and I was right. Whaja! Get their clothes ready!"

The younger woman had an air of confidence befitting the lady of the household.

"Have a seat in there, please. It won't be long." The younger woman pointed to the hall room.

Silently Jungsoon sat on the floor of the hall room she used to mop every day. The jar stand at one end of the courtyard displayed many more jars than she had had. The house was as she remembered, but the atmosphere was different. Perhaps she was more used to the house she was living in now.

"I packed the rest of your clothes and put them away. Wouldn't you like to take them along with you?"

"I would."

"Whaja! Bring out the blue bundle in the storage room."

Storage! My clothes? Jungsoon stared at the younger woman, amazed. They must have collected mildew and odor. But she was in no position to complain.

Taking the bundle from the maid she stood up.

"Let's go, Wonsup." Jungsoon held out her hand to her son. "Good bye!" Jungsoon turned to the woman.

"Good bye!" responded her husband's mistress. The maid followed after her, and Jungsoon heard the gate latch behind her.

The little house on the hill-top was crowded. The family of the landlord's sister had taken refuge there weeks ago. Jungsoon had added her sons to the household. The city had fallen into the hands of the People's Army, three days after the invasion began. Tanks rumbled throughout the city and in front of the prison gate. The invaders had opened the gate and set the political prisoners and others free. The prisoners waved red flags and welcomed their liberators. A handful of high government officials were rumored to have fled farther south, but most people stayed and watched their city flooded with red flags, slogans and pictures of Stalin and Kim Ilsung. People moved cautiously eyeing the red flags, People's Army personnel, and their tanks.

"Look over there! The smoke!"

Children rushed out from the room at the exclamation of the landlord. A column of dark thick smoke shot up into the sky over the city.

"Wow, they must have dropped bombs again some place."

"The United Nations air force and infantry have joined our army in the fight. It won't be long. We will be free of the Communists soon." The young landlord encouraged the family and relatives with this information. But the good news lasted for just a few weeks. Bombing shattered the city. Buildings burnt. Hope of restoring democracy dimmed as the invader's propaganda grew louder and more incessant.

"The valiant soldiers of our People's Army are pursuing the invaders farther south. Our true friend, The Generalissimo Stalin and our great leader Comrade Kim Ilsung..." ubiquitous loud speakers spewed forth the feverish harangue.

"Do you think your oldest brother is still down there in Kwangjoo? Oh, what's going to happen to him! Where can he be now?" Jungsoon fretted over Kangsup as the situation worsened.

Marches and rallies were now in the south too. Crowds of students were summoned to an athletic field and became fed up with new songs and the impassioned propaganda. Hyonsup was surprised to see the language teacher who had disappeared for a period of time. The thin light-faced young man said "Hello!" to Hyonsup, one of his best students.

"Now, all the territory of the south is liberated, except Pusan and the tiny Cheju Island. It will be just a couple of days until we sweep the U.S. imperialists and their instruments into the sea."

Another speaker climbed up the podium.

"Down with Rhee Syngman and his band!" students repeated after the leader on the podium.

"Let us volunteer to fight! To defeat the invaders quickly and to achieve our long-wished unification," the leader eloquently urged.

A complete silence ensued.

"Let us volunteer!" the speaker exhorted, and again "Let us volunteer!"

One, two, three—students slowly left their row. One of his classmates went to the front signifying his intention to volunteer. Some of the girls stepped forward to join the Women's Alliance. Hyonsup looked at the podium and the teachers below it. The language teacher's glance met his. He lowered his eyes. He thought the North invaded the South. Now, who's calling whom the invader! When he raised his eyes, the language teacher stood in front of him.

"See me after this is over."

A chill ran down his spine as the language teacher stalked off. He wished it were only a nightmare. Hyonsup turned around and studied a way out. Columns of students standing in silence left no path for him to escape. Blood rushed to his face. His heart pounded violently. The rally finally ended, and the column of students started to move from the far end. It would be just a little while until it was his school's turn to leave.

Soon, all the girls' schools would march out and then it would be the boys' turn. After the columns of the last school passed by him, Hyonsup mustered up his courage, took off his school cap, and slipped in and walked as naturally as he could. It was a long march to the outside. Finally he was outside the gate. Then he started to walk faster. Along the fence of a hospital were posted Communist slogans and the caricatures of President Truman and General MacArthur. Tanks rumbled by. Soon he broke into a run. The whole world seemed to have turned upside down.

Hyonsup stayed home reading books, working on science problems.

"Someone's knocking at the gate!" The landlord rushed in and whispered urgently. "Come on, Hyonsup, we must hide! It must be the People's Army soldiers!"

Hyonsup, carrying a book, rushed toward the main house and crawled under the hall room floor after the landlord.

"Who's there?" Jungsoon approached the gate and inquired cautiously.

"Is there a lady named Oh Jungsoon living here?" The man's voice was subdued and familiar. She opened the gate. Her mouth fell agape.

"Master! It's you! You are alive!"

The brother-in-law, aged and tanned, gave her a hard glance and stepped inside. He sat at the edge of the floor step leading to Jungsoon's small room. He looked about the shabby place.

"What are you doing here?"

"I live here. You see I—"

"Ah, I know. I first went to Donam-dong but Brother wasn't there. The woman told me where you might live."

He sat quietly for a moment.

"So, you went to the North, after all?" she asked.

"What's wrong with that?"

"Mother and Father had been worried about you," Jungsoon said meekly.

"Where are the children?"

"Oh, they are out some place. Kangsup is in Kwangjoo. He has a job there. Wonsup went out to play. And Hyonsup—" Something prevented her from going on. Suddenly she realized the man no longer belonged to her family nor was on her side. He stood up.

"Well, don't worry, Comrade, it will soon be a liberated land, and we will all live well." He stalked out, promising to come back. Jungsoon

136

was stunned and annoyed for a long time after he left.

The joy of reunion with the children was short-lived. Soon Jungsoon had to worry about the means of survival. She was behind in the rent. The stores that were open carried little grain, and the few vegetables she bought didn't satisfy their hunger.

"I have to go to Chang's restaurant and see if anyone is there. Perhaps I can borrow something from them even if they are closed."

"Mom, be careful!" Wonsup cautioned.

"Auntie, try to avoid those shell splinters in case there's a bombing. Fall on the ground and stay flat with your face down. Have a safe trip," the young landlord advised her. Then he called to Hyonsup. "Come on, stay with me. They might barge in any minute and you will be drafted by the Reds. Ah, I should have joined the army, then I would be fighting the Reds instead of hiding in the smelly dirt like this."

Debris of bombed buildings filled the streets. Destroyed tanks were overturned on the curbs. Most stores were closed and shuttered.

Although the Changs had opened the place with the ingredients in stock, few customers came. In the dark and deserted kitchen, Jungsoon offered to help. Two of the People's Army soldiers entered the place. Chang's wife rushed into the kitchen.

"Oh, they scare me, Auntie. Why don't you go see what they want."

Jungsoon wiped her hands on her apron and went to them.

"You open?" One of them asked in the dialect of Hamkyong Province.

"Yes," Jungsoon answered.

They took off their army caps and sat facing each other.

"What do you have, Comrade?"

The soldiers were young, their voices still unbroken. Probably they were much younger than Hyonsup.

"We haven't fully opened yet. But I can make some mandoos and noodles."

They looked at each other.

"Noodles! Is it cold?"

"No, hot. We don't have ice here."

"Hot noodles!"

The two hungry soldiers finished their lunch quickly.

"How much?" One of them took out some money and counted. It wasn't the currency of the south. Jungsoon sought the owner's approval glancing at Chang's wife half hidden behind the kitchen door. She waved and shook her hand left and right.

"You don't have to pay. It's on the house," finally Jungsoon said.

They looked at each other, grabbed their caps and fitting them on their heads walked out of the door, their height barely reaching hers. They reminded her of Hyonsup in the mornings when he grabbed his school cap and ran for school. They, too, must be sons dear to some mothers like herself.

Jungsoon returned home with some food and the grain. Chilling news greeted her. The young landlord had been killed. He had stepped outside to watch a bomber fly overhead and was struck by a shell splinter. The mourning continued for weeks after the hasty burial. Jungsoon comforted the landlady, cared for the baby, and helped clean the house. The landlady's sister-in-law asked the landlady to come with her to the rural area,

"Since your husband is gone, there is no reason for you to stay here. There is nothing for us to eat in Seoul. Let's all go to our house in the country. We can plant some of my cabbage seeds and in time we will have something to eat. And it will get your mind off the tragedy. What's happened has happened, Sis. Nothing is going to bring him back. Come. We must go on living. Think of the baby."

Heartbroken, the young landlady left with her baby and her sister-in-law for the country. She left the house in the care of Jungsoon.

"I will come back as soon as it's possible, Auntie."

Jungsoon and the boys had the tiny three-room house to themselves. Hyonsup and Wonsup were glad to have an extra room. But they ran to their mother whenever aircraft swooped over their roof. At night, they cowered into their quilts, listening to the aircraft roaring overhead and the booming response of anti-aircraft batteries. Too often, the bombs fell into their neighborhood. The thunderous explosion. Eerie light from the flames agitated their room.

"Mother, cover yourself with the quilt. Get under it. The cotton stuffing will make it harder for shrapnel to penetrate." Hyonsup whispered a tip he had learned from his departed friend, the landlord.

Chang's restaurant was closed. Supplies had run out. And because their downtown house was vulnerable to bombing, the couple moved to the less-exposed home of their relatives, the Kims. A vegetable market flourished in front of Kim's store. Jungsoon took a basket of bean sprouts to sell in the makeshift market. With her slim profit, she managed to buy wheat flour. That meant a few dinners with dumplings—cause for celebration.

Long, hot and hungry, the summer dragged on. Bombs, death, and propaganda. Until the cool September wind stirred through the smoking rubble of Seoul, there seemed to be no hope of change. On the shaded floor of Kim's store, Jungsoon chatted with Kim's wife discussing their uncertain future. Suddenly the store owner, Kim, burst in.

"It won't be long. It won't be long," he shouted, waving his arms.

"What won't?" Chang asked wondering.

"They have landed at Inchon harbor and are on their way to Seoul."

"Who?"

"The U.S. Marines. Another division is heading south from Inchon, and our R.O.K. Army and United Nations force from Pusan have crossed the Naktong river and are heading north. The People's Army is trapped. It won't be long."

"Are you sure?"

Jungsoon rushed the good news to the children. Neighbors gathered in excited knots. Intensive and devastating, the battle raged for a week. In the end, the city burned from the effect and the arson tactics of the retreating People's Army.

General MacArthur and his troops were lionized by the people of South Korea. The Taigeuk and United Nations flags few side by side. From the ashes and skeletons of buildings, emerged the people of Seoul, their backs straight, their heads high. Whole, or in pieces, the dead were collected. Hyonsup turned away and tried hard to avoid witnessing the carnage.

U.N. and R.O.K. divisions moved steadily northward.

Changs reopened the restaurant, but business was slow. Jungsoon went in and out to help whenever needed.

"Mom, I think I can sell some of those cigarettes to make money. I saw lots of kids doing that." Wonsup volunteered.

"No, I don't think so, son. Let me take care of our income. You go on back to school and study."

October was chilly. Through sleepless nights, Jungsoon worried about feeding and clothing her family. Unheated, the floor sent its chill through her bones. Memory of the dead still lingered in the tiny house. Wind rattled at the kitchen panels as if someone were hiding behind them. Once in a while airplanes ripped the sky and rushed to the northern province. It was during one of those nights when her brother-in-law returned.

"Help me, Sister!" The voice was urgent.

Her brother-in-law's face was half hidden by the hat pressed down to his nose and his coat hung loosely. He rushed inside the room without being invited.

Jungsoon lit the candle. Now she could get a better look at him. As he removed his ill-fitting hat and found a place to sit on the floor, she saw that his hair was messy and his face caked with dirt.

"Oh," she gasped. "What's the matter? Master, what has happened to you?"

Chayoung was obviously exhausted. He explained he had come a long way avoiding being spotted by both sides.

"You must be starved. I've got some leftover cold rice from the restaurant. I'll warm it up for you."

He devoured the food in silence. After washing his face and feet, as Jungsoon had asked him to, he sat staring into space, consumed by his thoughts.

"You're exhausted, Master. Go to Hyonsup's room and sleep. I will get a mattress and a cover for you." Chayoung didn't seem to have heard her. "Go on, Master. Have a good rest."

"Sister, I am sorry to bother you like this," he said. "Actually I shouldn't have come to you. But I didn't know to whom I could turn," the brother-in-law said.

"Oh, don't worry. You can stay as long as you wish."

"But, Sister! Do you know you can get into trouble by letting a person like me stay here?"

"But you are no longer a Communist, are you? You came back. You are not going to go back to the North, are you?"

"No."

A heavy silence followed. The brother-in-law sighed. "I thought the idea of Communism was social reform. Equal distribution of wealth, co-prosperity—all those ideals I espoused since I was a young man. It doesn't work that way. It will never work that way," he echoed bitterly.

"And me. Especially me. I am definitely a bourgeois. Look at my hands. They are the hands of the leisure-ridden yangban blood. I've never done any manual work, any hard work. I never worked the earth. How can I understand the soul of peasants and laborers? I was tired," he said wearily. "I simply wanted to come home."

How old he looks! Yet Jungsoon could still see a hint of the headstrong young man she used to serve.

"How different it might have been if you had married that attractive girl from Kyongsang Province and settled down."

"It's too late. Everything's too late for me now. I belong nowhere."

"If you decide to stay in the South, you will be all right, won't you?"

"I wish it were as simple as that. You are a wonderful person, Sister. Sometimes I've wondered if you were an ordinary human being. We really never have given you anything, have we? And that miserable brother of mine! I didn't think he could sink that low. Can you imagine a man of his position putting his wife in this situation!" He mused angrily. "I am nothing to you," he continued. "And yet, you would help me unquestioningly. I guess I'm no different from Brother. My family is all the same. No chivalry, no guts." He was talking to himself and incidentally to Jungsoon. Jungsoon felt a deep compassion for the wretched man. She had so many questions to ask. But this didn't seem to be the time to raise them.

"Master, you must get some rest," she said finally. "I will arrange your bed in Hyonsup's room. Come!"

"You are much too good to me, Sister. You can go to jail for just allowing me in the house. That brother of mine!" He shook his head. Then he mumbled on in despair. "You and I are people born at the wrong time and at the wrong place. Well, I don't have anything to lose anyway. No family or anybody depending on me. So, that's a relief, isn't it!"

He arose slowly, stiffly. "Sometimes, though, I wonder what she would look like—"

"Who?"

"You should probably know. The Japanese girl I was—she had my child. She'd be about—what? five by now?"

Like a child, Chayoung followed Jungsoon and watched as she prepared a bed for him next to Hyonsup.

"Tomorrow, Master, go see Mother and Father. They will be so surprised. Now, you may be a little cold since this room hasn't been heated for months. But here are some extra covers in case you get chilly during the night. Good night, Master."

"Sister," the brother-in-law called to the retreating Jungsoon.

"Thank you. I promise I won't bother you like this any more."

"Oh, Master, you are not bothering anybody. You know you are welcome to visit your nephews any time you want to."

Hyonsup was asleep. Chayoung looked at his sleeping nephew for a while.

"Hyonsup, wake up!" The uncle shook him.

"Uh?" Hyonsup opened his eyes half asleep.

"Hey, you go to the other room and sleep. You know I snore terribly. I don't think you will be able to sleep in the same room with me. Go on to the other room."

Hyonsup, half awake, stumbled out.

"Who was here last night?" Hyonsup asked in the morning.

"Sh—your uncle is here sleeping. Don't wake him up."

After the children left for school, Jungsoon washed dishes and got ready for work. The day was cloudy and she couldn't tell the time. She had the breakfast tray table ready for the brother-in-law and waited for him to stir.

"Master, are you awake?"

No answer.

"Are you there, Master?"

Still no answer. She opened the door.

"Wake up, Master! It's almost noon. Have breakfast and you can go back to sleep." Becoming bold she stepped inside. Near the pillow on the mattress lay a small bottle and a note:

Please don't let Mother know. To her I am a son already dead
and forgotten. No need to shock her twice. There was a way after
all, though cowardly. I don't expect heaven or hell. I just wish
to rest my tired soul in silence, like a piece of rock, like a piece
of wood. Thank you, Sister.

He lay on his back. In death, his face mirrored the frustration of his unfulfilled life.

Jungsoon rushed to find a doctor.

"An over-dose of quinine!"

Hyonsup took the news with heavy silence. He hadn't had that many chances to be close to the deceased. But he wanted him alive somewhere. The uncle owed him a Charlie Chaplin movie. Actually that wasn't it. Too many things were happening too fast. Everything was beyond his comprehension. Somehow, somebody should make this world a better place to live in. The back of the young adult walking inside the school building

142

to be excused reminded his mother of the time of her first visit.

Yoon Daeyoung met his son in his office with cold surprise.

"What brings you here?"

"Uncle is dead."

Daeyoung noted the evidence of poverty in the son who had run away from him. He was annoyed and angry that his brother had sought out the person he no longer recognized as his wife.

"I will send men to take care of it!" he snapped.

Two hired men came and removed the body to the crematory. Only Jungsoon and Hyonsup were witnesses. She took the ashes to the Han River bridge. The remains of Chayoung's tortured mortality swept downstream free and uncomplicated.

A month later a letter came bearing an army address. Kangsup was in the army.

"Mother, don't worry. I am doing just fine. I have taken the exam to become an officer cadet. After basic training, I will be a sublieutenant, a platoon leader. Wish me luck, Mother. I have to go to sleep now. See you, Mother. Cordially, Your son, Kangsup."

Jungsoon's heart swelled with pride. My son, a sublieutenant! Would she be able to see him soon? Would he be all right?

XV. The road to a refuge

Although Pyongyang is my home and capital,
And the walls have all been repaired,
If I must part from you, be left behind,
I'll stop spinning, and stop weaving,
Follow my own love with salt tears.

Unknown Kisaeng [15th century?]

Fall 1950. Pyongyang, North Korea.

Yi Chinjoo was wakened by the wall clock striking five. Dim light streaming through the chinks between the attic doors told her Kim Insoo was up there reading the Bible. Listening to her husband flip the pages and utter an occasional whispered prayer, she went back to sleep.

In the heavily bombed city of Pyongyang, buildings and streets had been reduced to ashes and rubble. Kim Insoo, the ardent Christian, now an elder and a suspected dissident, had been harassed and tortured by the police many times. Since the war, he confined himself to the attic and his Bible. He came down for meals, crossed the hall to see his ailing mother, and prayed with the family. Chinjoo, unable to emulate his zeal, tried to acquiesce with her husband but was more attuned to the sound of war.

When the mini-door in the dividing fence was flung open, Chinjoo held her breath.

"Good morning, Aunt!" It was the new neighbor. The Chois had moved to the south. "Is Mr. Elder home?"

"Do come in, Teacher Song. He is in."

The young school teacher had not been drafted because of his dysentery. He had made a radio, devoted his time to the underground church affairs, and admired Kim Insoo deeply. Since the war, the elders and some of the members met in secret at his home, held services, and hoped brighter days would dawn for them. Kim Insoo greeted the school teacher in the attic. A considerable time elapsed. The men's whispers grew louder, then the attic door was pushed open and the excited face of Kim Insoo peered down.

144

"Listen! The R.O.K Army has crossed the 38th parallel and are advancing northward. They recaptured Seoul a few days ago. It won't be long until they get here!"

Chinjoo and the children raised their eyebrows.

"Can it be true?"

Until the morning, the simple, four-tube radio clamored about hemming in the Communist forces in the Pusan perimeter far to the south.

"True! Ah, it's true," the young teacher assured them, excitedly. His homemade radio in his backyard air raid shelter had picked up the news.

Kim Insoo paced up and down the room, crossed the hall, and opened the door of the opposite room.

"Mother, stay with us in the master room."

"It wouldn't make any difference. It's all right here." The elderly lady answered feebly.

"Mother, what you need is good nutrition and restoratives. You just wait, Mother. Ginseng and antlers, I will buy you tons of those. I haven't been a good son, but I will make it up to you. You will see. Just be patient for a little while, Mother."

Kim Insoo mumbled on.

"It won't be long. We will soon be free. I knew something like this would happen. There are many signs."

"Here comes the airplane again. Under the quilt! We have to survive first before we see freedom." Chinjoo threw the cover over her head. The children followed her example. They heard the bombers and the retaliation of antiaircraft batteries. Kim Insoo's thoughts drifted into a bitter memory.

When a group of the Men's Alliance barged in and disrupted his church service, he reminded them of the freedom of religion the government professed to guarantee. They took him to the police station.

"Superstitious fanatic! Deny it! Deny and follow our great leader. You can even be a party member!"

He refused. He had a vision of the Disciple Peter. No, he wouldn't deny Christianity! The familiar concrete floor and the foul odors of the basement. Then the truncheon fell on his head as if it were a piece of firewood. The interrogation continued.

"Where is your God? Make him appear. If you do, I shall cook bean paste on my palm, ha, ha!" The policeman's laughter rang in his aching skull. He stood it with the determination of the martyr, Stephen.

"It won't be long. They'll be here soon. And the Americans, the people filled with humanism, the blessed country!" How could there be such a country which professes publicly that it believes in God? They say they even carry the phrase on their money. To him, that alone was the reason for adulation. "May God give them power to win the war!"

"Yobo! Get in here!" Chinjoo shouted.

"Ah, it won't be long!" Kim Insoo didn't bother to duck under the quilt. "We will all go south the first chance we have. Can you imagine? You and me and the girls, all in the free world, talking as we believe, doing as we please. I will build God's house there as Jacob raised Bethel in a strange land with the stone he put under his head for a night's sleep!"

Throughout the night, he sat like a prophet, mumbling, glowing in red whenever a flare-bomb flashed.

Toward morning, they were shaken out of their sleep by an ominous banging at the gate. Kim Insoo's face hardened.

"Into the attic!" Chinjoo hissed.

Kim Insoo didn't move.

"The first place they'd look for me is in the attic. I would rather go with dignity." Sliding his hands into the armholes of his cotton-padded gray chogori, he said calmly. "Listen, if anything happens to me, don't wait for me. You just go on south with the children when you have the chance. If I am alive I will follow you and find you wherever you are. Take Mother along to Wonjang-ni if you can. I am sure Teacher Song will be a lot of help to you."

Chinjoo followed him to the street. Helplessly, she watched her husband taken away by two Security policemen, his hair unkempt, his face unshaven. He did not turn back.

Although it was not a new experience, Chinjoo felt sick. With an icy heart she went into the kitchen. Steaming the potatoes for the children's meal, she felt the torture her husband would suffer. Darn! Couldn't he just keep his mouth shut and live like an ordinary fool? He has a spirit to go through fire and water for whatever he believes in.

"Leave two of them for your pa," Chinjoo instructed as she watched her children devouring the potatoes.

Dusk crept into the courtyard accompanied by the strong October wind. The lids on the jars in the jar stand rocked for a while, and the tin pail, put over a jar in place of its missing lid, fell off, hit the cemented

146

jar stand, and rolled on the ground. The man of the house was still missing. Chinjoo watched the gate in vain. Instead, she saw the mini-door pushed open. The wife of Teacher Song stepped inside,

"O, Sunhee's ma, our children's father isn't home yet. He went crosstown yesterday to visit Elder Ann. O, I told him not to go, but he did." Her voice trailed off into a sob.

"He will be home. Don't you worry. Have you and the children had anything to eat? Come on over. Let's fix something for ourselves."

Chinjoo walked to the police station to try for some information about her husband. The policemen had been shifted and the new ones knew nothing about Kim Insoo. When she persisted, one of them threatened her with a gun and she turned away. Teacher Song's wife and her two children joined Chinjoo. Air raids continued.

"Under the guilt! We have to stay alive to see your pa!"

Artillery fire rocked the floor on which they huddled.

"The gunfire is much closer now. Fighting must be going on just across the Taedong River," whispered Tongja as if she had taken over her father's place.

"Duck your head!" Chinjoo cried. A shell whined over their heads. A second later, a thunderous explosion. Again, again. The nerve-racking barrage continued. When it ceased, Chinjoo peered out and muttered.

"O, I wish your pa was here! Where can he be!"

A tap at the front gate and Chinjoo rushed out hoping against hope. Instead, it was a man from down the alley. Until a week ago, he had gone up and down the street shouting phrases, "U.S. imperialist and its puppet government." With an air of urgency he forced a flag into her hands.

"They are here. The R.O.K. Army and the U.N. troops are here!"

Chinjoo stared at the man of convenient allegiances.

"Are you certain?"

"Sure, I saw them. Here's a flag for you. Let's go welcome them!" The man scurried away.

"O, your pa should be here!" Chinjoo sighed fingering the Taigeuk flag with emotion. The freedom her husband so fervently had desired was a reality.

Night folded in. Somewhere in the neighborhood, dogs barked. Brassware, pots and pans clanged. In her master room, Chinjoo huddled with her three daughters and Teacher Song's young wife. They wished the clamor of victory would fade away and be replaced by a quiet, meaningful peace.

People crept out from the debris, exalting in freedom. Chinjoo met the man who lived down the alley.

"I've heard they've taken many men along, when they retreated, and killed them on the way. There are heaps of bodies left in the countryside." The man scuttled away.

"Let's go find your pa!"

Holding hands with horrified Sunhee, Chinjoo trudged miles north of the city along the unpaved country road. Whenever they heard of a place where the dead had been dumped, she rushed there. Some searchers had already uncovered the grisly hills off the main highway, in bushes, in furrows. They dug out the bodies, wet and rotting. Chinjoo stooped and examined, forgetting her youngest daughter turning her face away from the horrible scene. Victims were stabbed, slashed, and disfigured. Their hands had been tied behind them and joined with others by thick wire. Blood clotted around the torn wrists was grim testimony to frantic struggles to free themselves. It was an endless search. Chinjoo's blood-shot eyes examined one bloated body after another. At day's end most of the searchers left. Her legs worn out, her senses horror-numbed, Sunhee tugged at her mother.

"Ma, let's go home."

"You wait. Just one last place over that hill."

Sunhee dragged her body close to her mother.

"Isn't that your pa?" Chinjoo pointed at a body. The gray chogori. Her heart pulsing wildly, she stooped down and examined it for a long while. No. His height was much taller. It was some other woman's husband, another child's father.

"Ma, let's come back tomorrow."

"All right. Let's do that." Chinjoo slowly lifted herself, suddenly dead with fatigue, grasping tenaciously to the faint hope that her man might be alive somewhere.

Teacher Song's wife joined Chinjoo in the search next morning, but before noon, tired and losing nerve, the wife left. At week's end, the wife's brother came from a northern province and took the family back with him. The mini-door in the dividing fence was tightly closed.

Whenever the northern wind blew, the battered branches shuddered and the leaves fell on the debris of land and man. Atop the building that formerly housed the People's Committee headquarters, Taigeuk and United Nations flags whipped side by side in the wind. Men entered and left the building in a steady stream. One of them could have been her husband. The church where Kim Insoo once brought his family was reopened. She went to the church occasionally at the urging of the members, but the memory of her husband was too painful.

"Ma, the R.O.K. Army captured Chosan and reached the Yalu River. And the U.N. forces are advancing north from other fronts. My friend said that. Her brother is an R.O.K. army officer. Oh, we will soon all be free, all of our country," Tongja reported, coming home from school. She encouraged her mother with talk of the possible return of her missing father.

Hope was short-lived. A quiet snow whirled out of the gray sky, the day a church member brought the bad news. "Chinese Communist forces have come into the war. The R.O.K. Army was ambushed near the Yalu River."

Tongja's face darkened.

"Oh, they will be driven back soon. They won't be able to maintain their supply lines so far from China." Tongja brushed the bad news aside, her optimism backed by the prevailing news: The U.N. and R.O.K. troops on the east coast were nearing the Manchurian and Soviet borders. Children went to the rallies that urged 'Advance North!' as if their participation would speed the army's destiny.

Two weeks later Tongja announced.

"Ma, they've reached Haisanjin, the city on the border. I told you. O, now all of the country is free except the tiny northeast tip. Oh, pa should have been here!"

Then one afternoon Tongja came home without her habitual spirit. "I saw refugees coming from the North." Chinese Communist troops poured down from both sides of the Taibaik mountains. R.O.K. and U.N. forces were hit hard. Dark shadows swept over the women.

"It can't be!" Tongja didn't want to believe. Desperately watching the snowflakes settling in the courtyard, she repeated, "It can't be!" It had been barely a month since the city had been liberated.

Neighbors packed and left. Friends came and urged the Kims to go with them. But Chinjoo persisted.

"You go on. Don't worry about us. We will leave as soon as the children's pa comes home."

The United Nations forces were rapidly evacuating. Tanks, armored vehicles and hoards of pitiful refugees streamed out of the city. Tongja became restless.

"Ma, we don't have much time. They will soon blow up the bridges."

Chinjoo spent the afternoon in despair and disbelief, hoping against hope something dramatic would happen and reverse the situation. Her children, their faces distorted with fear, hovered around her waiting for their mother to make the decision. They were young, healthy, with a future, however uncertain. It was her duty to guide them and give them the chance. That's what her husband would have wanted. Chinjoo climbed up to the attic, fished for the one remaining silk magoja. She carefully scissored the pair of gold buttons from the moth-eaten jacket.

"Let's go. We are going as far as the uncle's home in Sariwon."

One button bought them food, grains, and other supplies for the road. She gathered Kim Insoo's pants, shirts, and fur hats, and pressed them on the girls. "You are all boys now, you hear me? Your name is Tongsoo. You all have letter 'soo' instead of 'ja' in your name. When you talk, talk like boys. But try not to talk at all."

Evening had arrived by the time the hasty preparations were completed.

"Ma, Grandma—"

"She can't be on the road in this weather." Chinjoo peeked into her mother-in-law's room. Trying to cover her emotion with her strong Pyongan Province accent, "Mother, we are leaving. We have to go, with the children and everything. I am sure Wonjang-ni uncle will come get you. There is some millet and rice left for you. We will be back as soon as things get better."

Folding her wrinkled hands in her lap, the elderly woman gazed at her daughter-in-law.

"I will be all right. Take care," she said quietly. Tears glistened in her hazy eyes. Chinjoo turned around.

Dressed in men's cotton defense caps or fur hats and carrying a bundle of quilts and clothing on their backs, the girls were ready to leave. At the gate, Sunhee hesitated glancing at the grandma's room.

"Sunhee, hurry!" Chinjoo called, trying not to look back.

Yi Chinjoo and her daughters trudged along the snow-covered

highway. Day followed day. Often they were by themselves, but more often they caught up with or were overtaken by eddies of the ever-increasing river of refugees. They searched the crowd for the man in gray clothes. Kim Insoo might possibly—possibly—be among the thousands making the southward trek. The cold millet cakes and potatoes ran out the first day. Reconnaissance planes and an occasional fighter droned overhead. Tanks and armored vehicles came from behind and rumbled past them. On each side of the road, fields and orchards shrouded in white and abandoned by their owners, mutely watched the refugees plod by.

"Oh, Ma, I am so tired. My feet are so sore," Sunhee complained falling behind.

"Come on, dear, see the little girl and boy over there? They walk faster than you do. Here, let me take it." Chinjoo took Sunhee's bundle and added it to her own. Tongja and Kwangja were always far ahead but when the distance became too great they rested on the roadside waiting for the rest of the family. Her neck compacted by the load on her head, Chinjoo felt as though her shoulders were being pulled off by the heavy bundle on her back. She came close to her youngest daughter.

"Come, dear, we are almost there. When we get to Sariwon uncle's home we will have food and rest. Just walk a little bit faster."

Sariwon. A lock was on the gate of the brother-in-law's house. That family, too, was fleeing south. Tired and discouraged, Chinjoo and the girls stayed in the neighborhood church for a week waiting for any new developments. Perhaps they had been too hasty in leaving their home. She hesitated and thought of going back. A new group of refugees arrived.

"Hello there, do you know how the situation is?"

"Still bad," a middle-aged man answered devouring the ball of rice distributed by the church volunteers. "Last time I heard, the People's Army was nearing Pyongyang. They must have taken the city by now."

Soon Chinjoo and the girls pushed south again.

They tried hard to keep up with men, but even Tongja and Kwangja sagged, and Chinjoo stopped for Sunhee who constantly fell behind.

"My dear, we will soon get there. When we get to Seoul we will settle down. You will have things. I bet they have lots of pretty things there. And when your pa joins us, we will be as happy as can be. Now, Tongsoo, give us some dried whiting." Hurrying her pace, she coaxed lagging Sunhee and distributed the strips of dried fish.

151

In December, the road was dreary. For many days they had not seen an army truck nor a retreating soldier. Their feet were now numb from the cold. Biting wind scooped up the icy snow and tore at their faces. Hills and small villages loomed ahead and eventually disappeared behind them. Tongja's sneakers developed holes and her socks felt the chill and pebbles along the road. Her thoughts mirrored those of her family's: If only she didn't have such a heavy load to carry, it would be so much easier to walk! Their overcoats pulled up to their necks and stooped with their heavy loads, they could almost number each painful step. Sunhee, half of her hair sticking out of her father's fur cap, tired and frozen, no longer asked "are we getting closer?"

"Around the mountain we will find a house where you can warm your hands. A nice, hot ondol floor where you can stretch your tired body. Now let's catch up with those people." Encouraging the children, Chinjoo plodded on. They came a mile or so more. Suddenly the refugees halted.

"Stay where you are!" A tall man in a fur hat and a chestnut-colored scarf warned. He traced a suspicious wire peeping out through the snow-laden underbrush. "It's a mine! Don't move! Everyone, go back as far as the tree over there! Go back stepping in the footprints you have made!"

When the line of the people had retreated a safe distance, he looked about. Planting his feet firmly, he carefully reached for a rock beside him. Then as if lifting a weight, he brought the rock over his head and hurled it. A deafening explosion followed. His companions watched breathlessly wondering if he were alive.

"It's clear, now!" The man sprang to his feet and motioned to the people to come.

Without being told, the people formed a line and stepped into the leader's footprints. To have a man like him on the road was comforting. He directed the group like an officer leading his platoon.

"Sir, you are doing a wonderful work for us all," Chinjoo complimented. But the man in front of her was too absorbed in his task to talk with Chinjoo.

"We must be approaching the 38th parallel. If lucky, we'll be crossing the line tomorrow."

Before long the short daylight gave way to dusk. Dark clouds loomed over the snow-covered mountain. Tired refugees saw a campfire in the mid-slope of the hill.

"There! There's a house. Over there, we will rest and eat."

Chinjoo and the girls mustered up their diminishing strength at the sign of human habitation. Refugees ahead of them turned quickly into the path leading to the small farm houses. The distance to the village was deceiving. Around the corner, appeared another mountain, and still many more hills—it fooled the refugees like a wanton maid luring a foolish gentleman.

Finally Chinjoo and the girls sat on the hall floor in one of the houses. For a sum collected from the refugees, the farmer's wife cooked a hot meal that rekindled life and hope in the people there. Around the fire, they talked about the mine in the afternoon: how lucky they had been; how kind the middle-aged man was who had saved the lives of the group that followed him. Leaning forward on his knapsack, the man with the chestnut colored scarf was quiet. On his knapsack was sewn three letters and Chinjoo guessed his family name was Son.

A fiftyish woman looked at Sunhee admiringly. "Why this young fella has the face of a pretty little gal."

Sunhee glanced at her mother who hurriedly babbled,

"O, do you really think so? You can hardly tell which is which when they're that young, can you, ha ha!"

A young man in an oversized parka eyed Tongja. Her head was wrapped in a scarf, her face hidden under a cotton defense cap.

"Hey, where do you come from?"

Tongja, standing by the fire, didn't answer.

"Hey, where do you come from?" He nudged her.

Tongja glanced at him once and evaded an answer with a smile. Chinjoo hastened to them.

"O, from Pyongyang. We are coming from Pyongyang. We've come a long way. Ah, I am glad we found this place. Nice and warm. The fire's burning real good now, isn't it!" Chinjoo bustled about, trying to divert the young man's attention. He nudged Tongja again.

"Hey, you must be a middle school boy. What grade are you in? I'm from Pyongyang, too. You must be in the fifth year of the middle school. Am I right? You didn't join the People's Army either, huh? Your ma must have had a hard time to hide you."

"No, he didn't go to a middle school. He is kind of slow. Not very smart, you know?" Chinjoo answered in a hurry.

"He sure is a shy one," the young man said and turned away.

The man with the scarf puffed at a cigarette, his dark eyes downcast and his hollow cheeks burning red from the heat of the fire. Occasionally he cast a sympathetic glance to Chinjoo and the children.

"Must be hard, going south with children."

"O, they're big boys, now. They take good care of themselves. Tongsoo and Kwangsoo, go over there and spread the quilts up on that hall floor and get ready for bed. You boys all must be very tired."

He smiled. Those were girls. A man who lived half a century was not to be taken in. Rich dark hair sticking from under their soiled caps, the raised bosoms under their crude attire, and the full buttocks would fool no one.

"I left a family behind," he reminisced softly, partly to Chinjoo, partly to himself. "I thought it would be only temporary, just falling back to the south of Taedong River, then advance north. I could have taken them along if I had known it would turn out this way." The low voice had a tinge of self-reproach.

"O, I am sure it will turn out all right. If you stay alive, you will find them again, I am sure."

The fire burned low and people curled up in their quilts.

In the morning Son and other refugees left. But Chinjoo and the girls hated to be on the dreary road again so soon. The warmth of the ondol floor and the burning fuel hole in the kitchen filled with the smell of cooking reminded them of their own home. She would stay there at least until they were completely rested. Perhaps she shouldn't go too far south. She would get home quicker once the situation got better. Refugees came and went. The farmer couple needed a hand. Chinjoo helped the wife cook and the girls still in boys' attire, helped gather firewood.

Days went by precariously. New arrivals indicated the situation was getting worse. After the last chores of distributing the cooked food and washing the dishes were finished, Chinjoo and the girls packed their things to leave early the next morning.

Chinjoo was awakened by a sharp cry, a flare, and thunder. Bombers roared overhead. Shell fragments burst into the straw-thatched roof and in seconds the farm house was a blazing torch.

"Get out, get out of here!" Chinjoo clutched the quilt over her head and scrambled outside. "Are we all here?" she asked breathlessly. "Hang on to the quilt!"

154

Plowing through the ankle-deep snow and tripping over rocks and dead twigs of the field, they ran without direction. Flames crackled into the air and lighted the area from which they were frantically scrambling.

How long they ran, they didn't know. Finally, they came to a stop in a field to catch their breath. Caps and fur hats were gone. Frightened faces matched their tangled hair. They could hear one another's rapid heartbeat. No one else was in sight. The flames died down.

A new day dawned over the mountain as if it had nothing to do with its predecessor's rampage. Chinjoo gathered up their things and folded up the quilts dampened from the night air. The girls woke up shivering.

"Ma, I can't go. I am freezing," said Tongja, who used to be the leader, her teeth chattering like wooden sandals.

"We have to cross the 38th parallel once and for all," declared Chinjoo. "Remember the man? He said we were almost there, didn't he?"

"But Ma, it's so cold." Tongja, shivering, whined.

"O, you will feel better once we are on the road. Give me some dried whiting."

"There is none. We have several dried cuttlefish left. That's all," Kwangja said.

A group of refugees trudged down the hill into the narrow road.

"Are you all coming from over there at the farm?" queried Chinjoo. "It was bombed last night. Oh, it was terrible. Were you there, too?"

"No, but we came by there this morning. You know there were some Communist soldiers in one of the houses there. They are all ashes now," an old man breathed with effort.

"Heavens!" Chinjoo gasped.

"We are now in the enemy zone. But I guess we have to keep going as well as we can." The man limped ahead.

Silently, they plodded on along the winding road. More pilgrims joined them. They had been told at the farm house that there were some Red guerrillas hiding somewhere in the deepest part of the mountains, but as yet there was no sign of them. A group of men covered with white sheets walked with Chinjoo and the girls for a while, went ahead of them, slowed down letting them catch up, and then rushed down the road again.

As they circled around a low mountain, fighters appeared from nowhere. Machine guns barked. The refugees ran back and forth in panic.

"Down!" Chinjoo grabbed her daughters and sank into the field. "This is it! This must be it! O, God!" Chinjoo closed her eyes and with

155

her face pressed against the icy dirt, clutched her daughters' arms and listened to the sounds of strafing. Planes swooped low and belched staccato fire. The barrage was returned by artillery in the surrounding mountains. Finally, the long, nerveracking moments came to an end. The roar of engines disappeared. Gunfire ceased. The world became silent. Cautiously Chinjoo lifted her head and saw Sunhee stirring. Several other refugees lifted their heads, but others remained motionless.

"Oh, Ma, we are caught in the front!" Two yards away Tongja stood up.

"Stay down!" Chinjoo made a frantic gesture. "Stay down! See, nobody is getting up yet?"

"They are all dead, Ma."

Chinjoo lifted herself slowly as if checking if she had been hit, too. Dead lay strewn like match sticks. The men in white sheets were among the dead. A gust of wind stirred the sheets. Underneath were combat Communist uniforms.

"Let's get out of here! We must stay alive!" Never in her life had she felt this more urgently. Without a complaint, the children rushed down the road.

Beyond the hill, at the end of the road they saw a crude sign.

"So, that's the 38th parallel!" Out of breath Chinjoo walked on with her teeth clenched. "Let's go, don't stop. Let's get past it."

At one time, crossing the painful symbol dividing their country would have been a haven for refugees. Not so any more.

Planes rocked the sky.

"Fall flat!" Chinjoo screamed to the children, and they flattened themselves on the roadside. The aircraft vanished. Silence. Cautiously, Chinjoo was about to stand up. Suddenly the whole earth seemed to explode. A high-pitched scream, impact, explosion. When first they had suffered these repeated sequences, they were in the familiar surrounding of the Pyongyang home. Now, they were exposed to an artillery barrage without a shred of protection.

"Please!" Chinjoo whispered.

A near hit in the hill nearby attacked their eardrums. The hill erupted. Earth, rocks and tree roots hurtled through the air, themselves projectiles. The concussions and explosions seemed to last a lifetime. But finally, the volley spent its fury on the South Korean hillsides. For the moment, the echoes of hate were silenced.

Alive, Chinjoo rose to her knees, screaming "Are you all there?"

"Ma," responded Kwangja in a hollow voice. "Ma, where's Sister Tongja?" At Kwangja's exclamation the family turned and saw Tongja writhing in pain, trying to get to her feet.

"No!" Chinjoo knelt beside her. A shell fragment had ripped through the child's leg. Blood streamed onto the cold earth.

"Ma, oh, Ma!" Tongja, unaware of what had happened to her until then, screamed.

"What shall we do? O, what shall we do!" Chinjoo stuffed one hand into the gaping hole and waved the other in the air. "Hurry, tear off my chima. Oh, don't cry, don't you cry. You will be all right!" Her hands shaking, Chinjoo dressed the wound with the strips of her chima. The children were petrified.

"What are you all standing there for? Come on, get moving! Here, lift Tongja onto my back!"

Kwangja took Tongja's load, and they started off again.

"Let's go. Every step will help."

Chinjoo, with determination born of desperation, stumbled along the dreary road, her legs becoming stiff, her chest bursting from her daughter's added weight. Few other refugees were in sight.

"Ma, I can't walk any more. Oh, I can't." Kwangja staggered, her long hair blowing in the wind.

"O, Ma, my leg!" Eighteen year old Tongja cried uncontrollably on her mother's back. Blood, soaking through the dressing, drenched Chinjoo.

"Let's make it to the entrance of that village!" Puffing heavily, Chinjoo led the children into a winding path.

Halfway to the village they saw a hut and a barn in flames.

"No more!" Kwangja collapsed by the flame.

Unloading her wounded daughter, Chinjoo joined Kwangja. Tongja's leg now resembled a dark red log.

"Kwangja, get some more strips of cloth!"

Tongja rested her wounded leg on her mother's lap. Through tears she stared at it in despair. She couldn't believe it. She couldn't believe it had happened to her.

"It will be all right. You will be all right." Chinjoo bound the leg with the strips from the cloth which Kwangja had pulled from the bundle.

Crouched on a rock warmed by the burning barn, Kwangja watched the weather-beaten beams sinking into ashes. They should have left home earlier. If only they had not stayed in Sariwon for so long!

"Ma, I think we are all going to die here!" she blurted out.

"Don't say that, you hear? We are going to live. We are going to live no matter what!" Chinjoo warned her while working on the wound. Sunhee, the youngest, sat by her eying her oldest sister's wound in pity. Kwangja stood up and walked around the hot ashes to get the heat.

"Where is everyone? They couldn't have all left for the south." Chinjoo stared desperately at huts of the mountain. There was no sign of life.

"What are we doing on this deadly road? Let's go into the highway," Sunhee suggested.

"Ma, I smell meat." Kwangja called, peering into the smoldering barn.

"Chickens are burning!"

Chinjoo could almost hear the preachings of Kim Insoo: "Don't eat the unclean food." But to her, the chicken meat was manna from heaven. They had gone without food the whole day.

"What are you all sitting there for? It might get hit again." A man hurried up the hill.

"Sir. Can you tell us how to get to the main highway?" called Chinjoo loudly.

"What do you want to go there for? It's worse. I've just come from there." The man scrambled up the hill without further delay.

"Girls," Chinjoo began to gather up the things. "Let's follow that man!"

It was said to have been an air-raid shelter during the Japanese occupation. Some said the People's Army had fought there during the advance of U.N. troops. The cave was hidden behind Archean rocks and crooked pines.

A long period seemed to have elapsed. Chinjoo could barely identify the human figures cowering at the back of the cave, as far as possible from the thunderous artillery strikes outside. Even the ceaseless wails of a middle-aged woman stopped temporarily. The cave shuddered with the shock waves from each concussion.

After a while, all became quiet outside. In the dark, Chinjoo felt for her daughters.

"Are you all there?"

"Yes, we're all here, Ma."

"Oh, my poor Okhee! O..." the middle-aged woman started.

"Come, come, we can't help it, can we? Be quiet," her husband reacted with irritation.

"I am going to get her!" The woman stood up.

"Sit still!" The man pulled her back.

They could feel the occasional vibration of war from afar. Someone struck a match to look for something in her bundle. Rocky walls of the cave and its frightened inhabitants were momentarily visible.

"Are you crazy? Snuff it off!" A man hissed angrily.

Pitch darkness enveloped them again. After the light, the darkness was more intense.

"Tongja, are you all right?"

"It hurts so!" Tongja moaned.

"It's all right. It will be all right. Here, let me spread another quilt over you." Chinjoo sought the bundle, and spread a quilt loosely around the shoulders of her daughters.

"Oh, Ma—" whined Tongja.

"Dear Tongja. Try. Try to sleep. You will be much better tomorrow. In the morning we will go out and try to find something to take care of it. Try to sleep. You are a good girl."

People dozed off. Even the grieving woman was silent. Tongja fell into a fitful sleep. The cold air of the cave mixed with steam of human breathing dampened the quilts that wrapped these worried people, living somehow between their dreams and hellish reality. In the deeper recesses of the cave, water dripped incessantly.

Morning light streamed in from the entrance. Some of the men ventured out to assess the situation.

"It's quiet now. I don't know what's happening, but for the time being I think it's all right," the man Chinjoo had followed to the cave informed the people.

"I will go and bury the child." The middled-aged woman's husband stood up.

"I will go with you!" Fresh sorrow struck the woman and she sobbed.

"No, you stay right here!" The husband's command was stern.

"Oh, Okhee, Okhee!" She broke into a wail after her husband left.

"Oh, she was such a darling. Oh, how smart she was! The teacher said she was the smartest one she'd had in years. How she used to show me how to read! Ah, the smart one always go first. I should've gone instead. The dull, old one like me should've gone first!''

Forgetting her own pain, Tongja listened.

"Don't you worry. Survivors must go on living. You've got your husband. You've got a whole life ahead of you." Chinjoo comforted her.

"I don't have any future. I should've gone instead. Oh..."

Chinjoo thought of her own husband. Where would he be now? 'If I am alive, I will come and join you wherever you are.' Would he? He would. He should.

"It's all my fault. I should've come up here in the morning as her father suggested, but I was foolish enough to stay, trying to get more of my possessions out of the closet. Oh, if only I'd grabbed her when she wanted to go outside. If only I hadn't gone back to get my ring. But how could I have known that shell fragment would hit her at that very moment!''

"Now, Auntie. Don't you blame yourself. Yesterday my daughter was struck by a shell fragment too. It's still bleeding. We are lucky she is alive—''

The woman wasn't listening. Then Chinjoo realized how terrible it was to talk about her wounded daughter to a woman who had just lost hers. The women's eyes picked out the children for the first time.

"Look like nice children. Coming from the North?''

"Yes.''

Overcome with fresh emotion, the woman buried her head in her hands, mumbling, "Our Okhee would have lived to be like one of yours. She was my only child. The child that I got after praying to Buddha for fifteen years. Oh, how could the merciful Buddha be so indifferent to me!''

Chinjoo scooped up spring water and returned to the children.

"Let me see now. How are you doing?" Chinjoo changed the outer dressing soaked with blood. Crouched under the quilt, Tongja, who had been the leader of the family, lost her speech. She didn't even feel the pain. Her mother applied the water to the swollen leg.

"Hurt bad?" The middle-aged woman peered at Tongja. "My, you are hurt pretty bad!''

"It will be all right. Get your mind off of it," Chinjoo comforted her daughter. "I will go out and see if I can find someone who might have some medicine. Then we will start south again.''

"You can't go anywhere. Soon the Communists will be overrunning this area. Auntie, I suggest you find some place near here to stay," the man who had led them to the cave advised Chinjoo, and left.

One by one the refugees took their leave, singly and in groups. The woman's husband returned.

"Let's go home. Soon they will be here. It's all over now."

Chinjoo saw no hope of going further south. But she should take care of her daughter's wound.

"Uncle, do you know any place where we can get some medicine for this wound? You live near hear, don't you?"

The man gave his wife a quick glance. Her mind adrift, she crouched in the shadows.

"I don't know. One drug store is a mile away, but it's closed. I just don't know."

"I've got something for that. Let's go. Let's go to our house!" The woman stood up. She had found a reason for living.

Relieved to have found someone to help them, Chinjoo and her daughters followed the man and his wife down the hill to the small village nestled against the mountainside.

XVI. The mother-in-law

You mock me I have done wrong
By borrowing grains from the Office.
Po I and Shu Chi gathered ferns;
I know all about their rectitude.
But do not blame me, friends;
This is a year of bad harvest.

Yun Son-do [1587-1671]

Winter 1950. South Korea.

Three days ago Oh Jungsoon and her two sons crossed the temporary bridge over the Han River, and walked southbound along the main highway. The railways by which she had traveled as a young woman lay parallel with the road. Demolished freight cars rusted by the tracks. Once in a while trains sped by packed with troops and war supplies. She didn't know how far south she should go. Pusan would be the safest place, but reaching it seemed as impossible as crossing the Pacific on foot. Very little money remained in her purse. The children were tired and their feet were blistered.

"Grandmother's house is on the way. We will stop by to see your grandparents. Let's try to make it before sundown."

It was well after dark when they limped into the familiar little town. Much had happened since Jungsoon had bid farewell to the mother-in-law. Her mind flooded with memories as they approached the home to which she was no longer related. A young woman answered the door.

"Oh, that old couple? They've moved several times. I don't know if they are even still here. Ask the people in that tavern across the street. They might know."

The tavern was filled with tobacco smoke and smelled of rice wine. Against a background of conversation and laughter, the patrons stared at them suspiciously.

"Oh, that old couple! They are back there some place. I believe the old man is dead."

"Where did they move?" Jungsoon was so eager to get the name of the place that she didn't hear the last words.

"That house over there," said the tavern keeper pointing to a dwelling farther up the street. "Last time I saw her the old lady was still living there."

In the back of the darkened house, they managed to find a room with no fence or a gate to protect it. A shadow moved across the small paper door.

"Mother?" Jungsoon whispered.

"Is someone there?" came the frail inquiry and Jungsoon recognized the mother-in-law's voice.

"It's Hyonsup. The children, Mother!"

"Who?"

"It's Hyonsup and Wonsup, Mother!"

"Hyonsup—Oh, come on in."

Jungsoon opened the door. Lamplight in the tiny room shone on an elderly lady, who lay stretched on her back, her white hair tangled, her eyes sunken, and her cheekbones raised high. It could not be the mother-in-law that she used to know.

"Oh, Mother!" Jungsoon sat down by the old woman, pushing away the lamp leaning dangerously close to her head. Smoothing her tangled hair the mother-in-law tried to sit up.

"Don't, please!" As she helped her lie back, Jungsoon sobbed quietly.

"I was burning my thumbs. They are so dry." The mother-in-law had been applying pork fat to her fingers. She melted this home remedy over the lamp. The tips now had become like hardened rubber and split open exposing the bone inside. Jungsoon resumed applying the pork fat for her, asking,

"Where is Father?"

"He was killed. They shot him, the Communists."

"Oh, no!"

"Somebody told them he had run for a national assemblyman. There are always informers, you know. National assemblyman! Why, he never was even close to being one." The mother-in-law sighed and sank back slowly, biting her lips from pain as she did. "When the Communist police occupied the local station, the first thing they did was to hunt for people who, they said, committed—treason. Since the officials at the time had fled, they came straight to our house and arrested him. I protested, say-

163

ing he was innocent and told them they would have to strike me first if they wanted to take him along, and that's exactly what they did. One man's rifle struck me down."

"Oh, Mother!"

"They just don't have any respect for old people," the mother-in-law said, matter-of-factly, her emotions drained but her spirit intact. "But that's not why I can't get up. You see this wound? I fell on the ice the other day, when I went down to the butcher's to get some pork fat for my dry skin. I guess now it's becoming a boil. It hurts so much!"

Jungsoon examined the mother-in-law's hip, and, as she suspected, the wound had become a boil as big as a wine bowl.

"You need some plaster patch, Mother. I will go get some."

"I don't think there's any pharmacy open this late. Anyway I don't have anything to live for. However, I guess the living should go on living until death arrives."

"Mother, you have everything to live for. You have your son and your grandchildren."

"Oh, children, how are you?" For the first time, the old lady saw the grandchildren standing mute behind their mother. "Sit down. Isn't this Kangsup?"

"No, Mother, that's Hyonsup. Kangsup is in the army."

"He is! Has time gone by that fast? Wonsup! Here, let me hold your hand," the mother-in-law extended her hand to the youngest grandson, who reluctantly gave her his. "Oh, you've grown up so much. My grandchildren! I thought when you grew up we would have a better time. But things are worse for you."

The old lady's bony hands caressed the boy's hand. Then suddenly her face froze in anger. "I don't have a son! He once passed through here and stopped for a while. I told him where his father's grave was. I don't know whether he visited there or not on his way back. I gather he had brought his woman and the child along but I didn't see them. Now he must be fleeing again."

Jungsoon felt the floor. It was only lukewarm.

"Mother, I will go heat the room."

In the dark corner of the kitchen was a small pile of dead leaves and twigs. Jungsoon burned them in the fuel hole to make the room warmer for the mother-in-law. On the mud counter, several bowls had been left with a couple of worn-out metal spoons in them. The mother-in-law used

164

to have meals only with silver spoons and silver chopsticks. Now she lay in the back room of a stranger's house and must have eaten her millet with those old spoons.

Under the lamp light, Jungsoon drained the pus from the mother-in-law's boil.

"Let's go south together, Mother." Jungsoon suggested quietly.

"I don't have any reason to flee. Even if they kill me I don't have much to lose except my ailing body. So, you go on with the children."

"Mother, if you are not going, we will all stay here with you."

At the foot of a hill there was a grave without a name. Remembering the once greatly respected father-in-law, Jungsoon wept. Hyonsup planted a piece of wood on which he had written his grandfather's name.

The next morning the family left. Jungsoon and Hyonsup, taking turns carrying the mother-in-law, joined the flow of the refugees heading south. The mother-in-law with sunken eyes remained quiet on Jungsoon's back, relieved because of the considerable amount of pus removed from her boil and the comfort of the plaster patch in place.

"Are you cold, Mother?" Jungsoon asked frequently.

"No, I am comfortable. You shouldn't be doing this. I am not even your mother-in-law any more."

"Oh, Mother! You are. You will always be."

In the beginning, the mother-in-law's body felt light, but trudging the snow-covered road mile after mile, the load became steadily heavier.

"I wonder if Chayoung is still alive. When the war broke out and the Communists came down, I thought he would appear, too. But I don't know. Perhaps it's just a rumor that he had gone to the north. Now he may have his own family somewhere, and someday he may come visit me. Don't you think so?"

"I am sure, Mother. He will."

Silence, then:

"I was planning your father-in-law's seventieth birthday coming next year. But I guess he may be having it in another world if there is such a world."

"Poor father! I am sure he is resting in peace."

After a while, Jungsoon asked a man with a loaded ox cart to give the mother-in-law a ride. He took her for a while but when the ox cart turned into a narrow path, they had to carry her again. The refugees came to a city and found people gathered from all directions. Some rested on the porch of a closed store, some rested sitting on their bundles along the road. With the help of the children, Jungsoon settled the lady on their bundles and covered her legs with a quilt. Under the eaves of a deserted tavern they found a country woman with a vending basket. Jungsoon bought some rice cakes. The mother-in-law couldn't quite finish her piece of cake.

"Poor lady, she must be terribly ill," a woman nearby commented casting a pitying glance at the mother-in-law's haggard face.

"Yes, she is. But she will get well as soon as we settle down at my brother's house a little past Pyongtack."

"Oh, is that where you are going?"

"That's the only place I know."

"It's not safe there either. We plan to go as far as Taegu."

A young woman nursing a baby in her arms, stared at Jungsoon, and as she met Jungsoon's eyes, moved closer and said,

"Excuse me, but you look very much like a lady I used to know."

Jungsoon searched the young woman's face but didn't recognize her.

"You look somewhat familiar, but—"

The young woman's glance traveled past the faces of Jungsoon, the mother-in-law and the two boys. Then she shouted out in excitement.

"Oh, Auntie, it's you! This is Grandma, isn't it?"

"Boonee! You're Boonee?" Jungsoon blurted out. Then grabbing hold of the young woman, she said, "Mother, this is Boonee. Do you remember Boonee?"

"Boonee—I know her." The mother-in-law recognized her. But her lips were stiff and her emotions too deadened to say more.

"Oh, how have you been? Let me look at your child." Jungsoon looked into the tiny face cuddled in the blanket.

"A boy, just two months old. My first one died of pneumonia when he was two."

"I am sorry to hear that. So, where's your husband? Where are you heading?"

"My husband is in the army. We've been living in Osan since we got married. I just left home this morning. I just left. I don't know where to go. With this baby it's too far south to my father's home. Frankly, I don't think he would welcome us either."

Jungsoon thought a moment.

"Let's go together to Pyongtack. We will think of something there."

"You wouldn't mind my coming along?" Boonee brightened. "I am sure we wouldn't be a burden. I will manage one way or another until my husband returns."

"Don't worry. We will all survive somehow. Let's go while there's still daylight."

With her hair in a permanent, Boonee had changed a lot. She tied her baby on her back, and carried her two large bundles in her hands. She walked beside Jungsoon. There were endless questions to ask and information to share.

"I can't believe that a nice man like Uncle could do a thing like that!" Boonee reacted to the changes of Jungsoon's life. "Grandma has changed a lot, hasn't she? I don't think she will live too long. There's no cure for the old folk's fall, they say."

"Hush. She will live longer than you think."

As the sun slipped behind the western mountains, the little group could see a town on the southern horizon.

"I don't think we can make it all the way to the town. But I have a distant cousin who lives in the outskirts. Let's go there and spend the night!" Boonee cried, trailing behind. While Jungsoon waited for her to catch up, she took the old lady from Hyonsup. The mother-in-law had also become restless.

"Are we there yet? Oh dear, I have to go—"

Jungsoon carried the old lady behind a deserted barn.

Boonee's cousin and her husband were upset by the arrival of the refugees at dusk.

"How are you, Uncle and Auntie? We haven't seen each other for a long time!"

They weren't too impressed by Boonee's boisterous greetings. Boonee sensed they were not welcome.

"Oh, this auntie here comes from Seoul," she said by way of introduction.

"Humph, some more beggars from Seoul," grumbled the husband of Boonee's cousin.

"Shh, Uncle, they are rich people. They only want to spend the night here. All the inns are closed, you know." The man took a hard look at the families in the courtyard and decided to accept them.

"I don't have a room to spare in my house, but there's the empty house of a neighbor who went south. Come, follow me."

As she followed the man across a small footbridge, Jungsoon became uneasy.

"We are not rich," Jungsoon whispered to Boonee.

"I know, Auntie, nobody is rich now. We've never been rich, have we? But don't worry. If he asks for money, I can give him some, but he wouldn't dare."

The man unlocked the gate to the two-room house and stalked into the master room as if it were his own. The long-deserted room smelled dankly of mildew and cold.

"You better use one room. There's no fuel to warm more rooms." Then the man lingered waiting for something. Boonee took out several ten won bills and handed them to the man, who stuffed the money in his tobacco pouch, and left saying "I will bring some twigs and firewood."

"Auntie, what do you say, shall we just stay here? Without money and food and in this cold winter I don't think we should be on the road. A few more miles south won't make much difference. Besides, there's no guarantee your brother would welcome us either."

Boonee was right. Not that Jungsoon's brother wouldn't welcome her, but the last time Jungsoon had seen them, the family could barely eke out a living itself. Any place would be as good as her brother's.

"But we don't have any money," Jungsoon confessed with a sigh.

"Don't worry about money. I've got enough to buy some grains from my cousin. But we aren't going to pay another penny for the rent!"

Hyonsup went into town for plaster patches for his grandmother. In the afternoon he returned with news and determination.

"Boys over seventeen are asked to report to an elementary school in town," he said calmly. "They give physical examinations right there and rush the boys to the army. Mother, you can get along without me, can't you?"

Hyonsup, a soldier already? Fighting was going on fiercely somewhere. And when she hadn't even heard from her first son yet? But the country needed him. Other parents sent their sons too.

"Son," Jungsoon touched his shoulder softly. "We will try."

Young men stood in line in the elementary-school field which served as a marshalling area. Parents, relatives and well-wishers milled about, waiting to see the young men off to the army, catching chances to hand snack sacks to their youngsters. Hyonsup said goodbye to his younger brother. After hugging Wonsup's shoulder, he added:

"Now, it's up to you. Take good care of Mother and Grandmother, you hear?"

Wonsup nodded, not really knowing what he had to do.

Jungsoon experienced a mother's pride and satisfaction as the line moved past her toward the waiting truck. She might never see him again. She grasped her son's shoulder.

"Take care of yourself. Don't worry about anything at home." Then she let go, staring through tears as he scrambled aboard the open army truck. Hyonsup, who lacked the nerve to face a dead man in the street, was going into the army. To kill. Or be killed! Jungsoon waved as the trucks clattered past her and disappeared into the downtown traffic.

During the week, the cousin's husband visited the house to collect rent. Boonee simply refused.

"If we had any more money, we'd spend it on food. We don't."

"I knew it! I knew from the beginning you were beggars from Seoul. Living in someone's house for nothing!"

"You're right, we are all beggars! How about you? The one who makes money from someone else's property is a thief!" Boonee fired.

"You! How dare you say such a thing to me? I let you and your flock stay here and I took care of you, and now you call me a thief?" The man shook his finger at Boonee. Boonee shook her finger back.

"Big deal. We could have just taken it ourselves, you know. This is war. You should be ashamed of yourself trying to suck blood out of fleas!"

At that instant, aircraft roared overhead. The house shuddered. Everyone, including the man, fell flat. There had been a close hit.

"The Chinese Communist army!" hissed the man lying motionless. Boonee cuddled her baby to her bosom.

"Oh, what shall we do, what shall we do!"

"Stay put!" the man shouted.

The bombing and strafing ended as suddenly as it began. Dark smoke curled into the sky above the house.

"It's the grain warehouse!" The man sprang up and ran.

"Crazy man," Boonee mumbled arising. Then her eyes lit up. "It's the grain warehouse! Auntie, let's go." Putting the baby down, Boonee rushed out. The aircrafts swooped in again.

"Wait, we can't go now," warned Jungsoon.

"But, Auntie, we need food. This is the only chance. Soon it will be all gone."

"All right. I will go. You stay here with the baby."

Local residents and refugees flocked around the grain warehouse gaping open among the flames and smoke. They scurried in and out, carrying away sacks of rice. The smell of burning grain singed Jungsoon's nostrils. She searched deeper into the smoldering building. Sacks of unhulled rice were ablaze. Others had been blown open, their contents lying in heaps on the floor. She managed to find a sack with a part of its seam torn open. Spreading her skirt, she scooped rice into it with frantic speed.

"Stop!"

Above the pile of the grain towered two Commuinist soldiers. Grabbing the end of the sack she had found, and clutching her skirt at her front, she fled. Bullets ripped by her head and dug into the earth. Spilling the grain, she ran frantically. She stumbled over a body halfway through the gunfire. The husband of Boonee's cousin! Somehow, she reached the alley and hurried over the footbridge with the shrunken rice sack.

"They are here again. The Communists!"

Inside the house, Jungsoon and Boonee hulled the rice in silence. Enough to last them six days.

"Now, where can we find any more food!" Boonee sighed.

Venturing outside, Jungsoon searched diligently throughout the bomb-destroyed farmyard. Holding her nose, she peered into what had once been the pig pen. Almost hidden in the hay and filth near the empty trough was a plump straw sack. She pinched it open. It wasn't flour, nor rice. She wasn't sure what it was.

"It's rice bran," Boonee identified. "Feed for the pigs."

Surviving for a week on the rice bran, Boonee's breasts went dry.

"Oh, my baby, my poor baby!" All evening Boonee tried to pacify her screaming infant. "Here, here, Baby." Boonee pressed her nipple against the tiny lips. But the baby refused to try this useless exercise again. Finally, he cried himself into a fitful sleep. During the night, a half-hearted artillery exchange awakened the family and the starving baby.

"Let me hold him for a while." Jungsoon took the baby and rocked him throughout the long night. His strength ebbed: he was too weak to cry any longer. A few days later the baby was a tiny, just-breathing skeleton. The tempo of war increased. Tactical aircraft crisscrossed the skies.

The baby's breathing turned to a pathetic rasp.

"Oh, my poor baby! Hang on just a little bit more! Soon we will have white milled rice and beef soup. Then you will have lots of milk."

"Let me hold him. Give him to me"

"No, it wouldn't do any good. Do sleep, Auntie. There's nothing we can do."

And Jungsoon fell asleep. When she awoke, the world was quiet.

"Boonee?"

"The baby died," Boonee said tonelessly.

They wrapped him in the blanket and buried him in the backyard.

Two days later the mother-in-law died. She had never been considered handsome but somewhere around the broad forehead lingered a chill dignity befitting a first-class yangban. Jungsoon had always envisioned the mother-in-law being buried with traditional pomp and ceremony: All her cousins and relatives gathered together, many days of mourning, hired taxies, and a long procession to the family graveyard. Jungsoon, with the help of Wonsup, strained to dig the frozen ground. The mother-in-law was buried in a shallow grave next to Boonee's baby.

"Wonsup, when the war is over and things get better, we should reinter your grandfather and grandmother side by side in the Yoon graveyard," said Jungsoon quietly.

"Come, Boonee," she continued. "Let's pull ourselves together. Here, have some food. I dug up some of the rice bran."

"I don't feel like eating. I am sick of it."

"O, you wouldn't want to starve to death before your husband returns. Have some and try to get your strength back."

"Give it to Wonsup. He needs it."

In a dark corner of the room Boonee sat, staring blankly for hours. Often, a bottomless sob would cause her body to quiver.

"Hush, Dear! The Chinese Communist soldiers out there might hear."

Snow piled on already deep snow. Sounds and tremors of warfare continued but distant. Wonsup was quiet in the room, weak and thinning.

Boonee regained some spirit and dragged her weak body to the well.

Bathed, she sat on the sunny hall floor and combed her wet hair.

"Oh, the sun feels good," she murmured.

"I am going out to see what the situation is," Jungsoon suggested. Then she shrank back. Someone was at the gate.

"Open up! It's me. I need to draw some water." Boonee's cousin stepped in with a bucket. "Our well is dried up."

"Oh! I thought it was a Chinese soldier."

"Chinese? Why, they've been gone quite a while. I think by now, the U.N. forces are as far north as Suwon.

"You mean we are in U.N. hands?"

"Yes, for about a week, now. Now what are you doing locked up in the house like this?" The woman drew the water and shuffled off adding, "Yes, that problem is gone. But we, the ones left behind, still have to worry about how we are going to eat, don't we!"

Jungsoon went through her clothes and chose something to sell. She crossed the footbridge and passed Boonee's cousin's house. Through the gate she saw a couple of foreign soldiers and a country boy. A queue of peddlers with food and cigarettes lined the street. A bucketful of rice in front of a woman caught her eye. Jungsoon asked the woman to exchange some rice for her chogori, the one and only silk which she had made for herself when she had been working. With a bowlful of rice and some cooked vegetables she returned along the street passing several foreigners walking through an alley. Nearing Boonee's cousin's house at the footbridge she saw a strange young woman by the gate. Her face heavy with make-up, she peered down the alley.

"Hello!" the young woman broke into a smile of greeting to soldiers emerging from the alley. Jungsoon hurriedly crossed the bridge. She slid inside the courtyard and closed the gate after her, out of breath.

"What is it, Auntie?" Boonee stared at her suspiciously. "Did you steal it?"

"No, no, I bought these."

"Oh, rice? My! it's white milled rice!"

Jungsoon went through her clothes but there was nothing more to sell.

"Auntie, we can't go on like this. I am going out to see what I can do."

"No, you stay here. I will go out. We can't have rice again, but we may find some cereal."

172

Boonee's cousin asked to borrow several quilts. Jungsoon stiffened, pretending not to have heard.

"Look, you think I am a dirty old woman. But at least it's not stealing or anything. You got to keep on living, you know. There isn't a soul to care for you even if you die like a rat. If you don't want to lend me some quilts, that's okay. There are a million other places where I can borrow them."

She was about to stomp off when Boonee cut in.

"We can lend you some quilts. We have extras."

Boonee's cousin turned.

"Yes, I opened up a whore house, that's what!" she spat as she left.

Jungsoon made several trips to the street market with extra bowls and spoons to sell. But the wheat bran and dried vegetables she got in return barely fed the family for another couple of days. For several days Boonee was pensive. Then one morning she dressed herself nicely, rolled up her coverlet, and walked toward the gate.

"Where are you going?" Jungsoon asked.

"Oh, just for a walk," Boonee answered.

Jungsoon blocked her way.

"Are you out of your mind? You are not going anywhere!"

Boonee's eyes shone strangely. Brushing aside Jungsoon, she hastened out of the gate. Jungsoon ran after her calling "Boonee! come back here!" Boonee, her head down and the coverlet tucked under her arm, crossed the footbridge and entered her cousin's house.

Boonee returned the following day—with a pound of rice and some canned food.

"Here, Auntie, cook some meals. I will bring lots more food tomorrow."

Boonee left. Jungsoon, sad of heart, looked at the sack of grain on the hall floor. Her child lay on the floor in another room with empty stomach. Slowly, she picked up the rice, emptied it into a pan, and washed it.

Icicles dripped from the eaves. Sunshine brightened the hall room and the piles of snow in the courtyard became smaller. Wonsup ran in and out the house, bringing both news and money. He insisted on helping the family and was hired in a pharmacy a refugee had opened.

"Mom, our army and the U.N. forces have taken Seoul back."

Jungsoon, too, earned some money making cakes for a bakery. Whenever she crossed the little footbridge and passed the house of Boonee's cousin she felt a weight on her conscience. Jungsoon returned the money Boonee gave her. At home, Wonsup played war games with children of the neighbors who had returned. They picked up new vocabulary: submachine guns, howitzers, carbines, M1s and MIGs.

A helmet was moving above the low fence. At first she thought it was Kangsup or Hyonsup. The soldier peeked through the gate left ajar.

"Ah, I am looking for someone. Do you know a young woman named Boonee?"

Jungsoon let the soldier in, staring at the earnest young man. He took off his helmet.

"I am her husband. I went back to Osan and someone said she came here to her cousin. I went over there and her cousin says she left a month ago. And out in the village someone said she was living here. I thought I would stop by and ask."

Jungsoon's mind whirled.

"Have a seat here, please," she managed to say. "She left here a month ago."

The children stared at her, amazed.

"And my child? Didn't she have a child?"

"Yes—he has been dead for two months now."

Seated at the edge of the hall floor he lowered his eyes. He stared at his helmet on his knee.

"I don't know where she could be. Didn't she tell you where she was going?"

"No," Jungsoon shook her head.

He stood up dusting his helmet.

"Well, I must be going."

"Auntie! Oh, how could you do this to me! You returned the money because it's dirty, right?" Boonee pushed open the gate and stormed in. Her husband stared, his mouth agape. The familiar face—but the garnish make-up.

"Isn't this Boonee?"

Boonee peered at the face under the helmet and froze, turning pale. She had never dreamed that her man would return alive and healthy, and had never prepared for it. The husband's eyes traveled from her face to the hundred-won bills in her hands, from the money to the heavy make-up.

His face twisted.

"Whore!" Finally he spat.

Boonee recovered from the shock.

"Yes, I am a whore!"

He exploded in fury, raining blow after blow on Boonee's face. She fell to the ground, cowering.

"You sound like you are proud of it! Was that all you could do?" he screamed and kicked her.

Jungsoon rushed in between them.

"Stop—please stop! It's not her fault. You know it's not!" Her hand shook as she wiped the blood from Boonee's face.

"You filth!" He trembled with rage. Then he walked heavily toward the gate. Boonee leaped to her feet and followed him.

"It's easy for you to say! What do you know about being hungry!"

"You could have starved to death!" Glaring at her, he walked out of the gate.

"Our child starved to death." Boonee followed, all the way down the alley, shouting after him, "Come back! Take me with you. Oh, take me!"

The children stood dumbfounded.

As if awakened from a nightmare, Jungsoon put her hand over Wonsup's shoulder and whispered,

"Let's go. Let's go to Seoul."

"But, Mom, it's not safe there yet. It might be in Communist hands again."

"Let's hope not."

XVII. The port city

Rough clouds gather around the valley
Where the snow slowly melts.
Where is the tree of the perfect plum?
In what lowland, what hollow?
I have lost my way, alone,
In the setting sun.

Yi Saek [1328-1396]

1951. Somewhere south of the 38th parallel.

Mountains hulked against the dawn. Humanity seemed to have left the earth. Even the wild animals, terrified by the war, had fled beyond the horizon. Only icy winds whined in the valley, whipping through the gaunt pines.

Chinjoo heard a crunch on the snow in the front yard.

"Wait!" she alerted her daughters.

The sound was repeated.

"Now!"

No sooner had the daughters crawled under the hall floor, than soldiers slipped in one by one through the millet stalk gate.

The leader of the Chinese Communist soldiers mumbled, gestured and tried to explain. Chinjoo couldn't understand, her eyes sweeping fearfully over the soldiers in their quilted uniforms. Finally the leader sat on one knee and wrote down two characters in the snow. Chinjoo stared at the characters and heaved a sigh of relief.

"O, you want me cook your breakfast?" Chinjoo mimicked eating.

The leader of the soldiers nodded enthusiastically, the fleece-lined ear flaps of his cap flapping against his frozen cheeks. He unloaded his backpack and released a sack of grain on the hall floor.

"It will be ready in half an hour, but I don't have any side dishes. I've got a scoop of bean paste and will fix some soup, but I don't know whether it will be enough for all of you." Chinjoo explained boisterously trying to keep their attention from the hall floor where her daughters were hiding.

Chinjoo started breakfast keeping up a steady chatter to the group of soldiers who squatted, easing their equipment to the floor.

"The wash pans are by the water jar there, if you want to brush your teeth and wash your face. I hope the water isn't too cold for you!" She didn't care if they didn't understand the language.

They sat at random on the hall floor and engulfed the steaming rice mixed with millet. Scooping up the rice into their bowls, Chinjoo heard a sneeze from under the floor. She stopped short. One of the soldiers looked about and down, then resumed eating. Hitting the scoop against the bowl unnecessarily, she managed several sneezes of her own and mumbled,

"This infernal cold! Never knows when to leave me!"

The Communists finished their meal, struggled into their packs, and, picking up their rifles, crunched off through the snow. When the last man was out of sight, Yi Chinjoo began to sweep the floor.

"They've gone! You can come out now."

Blue with cold, the daughters crept out of the dugout under the sagging hall floor.

"You should be more careful. You frightened the life out of me."

"Ma, I did all I could. My face almost exploded when I tried to hold it back." Tongja convulsed in a siege of sneezing. Tall Kwangja rubbed her cramped neck.

It had been more than two months since Chinjoo followed the Chin couple from the cave. The Chins helped Chinjoo and her girls make the half demolished hut near their house into something livable. She stuffed some pine branches into the loose millet stalk fence to ward off the winter wind. Tongja's leg showed signs of healing. She had stopped applying the ice and cuttlebone powder which Chin's wife supplied.

"The bone's all right. It just took a big chunk of flesh from your leg. You were lucky." Chin had examined the leg with some knowledge.

Then the Chins left for the home of the wife's parents.

While an occasional skirmish took place locally, the battle lines moved south. Several weeks ago, a number of People's Army soldiers noticed Chinjoo's Pyongan Province accent.

"You must have come from Pyongyang as a refugee," said the leader. "Why did you leave? Did you come by yourself? Go back."

Chinjoo insisted she had been living there for many years, and the

177

tobacco-smelling old lady who lived up the hill overheard and spoke up for her. Next time she might not be so fortunate. If some perceptive Northern soldiers should come, she might be forced to go with them.

"We've settled down in a bad place," Kwangja complained.

"What can you do? We can't go anywhere. We're stuck here, perhaps forever!" Tongja sighed, looking desperately at the encircling mountains. Long dreary months. Snow fell monotonously from the leaden sky. All they could see was ranges of mountains and valleys shrouded in white.

The sun lavished its warmth on the roof of their hut, on its sagging hall floor, and at the foot of the millet stalk fence. Gradually, the snow and icicles melted. Chinjoo stood idly on the edge of the hall and stared at the white-patched mountains. She saw the little old lady and her granddaughter trudging down the hill.

"Here they come again."

As usual, the old lady took out her tobacco-pouch as soon as she settled on the hardened earth floor, and her homely granddaughter, with a long braid down to her waist, sat down by the girls.

"My, you are learning fast. You've already finished one side of the socks?" the country maiden admired Kwangja's knitting.

"I went to Kaesung just the day before yesterday, and now look at my tobacco-pouch. It's getting thinner every time I look at it. Kaesung, far from the home of ginseng now, I can hardly find even a leaf of tobacco there." The old lady narrowed her eyes as she puffed at her two-foot-long bamboo pipe.

"Grandma, why don't you quit smoking. It's not going to do you any good," Chinjoo advised.

"It's a habit. You can't quit a habit so easily, especially a bad one!" She puffed again and glanced outside. "Finally the snow's melting. They say the year of heavy snow is the year of good harvest. Well, all the young ones have gone into the army, and the old ones are too weak to work in the fields. We've got no seed saved from last fall. How in the world are we going to have that good harvest!"

"Ma, we ran out of water again. I am going with Sunhee to get the spring water," Tongja called from outside.

"What did you say?" Chinjoo threw open the door. "You come right back in! A full grown woman trotting around at a time like this. Don't you know the People's Army soldiers are everywhere?"

"Why, Lady, let them go. One thing you don't have to worry about the People's Army soldiers, they don't rape. They are cruel, but never rape. In fact, I haven't seen them around here much lately. Let them go. They need some air. It's such a nice day."

Along the narrow, hilly path Tongja looked for a sign of spring. Through the scrub pines, between the rocks, the forsythias showed tiny buds. Spring might be just around the corner, but how much longer would she be trapped there? She picked a few buds.

"Do you think they will ever bloom?" she wondered, caressing the tiny bits of life.

"If we take them home and put them in a vase with water," the little sister answered. Sunhee felt sorry for her oldest sister. Tongja was pretty and the little sister had always admired her. She was now recovered from the dreadful wound, but over the past several months Tongja had changed. She was thin and pensive.

"Do you really think so?"

"I do."

Tongja was silent. Probably like the small forsythia bud, her maidenhood would never come to full bloom.

They had visited the cave once since the family had ended their journey from the North. The cave, now empty, either abandoned or undiscovered by the invading army, was less threatening after the initial unpleasantness of getting through the entrance.

"Sis, hurry, please. I don't want to be here very long." Sunhee rushed her sister.

"I am done. You hold this bucket." Tongja, herself, eager to get out of the dark cave, hefted the pair of tin water buckets with each hand and followed Sunhee out. A shower of snow and rocks bounced across the entrance. Tongja stopped, dropping the water buckets. A tall man blocked her way. Old, with a white beard, he gestured apologetically.

"I didn't mean to frighten you, young lady. I just wanted to ask the way—" The eyes shining under white eyebrows seemed vaguely familiar. The man seemed equally surprised. He looked first at Tongja and then at Sunhee, who stood frightened a few feet away. "O—you are, aren't you those children with a lady I met on the way to the south?"

Relieved, now that the man evidently meant her no harm, Tongja peered intently at the man. With a laugh, he pulled the familiar chestnut-colored scarf from under his chin. "Now do you recognize me?"

"Oh, yes, now I know," grinned Tongja.

When the daughters finally returned home accompanied by an old man carrying the water bucket, Chinjoo was relieved, but puzzled.

"Ma, you know the uncle with the chestnut colored scarf on the way here as refugees? Remember he detected a mine and saved people?"

"Ha, what do you know!" exclaimed the man. "We are all here again. So, you couldn't quite make it, could you, Auntie?" The man settled down on the hall floor ignoring the still-puzzled Chinjoo.

"But you are not—"

"Heavens, don't keep staring at me like that. Now, is this better? See, I just painted my eyebrows and tied on these false whiskers. That's all. Back then, your children weren't all girls either," the man chuckled. Chinjoo laughed, too, as the picture cleared.

"We thought you would be in the farther south by now, in Pusan."

"I couldn't make it."

"Oh, you, too, must be staying near here then."

"No. I went down as far as Pyongtack. But I decided to come back, to get back to my family. If lucky, I will have another chance to bring them all out. If not, I will at least be with them and know what will become of them. Hope this disguise would bring me safely to them."

Chinjoo thought a moment.

"Can we go with you, too?"

The man eyed Chinjoo to see if she were serious.

"You mean you've come all the way down here for nothing?"

"Well, my husband—" Chinjoo hesitated for a moment. But he seemed trustworthy. "If you go, would you find out what happened to my husband?"

After dinner, Son spread out a piece of paper and drew a map.

"Here, here are the R.O.K. and U.N. troops now. The central front now is at Chunchon and the east front is up close to the 38th parallel. Kimpo airfield is in their hands. Here, in the west, they are right on the other side of Imjin River."

"So, that's what's been happening. We were wondering what all the bombing and ground action were for," Chinjoo nodded.

"There is little chance for the Communist armies' massive maneuver. They are driven and beginning to retreat northward. This time it's not going to be as swift as it was last fall. The advance is slow. As a matter of fact, the U.S. 8th Army almost occupied Seoul in early February, but fell back again. So, if you want to get out of here, this may be the only chance you have. If you can cross this river and get to Munsan, you will be on your own. It's a risk, but you've got no other chance unless you want to go back, which is riskier. Well, as for your children's father—if he was taken by the Reds, he is as good as—I mean if he is alive, he will come and join you. If not, you will be glad that you have done the right thing. Take advantage of lulls in the fighting. Then you will be all right. Here's some of the South currency. You might need it. I don't need it any more."

Son took shelter there overnight and in the morning squeezed a card into her hand.

"In case you have trouble clearing your identity at a U.N. post, show this to them."

Chinjoo and Son stared thoughtfully at each other. Both wished they were one family and all they had to do was to take off on the southbound road together. The man's eyes shone under the white eyebrows.

"I wish you and your children good fortune. I promise I will find out what happened to their father."

Son, his disguise in place, limped off to the North.

The little old lady puffed at her long bamboo pipe.

"So, you—want to get out of here? Of course you realize it's an awfully dangerous thing." Her wrinkled neck in the soiled chogori collar contracted as she puffed at her pipe.

"Oh, we do, Grandma." Tongja was eager to go.

"Well, I know a ferryman in Changdan. He used to have a fishing boat and go out to the sea near Kangwha Island to catch squid. He used to take people back and forth for money along the river. I don't know if he still does, but I can find out soon enough."

The old lady reported: A small fishing boat was due to leave the next day, with other people lined ahead for the trip.

"Do you really have to go, Sisters?" The old lady's granddaughter wanted her new friends to change their mind.

"We have to. My children's pa just might be down there some place already and waiting for us. Don't you worry. We'll come visit you all when we can. If we stay alive, we are bound to meet again, you know."

"Dress lightly as though you are visiting your neighbors. Be ready by early morning. I will be here at dawn to show you the way," the old lady instructed.

Chinjoo searched her bundle and took out the buttonless magoja.

"Here. It's a little moth-eaten, but with a couple of buttons sewed back on, it will look as good as new, and will pay for your tobacco. I will leave all our quilts here. They are still like new, if you wash and redo them."

"My, that's a good silk." The old lady stroked the buttonless magoja, stuffed it under her chogori, and left with her sad granddaughter.

Pusan, South Korea.

It was too dark and foggy to tell which road the little old lady took. Along the slippery path, over the hills, and through the valleys sunken in the dense fog, Chinjoo stumbled on, occasionally turning to see if her children were all there.

"Where's Tongja? Oh, there you are. Grab hold of Sunhee's hand."

"Ma, I can't go!"

"Try. Try! Now, where did this old lady go? Find her. There! There! Follow her! There! There's the river!"

"Oh, Ma! I can't. I can't!"

"Try!"

The path lead through bushes entangled with tall weeds and scrub trees. Beyond that was the river extending to the endless horizon.

"Where's the boat? Where? Tongja, Kwangja, find the old lady. There, there's the boat. Oh, we're too late. People are already packed in it. Run. Run. Wait for us!"

Before they reached the riverside, the undergrowth parted and a voice bellowed:

"Halt!" Communist soldiers broke into the clearing.

"Get on the boat, get on!" screamed Chinjoo. "O, Tongja, come on, get in here!"

Frantically, the boatman pushed the boat away from shore before Tongja could get both legs aboard.

The Communists opened fire.

With Tongja's leg dangling over the side leaving a bloody wake, the boat chugged off.

Yi Chinjoo awoke in a small room, her heart violently pounding. Her eyes focused on the yellowing newspaper pasted on the wall. Listening to the noises outside and clinking sound of tableware in the neighborhood, she heaved a sigh of relief. She had had that nightmare again. Springing up, she examined Tongja's leg. The wound had healed leaving a three inch scar.

A year and a half had gone by since the ghastly escape that foggy morning; the winding path covered with dead branches and acacia following the other escapees to the secret launching place—the nightmare moment in the water when the shots rang out—then the headlong trek down to Pusan. It was a struggle to make a living here in the overcrowded port

183

city. Yet life finally offered some degree of safety.

August sunshine pierced through the chinks of the hut. Another hot, muggy day. Her daughters were still asleep under a cotton sheet that had partially slipped onto the floor.

"Girls, wake up! It's broad daylight. You will be late for work again."

"Already?" Kwangja lifted her head, mumbling. Tongja stirred but turned over to go back to sleep.

Chinjoo hurried to fix breakfast of rice and soup made with beef stock. Choosy Sunhee hesitated to eat, poking her chopsticks at bits of intestines and other cow innards.

"Have lots of it. We need fat." Chinjoo scooped more fat chunks into the hot soup. "You need a good breakfast to keep up with your job."

"Another day of that smelly rubber factory!" Kwangja groaned. "Ma, you should see. The room is stifling. It has windows like a prison cell, and a sickening, scorching smell of rubber. I know my lungs are coated with rubber, already. Oh, I wish I had enough money for school right now. Any school."

"You wait just a little bit more. I think I can make lots of money if things go the way they have for the last few days. Don't you worry. You will all get to go to school."

"Ma, I feel sorry for you, too. You, Ma, go around from place to place from morning till night, selling smuggled goods in an outdoor market."

"Listen, there's nothing wrong selling things in a market place. Didn't you hear 'You make money like a dog and eat like a lord.'? How do you think we can afford even this fat? It's a lot better than when we first got to Pusan. No money, no quilts, no nothing. It's a great improvement since then. Make money at whatever you can now, and you will have less worry in the days to come." Chinjoo lectured to the children while she hurriedly scooped up her rice.

Each had a place to go. Tongja was selected to be a secretary at a shipping company. Kwangja found temporary work in a rubber-shoe factory, but was anxious to continue her schooling. Chinjoo had started her lingerie-sales business with the small money earned at the waterfront. Little Sunhee followed her to the market and helped her arrange the things in the stall. Some money had been saved to pay entrance fees and tuitions, but they had only accumulated half of the amount. Chinjoo dreamed, as she was finishing the dishes, that as soon as the weather settled down and the new semester started, all her children would continue their education.

"Ma, I will be home late. I've got to work overtime."

"Again? That shipping company must be doing a mighty good business. If they have another position open, try to get Kwangja in, too."

Combing back her curled hair, looking into a worn-out mirror, Tongja hummed a well-known tune.

"You sound happy. You must be having a date or something with that navy captain," Kwangja jeered.

"Captain?" Chinjoo snapped around from stuffing the market goods in a bundle.

"Oh, she's just being silly, Ma." Tongja gave her younger sister a quick sharp glance.

"You are the one who's being silly, you know," retorted Kwangja.

"Now, listen to that girl, the way she's talking to her older sister!" Chinjoo clacked her tongue. On the other hand, she had some advice for her oldest daughter. "Women are ripened fruit, ready to be picked and eaten any time. Be careful. Working with all those men around. Don't make yourself too attractive. Set a good example to your younger sisters."

"Ma, this is about the hundredth time you've told me."

"I can't tell you enough. A good part of what goes wrong is the woman's fault. Don't get carried away even if men fall at your feet saying how beautiful you are, 'cause they'll say it to any woman. Men are all thieves. Just don't let it slip out of your mind for a moment."

"Oh, Ma!"

"Followers of advice will be benefited, so don't you think I am just nagging. Ma's advice is never wasted."

Silently, Tongja fitted herself into a pair of nylon stockings. Seeing the scar in her leg she frowned.

"Oh, I hate this! Ma, I need dark colored stockings. This shows."

"Don't you worry. People are too busy to notice a little thing like that."

Tongja, sullen, stooped out of the low wooden door and walked through the alley where the makeshift one-room houses clustered like crab shells. She was a secretary in a shipping company, a job that came as the result of steep competition. A young lady just turned twenty, in pink blouse and a flare skirt. She had changed as if she had bloomed after a long hard winter. Her once pale face glowed with health and color. Her gaunt figure was now trim and full. Even in a crowd, she stood out like a pearl. The scar—showed after all. A flaw in a precious gem. Chinjoo ran after her daughter, fished in her bundle, and handed her a package of shaded nylon stockings.

"Rush home as soon as you are through with your work. Don't pay attention to those sweet-talking men. Don't accept any invitations even for an expensive dinner, 'cause that's just the beginning to a lot of trouble. Men are all thieves!" Chinjoo's passionate voice drew the attention of passersby.

"Oh, Ma!" Tongja, her face red, dropped the package of the new stockings in her purse and hurried on her way, her back straight. A sight nice to watch even for a mother. But in the corner of Chinjoo's mind she carried a mother's concern. The city was full of men: soldiers, hoodlums, drifters, and smugglers. Although the battle line was up at the 38th parallel, and a cease-fire rumor persisted, fighting was still going on, and people lived as though there were no tomorrows. But what could she do? She couldn't lock Tongja inside the house and send the matchmakers around to hunt for a groom. Matchmakers lied as often as not. "So and so, president of a company, financially settled"—so on, ended up being either a marginally successful underwear dealer, or a balding company manager with a dozen kids. "Interpreter for a U.N. commander" turned out to be a house-boy in a foreign officer's home. Tongja talked of going to college, but she balked at going back to high school to make up the time lost and get her diploma. And besides, college cost much more than the family had. But she was a dependable and responsible girl. They had gone through hard times together. Perhaps Mother Chinjoo need not worry so much.

"Sunhee, let's hurry. It will be evening before we get there!" Brushing aside her concern over Tongja, Chinjoo grabbed her youngest daughter's hand, walked past the makeshift houses and plunged into the crowd. An endless crush of humanity surged in all directions against a cacophony of cars, trucks and streetcars. Another day in the bustling port city of Pusan.

In the hastily assembled market place they sold everything ranging from smelly fish to smuggled commodities such as lady's lingerie. When Chinjoo reached her stall, the couple next to her had already opened their shop and were helping a customer. With Sunhee's help, Chinjoo arranged articles on several yard wide wooden stands precariously supported by two pairs of spindly legs. It was muggy and hot. Two sailors, their contraband in sea bags, edged through the crowd to Chinjoo. One was a steady supplier, the other a stranger. Chinjoo bought five boxes of Coty powder and other American-made cosmetics, some blouses and skirts. There were two alligator purses and matching high-heeled shoes.

"Let's see. How much are they?"

The sailor looked about uneasily and mumbled the price,

"20,000 won per pair and the same for the purse."

"What? for those little things? You must be crazy. I wouldn't pay more than 10 won." Chinjoo shoved the articles away.

"As you please. Auntie, those are in great demand now. They sell like they have wings on them. At the least you will double your profit on the shoes alone. You can't even find them for 60,000 won anywhere, and some of the young women will pay anything just to get them on their feet."

Chinjoo's hand hesitated around the sack.

"Are you sure? Let's take a look at those again."

"Well, you don't have to buy if you aren't sure, Auntie. I've got millions of customers in line."

"I said let me take another look." On second thought, they did seem worth the price. "10,000 won a piece," Chinjoo declared.

The sailor shoved the shoes back into the sack without answering.

"Come on over here. I'll buy them." At the next shop, the owner had been listening intently to the haggling. He beckoned to the sailors.

"15,000 won. That's a lot of money. But I will take the chance!" Chinjoo held onto the sack with one hand and counted out the money with the other. The sailor shook his head disapprovingly.

"Come on over. Let me buy them." The voice from the next shop became urgent.

"18,000 won. I am going to be ruined!" wailed Chinjoo, waving the money in the sailor's face.

"Let's get rid of them," nudged the second sailor.

Chinjoo snatched the sack, stuffed it under the stall, and forced the money into the sailor's hand. The sailors sold the rest of the shoes to the owner of the next shop. Chinjoo sold nothing during the morning.

At noon, she bought some steamed mandoos for Sunhee and herself. Sighing over the slow business, she fanned unsuccessfully at the humidity. The midafternoon sun baked the market place. Flies settled on the littered watermelon peels by a nearby fruit stand. A beggar boy stood idly at the end of the alley against a crooked telephone pole blankly staring at the feast enjoyed by the flies. Near the rice-cake peddler's basket, a high school girl and a soldier bought a couple of cakes, and strolled off munching and giggling.

"I will tell you, all the gals are tainted now. There are no virgins any more. There's no virgin!" The muttering came from the shopkeeper next to hers.

"Mom, we can't even make today's shop rent," Sunhee mumbled to her mother.

"Don't you worry, dear. It's still too early and hot for people to shop around. Whew, what a day! Will you fan my back? It's so wet. It's as if I'd been standing in the rain."

"What a slow day. Have you made any sales yet?" called the young man who ran the houseware shop opposite her stall.

"No, I haven't even made my first sale today. Well, everyone must have all gone to the August 15th celebration or to the beach or something. It's hot just sitting still."

Sunhee, half fanning her mother and half examining the boxes of cosmetics, watched her mother arranging the items. A young lady with a parasol approached. Sunhee signaled her mother.

"Oh, may I help you?" Chinjoo greeted her like her own flesh and blood. The young lady didn't answer, but her eyes focused on the alligator shoes.

"How much are they?"

Chinjoo's eyes twinkled.

"60,000 won, Lady."

"It's expensive!" the young lady exclaimed. Her attention moved to other items, but came back to the shoes.

Chinjoo held the shoes in her palm and explained as best as she could.

"Expensive? Why, they are priceless. That kind is hard to come by and they are in fashion. Any high-society girl would love to pay anything for them. See the leather? And the finish of the shoes? I've never seen anything like these in my life."

"Still it's too high."

"Well, since you seem so attracted to them, I will sell them to you at 50,000."

The young lady turned away with her final offer.

188

"30,000 won?"

"No," Chinjoo definitely shook her head.

Chinjoo regretted it. She should have sold them. She might have been duped by the sailors. Nobody would buy them. In an hour another young woman approached and looked at the shoes again.

"How much?"

"50,000." Chinjoo carefully evaluated the customer. She's got to sell something this time.

"You can have it for 30,000 if you buy the matching purse too."

"How about 20,000 each?"

Chinjoo grew desperate.

"You can have them for 25,000." Chinjoo started to wrap the items.

"You can have these at 20,000 each," called the woman from the next shop. The customer headed in that direction. Hot blood rose in Chinjoo's throat. She grabbed the shoes in the wrapper and flung them at the storekeeper.

"And you can have these for nothing!"

The woman, hit by the sharp heel, screamed.

"You beggar from the north!" her husband roared, coming at her. Chinjoo, beside herself, twisted off a wooden stick and swung it at him.

"Stay out of this, you no good hen-chasing rooster! She is my customer, you hear me? We haven't finished our bargaining yet!"

"There's no such thing as your customer. She can shop wherever she likes," the man shouted at her once and went back to his shop.

Sunhee, white and shaken, stood quivering in front of the stall which tilted to one side. The merchandise was scattered on the ground.

"What are you standing there like that for?" Chinjoo put her arm around Sunhee's trembling shoulders and shoved her daughter behind the wooden stand. She picked a few things from the ground and tossed them inside. As she attempted to straighten up the tilted support, she suddenly felt weak and nauseous. Defeated. It was as bad as the bombs, the strafing, the heaps of rotting bodies. Too much for her to bear alone. Blankly Chinjoo stared at the hands of the man who was propping up her stall and gathering up the littered merchandise from the ground.

"Some people just don't understand business ethics, do they!" The young man from the houseware shop had retrieved her alligator shoes. His neighborly gesture helped her regain her composure.

Kim came from south of the Taedong River. He had left his young

189

wife in the north and came down to look for his parents during the brief U.N. occupation. But he was unsuccessful. Money ran out and the road to the north was blocked.

"I tell you, Auntie, at the age of thirty I've gone through more than most people experience in their entire lives. My parents left me in the care of my uncle when I was five. They left to seek a living and headed for Shanghai when things got rough during the Japanese rule. Uncle said the last letter he received was from Taejun. But they never came back, even after the liberation. So I gather they are still somewhere in mainland China. I've grown up and gotten along fine, but my lifelong dream was to find my parents. That's why I left my new wife on our wedding day." The young man paused, smiled, and then continued.

"That part of my life too, Auntie, you wouldn't believe. I was engaged to a girl. Then I was drafted by the Japanese and served in Singapore. After I came back a year after the liberation, I found out the girl had died. Anyway the 38th parallel had been drawn, so I lost my chance to come south and look for my parents. I was engaged the second time to a nice girl around the time this war broke out. My uncle and aunt were worried about this aging bachelor and urged me to marry. I only saw her twice—when I went to see her at the first arranged meeting in her country home with my uncle, and again on the wedding day. That's the day when I heard the Chinese army was moving south. I decided to come south, too. Now I am alone. The road is closed again. I should have taken her along with me, but how could I when I didn't even know where I was going. I had only this one address. And I was so determined to find them that I planned to go through every alley and street in the south." The young man told his story without emotion.

"You will be able to go back and get her, I am sure."

"Ah, fate settles everything. Poor girl. Of all the men, why did she have to hear about me? In fact, she had seen another suitor before me but she and her parents chose me instead. She would have been better off marrying him. I hope she isn't too old fashioned to marry another man instead of waiting for me. I will live on, somehow. I am used to living alone and I've got this business started on my own although it's still small. Excuse me, Auntie, there's a customer in my shop." Kim ran toward his place.

People straggled into the market place. The crowd, dispersed after

190

the celebration of the August 15th anniversary, mingled with the flow of rush hour. Many stopped at her stall and asked the prices, but Chinjoo had lost interest.

"How much is this? Don't you want to make money? I asked you how much this was." A middle-aged woman stuck her face close to the stallkeeper. Chinjoo peered at her customer. Her eyes grew wide. The woman was trying to recognize her, too.

"Why, isn't this Tongja's mom?"

"Ah, Bokye's mom! It really is you!"

They grabbed each other's hands.

"It's been five years—six years?"

"We were bound to meet again if we stayed alive, weren't we?" said Choi's wife, Chinjoo's former next-door neighbor who had left for the south soon after the liberation. "Oh, is this Sunhee? I can't believe that little child grew up to be such a fine young lady. Where's Sunhee's pa? Does he have a business of his own?"

A cloud crossed Chinjoo's face.

"He is still in the north."

"Oh, I am so sorry. But I am sure he will get here as soon as he gets a chance." The Chois had settled in Seoul, but became refugees again when the war broke out. They lived in the port city. Her husband worked at the dock, and she herself had a small fabric shop. It was a heartwarming reunion. They talked, occasionally interrupted by customers.

A young woman accompanied by a gentleman with graying hair noticed the alligator purse.

"How much is it?"

"The young lady asks how much it is," the gentleman repeated the question to Chinjoo.

"70,000 won," Chinjoo recited out loud. She didn't care if it didn't sell. The gentleman eyed the young lady.

"And the shoes?" he asked.

"70,000 won for the pair."

Without further words, the gentleman reached for his wallet, took out a hefty handful of 1,000 won bills and handed them to Chinjoo. Chinjoo wrapped the merchandise, unable to believe it was actually happening. The man took the package and walked away with his young lady.

"Must be a rich father," muttered Chinjoo, recovering her zest.

"Father! That was his mistress. Lots of those around these days," said Choi's wife, with a knowing nod. Choi's wife left after scribbling her address for Chinjoo, inviting Chinjoo to visit her, and promising her to come back again. Chinjoo enjoyed brisk business the rest of the day. It made up for all those disastrous hours early in the day. She sold cosmetics, soaps and lady's slips. When the rush was over, Chinjoo found time to breathe.

"Let's have some food, Sunhee. Go buy us some rice cakes, will you?" Chinjoo started to count the money in the pouch tied around her waist.

A couple stood in front of the stand staring at her.

"Aunt, you are alive!" the young man shouted grasping her hands. Chinjoo looked into his face.

"Ah, Mr. Teacher Song! And Kyungsoo's ma."

It was, indeed, Teacher Song and his wife. Teacher Song, the next-door neighbor in Pyongyang, who had frequented her house with the news of R.O.K. and U.N. advance, and the wife whom she had cared for a brief time while their husbands had been gone.

"My, two reunions in a row in one day! I've just talked with another good friend of mine!"

"Everybody seems to be meeting somebody, today. The crowd out there is awful."

"Ah, how did you come to Pusan? How did you find me? Ah, you are all safe and sound!" Chinjoo's mind flashed back.

"He was caught by the Reds and carried north. Then he escaped during the bombing," his wife explained.

"So, you have had your adventures, too. But I don't know what happened to my children's father."

Teacher Song's face grew grave. As he suspected, Chinjoo still didn't know. He had come across an old newspaper, saw Chinjoo's ad and rushed to meet her, but he didn't know he would be the first one to tell her.

"I looked all over for his body, but couldn't find it. We just left. He always said if he were alive he would come find us. So, at the last minute we decided to leave. I am not sure he is still alive. In my dreams I see him a lot. I ask him, 'Are you still alive?' He doesn't answer. Then I wake up with such a horrible feeling. If he is alive he should be here by now. I've advertised his name and my name in the newspaper for a year. Or is he back there but still in prison or what!"

Memories twisted Teacher Song's face—the forced march north.

"We have a sick man here," Kim Insoo had called out to the captors. One of the Security Policemen came to him.

"Who said that?"

"I did. Look at this man here, old and sick. He hasn't eaten for three days and he can't walk any farther. Perhaps if you can give him a little of your water, he will feel better."

"Shut up, and keep walking!"

For a while they plodded on, the aged sick man panting, dragging his weak body. Kim Insoo could not be silent.

"I beg you for the last time, please give him some water and let me carry him. Have mercy. I am sure you have a father of your own about his age. Think of it as doing a favor to your own father."

The column came to a stop. The Security Policemen held a whispered conversation, and Kim Insoo and the old man were taken away from the rest of the group into a nearby field. Wind blew through the fields bowing the tall weeds. The other captives, huddled in a pathetic knot, could hear the curses of the captors and the murmurings of Kim Insoo. A rifle butt flew in the air. The old man fell. Then Kim Insoo's voice, clearer this time:

"Forgive them, for they know not what they do!" The rifle butt smashed again. He dropped behind the reeds, his broad face upturned.

Sickened and terrorized, the rest of the group continued on, their hands tied behind them and roped together. Teacher Song saw no hope of survival. As they reached a river bank, fighter planes roared down on them. Captors and captives alike fell flat by the road bank. Now or never! As if it had been planned, the shackled captives scrambled to their feet and stumbled back the way they had come—away from the river. A short machine-gun burst, and the men fell like dominoes. After the planes left, the surviving captors found what they expected. All the prisoners were dead. All except Teacher Song. There and then, Teacher Song accepted the concept of Divine protection. He was alive, unwounded. He lay as he had fallen, the bottom body beneath the pile of riddled friends, covered with their blood, his eyes closed. The policemen left, quickly fording the stream. A village boy looking for crawfish helped Teacher Song dig out from under the stiffening corpses and free his hands from the bloodsoaked cords. Hiding by day and traveling by night, Teacher Song made his way to his wife's home in Hamkyong Province. He went back to search for Kim Insoo's body, but the road was blocked by the Chinese Communists. He should have gone back, no matter what. It lay heavy on his conscience.

"Then you must have left Pyongyang about the same time we did," Chinjoo was saying. "We started too late. And we were caught in the crossfire on the front. There were Communist soldiers disguised among us refugees. And the artillery fire coming after us—we just narrowly escaped. Tongja was wounded. She is all right now, though. You must have experienced the same thing."

"We came through the east coast," Teacher Song's wife said. "You see, there was a huge refugee evacuation by U.S. LSTs. Shortly after I arrived there with the children, my husband came. We hurried on to Hungnam, where we made the last ship."

Teacher Song had been quiet. How could he talk about his fortunate experience to someone who had had such misfortune!

"Aunt!" Teacher Song had made a painful decision. "I don't know whether I should tell you this. Probably it is best to leave it the way it is. But Aunt, I don't want you to live the rest of your life in false hope. Elder Kim has passed away. They killed him and others. After I left home, I was caught and was thrown into the same jail. Then we were taken up north, but we didn't have chance to talk," he continued with effort.

Chinjoo stared blankly at the man.

"Are you sure?" Her voice was hollow.

Teacher Song reached for her hand and held it fast.

"Aunt, be brave. Be brave just the way you have been!"

That was it. That was the end. The last glimmer of hope snuffed out. Her shoulders shook.

"Aunt!" Teacher Song and his wife placed their hands on her shaking shoulders. "Let's go to our house. You need rest. We will help you pack up the things."

Soon Chinjoo lifted her head and blew her nose.

"I will be all right. I have other children home. Thanks, but I'll be all right. Come and visit us when you can."

* * *

"How's your dancing coming along?" An office-mate approached with a smile as Tongja emptied the coffee grounds into the trash can. A large mirror on the wall in the lounge reflected the woman's freckled face.

"Oh, not so loud. If my mother finds out, she will kill me."

"You've got an old-fashioned mother, uh? Well, my mother would be proud of me, if I had a navy captain for a boy friend. Isn't he hand-

194

some, though! I saw you at the dance hall the other day. Well, I must confess I envied you. You were a perfectly matched couple." The girl powdered her face heavily and made a curve on her lip with lipstick. "Oh, I'd just love to go out with a navy officer. The army—well, their khaki uniform somehow reminds me of dirt and sweat. But navy officers. They look so clean. Well, a woman should be born pretty, you know. When you aren't, you just have to settle for an old man with money, don't you!" She brushed up her short eyelashes with mascara and chattered on.

"One thing fishy about this captain, though. Goodlooking, high position, bachelor—if he is. How come? Probably he is hiding half-a-dozen children and their mother—or mothers—somewhere. No, couldn't be. Kind of young for that. But you know what they say: Sailors have a girl in every port. So, take advice from an old miss. Don't give too much of your heart 'cause when it breaks it will hurt a lot. Oh, what am I saying! Well, what I meant was: Have fun. Are you coming to the dance hall tonight?"

"No, we are going to Songdo."

"Oh, to the beach! Wow, wait till your mother hears about this! I remember when you were first hired. You couldn't even look a man straight in the eye. Ha, ha! People learn fast, don't they! Well, have fun!" The young woman adjusted her blouse and left.

Eventually, the work day came to an end. Into the late afternoon humidity with heat capable of melting asphalt, poured the working men, office girls, soldiers and the executives of the business community. Streetcars jingled along adding to the din of noisy horns of cars carrying the presidents of private companies and government officers. The voices of the crowd, spiced with the accent of Kyongsang Province, joined the noises of the harbor to create a pandemonium made even more oppressive by the heat. Captain Lee took out his handkerchief and patted his forehead. The sun was still high. To make the most of the remaining daylight, people and cars vied with each other making their way through the narrow streets to the beach.

Overlooking the beach where the waves darted and broke, Tongja walked side by side with the handsome navy captain along the bridge that extended to the islet. Her heart swollen, she was conscious of her long curly hair blowing toward the shoulder insignia of his white uniform. She had known him for three months. After he had been introduced by her boss, they had gone dancing several times and had dinners together. He

195

was a nice escort and a good dancer. His fleeting smile made him even more attractive and exciting. "Sailors have a girl in every port." Would this be true with this sailor, too? Mother would kill her if she knew, but she wouldn't think about it now.

Two sailors and a lieutenant saluted as they passed by. Captain Lee returned their salutes and Tongja felt a tug of pride. A child beggar blocked their way and stuck out his dirty hand, furtively eyeing Tongja's purse. Captain Lee reached into his pocket and tossed him a crumpled 10 won bill. The child retreated bowing and examining it, then shouted to their backs.

"Cheap! 10 won can't buy nothing!"

Captain Lee grinned, his handsome teeth flashing in his tanned face. Tongja walked silently by him, and wondered what it would be like to be engaged to this man. Tongja tripped over a rock and almost broke her high heel.

"Careful!" His hand gently touched her shoulder to help her. Blushing, she tried to be sedate. As they approached the noises of the beach, she grew uneasy. Since the rush hour a week ago when her sister Kwangja spotted her walking side by side with him, she felt tainted.

"I can't swim," she blurted out by the beach house. At first he looked down on her incredulously, then responded a matter-of-factly.

"No problem. I will teach you how."

Had she come too far, perhaps? Should she have refused the very first tea. It was too late now to go back and erase the whole thing. Finally she came out of the beach house in a one piece swim suit with a bath robe around her shoulders, feeling naked. The officer in his swim trunks greeted her with a grin.

"Do I look funny?"

"No, it's just that I am used to seeing you in your uniform," said Tongja turning away from his bare chest.

"Come, let's go in!" Becoming a totally different man, almost like a high-school student, he held her hand and dashed toward the water. "Come on," he splashed water on her and laughed. With his cap off, his forehead was extremely white. She obeyed his command, like a tamed mermaid. She held her breath, put her head into the water, as he told her to do. Choking and swallowing water, she gasped.

He laughed. "Try again." She did. "Again." He taught her how to float. It was fun. She dipped her head, floated, propelled her arms, and kicked with her feet. "You are learning fast. Now let's have a race."

"All right!" Tongja became bold. She held her breath and swam in the direction Captain Lee was going. After a few strokes, she faltered. Captain Lee slipped his arm around her and pulled her toward the beach. She was conscious of her breast pressing against this man's side. She dropped onto the sand, exhausted.

"Hello, there, weren't you a little too ambitious?"

"It seemed so easy," she mumbled feeling silly.

He put his towel around her shoulders. It didn't seem possible that she and a man were sitting side by side, with their arms and legs uncovered. Beyond the crowded beach the water extended endlessly. Soft, fluffy clouds floated over the horizon.

"What do you suppose is over there, over the horizon?"

"Cheju Island," answered the captain matter-of-factly.

"I mean," Tongja glared at the man reproachfully. Surely she had expected a much more romantic response. But, what the heck, it was true. She had been there once, herself. "It's just a stretch of waste land, isn't it? I went to Cheju Island once with my mother. Nothing except rocks. What I had heard was right. It's the island of three plenties: plenty of rocks, plenty of winds, and plenty of women. Did you see all those woman divers there? They say men in Cheju Island stay home babysitting and women seafood divers support the family. Would you like to have a woman support you?"

"Why not? It would be a great life for any man, although I would hire another man for the babysitting," he chuckled glancing at the disappointed girl. She was beautiful and he was amused listening to her Pyongan Province accent slipping through her newly acquired way of speaking. A flawless creature. Her dark eyes fixed on the horizon, she seemed to yearn for a dreamland beyond the extent of the sea. His glance caressed down the soft, round shoulders, the arms that wrapped around her knees and her slender legs. Captain Lee's glance rested on the side of her leg.

"A shrapnel wound. It happened in the winter two years ago. Ugly, isn't it?" Obviously Tongja was aware of his stare.

"No," he shook his head. Her hair, still wet and parted in the middle, covered the sides of her face like a pair of satin drapes. "You are beautiful. That's all I know."

The day drifted into twilight as they chatted. The crowd began to thin.

"It's time to go home now."

"Yes?" Tongja woke up from a daydream. She meant "already?"

"I will take you to a nice dinner."

"I like Chinese," she responded, unabashed.

The driver, a sailor, arrived with a military jeep. The crowd had shifted from the beach to the city streets. Riding in an open jeep dashing through the heart of the city, her hair blowing behind her, she felt alive and excited.

"You are quiet," the captain said across the dinner table. "Are you worried about something?"

She had put her chopsticks down and was playing with her napkin.

"Perhaps. I need something to say to my mother, an excuse for being this late."

He thought for a moment with his head bent.

"Why don't you tell her the truth."

"Truth?"

"Why? Does she have anything against a navy captain buying a dinner for a friend's secretary?"

"Is that all I am to you—a friend's secretary?" she asked, unable to hide her disappointment. He didn't answer, sitting quietly as if it were his turn now.

"Our ship leaves for the East Sea next week on a new assignment," he said.

Tongja's heart sank.

"When are you coming back?"

"In two months, or three. I don't know. Plans are still being made. But it's war and you never know—" His voice trailed off.

"Must be nice to travel around." Tongja was moody.

"Sometimes. Much of the time, it's boring. Out at the sea, there's nothing much to do. Fighting a civil war, the navy doesn't fight at sea as much as it did in the Pacific war. This is more of a ground and air war."

"Oh, I hate war. I wish this would end soon. Don't you?"

"I agree. But I am so used to the navy now, I don't know what I would do in peace time. Maybe I should go to Cheju Island," he laughed.

"Take me to the dance hall."

Captain Lee arched his eyebrows in surprise. But seeing the sadness in Tongja's eyes, he followed her as she lead the way.

They danced away much of the night. Tongja buried her head on his shoulder, feeling the man's firm body. She remembered her first dance with him. It had taken nerve even to touch his hand. Now she pressed tightly against him, and let him carry her over the floor. Wouldn't he say anything before he left? Two months would be such a long time without him. Three months, forever. At least if they were engaged, she would know he belonged to her. But Captain Lee said nothing Tongja inwardly longed to hear.

"You should be home before the curfew," the captain said, concerned.

As the driver parked the jeep at the entrance of the makeshift houses, she wanted to cling to him forever.

"I will see you tomorrow at your office," he said opening the vehicle's door for her.

Through the low wooden door her mother's head appeared.

"Isn't that a man who just drove off?"

"Must be."

"Where have you been until this late?"

"Went to a movie—with a friend."

"Did you have dinner?"

"Yes."

"Come, sit down " Chinjoo faced her eldest daughter. "I've seen Teacher Song, today."

"Oh, did you?"

There was a moment of silence.

"Your pa passed away a long time ago."

"Oh, did he?"

"Teacher Song told me. He saw him killed." Chinjoo lifted her sleeve to her face. Tongja's reaction was slow in coming. Then, as if waking up from a dream, she mumbled,

"I knew it all along. Where else could he be?"

Captain Lee arrived in civilian clothes. They strolled along the street, had dinner and walked some more. They passed the army hospital fence. A poster presented a close-up of an army nurse. Someone had scribbled a mustache.

"Don't you think she looks better with a mustache?" Captain Lee tried to be cheerful. Tongja laughed. Then they went to the dance hall again. As they passed the dark army hospital fence on the way home, she whispered,

"Captain Lee, take me with you."

"I can't do that."

"Then I won't see you again?"

He looked down on her for a moment. Then he gently pushed her against the fence and held her tightly in his arms. She was dazed. That obviously was the sort of kiss she had seen many times in the Western movies. Her flesh melted in his grasp.

"I will see you tomorrow," Captain Lee said a few moments later as he left her at her door.

"This is our last night?"

When they came to the spot near the army hospital fence, Tongja waited—waited for the word that she was supposed to hear. 'Marry me!' or 'Wait for me!' or something. This night there was no kiss.

"Aren't you going to say good bye?" Tongja asked with grief. Lee's hands squeezed hers to his chest.

"Don't be upset when you hear what they say after I have left. You are a brave young lady, aren't you? I should have told you but I guess I was too afraid to do so. I am engaged. To a nice young lady just like you."

Tongja was stunned. Slowly, she came to herself and broke away from him.

"You are engaged?" she repeated stupidly.

"Please! She is a nice girl and I couldn't do anything to hurt her."

Tongja thrust her fist at his chest.

"You! Beast!"

She ran through the dark street, shoving and bumping into some people. The man started after her calling, then gave up and stood quietly until the billowing skirt completely disappeared into the deserted night.

Oooh—how could he! Tongja buried her face in her hands as she tried to catch her breath at a corner of the street. Then she hurried on.

Mother was right! They are all thieves. And it was her own fault. Falling for a strange sailor like that! For a few days she blamed the man for deceiving her, then herself, then him. When the height of her emotion passed, she felt numb and simply wanted him back. She just couldn't give him up to another woman!

The day of the captain's departure, Tongja walked down to the harbor. A mystic serenity seemed to embrace the earth. She sniffed the breeze, the salt, the seaweed. A warming sun and blue water created a false tranquility. She awoke from her reverie: Gunboats, destroyers, transports, battleships, LSTs, patrol torpedo boats—all kinds of naval vessels converged there from around the world like giant sea creatures searching for food. At the pier, a naval ship tugged at its moorings, its prow pointing to sea. Although military police were on guard at the gate beyond which civilians were prohibited, some relatives and friends of the crew gathered to get a glimpse of their loved ones. Good! she had arrived in time. She came here to ask him to take her with him. If not, to elicit his promise to return to her. She took off her high-heeled sandals and ran toward the ship. She stopped halfway to catch her breath. Captain Lee appeared on deck with a girl and other officers. He walked down the gang plank followed by the young woman at his heels. Taking her arm, they walked along the wharf. When they stopped, he caressed her shoulder. Tongja gazed at them stolidly. The woman held his hand, reluctant to let go. Tongja turned, her confidence gone. She gave way to tears. She didn't know how long she had walked until she came to the loose sand. The bathers gone, the morning beach was as lonely as herself. Oh, I've got to go home. She walked slowly along the sand.

Yi Chinjoo suspected something was wrong with her eldest daughter.

"You are working too hard. You've been working overtime so often since last June. Money is necessary, but your health comes first. Why, you even lost your appetite. Tell them you are a human being and need rest too. No more overtime!"

Chinjoo peered at her daughter who lay staring at the ceiling, a recently developed habit. Tongja didn't seem to hear what her mother said, so Chinjoo repeated.

"No more overtime work, you hear me? Come right home and rest. You don't even have to worry about cooking dinner. Kwangja will take care of it. Do you hear me?"

"I am not doing any overtime work, Ma," responded Tongja with a sigh, still staring at the ceiling.

"You aren't? But you came home late practically every day last month, and you didn't work overtime?" insisted Chinjoo.

Tongja was silent.

"Then—" Chinjoo's eyes narrowed. Her intuition strengthened her suspicion. "Kwangja, you take Sunhee out for a walk. Find something to do!" Then she faced Tongja. "Now, you tell me what happened. Was it a man?"

Tongja nodded slowly. Chinjoo's mouth fell agape. She wished it were one of those bad dreams.

"For how long? Since when? Who is he? Where? And all these late nights? He is a bachelor, of course, isn't he?"

"We just had a good time together, that's all. He is not here any more." Tongja whispered. It was not like Tongja. Could this be her trusted daughter?

"Good time together?" Chinjoo glanced apprehensively at her daughter's flat tummy. "Do you mean—you mean, goodness!" gasped Chinjoo not knowing whether to slap the girl or to cry.

"Oh, Ma! It's not like that. It's not what you think at all." Tongja seemed irritated, got up, and began to dress. "I—just had a good time. That's all. Swimming, dancing, dinners. And I found out he was engaged to some other woman. So it's over, and that's all. Now I need to go out and take a walk. I need some fresh air."

"Why, that double-crossing thief! I've got to have a word with him. Who is he? You tell me who that no-good young man is. I am just going to knock some sense into him."

"He did nothing wrong. I was the one who pushed things. And he isn't even here. So please pretend it has never happened."

Tongja went out. Chinjoo checked the urge to say more. Tongja fancying a man? It had never occurred in Chinjoo.

Tongja walked along the wall of the army hospital. So many places held memories. The Chinese restaurant, the tea house, even the glare of a jeep's headlights. When she passed the hospital fence, her eyes burned with tears. She blinked at the tattered poster, walked past it, turned and came back. Thoughtfully, she studied the text under the mustached nurse.

"Whew, that blazing summer has finally cooled off. I feel like living again." Chinjoo prattled on during dinner, savoring the pleasant weather and pleased to see all her daughters around the dinner table. She eyed Tongja. The oldest daughter seemed to have come to herself lately. Her appetite had returned. That was a big improvement. There was a remote possibility she would go to college. If she met a nice husband-to-be, then she would forget that first traumatic love affair. To keep her in a level emotional state was important. So Chinjoo had talked with Choi's wife, who gladly undertook the mission of finding an eligible bachelor or dependable matchmaker.

For a while there was silence. Chinjoo was absorbed in her accounting and inventory.

"Ma, I am going to be an army nurse. I am leaving next week for
training," announced Tongja, her voice controlled and determined.

"An army nurse?" gasped Chinjoo and other girls.

"Yes, Ma. After six months of training, I will be a sublieutenant."

"What? Are you out of your mind?" she shouted in spite of herself.
Crawling closer to her daughter, Chinjoo waved her finger. "You! You
don't mean that, do you? Young woman like you living with a bunch of
soldiers? Why, it's like throwing yourself into a lion's den. How could
you even think such a thing? Forget about going to work, too. From now
on, you are staying right here in this room!" Chinjoo shuddered with
indignation. An army nurse! It's as good as—No! Not her daughter!

"I am not going to work, Ma. I already quit my job. But I am going
to be an army nurse."

Chinjoo turned silent. They had gone through unbelievable hardships
together. Starved together. Escaped together. They fought the odds
together and had become one mind. Now when they could afford a few
things and enjoy life a bit, the world seemed to have turned against her.
Her daughter's mind seemed set and there wasn't anything she could do.
If only Kim Insoo were there! Chinjoo begged quietly, controlling her
voice.

"You are too young to understand. It might seem attractive, being
a lieutenant and all, but that's not all. Believe me it's not a dormitory
in a nun's temple. Think it over. Maybe you are too hasty."

Tongja heard but didn't listen.

For days Chinjoo coaxed, threatened, and begged. Nothing worked.

"All right! You do whatever you want to do! It's your business! I
don't care if you are attacked by millions of lions. Go on." Chinjoo regretted having said the last words. Tongja quietly packed her things and left.
All the hardships that she had gone through were just for that? The first
daughter, the one she hoped would be a proud example for the younger
ones, was now gone. There was nothing to look forward to. Chinjoo sat
in the middle of the room imagining herself rushing after Tongja, grabbing her by the arm, and smacking her across her face, shouting 'You
are not going anywhere!'

Packing her merchandise bundles, Chinjoo went to the market place. Until midday she couldn't keep her mind on anything.

"Listen, Mr. Kim. Can you tend the store for me a while? I've got to go and bring Tongja back."

Chinjoo rushed to the military depot where Tongja was to report. She bought steaming rice cakes. Somehow she would come back with her daughter and have the cakes at home talking about the nursing situation as if the whole thing had been a joke of the past.

The guard pointed at a crowd of young women in the hospital field. An army truck was parked there, and the young women slowly formed a line. Chinjoo recognized her daughter's fine features among the rest. She ignored the guard's warning and rushed to the girls. As Tongja approached the truck, Chinjoo struggled to hold back her tears.

"Here, you take these along. You will be hungry on the way. Write often."

Surprised, Tongja stared tenderly at her mother, taking the sack from her.

"I will, Ma. Oh, I will!"

The truck started noisily with its precious cargo, picked up speed and rumbled out of the hospital gate.

Many schools reopened and Chinjoo sent her children off to their respective grades in a girl's middle and high school. It was costly. Initial fee, tuition, books and uniforms. The school was temporarily located in a ramshackle shed in the heart of the crowded city. Chinjoo poured all her savings into their education.

Winter crept in. The war in the north dragged on with the rumor of armistice still given substance. Chinjoo's inventory at the shop had increased, but customers decreased. Pusan's population was thinning.

"I am going to pack and leave for Seoul, Auntie," said Kim at the hardware store.

"Do you really mean that? Do you think it's safe there? You might have to pack and run back down again," Chinjoo warned.

"No, Auntie. Sooner or later the war has to be over. Look, there! The fabric-store owners have gone to Seoul already, and one down this aisle. That one on the corner has left too. I guess I might as well find something to do up there. I can't just sit here and stare at those aluminum pans all my life, can I, Auntie?" The young man who, like Chinjoo, came from Pyongan Province, had been good to her and helped her in many ways.

"Well, you go on. And if you find a good place, will you let me know? I guess going there a little ahead of everybody would help, wouldn't it? And thank you for everything."

XVIII. From the ashes

By moonlight I sit all alone
  in the lookout on Hansan isle.
My sword is on my thigh,
  I am submerged in deep despair.
From somewhere the shrill note of a pipe. . .
  will it sever my heartstrings?

                              Yi Sunsin (1545-1599)

June, 1951. North of the 38th parallel.

The front! Mud. Sweat. Gunfire! A lull came after intense fighting. It was one of the fiercest tug of war between the offensive U.N. and the Communists' stiff resistance. Putting down his heavy M1, Private Yoon Hyonsup flopped on the ground in front of the bunker which, until the day before, had belonged to the Communists. A few days ago they had taken a hill deeper in the so-called Iron Triangle, the unconquerable mountainous bastion. He could still hear the unearthly cacophony of bamboo pipes and gongs hammered by the Chinese Communists launching a series of attacks from every direction. Isolated after a U.N. force on the right flank and the R.O.K. troops on the left withdrew, his regiment defended its position without food or air support. It was a resistance in the face of death that dragged on for three days. Finally, the main force arrived and the Chinese were driven off. The rocky slope festered with the dead of both sides. Captured field guns and horses saddled with sacks of grain watched mutely as their new masters' armored vehicles struggled through the muddy road. Hyonsup rubbed off the mud clinging to his boots. After the monsoon rain, the direct sunlight in the high altitude steamed his soiled uniform and baked his neck. Gulping a mouthful of water from his canteen, he sprinkled a few drops on his face.

Several yards away, Hyonsup noted a swatch of torn fatigue. Whose? His brother, Kangsup might have fought on this very spot, leading his platoon. Or he might have been a part of that daring Tiger unit that Hyonsup had heard so much about. Or he might be dead like one of

206

those—Hyonsup turned away from the rocky slope. Still rubbing his face, he fished through his back-pack for a cigarette wrapper he had picked up and saved. "Mother, it's hell here," he scribbled. "Yes, I've killed. Many times. We've got to kill. There are bodies within a few meters of me and at any moment, I may end up just like one of them. I no longer have any feelings." Hyonsup stopped.

A gust of wind assaulted his senses with the smell of gangrenous flesh. Service Corp men hurried by with stretchers for the dead and wounded. Soldiers with shovels hauled bodies into the woods for burial. Hyonsup crumpled the cigarette wrapper, flipped it away, and got to his feet.

It had been a month since Hyonsup had slept stretched out at full length. Finally, his detachment had been relieved from the spearhead a-ction and were back at the third line. Aircraft roared above the command post in the valley. Summer's dark green foliage covered the bomb-cratered hills. A scattering of farm huts, trampled by the rampages of war, rotted at the foot of the hill. Over the hill was a tiny village. Some of the combat-weary men welcomed the hamlet as at least a symbol of "rest and rehabilitation."

Hyonsup sat down by a tree at the edge of the hill, rubbing off the sweat drops dripping under his helmet. What is there left to live for now? His future might be a matter of seconds. So the only thing to do was to grab whatever those seconds might bring. Along the narrow footpath toward the village, Hyonsup saw a small moving object, far above him on the hillside. A girl? He had never been intimate with a girl. Once or twice he fantasized when a high school girl swung along the street, or when he sat next to a young woman in the streetcar, savoring the mystic experi-ence for the future. But would there be a natural fulfillment for him? In a few days, he would be back at the front. He might never come back. He might never experience a girl. He focused on the moving object: a country maiden carrying a water jar on her head, walking along the banks of a deserted paddy field, her long chima fluttering behind. At times, she was half hidden by the high weeds. Then she was completely exposed only to disappear again into the tall millet stalks. She reappeared fleetingly and then was screened by pine trees. At last, she came into clear view. Then she slowly faded into a familiar figure: his mother beckoning to him, "Hurry, Hyonsup!"

Private Yoon walked toward the tent. On the way he stooped and picked up another cigarette wrapper and wrote, "Mother, I am fine. We will be sent back to the front line. I wish you good health and a long life, no matter what happens to me."

The corporal snapped orders over the clumping of army boots. Hyonsup crumpled the cigarette wrapper and tossed it into the wind.

*   *   *

Through the window of the restaurant she had begun to restore with the help of her son, Wonsup, Oh Jungsoon anxiously watched the people passing by. She had opened the place herself and was already serving customers. The owner Changs hadn't come home yet. Most of the neighboring stores were still shuttered as they had been left by their owners who had fled south to take refuge. Here and there, looters had broken down wooden doors. Ashes and ruins stifled initiative. Skeletons of buildings rose starkly from the busy streets.

When they first went in through the door smashed by looters, darkness and stench engulfed them. Fighting nausea, they found cupboards and desk drawers thrown open, their contents strewn on the floor. Valuables were gone. Tables and chairs were knocked off and broken.

"Mom!" Wonsup had screamed. "Look, the corpse!"

She didn't know how long it had been there. It was bloated, blackened. The smell was sickening. There must have been fighting in the street. Walls were pockmarked with bullet holes. Several men from a district volunteers service came and cleared the body away. It took perseverance, courage and days of debilitating nausea to clear the mess. But eventually the restaurant was again fit for human lodging. She started it modestly. Dishes for ten or so. A handwritten sign outside enticed passers-by. Food ran out many times. Jungsoon borrowed money at five percent and expanded the menu. It had been difficult even to pay off the interest, but gradually the business had picked up and now she was out of debt.

People, deadened by refugee life, returned at an increasing tempo to the old capital city. Some came to reclaim their property, some had no other place to go, and others came to explore new business prospects. Thus Jungsoon's lot improved. Businesses and banks were reopened as were several hospitals. Jungsoon sent Wonsup back to school. Boys and girls whose minds would forever carry the scars of war, were now students once more. The teachers were devoted. They, too, were marked by years of privation and pain.

"Though fierce fighting is taking place only 30 miles north of us, we've got to concentrate on education. Someone said, 'Knowledge is power.' We cannot progress without it. We've got a lot of catching up to do." The physics teacher was quietly determined to lead the way.

Jungsoon heaved a sigh of relief. Now all she had to do was to broaden her income. Business was slow in the afternoon and Jungsoon sat on a chair cleaning the soybean sprouts. She thought about Hyonsup. He is so young. Would he be all right? And Kangsup? She had been too busy fending off starvation and taking care of the rest of the children to wonder much about her eldest son. Where would he be now? He must have written while they were away. Would he be still fighting at the front? Or relieved and transferred to the rear? Jungsoon glanced at the door, checking for customers. A woman swung open the door and strode into the restaurant. It was Chang's wife, the owner.

"Goodness gracious, it's you at last! It's you!" Surprised, Jungsoon greeted her, rose, and extended her hands and held hers in a warm grasp. There was a moment of silence and Jungsoon realized that her greeting was met with a cold stare. Chang's wife, her hair combed back, her face made up, showed no trace of the privations of the recent past. She let go of Jungsoon's hands, darted around the house, the kitchen and its contents.

"So, you've come here and opened your own business," Chang's wife blurted out.

"Oh, I thought I could make a headstart and make a living until you all came back. Oh, you should have seen how this place looked when I first got here. Most of the chairs and tables had been taken. I've fixed the broken ones. And these benches, we made out of the firewood we bought at the market. And there wasn't even a—"

Chang's wife wasn't listening. She bustled in and out of the kitchen and to her residence in the back where she found many items missing.

"Oh, the good china set is all gone. What are those that look like farmers' bowls?"

"Those are the used ones I bought. There wasn't any china left here when we came."

"There was a whole bunch of good napkins here and table cloths. Oh, I wonder where they went."

Jungsoon felt it best not to answer. It was heartbreaking to be misunderstood by someone as kind as she remembered Chang's wife to be.

A month later, the Changs moved into the restaurant. Chang, although sympathetic, was determined to make changes.

"Auntie, we don't want to be this way, but we have to. We are going to rebuild this place and I am bringing my skilled, experienced cook up here. You know what I mean. Down in Pusan we turned to Chinese cuisine. People like Chinese food very much these days. And we might as well start thinking of the future. We want to expand. Open a Western section too. We may even add Japanese food. Really, I didn't mean to disappoint you, but Auntie, you can stay and do other jobs—like cleaning. We've got lots of linens to be washed, and dishes to be done. Auntie, you understand, don't you? It's a whole new world."

Jungsoon slumped. She realized her means of livelihood was now tenuous.

"We want you to be with us. Please stay!"

Chang's wife listened as her husband explained. Then, with little interest, added. "Yes, why don't you?"

A postman shuffled along the deserted alley, peering at the address plates on the gates.

"A letter for you!" he shouted and slid an envelope under Jungsoon's gate. Jungsoon dried her hands, wet from laundering, and picked up the letter. It bore an army post mark. Her heart leaping, she tore it open. Kangsup had been wounded, treated in the field hospital and transferred to an army hospital in Pusan. Kangsup is alive! But how is he now? How bad is he?

"Go, let your father know."

Wonsup went to find his father. The bank was closed, half of the building was in ruins and bullet holes pocked the gray stone walls. At his father's residence, he found an old lady whom he had never seen before. Perhaps she was related to his father's present wife. She explained that the Yoon family had gone south and hadn't come back yet. Wonsup left a message and departed.

"Poor Kangsup!" Jungsoon sighed. She read the letter many times. It said he was recovering, but how soon? How severely was he wounded? She pictured the boy lying in the hospital, his face lined with suffering. She felt the pain herself. "Oh, if only I could fly there!"

Her hopes were fulfilled when the transportation to the Pusan hospital materialized. Chang arranged for her to ride in the restaurant's truck

210

dispatched to Pusan for supplies. The driver let her off at the hospital.

Pale and thin, Lt. Yoon Kangsup rested in a wheelchair in the shade of an oak tree on the spacious grounds of the military hospital. His mother rushed to him, knelt down, and squeezed his hand resting weakly on the armrest.

"How are you? Is everything all right?" Jungsoon's glance swept down to his feet on the footrest.

"Mother, how wonderful to see you. Yes, I am just getting some air. I'm very weak. I needed sunshine and rest, that's all."

"I should have come sooner, but with no transportation available I couldn't make it. Hyonsup went into the army in January. So where did you get hurt?"

Kangsup lifted his shirt and exposed his heavily bandaged torso.

"Shrapnel in my chest and thigh. The doctors dug it out. That was the hard part."

Jungsoon looked under the dressing and was appalled at the damage. The wound reminded her of the mother-in-law.

"Your grandmother—she passed away. Grandfather too."

Kangsup didn't respond. His face saddened.

"Have you heard from Father?"

"No. He left when the Communists came and hasn't come back yet."

"He may be here somewhere in Pusan. But what do I care!"

"Hush, son. All of us are having hard times. Are you coming home soon?"

"I don't know, Mother. If I get well enough to fight, they will send me back to the front. If not, I will be discharged."

"Come home when you are discharged."

* * *

Oh Jungsoon gasped when Yoon Daeyoung strode into her house. With his felt hat pressed down and his hands in his coat pockets, he stood in front of the crooked stone step like a statue. After recovering from the initial shock, Jungsoon managed to say,

"Do come in."

Daeyoung didn't move. Jungsoon hesitated, then said,

"Do sit down."

Reluctantly, he sat on the edge of the hall floor without taking his shoes off.

211

"Kangsup is in the army hospital in Pusan," she said.

"So I heard." He looked down, avoiding her glance. "Is he badly hurt?"

"Yes. The doctor explained the whole thing to me. First the doctors thought they would have to amputate his leg. He had several bullet wounds. One bad wound on the chest and another bullet in his thigh. That was the worst one, the doctor said. In addition to that—"

"But he is all right, now, isn't he?" Daeyoung interrupted, irritated at the details. "I mean he is not going to be handicapped or anything."

"No, oh no! He just needs to recuperate. The doctor said he may be discharged soon."

"Well then, there is nothing to worry about." He got up. "If he comes back, send him home to me. We haven't moved back completely, but by the end of the year we will have." He hesitated a moment. Still avoiding her eyes he asked, "Do you know what happened to Mother in the country? I stopped there on the way. I know Father passed away. But Mother?"

"She is gone too. We took her along south to seek refuge, but after a month—. When you decide to reinter their remains, the children will show you where they are buried."

Daeyoung walked away, his glance still downcast.

*   *   *

Kangsup, pale and weak, returned to his mother. He stayed home for a while not knowing what to do. A college was reopened but he showed no interest. He came and went sometimes visiting his father's home. He was dissatisfied. There would be a quarrel with his father and he would return to his mother again.

"Why don't you find a job? It will keep you busy."

"I will, Mother, as soon as I get my strength back."

In the beginning the response was mild, but as the days went by, he raised his voice at Jungsoon.

"Do you think jobs grow on trees? I've looked all over. And no one's going to hire a discharged service man!"

True, jobs were scarce, but he made no effort to find one. Kangsup was content to stay home while Jungsoon went to work and his brother went to school.

Restaurant-owner Chang made frequent trips between Seoul and Pusan. By late spring, most of his business had been transferred from

212

Pusan to Seoul. Ashes and the debris of war were removed from the streets. Crippled buildings were gradually being rebuilt.

In the attractive new building, Chang's business flourished and four cooks were kept busy. Young waitresses and hostesses were hired. The cooking and dishwashing Jungsoon was assigned to before was now reassigned to younger people, and she was relegated to the post of cleaning lady.

"Mom, my tuition fee is way past due. I might be expelled."

Jungsoon borrowed the tuition money from Chang, and put it in the chest drawer. Wonsup went to bed relieved and happy. Next morning, the money was gone. They tore the room apart but the money had disappeared. Comforting the distraught Wonsup, she rushed to the moneylender and arranged a loan.

Jungsoon eyed her eldest son. He appeared uninterested, but, nevertheless, nervous.

"Did you, by any chance, use that money?"

"How can you say such a thing to me! Me? Use my brother's tuition money for myself? Of course not."

Jungsoon returned from the restaurant tired and sad. Kangsup was gone, and Wonsup accosted her, obviously upset.

"Mom, you know what? There's this big syringe in the desk drawer."

She had suspected something wrong with Kangsup, but her heart sank with the horrifying fact.

Kangsup came home drunk and high spirited.

"Mother, I am going to take you right back to Father's home where you belong. Today I chased the bitch out of the house. I threw just about everything at her. Boy, was she scared! Ha, ha! It won't be long, till we all move into the house. You will see." He gagged, threw up, and fell asleep with his arms thrust out on the mattress. Jungsoon pushed up his sleeves. The skin, pale and taut, was patterned with countless needle punctures.

Kangsup's addiction to morphine started with the heavy anesthetics involved with treatment for his wounds.

"More, more!" he had screamed. Only the drug relieved his pain. During the recuperation period he seduced an army nurse who provided injections. As the time passed the dose had to be increased. Now he realized it was impossible to exist without it.

"Kangsup! Oh, why didn't you tell me? We could have gone to

doctors. You can be hospitalized and cured.'' Jungsoon tried to talk him into seeing a doctor.

"Don't worry. I am not what you think. I will be all right.''

But his health deteriorated rapidly. He was hardly recognizable even to his own family.

"Let's go see a doctor.''

"A doctor! You know what they say, 'Doctors are licensed thieves!' Mother, it would cost you a fortune. And you don't have a fortune.''

Soon he even gave up being defensive.

"Mother, will you give me some money? Will you, Mother? This is the last one. Honest. Never again! Please!''

His lips were purple, his shivering uncontrolled. She gave in the first time, but when he asked the second time she refused. She simply didn't have it. One afternoon when he fell asleep she called a doctor to the house.

"Oh, you know, he was a lieutenant and he got badly wounded. And those army doctors, they just poured drugs into him. That's how he got started.''

The doctor quietly examined him.

"Is that what he says? Auntie, it is highly unlikely. Perhaps one in a million.'' The doctor stared at the unconscious man with contempt.

"Is there any way that he can recover? Will he be all right soon?''

The doctor let go of the young man's arm, shook his head, and said dully,

"He is a hopeless case.''

* * *

Through the window, Jungsoon and Chang's wife peered at the marching students. Undaunted by a steady rain that wilted their placards, they moved on shouting,

"We are against the armistice! On with the advance north, and the unification!''

"Your children must be out there, too,'' mumbled Chang's wife.

"I guess.'' Jungsoon scanned the rows but dark school uniforms made recognition difficult. It was a long parade. When it was over, Jungsoon returned to work.

Although business was slow in the afternoon, the cooks were busy preparing for the post-rush-hour crowd. Jungsoon helped slice meat in the kitchen, then swept the dining-room floor. As she shoved chairs back and forth, a young woman with a baby cuddled in her arms entered, and took a seat in a far corner. The baby was well dressed with a knit wool cap, cape and quilted blanket. It's mother wore an attractive silk ensemble. She caressed the infant while picking a few bits of lint from the blanket. She spoke to Jungsoon.

"May I just wait here for a—Oh, Auntie!"

Their eyes met.

"Boonee! Is it you, Boonee?"

The cook and Chang's wife peeked out from the kitchen.

"This is not a dream, is it? Oh, what a small world!" Jungsoon ran to her.

"Oh, Auntie—" Memory flicked across Boonee's healthy face. Jungsoon paused.

"You had another baby? Let me see—So, he came back to you after all."

Boonee shook her head.

"I am married to another man. It's a long story. You see—after you left—You know, Auntie, I would have pretended not to know you if you were somebody else. But you know all about me and—"

"Boonee, I don't know anything about you except you have been a good woman and now are happily married."

"Auntie, come visit us. We have just moved into a house in Ahyundong. Sungjin's daddy started a middle school in the countryside, but wishes to settle down in Seoul."

"Auntie, could you come and help here?" Chang's wife called from the kitchen. Customers were arriving.

"Auntie, I wish we could go to a movie together. Sungjin's daddy is supposed to meet me here, have dinner and go to a movie."

"I am too old for those things. You go on. I have to go now."

"Can we taste some of your dishes? You know, I like your bulgogi. I will order as soon as my husband comes."

"I don't cook any more."

"You don't?"

"No. But there are lots of things to do—cleaning, sweeping."

Boonee's eyes followed the lady in the soiled apron as she hurried to the kitchen.

"Auntie, take off that apron and serve some of the food. We need lots of hands. Who was she?"

"Oh, a young lady, a good friend of mine."

Jungsoon, moving between the kitchen and dining room, noted that a young man had joined Boonee.

"I would like you to meet my husband. Yobo, this is the lady who taught me how to cook and sew."

"Ah, is that right? Pleased to meet you, ma'am. Thanks to you, she is quite a cook." The man stood up and bowed.

"Not at all. She is quick to learn, that's why," smiled Jungsoon taking a good look at Boonee's man. When most men insisted on marrying virgins, Boonee was extremely fortunate to find an attractive husband who accepted her despite her tainted background.

Finishing their dinner, Boonee's family stopped by the kitchen.

"Do come visit us, Auntie. Here, this is the address."

"I will, of course. Good-bye." Squeezing the address slip in her fist, Jungsoon silently wished the couple all the happiness as they walked out the door, the young man holding the baby and making way for his wife.

* * *

Usually Kangsup was gone several days. Then he appeared out of nowhere, sometimes feeling well, sometimes down. Jungsoon worried more about him when he was away than when he was home.

"Come home. Come home, dear!" begged Jungsoon.

"Mother, I said I am all right now. What are you crying for?"

When he left, so did some of Jungsoon's belongings.

Hyonsup came home on several short furloughs. Other parents gave their sons substantial pocket money when they came home on leave. Hyonsup must need some money too, to spend in his spare time.

"Here, dear. I wish I could afford more."

"Mother, I don't need money. Here, this is three months' salary. Hyonsup squeezed several ten hwan bills into her hand, joking at the sum the government doled out as salary. "It's worth three packs of Wharang cigarettes, they say. I don't smoke, so the money was saved." He had grown taller, more mature.

"You are all right, aren't you? Everything is all right with you, isn't it?" Jungsoon eyed her second son, closely. Knowing what his mother meant, Hyonsup laughed,

"Mother, I am all right. The war will be over. The armistice is going

216

to be signed soon."

That fall, Kangsup died. On a rainy day, Jungsoon followed the policeman who had found him dead in the street. She knelt down and lifted the straw mat covering her son's stiffened body. His back was curved like a shrimp. Dressed in his faded army trousers, now drenched by the rain, he lay on a heap of fallen leaves.

Jungsoon walked home along the wet street, following the hired cart carrying the inexpensive coffin covered with a white sheet. A healthy young man, who had dreams, and fought for his country. She recalled another woman worse off than she, who had given her five sons to the country. Jungsoon remembered a little boy saying: "I will be a pilot when I grow up!" chasing after a toy glider that swooped over the roof. The little boy was gone forever, the pilot he had never become!

XIX. Prosperity

The wedding candles flicker in the bedroom
when I meet this gentle lovely girl.
I look here, I look there, I look once and again:
She is fifteen years old,
and her face is a peach flower.
Golden hairpin and white gauze skirt,
shining eyes cast sideways,
and lips half-parted in a smile—
this is my loved one!
Give me a song to murmur
and gentleness under the quilt,
and what more have I to say?

Anonymous

1954. Seoul, South Korea.

"Dear Ma: I wish I could have written sooner, but really what could I say to make you happy other than leaving everything here and coming home? It isn't exactly a young woman's dream place, but it isn't as bad as you feared it would be. I've been promoted. I am a first lieutenant now, and in some ways enjoying my life. No life is really better than another. It's rather the person's choice that makes her what she is, although there are times I wish I had chosen otherwise. But it doesn't matter now. Ma, I am engaged. . ."

"Engaged!" Chinjoo gasped. "Engaged without parent's consent?"

"Mom, Eldest Sister is engaged?" Sunhee, curious, came closer and placed an arm around Chinjoo's shoulder. "How can she be engaged when we didn't have any engagement ceremony for her?"

"Sh, I am still reading."

". . . to a wonderful man. He is a gentle, responsible man any mother would wish for a son-in-law. He is in uniform like I am."

Engaged. . . a wonderful man. . .

Chinjoo read Tongja's letter over many times. She couldn't decide

218

whether the situation was an improvement or not.

"Oh, Mom. When is she going to have the wedding? Is she going to have it here? Is she coming home soon? Oh, I can't wait until I see them!"

Blankly, Chinjoo stared at her noisy youngest daughter as she folded the letter away. Her eyes ran over the fancy wall and ceiling papers, and on the three-tiered wardrobe that had recently replaced their wicker trunks. The decorative metal hinges and door rings shone brightly near the window. Slowly the frown cleared away from her face.

"Yes, she is going to have the wedding right here! A big one! This house is a little too small for a big wedding though, don't you think?"

Chinjoo had made a trip to Seoul after the young hardware-stall operator had packed and gone. Just before crossing the temporary bridge over the Han River, the bus broke down and Chinjoo waited at the depot. While waiting, she and Sunhee roamed through the deserted industrial area. Abandoned factories with thick chimneys were dark with soot and stain. Under the roofs of half-demolished buildings, smashed windows stared like hollow eyes.

"What are you looking at, Mom?" Sunhee asked restlessly.

"I am looking at that big field. Let's go over there, across the street to that real-estate office."

"Mom, I thought we were going to have a store in the heart of Seoul."

"Who said we weren't? You just come along."

In the small real-estate office, an elderly man absorbed in the game of changgi with a colleague, looked up and asked halfheartedly,

"Are you looking for a room or a house?" He was concentrating on his next move.

"Sir, I am looking for a piece of land."

The man didn't comprehend. Chinjoo continued,

"Sir, do you know who that land belongs to?"

"Land?" The man turned to her, still holding a round piece of wood. "Which land?"

"The land over there in back of those buildings." Chinjoo pointed through the door. Reluctantly, the bearded elder rose and craned his neck toward where Chinjoo was pointing.

"That's not land. It's a bunch of hills and creeks." The man eyed her as if she were out of her mind.

"Do you know who that belongs to? I want to buy some if it's for sale."

The elderly man put down his game piece.

"You really want to buy it?"

"Why do you think I asked?"

The agent put away his game and became as serious as Chinjoo.

"Let's see, the last time I saw the owner he was interested in selling, but that was before the war. Let me see. The owner is dead. Killed in a bomb barrage. I will go see his son, since he is the one who owns it now." Still in doubt, the old man scrutinized the woman. "By the way, Lady, do you have that kind of money?"

"Whoever heard of anybody buying land without money? Yes, I've got the money. But it all depends on how much he is asking." Chinjoo tapped the large handbag under her arm.

"Wait here, Lady. I will be right back. He lives nearby."

The son was anxious to get ready cash and delighted to find someone interested in buying his unproductive land. The bus had been repaired and drove off. Chinjoo had been too busy to notice or care. Chinjoo's second offer was accepted, much to her surprise. After putting her seal on the necessary documents and paying the young man the price agreed upon, Chinjoo was a land owner.

"That's a good piece of land. Soon people will build factories and houses there." The real-estate dealer, surprised and delighted to have his windfall deal close smoothly, encouraged that foolish woman who had bought the wasteland: too dry for a paddy-field; too rocky for planting other grains; too wet for building because of a stream which flooded every monsoon season carrying avalanches of rocks from the upstream. It was a piece of earth tabbed by real-estate people as "a dog."

In Seoul, Chinjoo rented a store in the mall at East Gate, a newly built business area. She expanded her line of merchandise. Former residents and newcomers continued to pour into the city, and her business picked up fast. After paying several months rent for a room near the mall, she purchased an inexpensive house in the northern outskirts. The solidly built house, with a big hall room and kitchen and three other rooms, would have cost her twice the amount had it been located within the city limits. The girls helped clean the house, hang new wallpaper, and lay a new floor. Chinjoo sat down in the master room extending her legs on the shiny ondol floor covered with waxed yellow paper.

"Can you believe it? This is our home! Not a makeshift one-room hut, or a rented room. No more crooked pillars. See those walls over there? They are as straight as can be. This is my home and your home! Let's celebrate!"

Chinjoo barbecued ten pounds of beef ribs for the children. They had not had a celebration since long before the war. Holidays had passed by like any other ordinary days. Birthdays had gone unnoticed.

"Eat to your heart's content!"

That night Chinjoo dreamed of her husband. "I will first build God's house there as Jacob built Bethel. . ." Then she dreamed of the rugged Kim Insoo putting his arms around her waist. She woke with mixed feelings. It had been a long time since she had thought of her husband. Getting by on her own seemed to have become a lifelong business. How he would have loved to conduct Chinjoo's business himself!

With the government's return to the former capital her business flourished. After the rush hour, people poured into the mall jostling through the aisles, some window shopping, but most in a buying mood: anything, from cosmetics to foreign-made lingerie, underwear and socks, even handkerchiefs. Children returned to school. Kwangja, a freshman majoring in English literature at a women's university, would go through Chinjoo's bundle when she came home after closing the store.

"Ma, this looks good! This is just what I want." She would help herself to the things she liked. She spent considerable time at movie houses with her friends.

"You come home right after the movie. A big girl like you should be very careful. Hoodlums and pickpockets are in the street. You hear me?"

Sunhee, the youngest, was attached to her mother and often came directly to the shop after school and stayed until closing time. When the day's work ended at nine o'clock, Chinjoo headed home with a tired body and a sack of money. Sunhee quietly rode at her side, while Chinjoo leaned against the window sill of the ramshackle bus, staring out into the dark, swaying as the bus jolted over the unpaved road to the northern outskirts. Lighted houses clustered at one spot, a few barns and huts slipped by into the night. The rest was an expanse of dark land, including a cemetery.

"Look at that empty land. Wonder who it belongs to."

"Oh, Mom, who cares! I don't think anybody would want to live there. Why are you always thinking about useless land?" Sunhee would respond sullenly. By that time of day, she was hungry and tired.

But Chinjoo, her eyes narrowed, thought aloud,

"Look at that. I bet nobody thinks it's worth anything. You think someone owns it?"

"There you go again, Mom. You asked me that many times before."

"Well, I am just curious. Wonder who it belongs to."

Counting the money at day's end was immensely satisfying to Chinjoo. First she set aside the girls' tuition, then the food money. The remainder was for saving. Even after the currency revaluation, the little safe had become hard to close.

"Why don't you put that in the bank, Ma?" Kwangja suggested. Chinjoo had a better idea. She took time off one afternoon and with Sunhee headed for a small real-estate office.

"What do you want that useless desert for, Lady?" The real-estate man stared at her over his glasses.

"I just want to buy some."

The woman's positive statement sounded absurd. At last he signaled to the messenger boy.

"You know the elderly Koo, don't you? Fetch him."

The boy nodded and ran out. In about ten minutes, he returned accompanied by a ruddy farmer who had obviously been located in a tavern. The smell of sool permeated his soiled beard. Eying the possible buyer he was hopeful and bemused.

"The land up to that tree and barn—is that what you are interested in?" The rumpled farmer outlined the area with a dirty finger.

"One thing, though, sir, tell me about those mounds over there," said Chinjoo pointing at the end of the land.

"Aw, just a bunch of graves made during the war. Some marked with names have relatives. Others are unknown. But don't you worry. They aren't gonna hurt you," guffawed the owner, rubbing his mouth and beard with the palm of his hand.

When Chinjoo counted out the money to the owner of the land, Sunhee was unhappy.

"Mom, what's the use of buying another piece of barren land? Nobody would take it even if it were free. It cost as much as our registra-

222

tion fees for two semesters.''

"But you just look at that!'' Chinjoo cast a proud glance around the land that had just become her property. "Where can you buy such a big chunk of land for such a small amount? Don't worry. Your registration fee is already put aside.''

Sunhee tucked her hand under her mother's arm, casting a reluctant glance at the ugly mounds at the far end. The grim scene reminded her of the time she and her mother had gone on a nightmare search for her father's body.

"Mom, let's go home!''

"You're right. Let's go home, now.''

Seoul, the old capital, was regaining its former appearance and personality. Crowded and clamorous with the din of reconstruction and traffic, new blood coursed through its old veins. Businesses, restaurants, and teahouses boomed. And women lavished money on their clothes. Toward the fall, Chinjoo acquired a fabric store. Customers crammed into the mall and bought fabrics to make Korean as well as Western-styled dresses and suits. While at the store, Chinjoo met many friends from the north—elders, and church members from Pyongyang, even Sariwon brother-in-law's family. Reunions were heartwarming except when she had to explain about her husband. Some already had heard about his death. Without her husband, her relationship with former friends was not quite the same. Chinjoo worked long and hard planning for herself and for the children, and the Sariwon brother-in-law's family was doing the same.

Lively Chinjoo traveled back and forth checking the value of her lands. She was elated to learn the land on the other side of the Han River had tripled in value. She had to restock and expand her inventory, securing fabrics from wholesalers as well as silks from Hong Kong dealers. After dark, she would hurry home, where the children had things to discuss with their mother.

The season changed. Parents had to have their sons' and daughters' new school uniforms made.

"Why, these uniforms will cost me a fortune.'' Then suddenly Chinjoo saw a road opening to another business. "Come here, Sunhee. How many are there in your school?''

"Students? Oh, maybe two thousand including middle school. Why?''

"Just asking.''

Myong-dong streets bustled during the lunch hour and after work. Chinjoo had long eyed an empty lot between two burned buildings. The price was higher than she had expected, but she borrowed the money with her land as security. She contracted for the erection of a modest building and hired two tailors, five seamstresses and two attendants. Then she went to the schools, starting with Sunhee's, and offered school uniforms at a lower price than those produced by the leading tailors. She secured contracts from two schools, and by the time orders started to come in, there were ten tailors, twenty seamstresses upstairs and five attendants downstairs. Office girls and affluent women came to have their suits and dresses made. It was not unusual for Chinjoo to work through mealtime.

"Oh, my legs. They hurt like anything! Sookee, give them a little massage. There! there! Ah, they feel good!" Chinjoo sat on the floor when she came home, her legs outstretched, as Sookee, a newly hired maid and cook, went over the legs with her hands. She had never had a maid, but here in the south every family who could afford to have a maid had one. Besides, she needed someone to take care of the housework. After a hard day, it was satisfying to come home and have the house in order and find her growing children occupying themselves with their studies.

"How's everything with you girls? You need anything? Got enough money? I've been so busy I wouldn't know if one of my daughters was missing. Kwangja!" Chinjoo called turning toward her daughter's room.

"Come here! Let me take a look at you! You need any money?" Kwangja came in with a smile but seemed anxious.

"Yes, Ma, I need some money. But first, Ma, let me massage your legs."

"Sookee already did it."

"This is different. I have a magical hand, Ma." Obviously Kwangja had a favor to ask. Chinjoo enjoyed every minute of her service.

"Push that bundle toward me. I've got something for you. This skirt will sure look nice on you." Chinjoo took out a foreign-made pleated skirt and a pair of white-and-brown saddle shoes.

"They look nice," Kwangja gave a short response but had something else to say. "Ma, I want to enter the Miss Korea contest."

"Miss Korea! Why, isn't that where you go half naked and walk around in front of a million people?"

"Ma, it's not like that. It's a competition and you get lots of good opportunities. It's an honor. Wouldn't you like to be the mother of the most beautiful girl in the whole country?''

"Don't you be silly! I know you are a beautiful child, but not that beautiful.''

"Ma, they don't judge by the face any more. Look, I have a beautifully balanced body. Look, Ma. All my friends are dying to be me! Ma, I've already entered.''

The mother's face froze. Her head jerked and the pair of saddle shoes flew at her daughter.

"You! sit and listen! You are not going to go around showing your naked thighs to a herd of men. They aren't for sale. Is that all you've learned hanging around with those no good friends of yours, huh? You are not going to go into any such thing! You just go right back and cancel it first thing in the morning, you hear?'' Chinjoo grabbed her by the shoulders and shook her violently. "Now, get back to your room and do what you are supposed to, like studying!''

Kwangja didn't dare to respond and went straight back to her room. There was a brief moment of sniffling, then the entire house became hushed.

"Miss Korea!'' Chinjoo muttered shaking with rage.

The maid quietly moved around getting the mattress and coverlet ready for her bed. Problems! They always came when things looked so perfect. Why, in her days, girls had bundled up with layers of clothes, and even a bare ankle seen by a relative had been the cause of much talk. Now, stalking half naked in front of a crowd is an honor? What's this world coming to! What if she runs off, though? Suddenly everything looked so hard for her. She fervently missed someone she could consult and come up with a plausible solution. How she wished Kim Insoo were alive somewhere, even if with another woman.

All the neighborhood seemed to have gone to sleep. Chinjoo quietly opened the door to Kwangja's room. Her daughter was asleep, dried tears on her face. Was she really that beautiful? With her busy life Chinjoo had missed the little girl changing into a woman. The most beautiful woman in Korea? It couldn't be. Perhaps she was a little old fashioned? Perhaps she should have let her enter? No! Chinjoo tucked the blanket around Kwangja, feeling proud and wishing her the best future a decent woman might long for.

* * *

225

Twenty miles north of the 38th parallel, in what was recently a North Korean zone, an R.O.K. mobile army surgical hospital was on line. Lt. Kim Tongja and Captain Cho were enjoying a rare moment of leisure around the campfire with several other officers. Struggling with an onslaught of memories, Tongja fell silent. The military demarcation line was a short distance north. Four years ago, she and her family fled from somewhere up there beyond this familiar terrain. Although the MASH unit was located on the center front, and the refugees had struggled along the highway on the west, the sparse pine and tussock grass triggered scenes of the long, perilous refugee period. That no-man's land where they had been trapped was now North Korean territory. Had they not had the courage to make a run for the boat, they would still be there suffering under the Communist rule. Would their house still be standing? And the Grandma they left behind. And her father was there someplace, his bones buried under an avalanche of clay and dirt.

"Lieutenant Kim, you look pensive."

"Me? Oh, no." Tongja startled, turned to Captain Cho and smiled. He seemed to want to say more but was interrupted by other officers joining the circle. In the afternoon they had gone on a pheasant hunt. Now they watched the pheasants roasting at the campfire. Brightly colored feathers were scattered by a fitful wind. The officers and nurses joked about their marksmanship.

Tongja, her face glowing in the campfire, sat listening to their banter. When she stirred, her lieutenant bars glowed in the firelight. The war was over, but there had been sporadic clashes along the demarcation line. Enough casualties were brought in to keep them busy. It had taken many months for Tongja to adjust to military life. At first, she had to deal with men's advances. Unlike some of the other nurses, she was too shy to joke with men. Massive Communist attacks created massive casualty lists. She often lacked courage to face the physical and mental agony of young men who had narrowly escaped death, and who still might die in hours, or minutes. More than once, she fought against tearing off her insignia and running home. The turning point came when she was assigned to work with the even-tempered Captain Cho. She realized she needed someone like him to deal with the rugged existence. She allowed him to approach her while she cautiously approached him. To her, their relationship was comfortable, if for no other reason than it protected her from the advances of other men. If only she didn't give him too much of her heart! She knew

226

only too bitterly he might not be all she thought he was. There may be another girl or girls in his life. He may also be a married father, although he looked a little too young for that.

"Hey, we need some salt!"

A private went inside the tent and returned with little packages of salt and some tin plates.

"Mmm, nothing can beat the taste of this!" the major said.

Tongja took the piece Captain Cho offered her. As she was struggling with the hot meat, two figures approached through the darkness.

"What's a civilian doing here?" muttered someone.

A few feet away from the campfire, the visitors stopped. One, in uniform, came closer.

"Lieutenant Kim, someone's here to see you."

"Me?" Tongja lifted the tin dish from her lap and rose wondering. Wearing a pair of dark pants and striped shirt, the civilian approached to within a dozen feet of her. Captain Cho eyed him closely.

She came close and stared into his face.

"How are you?" His eyes searched her face.

"It's you!" she whispered. Captain Lee. They took a few steps to be out of earshot of the crowd. "What are you doing here?"

"Is that all you can say? After hitchhiking more than two hundred miles all the way from Pusan? Is that all I hear?" Out of uniform, he seemed older and a bit heavier. Shabby from the long and tiring journey, he was not the compelling figure he once was.

"You quit the navy?"

"Yes. Last summer, right after the armistice. I am preparing for the bar exam. Oh, I am so rusty. I can't seem to concentrate. How about you? How are you doing here?"

"Not too bad. Aren't you—married now and have children?" She asked, considering herself a bit bold, as they walked slowly through the hospital tent area.

"No. She died last summer. She had been ill for a long time. T.B. Nowadays they say they have cures. But I guess the cure came a little too late for her. We had been engaged five years. She had been in and out of the sanitarium."

Tongja listened without emotion. After a brief silence he continued,

"I just wanted to see you. It took a long time to find out where you were. I—hoped that you would come to see me before I left Pusan—"

227

I did! Tongja checked the urge to say so. They walked on in silence. Then she realized they had walked around the whole hospital area. Embers of the campfire glowed dully. Most of the men and nurses had retired to their tents.

"Can I help you with anything, Lieutenant Kim?" Captain Cho asked stepping from the surgical tent.

Tongja thought for a moment.

"Yes. Could you put up my guest in your tent overnight? It's too late for him to go back home."

"Sure!"

The men shook hands. Tongja thanked Captain Cho and watched them disappear inside.

Captain Lee spent the next day at the MASH compound. He tried to find a chance to be alone with Tongja but couldn't. At the end of the day, he left, obviously disappointed. As the jeep with Captain Lee rattled down the dirt road, she was overcome with indecision. Had she done the right thing?

All evening, her mind wandered so erratically that the head nurse found her performance inefficient. Captain Cho was reserved and quiet. Just before bedtime, she stepped out to enjoy the evening air and to think things through. As she rested beside the stream, Captain Cho approached. He squatted next to her, throwing stones into the dark water.

"Can't get to sleep, Captain Cho?" Tongja asked quietly.

"Obviously, I'm not the only one who can't get to sleep," he replied. "Nice chum, that ex-naval officer."

The wind blew a lonely song through the pines. An owl called in the far-away darkness, his voice echoing from the low mountains.

"I—my term of office expires soon," he said, "and I am thinking of going back home to finish my internship, then, probably start a practice. I may develop a pretty good income if people overlook the bad image of an army doctor."

"That would be nice. Anyway the war has ended and there's no reason for you to stay here."

"How about you?"

"Me? Oh, I will just stick around for a while. I don't have anything better to do."

"You don't have your family?"

"I do, but I sort of ran away, and I feel uncomfortable going back

228

without accomplishing anything.''

"You should get married!"

"Oh really?"

"You like him?"

"Who? Oh! I did once," said Tongja softly. "But no longer."

Captain Cho pulled her to her feet, clasped her in his arms, and whispered,

"Then marry me!"

She felt his unshaven chin against her cheek. The buttons on their uniforms pressed hard against her breasts and she felt his rugged warmth. Suddenly she knew she was free, free of the first painful love. Free to trust, and love another man, an army doctor named Cho.

*   *   *

"Kwangja! Are you sure those flowers have been delivered to the wedding hall? Where's my purse? Sunhee, are you ready? Hurry, or we'll be late! Now, how do I look? Am I dressed too colorfully for the mother of the bride?" Chinjoo, dressed in a jade floral ensemble, looked at her reflection in the dresser mirror.

"You look just perfect. Young and beautiful," complimented Kwangja, patting down a strand of her mother's hair.

"That's what I mean. I shouldn't look prettier than Tongja. She is the queen today. Nobody should look prettier than the bride. There! There's the taxi!" Chinjoo picked up her purse, glanced at herself in the mirror one last time and rushed out.

Relatives and friends crowded the tastefully decorated ceremonial hall which was newly opened. Chinjoo peeked into the waiting room where the bride was being tended.

"Is everything all right here?"

"All right, Mother-of-the-Bride! We are taking good care of your daughter, ma'am. Do have a seat out there and catch your breath."

Kwangja's friends were there to help. Chinjoo took a seat in the front of the hall and tried to calm herself. Choi's wife and the Teacher Song couple were there too. Sariwon sister-in-law hurriedly rustled in and settled next to her.

"Oh, how proud would the father of the bride have been, had he been here!" sighed the sister-in-law, giving Chinjoo's hand a loving squeeze.

229

As usual the ceremony was late in starting. Some people were always late for everything. Kwangja had asked the dean of her college to be master of the ceremony for her older sister. He appeared at the podium and the murmur of voices stilled. Chinjoo's heart thumped loudly again. The bride, dressed in a rented lacy Western dress, her head bent modestly behind the misty veil, her white-gloved hand gently resting on the Sariwon uncle's arm, moved slowly from behind in tune with the wedding march. Chinjoo dabbed her handkerchief to her eyes.

Choi's wife took her elbow.

Tongja! A lot of things had happened to that child. The painful memory of her shrapnel wound, a love that had ended with her broken heart. Yet she survived them all, and there she was, more beautiful than ever before. And her father—it should have been Kim Insoo walking proudly down the aisle with her daughter's hand over his arm this wonderful day. Chinjoo sniffled once and turned to the podium. The symbol of love: Captain Cho gave his bride a diamond ring, and she presented him with a gold necktie pin supplied by Chinjoo.

Man and wife!

When Tongja and her fiancé first came into the house after the long separation from her family, Chinjoo was so glad just to have her daughter home, she hadn't given Cho a careful evaluation. Now the groom, reserved and handsome in his rented tuxedo appeared to be a fine young man any mother would be proud to have as a son-in-law. Tongja, her first-born, was now safe in his hands and would be taken care of. As the bride and groom marched down the aisle, a sigh of gratitude escaped Chinjoo's lips.

Then it was off to the groom's home for the traditional ceremony and the reception. Mr. Cho's parents were just as delighted and proud as was Chinjoo. They insisted on observing all the traditions. Having experienced the weddings of their two older sons, the parents had saved all the clothes for the bride and groom. The older daughters-in-law helped dress their new sister-in-law.

Hidden behind the colorful bridal gown, her hair together with a long artificial hair piece, combed smoothly into a chignon, which was pierced with a gold hair-bar, Tongja slowly walked out of the room assisted by a sister-in-law on either side. On her head was a little diadem decorated with beads and golden thread, from which dangled a short tassel covering the red dot in the center of her forehead. The bridegroom waited in the middle of the hall room. He wore a long robe tied at his waist with a golden belt, silk boots and a silk hat. They faced each other. Tongja made a deep curtsy and the groom a deep bow, his forehead and knees touching the floor. Each took a sip from a wine bowl.

The parents-in-law sat proudly behind a table on which were a string of threaded jujubes (Chinese dates) and a roll of dried meat spread with pine-nut powder. They were now ready to receive curtsies from their new daughter-in-law. With her sisters-in-law assisting, Tongja brought her silk-draped hands to her forehead and curtsied. Slowly, cautiously. She was shaky. She had never done this before, except simple curtsies to parents and Grandma on those New Year's days when she was very young. The grown-ups tossed coins to youngsters after the curtsies. She had practiced several times before coming out to the hall room. She made it, but getting up as smoothly and slowly as she had gotten down was a struggle. She hung on to the two sister-in-law.

"Why, that's just like a boy doing a curtsy." A young lady on the groom's side whispered and giggled.

"If it's so easy, why don't you go up there and do it yourself!" Kwangja challenged her.

People were watching, from the courtyard and open-doored rooms.

"I can't see the bride. I can't wait till she faces this way," complained a relative on the groom's side who had missed the ceremony at the wedding hall.

Having received two more curtsies, the father-in-law loosened a handful of jujubes from the string and tossed them into the bride's lap.

"My dear, have lots of sons and daughters, and lead a long happy married life!"

Lifting her right hand, the mother-in-law made a gesture of covering the pine-nut-powdered meat, symbolically covering the daughter-in-law's flaws that might be found during her life in her household. After that, it was a continuous round of curtsies to all the relatives on the groom's side—cousins and the brothers-in-law couples in order of seniority.

People scattered into various rooms where a meal was served. In the hall room, a table was set for the bride and the groom. Finally, Tongja was seated at the table in a rainbow-colored sleeved chogori and a bright red chima. The groom, his light face beaming, sat crosslegged beside his new wife.

"Oh, the bride is a beauty!" relatives exclaimed.

The groom was supposed to feed the bride. He lifted a spoonful of the noodle soup and brought it to Tongja's lips. She was supposed to decline shyly and without a word. Oh, how she wished she could eat all the soup! In the rush and excitement she had hardly eaten anything. Slightly turning her face away she declined the second feeding as well. On the third, she was allowed to take a nibble. A couple of noodle bits went into her mouth and she had a hard time chewing in front of the people watching. Although her eyes were downcast, she knew the table was laden with food. Captain Cho was also hungry, and having finished his ceremonial duty, started to devour his noodle soup. The long noodle is the symbol of long life. Women and children disappeared into other rooms, and Tongja reached her hand under the table and pinched her new husband's knee.

"I want some food," she whispered.

"How?" he whispered back turning to her in surprise.

"Give me that piece of cake," she breathed, with her eyes still downcast. The groom took a piece of the sweet rice cake and passed it to his wife under the table.

"Mother is watching you," warned her husband.

All the doors were left open and from the master room she knew her mother-in-law and other ladies watched her while having their own meal.

"Lift your sleeve in front of me."

The groom lifted his hand so the wide sleeve of his chogori would hide her face. Tongja wolfed down the piece of rice cake. The eldest daughter-in-law of the house, thinking his raised hand was a signal, rushed to him.

"Master, do you need anything?"

"No!"

"I thought—Why, you are blocking her face."

Tongja stopped short. The sister-in-law retreated casting a suspicious glance at Tongja. It was a struggle to finish the tiny piece of cake, chewing it whenever she could. And that was all the food she had on her wedding.

Chinjoo returned home from the wedding hall, exhausted and empty. Tongja had been home barely two months, but her presence was still felt there. Her skirt, blouses and even her army officer's uniform still hung in her room. Chinjoo stood at the door of Tongja's room. She day-dreamed: Tongja would bound out any minute all dressed up for a date. But no. Now she had become someone's wife, whisked away to the groom's house, and Chinjoo wasn't supposed to visit until a proper time had passed. She now belonged to Cho's family and was too far away for her mother even to worry about. Chinjoo sniffled.

"There I go again. Lately I have become silly, have I not, Sunhee? I guess your ma is getting old, shedding tears on every tidbitty thing!" Then she busied herself about the house.

Sunhee, also feeling sad and lonesome, comforted her mother.

"Not at all, Mom. You are so young. In fact at the wedding hall, someone from the groom's party asked if you were the bride's sister!"

"Really?" Chinjoo stopped picking up the things on the floor. "Well, I guess I was sitting in the shade, so they couldn't see my wrinkles."

"Mom, is Oldest Sister coming to visit us?"

"Of course. She is coming home in three days and we will have a homecoming party. So, let's start cleaning this place. Three days will pass in just three winks. Soon it will be your turn to get married and go away."

"Oh, Mom, I am not going to marry anybody. I am going to live right here with you."

"That's what all little girls say, but we will see."

The in-law's, who at first had been reluctant to accept an army nurse into the family, having finally given in to their third son's strong admonitions, made an effort to cover the new daughter-in-law's failure to conform to their family tradition. Table setting was a case in point. It had to be done just so: rice bowl, soup bowl, and silver spoons and chopsticks from left to right of each person. Sauce mix, kimchees and other pickles in the center with other side dishes neatly arranged around them. Each had to be covered with a lid until the appropriate persons were seated at the table and ready to eat. Tongja managed to place the silverware between the two bowls and place the dishes anywhere there was space. Once, she had set the dinner tray-table of the parents-in-law and was about to bring it to their room, when the first sister-in-law hurriedly called her back and rearranged everything.

Tongja complained when she came for a visit.

"Ma, I wish we could have our own home. He doesn't mind the way I do things, but his family does. They have a house set aside for him, but we are supposed to live with the parents-in-law for at least one year. And the second-son couple are still with them. Oh, sometimes I feel that putting on an army uniform and tending wounded soldiers at the front would be much easier for me. I know they talk behind my back.''

"Don't you pay any attention to that. Just do what you have to do the best you can. Try to learn their ways.''

But Chinjoo wanted to make it easier for her daughter if she could. She paid a visit to the in-laws.

"Well, Sir, and Madam, don't you think your son should have his own home? Ah, I understand. But your third son is different. He is a skilled surgeon. He needs to have a practice. If you can't afford to offer anything to start his profession, why, I can provide some land. Times have changed. Young couples today think differently from us old folks. They'll be much better off if we leave them alone. Don't you agree?''

The in-law couple were astonished to have the mother of their daughter-in-law advise them, and especially to have her say "you can't afford to offer. . .'' stung their once-well-to-do, now not-so-well-to-do family pride. The couple exchanged glances, then acquiesced.

"We were already figuring out those things, Madam. I will have men fix the house in Ankuk-dong and ready it for them. About opening his practice, I will talk it over with my son. If he thinks he is ready, we will look for a proper location and a building. Of course, if you would like to contribute to his starting, you are welcome to do so. I am certain, though, he will want to pay you back,'' concluded the father-in-law.

Chinjoo's land across the Han River had gone up ten times in value in four years. The area had become an industrial site. Modern technology and skilled manpower moved into the area. The stream had been diverted and the wetlands were transformed into a dry base on which factories and other firms prospered. Chinjoo leased her land and helped her son-in-law open his office.

Tongja was happy to have her husband settled and starting his profession. A son born to them added to her happiness. She often visited Chinjoo in the tailor shop to take her mother to lunch. It generally ended with Chinjoo treating her.

One day, they had lunch together and walked toward Tongja's home. The city was undergoing dramatic changes. Foreign investment was instrumental in the construction going on everywhere. Restaurants and stores were booming and streets were crowded with people. Ruins had been replaced by multi-story buildings, which housed a variety of department stores. And women were anxious to obtain Western fashions. A trim young woman walked out of the building whose sign read USIS.

"Why, look at her, she is almost as tall as a Western lady," observed Chinjoo.

"Ma, that's Kwangja," Tongja answered.

Hearing her name, the girl turned around. Chinjoo gasped.

"Kwangja! What are you doing here in the middle of the day? Don't you have classes?"

"I came here to look for some books. Remember the graduation drama our English Department is going to present?" Kwangja was holding an armful of books. "Oh, I've got to run. Ma, do you have some money? I might go to see a movie with a friend after the rehearsal. It helps me act."

"You sound as if I own a mint." Chinjoo opened her purse and as usual handed a dozen ten hwan bills to her.

"See you, Ma." Stuffing the money into her purse she walked away contented.

Chinjoo parted with her eldest daughter.

"Go on. Take good care of your baby. Don't just leave him in the hands of your maid all the time. He needs a mother's attention more than anything else. Now, I've got to go to the mall and see how the Chois are doing. Go on, you need to prepare dinner for your husband, don't you? Fix him a good meal. Don't make him think his home is a hotel just to stop by and spend the night."

The land to the north of the city was developed by the government into residential areas to accommodate the ever-increasing population. Chinjoo followed suit and turned her land between the city and the developing zone into a subdivision for housing. She invested in building houses on her land and made more money than she had ever dreamed of.

A muggy day. Chinjoo made the rounds from the construction site where several houses were under way, to the shop in the mall which Chois rented from her, and the tailor shop. She had been tending customers until mid-afternoon. Everything was under control. Kwangja dashed about, taking up oil painting in a private studio at one time, and at another, working on a play production. Sunhee was in her second year of high school and doing superbly. She was the sweetest thing to come home and talk with and to listen to.

"You know what, Mom? I want to go to an engineering college."

"Never heard of such thing. What's a pretty little lady like you have

235

to do with engineering. Leave it to men.''

"Mom, you don't understand. My teacher says we have to study with an industrial future in mind. Now women have to major in engineering and shipbuilding, too. We have too many literature and home-economics majors." Sunhee recited the young teacher's strong opinion that so impressed her.

"Still, home economics is the right thing for you to do. A woman's job is to make a happy home, nothing else."

Their new house was closer to the heart of the city, and was large for her family of four. Kwangja and Sunhee each had her own room and kept herself busy, and the gentle maid was always out working. Chinjoo finished her accounting for the day. She was at leisure. Looking at the clean wall paper and the furniture inlaid with mother-of-pearl, she felt the presence of someone who should have been there to share. How he loved to do the accounting himself! Chinjoo crossed the hall to Sunhee's room. At the end of the room Sunhee bent over her experiment, smelling of chemicals. Unlike other girls, she truly liked science. But a girl should major in something else. Chinjoo tried to talk to her, then decided to leave her alone.

"Whew! It's still hot!" Chinjoo muttered to herself and stepped down into the courtyard.

The long July afternoon finally gave way to dusk. The jingle of silverware washing had long disappeared. Sookee, who had been doing the ironing in the hall room a while ago, retired to her room, too. From the inner city came the roar of automobiles, and whistling of streetcars. Lights burned in the children's rooms. They were all at their work.

Suddenly, the daughters heard a strange sound. They hushed to listen.

"Yaart! Yaart!" came their mother's voice, breathless with effort. At almost the same time, they all opened their doors and burst out into the darkened courtyard.

"Mom, you need any help there?"

"No!" Chinjoo panted.

"Sounds as if you are lifting something heavy."

"I am not lifting anything! I am just exercising."

"What did you say, Ma?"

"Karate! You know, karate? It's good exercise!"

XX. Through the narrow gate

However high a mountain may be,
It still is lower than the sky.
Climb, climb again, and higher, who says
You will not gain the summit?
People complain it is too high,
With no trial, no attempt, no will.

Yang Sa-on [1517-1584]

Fall 1954.

Hyonsup came home after completing his military service and began to study for the college entrance exam. While finishing his final high-school year in pursuit of his diploma, he disciplined himself to weeks of study.

"I need to loosen up my hardened brain," Hyonsup explained. He spent long hours at his best friend's house sharing books and ideas for the preparation.

In the dark corner of the cupboard stood a brass bowl waiting to be exhumed. Jungsoon thought it was now time to empty the treasure.

"Here, buy the books you need."

"But you need it more than I do, Mother."

"That's your money. Remember you gave me your salary for the last three years while you were in the army? I saved it."

"Mother! You kept it all this time? Thank you. I really need books now more than I needed cigarettes then. Honestly, Mother. You should have used it."

Nevertheless, his determination to get a higher education became increasingly shaky. Even if he passed the examination, where could they find the enormous college entrance and tuition fees for him? They simply didn't have that kind of money. Yet it was obvious that without higher education there was no guarantee of a position paying enough to raise his mother above degrading toil.

"Perhaps I should get a job instead," Hyonsup thought uncertainly.

"My dear, you worry about the exam and let me worry about the rest. We will manage. Somehow.''

Having absorbed only the heat from the cooking, the floor stayed lukewarm for a short while and was cold the rest of the night. Midnight. The neighborhood slept. Even Jungsoon, who had been darning the children's clothes, dozed. Only Hyonsup wrapped in layers of quilts, was awake studying. Occasionally, he patted cold water on his eyelids to keep him awake. He worked until his hands became too cold and stiff to turn any more pages of his books.

"Go to bed, dear. Go to bed," murmured Jungsoon, as she awakened and saw the figure hunched over the small desk.

The little window in their room fogged with their breath. It froze.

This February morning was unusually cold. Jungsoon, wrapped to her chin in a scarf, hurried along the deserted street where street lights were still bright. She finally came to the Engineering College of Seoul National University. Her heart pounding, hope swelling inside her, she gazed at the university sign illuminated by the night light. It was an extremely narrow gate that the talented, motivated students from throughout the country were trying to squeeze through. Wall posters put up by students already enrolled at the university encouraged would-be students from their respective high schools. There was one for the students coming from Hyonsup's high school, too. Jungsoon carefully looked about. Unwrapping her bundle, she took out a hefty piece of sweet rice cake she had made early in the morning, and pressed it against the cold iron gate. She pressed it as hard as she could, walked away and came back to make sure it had not fallen off. When she hurried back to fix breakfast for the boys, the morning rush hour had begun.

It was the beginning of the exam week. Each morning Jungsoon cooked hot rice and beef soup for her son. She slipped some money into his pocket.

"Buy yourself a good lunch. But not the hard boiled eggs. They say if you eat hard-boiled eggs you will not pass the exam because the eggs are too slippery. The eggs slip and you fail. But, if you paste a sweet rice cake at the gate, then they say you'll pass because your name will be stuck up on the wall just like the sweet rice cake when they announce the results." Jungsoon smiled hoping inwardly that it would really work.

"Oh, Mother. It's all superstition!"

"Well, no point in doing what's said to be bad."

Until the announcement of the results, the whole family lived with nightmares of failure. After a fitful night, the morning came when they arose early to go to school to find out the results. Rapid footsteps sounded in the courtyard and a voice at the door called,

"You passed! Oh, Hyonsup's mom, he passed! Look here!" It was the landlady who had been interested in Hyonsup's effort.

"Really? Where? Let us see." Hyonsup snatched the newspaper from the landlady. Three sets of Yoon eyes searched the finely printed columns.

"Oh, here! Here's Older Brother's name!" Wonsup shouted peering over his brother's shoulder.

Without a doubt, it was the most uplifting day in the life of the small family. The family feasted on rice, two pounds of beef, and several vegetable dishes.

"You have worked hard, Hyonsup. I am so very proud of you!" Then Jungsoon remembered something. "You know, Hyonsup? It was not a superstition after all. I think the sweet rice cakes worked too," Jungsoon smiled. Hyonsup stopped eating and searched her face.

"You mean, you actually did stick the sweet rice cakes on the gate?"

"Why not?"

"Mother!"

Next day, Jungsoon worried. Where could she get the entrance fee? Tuition at the government-supported university was only one quarter of that of a private university, but the entrance fees plus books and school uniforms were still too high for Jungsoon's income. For Hyonsup, the worst part was over and he browsed through newspapers and magazines.

"Hyonsup, will you go and talk to your father? He might help."

"Father?" He brushed aside his newspaper. "Mother, I am not going to go to him asking for help. I know he wouldn't. Even if he would, I wouldn't accept it. I don't even think of him as my father."

"Hush, Son! That's not the way to talk about your father."

"Mother, why are you still protecting him? He's not worth it. Think of all the things you have gone through. Look what he has done to you. See what he has put us all through."

"That doesn't make any difference. He is still your father."

"Well, I am not going, Mother. I would rather go to someone else and beg."

* * *

Dingy stains had been steamed away. The stone Doric pillars of the Special Commercial Bank were smart in new paint. The Special Commercial bank stood tall, surrounded by other business houses. At the intersection the traffic was heavy, and smartly-clad people crowded the street in the bright afternoon sunlight. Jungsoon hesitated at the gate, gathered her courage and approached the guard's office. A uniformed man glanced at her unconcernedly.

"May I—Could I see Mr. Yoon Daeyoung?"

He looked her over from head to toe.

"I beg your pardon?"

"May I see Mr. Yoon Daeyoung?"

"You mean the president of the bank?"

Jungsoon's eyes grew large for a minute. Her throat was dry.

"He was the chief of the business department when the war broke out."

"Well, he is the president now."

"Oh! Well—may I see him?"

The man's eyes narrowed.

"Who are you? What's your name?"

"Well—I—I am a relative of his."

The man dialed the phone.

"His secretary says he is out to lunch, ma'am."

"I will come back later. Thank you."

Disappointed, Jungsoon turned to go. But she couldn't leave without some results. She had taken an hour off from her job after the hectic lunch time. Jungsoon paced up and down the busy street. Clean-cut executives and junior executives went in and out of the nearby buildings. Affluent women passed with wool coats and expensive handbags. At the entrance of an alley where makeshift markets flourished, shabby men with A-frames on their backs idled, waiting to be called to carry people's bundles. Young unemployed men also wandered through the alley. Jungsoon traversed the street several times. On the third trip, she noticed a woman with a familiar face coming toward her. Jungsoon stopped short and so did the other woman. Each took a few minutes to recognize the other. One had become poorer, the other, richer since their last meeting. Slowly the powdered face above the mink coat became soft. She extended her gloved hand.

"Hyonsup's Mom?"

"It's you! Oh, you look as young as ever." Jungsoon complimented her realizing how shabby she looked in comparison. Chung's wife was wordless.

"How are you doing? And the children?" asked Chung's wife at last.

"Fine. Fine. And you?"

"You know? I saw you working the other day at the Moon restaurant. I thought I was mistaken. But I was right." Compassion showed on her face and Jungsoon felt ashamed. "Before the war, I visited your home at Donam-dong. But there was this woman. And I learned—Oh, how could he do such a thing!"

"It happened a long time ago."

"Well, we've got a lot of things to talk about." Then Chung's wife looked at her gold watch. "Listen. I've got to meet someone in a hurry. Here, here's my address. Come and visit me, will you?" Chung's wife waved good-bye.

Jungsoon returned to the bank. As she stepped down on the driveway leading to the guard's office, a black sedan sounded its horn and approached from behind her. Jungsoon, startled, gave way. The car quietly slid through the gate and stopped at the building's rear entrance, where a crowd of young men waited attentively. One of them opened the car door and as soon as a gentleman emerged the young men accompanied him inside. Jungsoon, beset by conflicting emotions, recognized the father of her children.

"That's him, the president. I guess we can call again now."

It seemed such a long while. At last, the guard put down the receiver.

"The president wishes to see all his relatives at his residence."

Her hope evaporated and her strength drained. Blindly, Jungsoon walked back to the crowded street. Her shoulders sagged. Why such a distance between him and her?

With the address slip in her hand Jungsoon hesitated many times. No. She had suffered a self-imposed guilt for what had once happened to Boonee. Even though all was changed now, the past persisted and somehow she felt responsible for her part in Boonee's life. How could she visit her now and ask for a loan? Jungsoon climbed the hilly alley in the newly developed residential area. She found the address in front of a new house with a dark blue tile roof.

"Do come in, Auntie. I was just thinking about you and was planning to visit you in a day or two.''

Boonee picked up the room while Jungsoon looked at the sleeping child.

"Oh, sweet baby. He looks a lot like you," commented Jungsoon glancing, in turn, at Boonee and then at the baby. Apologetically she handed the fruit sack to Boonee. "Oh, I didn't bring anything except this fruit."

"Auntie, you shouldn't have done this. We can certainly live without the old custom. You can't afford it." Boonee, having put things in order, came and sat facing Jungsoon. "I am glad you came. People usually don't make friends with the likes of me when they know my past."

"Don't say such a thing."

"Well, I try not to, but I can't help it. I still have nightmares about those days. After you left, my whole world became dark. I didn't have a single reason for living. The next day at dawn, I just took off, and walked and walked. I didn't know and I didn't care whether I was heading north or south. I didn't have any place to go, or anybody to help me. Finally I fell at the foot of a mountain, cold and exhausted. I just sat there on the cold dirt, wishing the end would come soon. Just sat there staring at the cold dirt—oh I don't know for how long." Boonee brushed away a tear. A pair of thick gold rings on her finger cut a bright arc through the air as she did so. "Then I felt someone beside me. I was too weak to look up and see who it was. I didn't care if it were a man, soldier, or any other man—let him have me. I didn't care. I couldn't care. He must have called me many times. I heard but didn't move. Finally he lifted me and carried me to his house. He called neighbor women to take care of me. That was Sungjin's daddy. He was on his way from his morning prayer session at the country church. Oh, my horrible past. I don't deserve him. Sometimes I feel like destroying myself, especially when Sungjin's daddy is understanding and generous. Oh—if only we could go back again!" Boonee fought tears again.

"Come, dear. You deserve everything that you have now. You've been a good woman all your life."

"You know how I used to talk about my future in your house? Actually I was looking forward to Grandma's arranging a marriage for me."

"I don't think any of us could have done a better job. You have such a wonderful husband."

"You never know what fate has in store for you. I never dreamed Grandma and Grandpa would die so miserably. Can you imagine? Poor Grandma!"

They were silent as memories swept over them.

The curfew was only an hour away, but she couldn't ask her for help, especially money. It wasn't right.

"I—I have to go now."

Sensitive Boonee knew that something was wrong.

"Auntie, what's the matter? If you need something and I can help, please tell me."

Jungsoon summoned up her courage.

"Can you lend me some money? Hyonsup needs the entrance fee for college."

"How much?"

"5,000 hwan."

Boonee, without further words, got up, opened the dresser drawer, and handed her a bundle of the new money.

"I will pay you five percent a month interest."

"Oh, Auntie, I wish I could just give it to you. But Sungjin's daddy needs it to finance the school. The school he opened in the countryside is growing, and he needs to buy equipments and things. Auntie, pay me back when you can."

"Thank you, Boonee, I will pay you back as soon as possible."

Hyonsup was home, excited.

"Mother, guess what! I scored the highest in the entire college! Boy, is this really true!" Hyonsup closed his eyes not believing it himself.

"Good for you, son! I am so proud. Now, here's your entrance fee. Go and register early."

"No, no, Mother. My entrance fee and the tuition are waived. It's like a scholarship!"

Joy engulfed Jungsoon. She wasn't used to such good news. A cloud lifted from her mind and she gazed at her son with the pride only a mother could know.

"Well! Things do come out all right, don't they?"

Jungsoon immediately returned the money she borrowed from Boonee. Boonee's husband was there, too. Taking the money Boonee said,

"You could have used it for other expenses. Sungjin's daddy says he won't be needing it for a while." Boonee smiled and glanced at the understanding man. A middle school principal in a countryside. A thoughtful young man who had rescued Boonee at the point of no return. Jungsoon bid farewell to Boonee and her soft-spoken husband. To her, he was someone as saintly as Buddha or Confucius.

* * *

New semesters moved in fast. It seemed they just paid the first-semester fee and the second semester's was staring them in the face. Although Hyonsup's tuition was exempt, to send Wonsup to high school was still a struggle. With Wonsup preparing for his college exam, Jungsoon's worries mounted.

"If I do well, I can get a scholarship like Older Brother, but Mother, my registration fee for the last high school semester is way past due. I won't be able to graduate if I don't pay," Wonsup wailed, even though he well knew the situation.

"Don't worry. I will get the money, somehow."

Throughout the night, Jungsoon slept little. She had already borrowed from the Chang couple twice before. Although it was deducted monthly from her pay, asking for a loan for the third time would be a little too much. The only person she could think of was Boonee. She climbed the hill again. Halfway she faltered. "Even a flea has a face," she muttered, wending her way down the hill. She remembered Chung's wife.

As their wealth increased the Chungs had moved several times and were now living in a newly built two-story house. The front door was hidden behind well-tended evergreen shrubs and trees. A gate hung over the paved driveway leading to the front entrance. She carefully pressed the button. A young woman approached asking,

"Who's there?"

"Hyonsup's mother. Tell your auntie I am Hyonsup's mother."

The maid returned, opened the gate and led the way to the front door.

Chung's wife was in the master room playing the kayakum, a musical instrument. The room was expensively decorated in Korean style with the furniture inlaid with mother-of-pearl, the wall and ceiling papered and the floor of shiny ondol. The mistress of the house wore a silk chogori and chima. Her attractive hair style was clearly the work of a beautician.

"Are you going out?"

"No, I always dress up when I play the kayakum just to keep the mood."

"How long have you played the kayakum?" Jungsoon asked and admiringly touched the strings on the wooden board.

"Not long, but I am learning. Well, I have to have something to occupy my time while my husband is away." Chung's wife put aside her instrument and turned to her. "Do you know Hyonsup's father is the president of the bank? Do you ever hear from him?"

"No."

"I see you still cherish that chignon of yours!"

"Well, I don't know any other way," Jungsoon smoothed down her hair, embarrassed.

Chung's wife noticed Jungsoon's hollow cheeks and tired eyes.

"Why, look at you. Whoever made you this way will be punished!" She shook her head in disapproval.

"Oh, I am all right." Ashamed, Jungsoon smiled awkwardly. "I should have changed, but didn't have enough time."

There was a brief moment of silence.

"It's so quiet." Jungsoon's eyes roamed around the room. "The children must have gone to sleep."

"Children?" Chung's wife saddened. "I don't have any children."

"You didn't have any children?"

"No."

Jungsoon was as disappointed as Chung's wife. She knew the younger woman had read Ujeekawa's magazines and planned to make those pretty little dresses for her children.

"It's so unfair," started Chung's wife. "If I were you, my husband would have carried me around on his back, proud—having given him so many sons. I don't even have a daughter. I wanted to adopt one, but he wouldn't allow it. Now he has—another woman—and has his wish granted, two sons."

Behind the finery was a broken heart.

"You were such a happy couple."

"But he comes home regularly, every other day. He invites his friends and has parties in that living room. But when he is gone—They say 'There's nothing like hungry sorrow.' To me, there's nothing like a brokenhearted woman's sorrow." A sigh escaped her lips. "Well, compared with you, let's say—I am a little better off."

With difficulty, Jungsoon mentioned the reason of her visit. Chung's wife gave her the money. Then she watched as Jungsoon stuffed it in her money pouch. She closely examined Jungsoon's chogori collar.

"Oh, look at the way your chogori collar curves. You used to have such a knack in sewing, and you still do." Chung's wife thought for a moment. "Hyonsup's mom, do you think you will have time to sew? I've got a pile of clothes to be washed and remade. I will pay you a little more than I usually do."

"If my sewing suits you. Thank you."

"Come, Hyonsup's mom, follow me." Chung's wife led her into the hall, past the living room decorated in Western style, and to a closet room. She produced an impressive array of clothes: Yangdan, brocade, silk, embroidered, imported, summer, winter, all kinds.

"Those are all to be washed?"

"Yes, they pile up fast. I kept putting off taking them to the seamstress."

Jungsoon took the large bundle and prepared to leave.

"Thank you for everything. I will pay you interest monthly on the money."

"Forget the interest. You can deduct your sewing fee from the loan if you want to."

As the maid latched the gate behind Jungsoon, the kayakum music resumed. Chung's wife poured her grief into the strings.

Redoing Chung's wife's clothes took most of Jungsoon's time after her work at the restaurant. None of the beautiful wardrobe had been worn more than once. Some were too good and new to be torn apart and washed. She did them all carefully, putting her heart and soul into the task. Her fingers ached from pulling the thread and taking the pieces apart. The delicate materials required gentle handling. She washed by hand, starched in the right amount, dried and ironed them, and then sewed them together. Shading her lamp with a dark cloth, she worked until three in the morning trying not to bother her sons sleeping in the other part of the room. Wonsup awakened.

"Mom, are you still sewing?" he asked, rubbing his eyes.

"Oh, I'm almost done. Turn over and go back to sleep."

Days went by. Chung's wife introduced Jungsoon to more customers and it became a routine of endless labor in the evening. If only she had a sewing machine, the job could be done so much easier and faster!

The joy of Wonsup's passing the college entrance exams was short-lived. Soon his education became an additional financial burden.

"Mom, I think I will get a job," Wonsup suggested gloomily. Yet it was evident to him that he couldn't get a steady job anywhere.

"You've got to continue to study."

"What's the use, Mom? Even with a college degree, I won't be able to get a job."

"It seems so now. But you will see, your education will be helpful throughout your life. You don't study just to get a job. It enriches your mind. It gives you confidence."

"What's the use of a rich mind if we're starving!"

"I would rather starve with a rich mind than without it."

"But how can we get the money?"

This time the answer didn't come as fast. Jungsoon sighed.

"Don't worry, we will get the money, somehow."

"How?" Wonsup quizzed sardonically.

Wonsup came home from school with a question.

"Mother, you know what one of my friends said today? 'Hey, Wonsup! Our next door neighbor is the president of the Special Commercial Bank. You have the same family name and you look a lot like him. Are you, by any chance, related?' I just laughed and didn't say anything."

"That's right, son.. Don't say anything that would embarrass your father in his position."

"But is he really the president of the bank?"

"Yes, he is," Jungsoon answered quietly and continued her work.

Next day, Wonsup brought his book-bag home full of money. Jungsoon was frightened.

"Where did you get this?"

Wonsup smiled slyly.

"From Father."

"Father?" Hyonsup glared at his younger brother. "How did you meet him?"

"I went to see him," he whispered, hanging his head.

"What? You went to the bank?"

"Yes."

"Why, you idiot! He is not even our father. He abandoned us, remember?"

"Enough!" Jungsoon warned Hyonsup.

"Then how can I get my college entrance fee? Can you get it for me, huh?" Wonsup challenged his older brother. Jungsoon sympathized with her youngest. She put her hand on his shoulder lovingly.

"That's all right. Next time, dear, just tell me when you want to go. What did he say?"

"He said 'Careful!'—just 'Careful!'"

As the winter advanced, Jungsoon quit the job at the restaurant at the urging of her sons, and made sewing her main business. Chung's wife gave her new fabrics to work on, and Jungsoon acquired other customers including some in her own neighborhood. People appreciated her workmanship. Jungsoon went through her days and nights in a daze, but her hands moved fast and surely as if they were independent of the rest of her body.

With dinner over, Jungsoon resumed her work. Wonsup, who had worked diligently to get a scholarship, was excited. He stole surreptitious glances at his brother. Finally, alone with his mother, he took money from his book-bag and handed it to her.

Jungsoon was aghast.

"You went to your father again!"

"Sh, Mom, I want you to buy a sewing machine."

"Did you tell him that?"

"No, I told him I needed it for my registration. Mom, don't tell Older Brother or I will get into trouble again."

It had been a long time since she had had a sewing machine. Even though it was hand operated, she was thrilled at the speed her work was accomplished. She sewed throughout the night, her eyes growing dim, blinking when she tried to get the thread through the needle. The noise made it hard for Hyonsup to concentrate on his work. Wonsup, not bothered by the sound of the sewing machine, worked and went to bed when it was time, but Hyonsup sometimes put down his pen and paced the courtyard. Although he didn't complain about the noise, Jungsoon felt guilty. Somehow she should get a house with another room.

With the sewing machine, she gradually increased the amount of work. More customers were added, including Boonee. Hyonsup found a teaching job in a night school. Wonsup tutored students privately which helped with his expenses, and studied hard in fear of losing his tuition scholarship.

"Why don't you get some exercise, too. Go out and get some air, play pingpong or something."

"It's all right, Mom. Just wait until I get through college. I will take good care of you and you won't have to work at all. We will get a great big house and have a maid like we used to. And you can just visit relatives and friends and have a good time, like Grandma did."

Jungsoon was overwhelmed at his compassion and understanding. Would such a time ever come? A most remote possibility. Nevertheless, Wonsup's vision was heartwarming and she was deeply proud of him.

Sandwiched between houses in an inexpensive neighborhood, the small two bedroom dwelling was fenced in with rotting pine timbers. But it was a joyous occasion when they moved into this new house.

"I am proud of you all. We've put all our efforts into this. Can you believe this is ours? No more rent."

No rent. That was important. A great improvement after a long, long time, but the house looked so small that the boys were not impressed. It didn't measure up to the houses they had lived in when they were little, and they knew from visiting their friends' homes, what a house was supposed to be like. After overcoming those initial mixed feelings, however, they became spirited and joked as they carried their new desks into a room of their own.

XXI. Blue-eyed teacher

"What was love like?
Was it round? Was it wide?
Was it long? Was it short?
Could you pace it? Could you span it?"
"It was not long enough to tire me,
but it was enough to sever my entrails."

Anonymous

Fall 1958. Seoul.

Having her eldest daughter married with a happy family, her businesses on safe ground, Chinjoo prepared for the approaching winter. The family stuffed a hundred cabbages and secured sacks of rice and the coal to last through winter. Chinjoo was glad to see the preparations complete. However, she worried about Kwangja. Still unmarried at the age of twenty-five, Kwangja was unconcerned about her marital status. She had graduated from college, taken a job as the interpreter in a business firm, and earned enough to satisfy her personal needs. Chinjoo acquired a couple of eligible bachelors' photos through Choi's wife, and showed them to her. Kwangja wasn't shy. She scrutinized them.

"Well, what do you think?"

"What can you tell from pictures, Ma?"

"We can always arrange a date."

"This one looks too babyish."

"But he is twenty-seven, just the right age for you. How about the other one?"

"Looks like a grandpa."

"Well, then you better find someone in between real quick. Otherwise, you will be a grandma yourself before you even get married. You won't be twenty-five forever." Chinjoo examined the pictures and commented, "To me, they look like a pair of fine young men."

A bright afternoon. There were always people in the street. Unlike the morning rush, the flow was sluggish. Some were well-clothed with places to go. Some were poorly clad and had nowhere to go. Nevertheless, in traditional costumes, in suits or dresses, all had a purpose to go after and a reason to be out. On telephone wires a flock of swallows sat like music notes written on staffs. A bus lurched to the curb and the birds scattered. In a Western two-piece suit her tailor insisted on making for her, Chinjoo visited Choi's wife, who still had their business in the mall.

"My, you look as young as one of your daughters," she greeted Chinjoo smiling.

"It must be this suit. One of the tailors insisted, so I thought I would give it a try. I will tell you, though, it's a lot easier for me to walk freely in a chogori and chima. This tight skirt is not for me."

"Sunhee's mom, you haven't got anything to worry about. Your business is better than ours. And we came down here five years before you did. Your children are all grown, healthy and on their own. Now, all you have to do is to take care of yourself." Choi's wife snapped her fingers. "There are a couple of suitors I have in mind."

"Ah, that's exactly why I came by today. We have to do something about Kwangja, otherwise she will be an old maid in no time."

"Not her! I mean you!"

"Me? Why, what a terrible thing to say. Don't even joke like that!" Choi's wife leaned forward and became serious.

"I am not joking. Look, your children are grown and they'll soon be all gone. Even now, do you think they care about their ma? They've all got their own lives. And what do you get? Do you think they will take care of you when you are old and gray? A once-a-month visit would be too frequent for them. You are mourning your husband much too long. Think about other men. Don't you remember the old saying? 'A man buries his wife and on the way home remarries.'?"

"Sunhee's pa just might be alive somewhere in the north." Chinjoo narrowed her eyes. The old wound hurt afresh.

"He is not! You know he is not. Even so you have to live on. Those men who left their families behind in the north have married here. And I am not surprised. There's no way you can find him, not in this life anyway. We live while we have a life to live."

"I've got to go now." Chinjoo got up and waved her hand. "I am not in any hurry, so find someone for Kwangja first, you hear me?"

That night Chinjoo tossed and turned. She had many short

251

nightmares.

"Why, that no good friend of mine! Shouldn't have gone to her in the first place. Marry again at forty-five? How terrible!"

A ray of sun shone on her face and awakened her from a sound sleep around dawn. The maid was doing the dishes in the kitchen. Chinjoo glanced Sunhee combing her hair before the mirror. A freshman in a co-educational university, a science major, Sunhee relaxed after the hard work to get through.

"I'm still tired. I feel like I can sleep for days."

"Mom, I need some money."

"What did you do with the money I gave you yesterday?"

"Mom, that was just enough to buy notebooks. The way prices are going up these days, you wake up in the morning and it's not the same as the day before."

Chinjoo took a little money out of her purse.

"That's all I've got. The way you girls are spending money, you must think it grows on trees."

Sunhee left. Chinjoo moved around slowly, freshened herself and faced the breakfast table the maid had just brought in. Kwangja quietly slid into the room.

"You still here? Aren't you late for your work? Well, if you need money, I just gave the last change to your sister."

"No, Ma, it's not money." Kwangja sat near her mother. She seemed to be gathering up courage to speak. But it didn't take long for her to ask,

"Ma, can I invite an American friend for dinner tonight?"

"An American friend? Why, yes, but I don't know what she would like—and—"

"It's 'he'. He wants to try some of our food. So, don't concern yourself about what he likes," Kwangja explained breathlessly.

"He?"

"Oh, he is very nice. Actually he used to be a teacher. He helped me a lot when I was looking for the materials for the school drama. Okay, Ma?"

"All right," Chinjoo gave a casual answer. She knew there were some Americans from whom a group of Korean students took English conversation lessons. The students invited the teachers to their houses on occasion.

When the tall blue-eyed foreigner in a civilian suit walked into the house, Chinjoo didn't know what to say. She was only used to seeing Americans, some in army uniforms or gray-haired businessmen often puffing a pipe as they walked along the sidewalk and crossed the streets. To greet a young non-military American was quite an experience.

The foreign guest waited at the stone step. He glanced once at Kwangja who was taking off her shoes, then, he, too, removed his. Chinjoo stood watching and said,

"Come in, please!" and showed him in as she would a visiting teacher. The American guest looked at Kwangja and followed her into the master room.

"Do sit down!" Chinjoo politely pushed a cushion mat toward him.

"My mother!" Kwangja said to him.

"How do you do? Thank you, Mrs. Kim." He eased himself crosslegged onto the mat.

"Ma, this is Mr. Hanson. Mr. Steve Hanson."

Except for his extremely pale face and hairy hands, the dark-haired young man in a navy blue suit didn't give her too strange an impression.

"You feel at home, Mr. Hanson. Kwangja, ask your teacher to have some more of this meat. I heard they like meat a lot. Here, would you like to try this vegetable dish? No, no. That's kimchee, too hot. Kwangja, I think he might like this. Push the dish closer to him." Chinjoo was so concerned about making the foreign guest feel at home, she paid little heed to her daughter's relationship with him.

"This is just fine! Thank you!" The American guest didn't take his eyes off Kwangja, who translated her mother's words. The couple appeared to be in love in spite of Kwangja's pretended indifference. Sunhee and the maid quietly giggled at each other.

"Why, these naughty girls, what's so funny?" chided Chinjoo. "Sookee! bring some soojungkwa in!" Chinjoo wanted to see the dessert properly served. "This girl is slow. I will go get it."

Chinjoo went down the stone step, putting on her rubber shoes. She noticed the size of the guest's shoes placed next to Kwangja's high-heeled ones, which were considered big for a girl. His looked rowboats.

It was time for the guest to leave. Kwangja wanted to see him off and stepped outside with him. Chinjoo began to fret. She seemed to be taking a great deal of time just to say good-bye. When she finally returned, Chinjoo offered advice.

"Don't go around the neighborhood with a foreign man like that.

They will talk. They will think you are some kind of—"

"Ma, I go to movies with him all the time. I don't care what people say."

"I wouldn't be so sure about that! Learning English from him is one thing, and going around with him like that is another."

Kwangja turned silent, deciding enough was enough for the time being. But the next day after coming home from a date with Steve, she announced,

"I am going to marry the American."

Chinjoo was overcome. What had gone wrong? Her daughter marrying a foreigner! No!

"Let me sit down." Chinjoo felt dizzy. Sunhee and the maid were frightened and helped her to the mat. Chinjoo peered at Kwangja, who was silent like a defendant waiting for the final sentence. Chinjoo mused: Tongja had done as she pleased. Nothing she could do would prevent it if this child's mind had already been made up. She remembered Kwangja when she had wanted to enter the beauty contest, and her feelings afterwards.

"Is he a bachelor?"

"Of course, Ma. He is only twenty-five, the same as I am."

"He looks more like forty-five to me."

"Ma, they are tall and mature early. That's why."

"Does he have his parents' permission?"

"Ma, he needs only their blessing. He makes his own decisions. He said he would write and let them know. In fact he has already written about me several times in his letters home. Ma, I do really like him and he likes me. He says he—Ma, if we cannot marry, then my memory of him would last so long it would be impossible for me to marry another man anyway. I might not get over it at all." Tears ran down her cheeks.

There was a silent moment. Chinjoo was again reminded of the beauty contest.

"Go to bed," said the mother softly. "We will think it over another day."

In the clean, efficiently designed building, students mixed with other Seoul residents moving in and out, some with arms full of books. Others used the reading room. The American flag stood in the vestibule. Chinjoo paced up and down the clean tile, then spoke to the man at the desk. They exchanged a few words, Chinjoo showing him her address book. He went inside and Chinjoo retired to a corner waiting. He came back with the address book. Chinjoo thanked him and offered him some money which he pushed back to her. She thanked him again and rushed to her tailor shop.

Throughout the day, she searched the faces of her customers. Finally a college student arrived to have his new uniform made. Chinjoo nervously called him to her.

"Do you speak English?"

"A little, ma'am," the young man answered, wondering.

"Now, here it is. Can you talk to an American on the phone?"

"Not really, ma'am. But I can try."

Chinjoo picked up the phone and asked the long distance operator to get the number she had obtained from the United States Information Service. Chinjoo put down the receiver and waited.

"If the call goes through, I will make your uniform at half price. I want to find out if this man has a wife in his country. How do you say if you want to talk to Hanson's wife?"

"Uh—'I would like to talk to Mrs. Hanson, please.'"

"Very good, very good."

When the phone rang, Chinjoo handed it to him. The young man cautiously asked,

"I would like to speak to Mrs. Hanson, please!"

"This is she speaking."

"I beg your pardon?"

"This is she speaking. I am Mrs. Hanson."

The young man froze.

"What do I do, Auntie? She is there. Mr. Hanson's wife!"

Chinjoo's face twisted with anger.

"Why, that—Tell her her husband is fine here. Tell her he is involved with another woman here."

The young man took a moment, then said,

"Your husband is doing very good here in Korea. Oh, your husband is there with you?—Funny—he is right here too. Oh, your son! That's right—Steve Hanson. That's him. Excuse me. Oh, Auntie. That's his mother."

"All right, tell her you would like to speak to Steve's wife."

The young man returned to the phone.

"No? No wife? Auntie, he is not married, unless he was married last week."

"Last week?" Chinjoo's eyes questioned for a moment, then her tightened muscles relaxed into a smile. "No, he didn't get married last week. Tell her her son is doing fine."

"No, he didn't get married last week!" said the student to the puzzled lady on the phone. Then the young man glanced at Chinjoo helplessly. "What do I do? She asks many questions, but I don't know what to say. I don't understand what she is saying."

"Tell her her son is—Ask her what she thinks of—Here, let me talk— Oh, tell her—good-bye."

"Hello, hello—"

"Good-bye." The young man put down the receiver in a panic, "Hello" still echoing in the receiver.

"Do you still think you want to marry him?" Chinjoo searched Kwangja's face to make sure. If there were a hint of hesitation, then it might be easy to dissuade her.

"Ma, this is not yesterday's, a week ago's, nor even a month ago's business. I have thought about it for such a long time. And he, too. I've asked him many times the same question that you asked me now. I even asked him to go home to the states and think about it. He went home last summer, and came back with the same answer. Ma, I am sorry to have to be this way, but—" Kwangja was becoming emotional.

Oh, Yobo, where are you when I need you most? You ought to be here! Chinjoo cried in her heart. Finally after a long pause Chinjoo sighed softly,

"Do you think he will like a gold necktie pin for an engagement present?"

"Huh? Oh! Yes—yes—I am sure he will!" Kwangja wiped the tears from her cheeks. She was overwhelmed with surprise and happiness. She hugged her mother.

The hired sedan decorated with colorful streamers was waiting. Covered with confetti, the groom walked toward Chinjoo and gave her a kiss on the cheek. A strange custom. Nonetheless she felt a strange warmth. Their baggage loaded in the trunk, the newly-wed couple got into the car, waved to her, and the vehicle slowly moved away from the crowd.

They were spending their honeymoon in Onyang Hot Springs. Chinjoo felt warm and satisfied. On the other hand she felt that a tall Yankee had walked off with her daughter.

Kwangja! She had been pretty and happy all day long. Strange though, that Kwangja, even when she was little, in the confused period after the liberation, had observed a Russian officer, saying "He looks handsome!" Perhaps she was destined to marry a foreigner. One misgiving lingered. She hated to think that Kwangja and Steve would be stared at when they walked in the street. Perhaps she should have said "no" that one morning and "yes" to the beauty contest.

"Mom, let's go home!" Sunhee tucked her hand under her mother's arm, and so did her oldest daughter, Tongja, on the other side. Chinjoo slowly walked away with her daughters.

"He is a fine young man, isn't he? He will take good care of her, won't he?"

"Oh, Ma, sure he will."

"Deep down in our hearts, we human beings are all the same. Don't you think so, too?"

"Of course, Ma."

"If only people could see that!"

XXII. The next generation

Even a foolish fellow can know and act.
Is it not easy, learning the Way?
Even a sage cannot know all and act.
Is it not difficult, learning the Way?
While I study and work, easy or difficult,
I do not see old age creeping upon me.
                                    Yi Hwang [1501-1571]

Spring 1959. Seoul.

Getting off the bus, Hyonsup walked rapidly along the empty street
and ran into the red brick building. The mid-term exam of the required
freshman course which he had put off was only a week away. He had
missed the last several classes. It had been a hectic time of year and would
be so for a few more weeks: the school, a thesis, lab experiments, teaching
at night school, tutoring a high-school student, plus comprehensive study
for the competitive tests for the positions open in an industrial firm. After
the night school teaching job and working on the thesis, he had overslept.
One more week like that and he wouldn't be able to finish the course and
graduate in the spring.

As he feared, he was late. Class was under way when he opened the
door and tiptoed into the room finding a vacant desk. He stole a glance
at the textbook of the student in front of him to determine how far the
recitation had progressed. He peered over the girl's shoulder, but couldn't
get the page number.

"May I—Where are we?" he whispered.

The girl didn't turn or answer but quickly showed him the page, and
her undivided attention went back to the professor. She was one of the
few female students in the whole school. Probably one of those proud
ones with brains and no looks. But it was none of his concern.

At last the class in Korean history was over and the professor
announced what the exam would cover.

"Don't think just the orthodox school will be counted. I will test your ability to develop the circumstances of those periods using various chronicles, including the stories I have told you. So those of you who have missed classes and who think they finished our history in high school, don't count on your luck."

What chronicles? Students were leaving. Hyonsup was disturbed. Before the girl finished packing her things, he mustered up courage.

"Excuse me, but may I borrow your notes?" His eyes took in the girl from head to toe. Wow! a far cry from what he had envisioned. Brains and looks! But she was awfully young. He asked again,

"May I?"

She hesitated, but then felt sympathy toward the man who appeared old for a freshman.

"If it's for a few hours."

"It won't take that long. I will just look through them until the next period."

"I hope you can read my handwriting," the girl said affably, and went out into the hall.

Hyonsup quickly skimmed through the notes. The legible handwriting resembled the papers in a register's office: Three Kingdoms, United Silla, Period of Koryo, Yi dynasty. Admiral Yi Soon-Shin and his world's first ironclad warships. The Hermit Kingdom and the Western influence. All familiar themes he had learned by heart during the college exam preparation periods.

Hyonsup rushed out into the hall, found the girl and returned the notebook.

"Thank you very much."

"You are welcome." She carefully tucked the notebook in her school bag and walked down the hall. Hyonsup enjoyed the way she walked.

The day was rapidly drawing to a close. Streetcars, buses, taxies, sedans, and people flooded the streets and fought to get ahead of one another. Blushing coldly, the sun hung behind the snow-dotted western hills. Windows of tall buildings reflected its weak, pink shine. Hyonsup alighted from the crowded bus and walked rapidly along the busy street. Occasionally, he touched his hair and smoothed down a wayward cowlick. He had only an hour before night school, and after that, he had to do the final editing and copying of the thesis.

"Hey, Yoon, where are you rushing to?" It was his classmate, Chun.

"Have you had your graduation picture taken yet?"

"That's where I'm heading. I have put it off for so long. This is the last day, I believe?"

"It is, but don't worry. I've asked my kid sister to wait in line for me."

The photo studio wasn't as crowded as he and Chun had feared. Two girls waited inside. Hyonsup recognized one of them as the girl in the history class whose notes he had borrowed. Hyonsup nodded to her. She smiled.

"What took you so long?" Chun's sister asked her brother.

"What's the difference? There's hardly anyone here."

"I've written in your name and they called your name many times. I was so embarrassed," the sister complained and turned to her friend for help. "Isn't that so, Sunhee?"

"That's right! There were many more people then," Sunhee agreed.

Chun and Hyonsup had their pictures taken and returned to the waiting room. Chun said with surprise,

"You still here?"

"What do you mean? You said you would treat us if we reserved a seat for you here."

"But you hardly did anything!"

"We did! There were long lines!" Even Sunhee joined in the chorus.

"All right, tea. Yoon, how about joining us?"

Hyonsup glanced at his watch. There was a bit of time to spare.

"All right."

It was a short walk to a teahouse. The four young people found a quiet table walled off by tropical plants, near the aquarium.

"Tea, that's all? You promised to treat us to a nice dinner," the sister wailed.

"Ha! listen to that!" Chun muttered turning to Hyonsup. "This is a good lesson to learn. Never promise your kid sister anything. What do you say, Yoon? Join us?"

"No, really. I have to go. I have to proofread and copy my thesis right after night school. And there are many other things I've put off."

"That reminds me. I've got to work on that, too. Hey, kids. I'm busy this evening. I will owe you a dinner." He stubbed off his cigarette in the ashtray. Then he had an idea. "Listen! You want to go to a movie? There's a good movie in town, what's it called—"

"'For Whom The Bell Tolls'?"

"Yeah, something like that. You want to go?"

"Yes!" The sister was delighted at her brother's unexpected generosity. The ticket price for this noted film was much higher than usual, it being a longer film. But the brother had his own plan.

"Now, since those tickets are expensive, you have to earn them."

"How?"

"Copy my thesis."

The sister exchanged glances with her friend.

"All right! But you have to pay me in advance. Now. We want to go and see the movie this evening."

The brother fished in his pocket and handed over several 100 hwan bills.

"That's enough for two of you, right? Now, Sunhee, you have to copy this gentleman's thesis. You want to do it?"

Sunhee thought a moment, eyeing Hyonsup as if expecting his permission.

Chun turned to Hyonsup "What do you say?"

"That seems to be a good idea!" Grinning, Hyonsup opened his briefcase and pulled out a notebook, and pushed it toward the girl. Sunhee, picking it up, examined it, wondering if she could carry out the mission.

"Brother, this money doesn't include the price of the paper to copy it on," the sister said.

Hyonsup reached in his pocket and took out some money.

"Ah, never mind, Yoon. Here—here's the money for the paper."

The sister, having gotten what she wanted, signaled Sunhee, who carefully stuffed the notebook into her book-bag. The girls left, giggling.

"Whew, that spoiled sister of mine! You got one?"

"No."

"Good for you! Now I feel like I've got two. Cute, though. From the north. She's in the pulp-and-paper department. Pulp and paper—can you imagine that! I've tried to talk her out of it. 'What's a pretty one like you doing in pulp! How about home economics, music, nursing—anything but pulp and paper.' But she enrolled in that discipline anyway. In a couple of years probably she will be hunting for a husband rather than pursuing pulp and paper." Chun finally stopped talking.

"How did she get into the college?" Hyonsup asked.

"Well, there's no law against females entering. It has been always boys who applied and they naturally assumed everyone who's coming would be a boy. Anyway it had been a point of lengthy discussion in the admissions office, but they decided to let her take the exam as long as she was competent. I guess they just decided to let her in to see if she could do the work. Well, they must've liked her looks, too, who knows!" chuckled Chun.

*　*　*

"Mother, see this newspaper? Father has become the minister of finance." Wonsup pointed at an item in the morning newspaper.

"Let me see." Hyonsup snatched the newspaper from his youngest brother. In a minute he put it down, disgusted. "Well, one thing I'm sure of, it doesn't have anything to do with us!"

Jungsoon took the newspaper and scanned the story and the photograph. Evidently he had reached the goal he had set many years ago. In her heart she wished him success. If only he would do something for his children! But it didn't matter now. She was capable of supporting the children by herself. And the worst seemed over. Hyonsup was graduating. He had taken tests for a respected company in industry and was awaiting the result. Wonsup was going on his junior year, and if Hyonsup got the job he would take care of Wonsup's registration fees. Hyonsup seemed confident and happy, relaxing from the long, hard work.

An early March wind blew against her face and up her sleeves making her shiver. Jungsoon sat in the midst of Hyonsup's friends and other students, her back slightly bent, her pale face haggard and drawn. She had come to Hyonsup's graduation with Wonsup. When her son's name was called, he walked up the aisle in his academic regalia to the platform to receive his diploma. His mother's eyes followed him, dimmed by tears. After all those painstaking long years, he had finally made it. She dabbed her cheeks with her handkerchief. An achievement worth all her endless days and nights of debilitating toil. That moment seemed worth her whole life and more.

The ceremony was over.

"Now, Hyonsup's mother, won't you look here for a moment and smile, please?" Hyonsup's friend was taking pictures. Jungsoon tried to smile, ending up with quivering lips.

At a far end of the university grounds hidden behind many other groups taking photographs, Hyonsup saw a young lady.

"Excuse me for a moment!" Hyonsup was surprised to see her there and went to greet her.

"Hello, how are you?"

"Fine. Congratulations!" Sunhee smiled. "My friend's brother, Mr. Chun, is graduating, too, so I came," she said as if to assure Hyonsup she hadn't come for his graduation.

"I see." A wave of disappointment crossed his face. After all, she had simply allowed him to borrow her notes, had a brief cup of tea with him, and copied his thesis. It would have been presumptuous to expect her to be there because of him.

"Did you like my handwriting?" Sunhee asked.

"Ah, yes. The professor must have liked it, too. I wouldn't be here, otherwise."

Sunhee's smile displayed dimples in her cheeks. A moment of silence. Then she turned.

"Oh, I have to go now. Good-bye, Mr. Yoon."

"Good-bye." His thoughts following her, he walked back to where his mother was waiting.

A modest graduation party was under way at a Chinese restaurant.

"Ma'am, you must be proud of him." Hyonsup's friends, mostly high-school chums, complimented the middle-aged lady.

"Oh, he is most fortunate to have good friends like you," Jungsoon replied. This was one of the rare moments of satisfaction in her life. Seeing her other son in college uniform, Jungsoon gave a sigh of relief. Her long toil to get them to their academic goals was half over.

The party ended. Coming home with two grown sons, she felt proud. Hyonsup helped his mother cross the street.

"Don't treat me like an old lady," laughed Jungsoon. Her jaw muscles felt strange. She wasn't used to laughs. Hyonsup looked at her in the dark rayon turumagi with a scarf over the sagging shoulders. He felt great sympathy and appreciation for his mother.

"Mother, guess what. I've got a job!"

"You do?" Jungsoon almost choked over the unbelievable news.

"Yes, Mother. I am one of the five they selected."

"Oh, I am so proud of you!"

"Now, Mother, you don't have to work so hard. Quit sewing to-morrow!" Hyonsup couldn't get over the good fortune. He had taken

263

the tests but to be one out of fifty had seemed such an improbability. Now he felt as if it were the beginning of something big. He would make it somehow. He would make that wonderful old lady look like a queen, someday, somehow!

* * *

"Mother, I told you to quit doing that!"

"I am not working hard. I don't have much to do the whole day. Don't worry. If it's too much for me, I will quit."

Still bending over her sewing machine, Jungsoon went through the separated pieces. Hyonsup had worked almost a year, but there wasn't any miraculous change in their finances. He should get married and have his own family. He never wanted to discuss it saying it was too early for him to consider it. But Jungsoon worried. She went to Chung's wife with a couple of photographs of Hyonsup. Chung's wife said she knew quite a few people who were looking for a groom. They said the brides' families asked too much these days: What school had he gone to? Does he have a good job? Is he from a well-to-do family? Does he have to live with his parents? With the first two questions there could be no problem, but the latter two would. The small house of the groom would go against him. She should make extra money to improve the house. Or perhaps change it into a three-bedroom house. It should have at least three: one for the newly-wed couple, one for Wonsup and one for her. Jungsoon found many reasons to work.

* * *

At Chinjoo's prosperous residence, Chinjoo was absorbed in going through young men's pictures.

"This one looks like a sissy." Chinjoo put one photo down and looked at another. "This one has too narrow a forehead. A sign of a small mind." She put it down and looked at still another.

Having married Kwangja off, she had only one more daughter to worry about. Two girls had chosen their spouses themselves and gone. Now, for the last time, she would look for a young man in the traditional Korean manner. This time for Sunhee. She would select the best one for her. Sunhee was only a sophomore, but it was never too early to start. She would be a junior in a month. They would be engaged, and, as soon as she graduated from college, she would be married.

Chinjoo stopped, went back to the one she had just put down.

"Come here, Sunhee. Take a look at this one. I got this one from a nice customer of mine."

"Oh, Mom, I have to study."

"Come here. We should get started soon. You aren't going to stay twenty-one forever. Pretty soon twenty-two and twenty-three, and a woman over twenty-three is over the hill, you hear me? Come take a quick look. It won't hurt just to take a look, you know."

Sunhee came to her mother, took the picture, stared at it, and put it down on her lap, obviously shaken.

"What's the matter? You don't like him? Why, to me he looks young and dignified."

Sunhee, to make sure, picked up the photograph and studied it.

"Oh, you like him? That's his graduation photo. He has a job now in that—what's the name of it—I forgot, a leading industrial firm. Anyway. Why don't we arrange a date? How about tomorrow? You know—'Strike while the iron is hot.'? Meet me at the tailor shop at five o'clock, right after school tomorrow. I will have Chung's wife make the arrangements."

A tea house of leading quality served as the first meeting place. Hyonsup was chaperoned by Chung's wife, and Sunhee, by her mother. The older women quickly appraised the young people, and made the polite remarks demanded by the occasion.

"His mother was very busy and didn't feel good. So I came. You don't mind, do you?" said Chung's wife, a good customer of Chinjoo's who came regularly to have her Western suits and dresses made.

"No problem at all. I happen to be busy all the time, too. Now, young man, you must be happy working with such a fine company."

"Yes, ma'am. It is an excellent learning experience."

Sunhee stared at her coffee cup as the others talked.

"Now, we ladies have something to talk about in private. So, let's move and leave these young people alone." Chinjoo hustled Chung's wife away.

Hyonsup smiled kindly.

"Mother said it was a young lady whose last name is Kim and would graduate from college soon, but I never dreamed it would be you."

"I didn't know either until I saw your picture," she answered.

"So you did know then whom you were going to meet?"

265

"Mother doesn't know we've already met," she explained. "I didn't tell her."

"What a small world!"

"Disappointed?" Sunhee searched his face, waiting for his reaction. Hyonsup stared at her quietly. A beautiful woman, young, but—"I was expecting somewhat older woman, around my age."

"You think of me as a girl—like my friend's brother does?"

"Well, no."

"How old are you?"

Hyonsup stared at her again, a bit taken aback.

"Didn't your mother tell you?"

"No. Maybe she did and I forgot."

"Twenty-seven. You know, a young man has military duty, and also the war. Upsets one's schedule," he chuckled.

Chinjoo, watching the interplay through the branches of a tropical plant, saw Sunhee follow in Hyonsup's laughter without reservation. O— that girl! Chinjoo wished she could call her aside and give her a tip. A girl was supposed to be shy. She should have told Sunhee that before she came! Tsk, tsk!

Chinjoo turned to Chung's wife apologetically. "She is usually shy."

"Oh, I don't think anything's wrong. They seem to be getting along fine. Today's young people—they just naturally get acquainted. They know how to, better than we think they do. Certainly more naturally than in our day."

"But he will think she is too forward."

"Don't worry. He is an understanding young man."

At last, the chaperons reappeared and took the young people out. Hyonsup followed Sunhee as they walked away with their chaperons.

"How about meeting me at the Dragon tomorrow?" he whispered.

*   *   *

"You seem to be getting along fine with this young man. One thing bothers me though. The age—he is six years older. Do you think this young man just might have married once before?"

"Oh, Mom! A man has to go to the army. It's natural to be that age by the time he settles down with a job."

The mother's eyes twinkled behind a new addition to her life, eyeglasses.

266

"Why, you naughty girl! Siding with him already?" she chided. "You like him, don't you?"

Sunhee nodded as she sat down by Chinjoo, slipping her arms around her mother's waist, blushing.

Sunhee became unusually pretty. And lately she seemed much concerned about how she dressed. She stood in front of the mirror longer, and often asked her mother to have new clothes made.

"Are you going to have a fashion show or something? Where did you hide those skirts and one-piece dresses I had made at my tailor shop last week?" Chinjoo reproved but not unkindly. After all, this was the last daughter and Chinjoo knew she could afford to give her last daughter, Sunhee, what she wanted.

The relationship with Hyonsup was sailing along smoothly with her mother's blessing. Sunhee never had a brother and she almost regarded him with the same respect. She liked to be a little spoiled by him. Sometimes she phoned him at his office in the middle of the morning and asked him to buy her lunch.

"You should be in school," he would chide. "Have you finished all the class periods? Besides, my money is running out."

"Then I will bring my own money. I've got a piggy bank about this big."

"You should be in the classroom."

"I don't have any classes until two o'clock."

"Then study, read books, or prepare for the exam."

"You treat me like a child."

"You are a child."

"All right, I am going. And I will never call you again as long as I live."

"Now, you seem to be coming to your senses. Good-bye."

But, Sunhee, before the week's end, would call him.

Lunch hour. Sunhee and Hyonsup had noodles at a Chinese restaurant. When they came out, the sidewalks were crowded with people watching the waves of students marching in the middle of the street, shouting,

"Down with the dictator! Down with Rhee Syngman!"

Shouting and waving the placards, columns of students strode by. Sunhee had demonstrated the day before. She was afraid and worried about

267

the situation of the past several months. She moved closer to Hyonsup's side.

Soon sirens screamed and armed police trucks rolled through the street. Gunshots. People scrambled into the buildings.

"Let's get in here for a while." Hyonsup shoved Sunhee into his company building. "You stay here. I will go upstairs and find out about the situation."

As the sounds of strife died, people emerged from the building and Hyonsup hurried down the stairs from his department.

"Our company is sending its employees home. You go home quickly before it gets worse."

"But my mother. She must be still in her shop." Sunhee's memory of the road for refuge was still vivid. "I want to go with my mother. Come with me, Mr. Yoon. The shop is just around the corner."

Chinjoo had dismissed her employees. Fitting wooden shutters against the showcase windows, she closed the shop.

"Ah, it's you two! I was worried about you. Students have been killed in front of the government building. The army is taking control of the situation. I am so glad you are here."

"Here, let me help you, ma'am." Hyonsup lifted the wooden door and fitted it into the rail.

"Over there. Thank you. I hope things won't get worse. I think that President Rhee should step down. That's the only way this trouble is going to end, don't you think, Mr. Yoon?" Chinjoo eyed Hyonsup and thought proudly that Sunhee had good taste.

Hyonsup glanced at his watch.

"We've got to go home, ma'am. The curfew starts soon."

"Wouldn't you come with us, Mr. Yoon?"

"Thank you, ma'am, but I have to go and see if my mother is home safe. And my brother too."

"Oh, your mother! Of course. I would love to meet her. Go on home! Let's hurry, Sunhee. Good-bye. Come visit us at home when you can!" Chinjoo grabbed her purse and rushed her daughter out, and, locking the front door, signaled Hyonsup to hurry to his mother.

Revolution against the regime engulfed all of South Korea. The aging, wrinkled gentleman with white hair, once the hope of the country, a respected patriot, a conscientious leader, now branded as a merciless dictator, had stepped down. A key government figure and his family had committed suicide. Streets were littered with crumpled newspapers and leaflets. Trucks roared by, carrying elated students who shouted their victorious hurrahs. Sunhee walked with Hyonsup. She hadn't seen him for a week and missed him deeply.

"Well, what now?" Sunhee asked. She felt sorry for the elderly statesman whose name she identified with freedom and dignity ever since they had crossed the 38th parallel. Somehow "dictator" seemed too strong a description of the aged patriot. "Don't you think he was just uninformed? It's the men that surrounded him who were responsible. Making him believe his running for the fourth term against the constitution would best serve the country. It is still much better than in the north, though."

"It's not enough. Here in the south we are talking about a democratic government. Of course there's no guarantee the next leader will be better. But the idea is to change the government and give the opposition a chance."

Sunhee listened, her mood subdued. She liked to hear him talk, and was proud to be his girl. Cautiously she looked up at him. She wanted to touch him.

"May I place my hand on your arm?"

Hyonsup, his hands in his pockets, was deep in thought of a less-personal nature.

"I don't know. I'm not a political-science major. But power! It must be such an attractive thing that, once a person obtains it, it can never be let go, except by force," he concluded.

Here and there, they saw groups of responsible students sweeping and cleaning away the mess in the streets.

XXIII. Meeting again

The hills have stood from of old;
*   but streams are never ancient waters.*
Day and night they flow on:
*   how can they ever endure?*
Famous men are like the waters:
*   they pass and they cannot return.*
                    Hwang Chini (early 16th century)

Fall 1961. South Korea.

Another major political upheaval, a military junta had rent the nation. There were frequent changes of governing figures. Amidst hopes, promises, and thwarted expectations, two summers had passed. Leaves fell on the streets where so many historical events had taken place.

Only Jungsoon's home remained the same: small, seemingly untouched by the ebb and flow of violent politics. Her sewing machine droned deep into the night. The timbers propping up her house were as slender as her thin wrists. She made regular deliveries to Chung's in the other part of the city.

Chung's wife, attired for a party, touched and examined the finished clothes.

"Well, I hear Mr. Yoon Daeyoung is out of prison. I will say he is the shortest-lived minister I've ever heard of. Do you hear from him at all?"

"No," Jungsoon shook her head. "I am sure he has a lot of other things on his mind." She still felt sympathy for her former husband. All she saw of him were the pictures in the newspapers with the rest of the cabinet members of the toppled government.

"How is Hyonsup doing with the young lady? I didn't expect they'd like each other right away like that. You know what they say: if the marriage for which you did the matchmaking succeeds, you get a bowl of wine, and if it fails you get three slaps across your face. Hurry up with their marriage. Let's see if I can get a bowl of wine. I hope this time my matchmaking succeeds. When are they going to be engaged?"

"Hyonsup seems to like her very much, but he doesn't answer clearly when I ask him about the appropriate date for their engagement ceremony. But I am sure Hyonsup will not earn you a sore face."

Jungsoon carefully wrapped the clothes to be done. The bundle was smaller each time she came.

"I've sent all my yangdan clothes to the dry cleaners. It's amazing. They come out just like new, all cleaned and ironed. It saves taking them apart and sewing them all over again. Of course, I still want you to make the new ones the way you've always done. You should take it easy now, with Hyonsup having a good job. Doesn't he say so, too?"

"He does, all the time. But I don't have much to do. It's just to pass time. That's all."

With the bundle under her arm, Jungsoon bid Chung's wife good-bye.

She got off the streetcar. The night streets were empty except for movie goers pouring from the theatre. A chilly night wind blew through her sleeves and penetrated her bones. She should have worn her turumagi. Most stores were closed. A drunk across the street disappeared unsteadily into an alley. Jungsoon hurried on. A tiny store was still open. Her white thread had run out. Seeing a customer with the storekeeper she felt it safe to enter.

"Do you carry white thread?"

"Yes, ma'am. How many?"

"Two bunches, please."

An elderly gentleman paying for his sack of cookies turned at the sound of her voice. Jungsoon's glance met his, turned away, and then snapped back. Her heart thumped violently. The man looked at her equally surprised.

"Is it—you?"

"How are you?" Jungsoon's voice trembled.

Yoon Daeyoung stepped over, making room for her to pay for her purchase. He went out and waited for her.

"Just bought a sack of cookies. Taisup likes them," he smiled awkwardly as he lifted the sack.

"I am sure he does."

"He is working hard to get into the middle school. He likes to munch cookies while he studies."

"It helps, doesn't it?"

Silently they walked side by side. Daeyoung's face, under the street light, had aged. His hair was turning gray and his once-smooth forehead

271

was wrinkled. His shoulders wrapped in a gray overcoat sagged and the sack of cookies seemed to weigh him down. This was an entirely different man from the powerful figure she had glimpsed in a sedan in front of the bank. No power. No friends. No future. An old tiger with no teeth.

"How are you doing? How's Hyonsup? He must have graduated from college by now."

"Yes, two years ago. He has a job now. Wonsup is senior. After his graduation in the coming spring, he will enter the army to finish his military duty."

"Ah, already? The time seems to have gone so fast."

"I should have let you know."

He didn't answer and walked on.

"I suppose the children hate me."

"Oh, don't say that. I don't think that's true."

They walked on in silence. Jungsoon couldn't believe this was happening.

"I feel sorry about Kangsup. That child. He should have come to me when he was in his right mind. Well, it does no good to talk about those things now." Clearing his throat, Daeyoung continued. "I—uh—I have done a lot of thinking. I wanted to talk to you about—"

Jungsoon was aware they were nearing an alley leading to her home but decided to go on.

"You must have read a lot about me in the newspapers. I haven't much left. I—uh—didn't have as much from the beginning. Some claimed that I had taken bribes and had made a fortune—You know that I am not the type."

"Oh, I do. I know."

"But I have some insurance that I want you to distribute among the children when I am gone."

"Oh, you shouldn't be talking that way. You are still young."

"I am old. Much older than I wish. Well, it will come to everybody sooner or later. Sooner to me." His voice had no spirit and he talked very slowly. "I have a stomach and bowel problem. It's been going on for some time." He paused. "By the way, are you also going this way?" He turned to her.

"Yes, I am," she answered quickly.

"Well, looking back—of course I have done a terrible thing—to you—putting you through all that trouble. I know—you've had a hard time—"

"Oh, no need to talk about those things. It's past."

"But I want you to know that I really didn't mean to—It—it—so happened."

Jungsoon felt colder than ever. She shivered.

"What's the matter?"

"Oh, nothing."

"Of course, Taisup's mom had to go through a lot of things, perhaps different from yours, but a lot of things—She has changed too. She has changed a great deal."

They walked through the cold street. The lights in the houses shone dimly. Warehouses and abandoned buildings loomed dark against the starry sky. He seemed to have an endless story to tell. He didn't seem to be aware to whom he was talking. Jungsoon walked close to him, listening silently. The wind made the trees shudder. Leaves fell on her shoulders.

"And Taisup, he seems to be a bright one, but his mother is spoiling him somewhat. He likes sweet things. Cookies, candies. He always looks for something in my hand when I get home. His teeth are terrible, full of cavities. I guess he will have to have his teeth fixed before he goes to high school. I wish I could be around until he graduates from college. But I don't know."

"You will be, oh, you will be."

"I want to talk to Hyonsup. He is still my son. First son, now that Kangsup's gone. Tell him to take care of Taisup, will you?"

"I will," Jungsoon nodded.

"Now, wait a minute. I am almost home." He paused and turned to her. "You've passed your home?"

"Oh, don't worry, I will go back. It's just around the corner."

"This is Yongsan. Wonsup said you live in Gongduck-dong."

Jungsoon insisted it was all right.

"No, it's not all right. I won't let you walk all the way back alone at this time of night."

He stood at the curb and hailed a taxi cab.

"Gongduck-dong, please!"

She stooped into the cab, while he put some money into the driver's hand. Then he held out the sack of cookies toward her.

"Here, say hello to the children for me."

Jungsoon shoved it back to him.

"No, please! They've all grown up. They don't need them."

The taxi cab left the man standing forlornly at the curb with a sack of cookies.

"Mom, you are late! We thought you got lost or something. What happened?" asked Wonsup. He had just returned from a hike.

Jungsoon stood in the middle of the room unwrapping her scarf. The night's events seemed like a dream, or a nightmare, leaving her confused. Wonsup had already prepared his mother's bed. The floor underneath was lukewarm. Jungsoon sat down, covering her stiffened knees with a quilt.

"Hyonsup! Can you come here?"

Hyonsup appeared with a sleepy look.

"Yes, Mother?"

"Come sit down. I want to talk with you. I've seen your father."

Hyonsup stared at her.

"I met him on the way home. He has grown old and tired. I know how you feel about him. But still there are some things you should understand."

"Oh, Mother. There you go again!"

"Now, you listen, son!" Jungsoon commanded quietly. "He is very tired. Old and lonely. Although you may not believe it, he still holds you in high esteem as his son, now first son. Go see him and talk to him. People have chances only so many times. By the time you feel sorry, he won't be here. There is no need to hate a man when there's nothing left in him to be hated."

Hyonsup sat with his head bent, wondering how a man who had seemed so unforgivable to him could become a pathetic figure.

* * *

Baking sweet potatoes and chestnuts sent their sweet odors into the air. Cabbages and radishes were piled in front of vegetable stores ready for the pickling season.

"It smells good. Makes me hungry."

Sunhee approached the street stall and bought a sack of baked chestnuts. She slipped the chestnut sack into Hyonsup's trench-coat pocket. Peeling the skin off one, she placed half of it in his hand.

"That's for you and this for me. Now, that will keep us warm while

I peel another one. Hot!"

Hyonsup, munching his half, groaned, "Ah—this bag is burning my side!"

"Oh, I am sorry." She slipped her hand in Hyonsup's pocket and retrieved the sack.

They passed dark buildings abandoned for the night, lighted showcase windows, jewelry stores, furniture outlets. Crossing the street, headlights silhouetted the couple. Whenever they passed a dark doorway, she wished he would push her into it and kiss her as men did in those foreign movies. But her man, shackled by centuries-old Confucian ethics, was not the one to attempt it. She couldn't make up her mind whether or not he was handsome. Sometimes he appeared handsome. Other times he was just—average.

From a nearby alley came shouts,

"Haart! Haart!"

"What's that?"

"A taekwondo place."

"What is it, actually?" asked Sunhee. "I've heard a lot about it but—"

"Well, it's a form of martial art. Karate in Japanese, kung fu in Chinese, and taekwondo, etc., in Korean. Each developed a bit differently. It was started in China by a monk a long time ago. You see, there was this temple hidden deep in the heart of a mountain, and many young men with diehard determination to become monks flocked there. Once they arrived in the quiet uninhabited valley and followed the monotonous religious routines day and night, all they seemed to be able to think about was women. So the head of the monastery thought of a device that could divert their desire and energy to something spiritual as well as physical. That was the beginning." Hyonsup concluded with a laugh.

Sunhee was silent. She was reminded of that hot summer evening long ago when her mother had practiced karate.

"I am thirsty. Would you buy me a cup of tea?"

"If you find a place still open."

The small teahouse had only a few customers. With an oval table between them, Hyonsup and Sunhee faced each other.

"Here, have some more." Hyonsup pulled out the considerably reduced sack of chestnuts.

"I'm sick of chestnuts." Sunhee pushed the sack aside.

275

A waitress took their order. She came back with the tea. Sunhee took a sip.

"That makes me feel good."

"Now, young lady, with all your wishes granted, are you satisfied?" Hyonsup grinned at her. It was always refreshing to watch her: beautiful, vivacious, and natural. Would it be fair to ask her to be the wife his mother expected for him? Or even remotely to suggest that to her? Whenever he eyed the carefree college senior, he was afraid she might not be a dutiful daughter-in-law. 'Someday, somehow, I will make my mother appear like a queen.' His love for Sunhee weakened this resolve.

Sunhee became thoughtful. Her cheeks were rosy from the hot tea. She looked at the table, the tea cup and her empty ring finger. It took her a while to speak.

"Listen, Mr. Yoon. We've walked up and down the night streets and gone to movies. That's all we've done the last two years. I think our relationship should be a little more meaningful than that, don't you? You think—I am all right, don't you? Or is your mother still distributing the pictures of you and going through other candidates?"

"I don't have any more pictures."

"Am I—competing with anyone else?"

"That can't be. You know I can't afford two of you."

"Then what is it? I want to know where I stand. I need some definite idea as to our status—like being engaged."

Hyonsup was taken aback.

"You are too young. Your thoughts should be focused on your studies."

"I will be through with school in several months. You still act like an older brother or something. Thanks, but no thanks. I've been treated like a baby by my mother and two sisters all my life. But your treatment is the worst of all. Now, I say this risking my pride. I could attract an army of young men right this minute if I wanted to. But that's not what I'm interested in. My mother keeps asking me when my engagement ceremony will be. Yesterday, she became emotional and yelled, 'If this young man is not interested in you, start looking for another, or else you will be a spinster even before you graduate.' What do you suppose I should tell her?"

Hyonsup was silent, listening to the lecture he knew he deserved but didn't expect from Sunhee. He knew the time would come sooner or later.

But not yet. It would, at the least, put unnecessary financial pressure on him. On the other hand, she was right. There were times at night, lying in his bed staring at the ceiling he pictured her beautiful body next to his. Hyonsup, the Intelligent Harmony, marrying Sunhee, the Enchanting Maiden—Yoon Hyonsup and Kim Sunhee. Kim— "You, Kim of Kimhae?" asked Hyonsup suddenly grinning.

"Yes, why?"

Hyonsup laughed in an attempt to clear the moody air.

"I just remembered something. My grandmother ought to be here. You see, years ago, this one pretty young lady from Kyongsang Province was to be engaged to my uncle. Well, those trivial things they always ask about their family. I remember my grandmother snapping, "Kim of Kimhae? That's not yangban?' "

Sunhee tried to find the meaning behind his lighthearted reminiscence. To her it wasn't funny.

"So, that's what's been bothering you! Why didn't you say so in the first place?" Sunhee reacted unexpectedly. She stood, picked up her purse, and walked out.

He was left alone at the table, wondering.

"Something wrong?" Chinjoo searched her daughter's face when she stormed into her house.

"Oh, men!" She threw her purse on her desk, went to the bathroom, washed, came back and flopped on the cushion mat facing the wall.

Chinjoo was in the master room going over her books. It was quiet, with two of her daughters married and gone. She heard Sunhee storming around in her opposite room. Chinjoo decided to check.

"Are you in bed?"

Sunhee didn't answer. Chinjoo opened the door cautiously and looked over the edge of her glasses.

"Did you see him, today?"

Sunhee abruptly turned to her mother.

"Mom, Kim of Kimhae isn't yangban, is it?'

Chinjoo took off her glasses.

"Of course it's yangban. Don't you know King Kumhai who founded Karak Kingdom? That's the ancestor of your Kim. Haven't you heard about famous generals Kim Yu-shin and Kim Chun-chu? Those are all Kims of Kimhae. Kim Chun-chu became the King Muyol of the United

Silla. They and all other Kims of Kimhae were responsible for the prosperity of those times. Why do you ask?"

"Just curious. Some people don't know." Sunhee shrugged. She was amazed at her learned mother.

"Well, whoever they are, they must have dozed off in history class. Tell them you are the descendant of King Kumhai, that when it comes to nobility there's nothing like Kim of Kimhae!" Chinjoo put on her glasses and returned to her room.

* * *

"How are you, Miss Kim? Can you believe you actually could live the whole week without calling me?" teased Hyonsup as he walked along the wall of Kyongbok Palace with Sunhee. Hyonsup didn't think Sunhee would be upset an entire week. He must have really offended her.

"I would never have come if you hadn't called me first."

It had been a struggle for Sunhee not to call. But she had checked herself whenever she wanted to go to the phone. And finally when the call came for her she quivered hearing his voice again. She missed him so much! And a most unlikely suggestion had come from him,

"How about a walk in an old palace?"

They strolled about the ground of the old palace. Hyonsup had worked overtime in the past and was entitled to a day off. There were few visitors other than a small group of elementary children. They and their teachers peeked into places of interest at a good distance from Sunhee and Hyonsup.

They went past Royal Audience Hall and up to the Throne Hall.

"May I usher my lady to the throne?" Hyonsup watched Sunhee mounting up the stone steps.

"You may!" Sunhee played along. "Here comes the daughter of King Kumhai!"

Surviving many invasions, revolts and wars, the fourteenth century structure still stood, through tireless repairs and repaints. Since the throne was just for looking at, they sat on the stone step side by side overlooking the Royal Audience Hall, where kings of the past dynasty had audiences of their ministers and royal subjects.

"You know? My mother says Kim of Kimhae is—Oh, this whole thing! Don't you think we are acting silly?"

"We? It's you! Nobody cares about such things any more. Things have changed. Money, that's yangban now. The new industrial and business clans are in power. And those systems that led to power and authority in the old days are obsolete. We've had our time through a good part of the Yi dynasty. And you had yours many many centuries before us. Who cares! The only thing we have to do with our ancestors is share the blame that led this country to disaster. We, yangbans, concerned ourselves with factional and personal struggles when there were imminent dangers of invasion from outside. And within, the misery and cries of the poor. We tinkled our silver chopsticks and wasted beef and wine. We were sunk in luxury. And another thing. Anybody who dwells on the past and on how well he had lived, is simply confessing how miserable he is now. I guess I've made this speech in spite of myself because I don't have anything now to offer you.''

Sunhee listened. Her heart softened. She regretted her reaction of the other day.

They walked toward the garden passing a pond of lilies.

"I visited my father yesterday. A strange reunion after almost nine years. I couldn't believe my eyes when I stepped into that small house. His fortune has been reduced to that piece of land and this house. I was moved to see how far a human being can fall in such a short time. And his wife received me as if I were a guest of honor. My father, once a first son of a first son of a respected family—forgive me—who knew only how to be waited on was now out in the courtyard taking down his underwear and socks from the clothesline. I almost turned back thinking I had the wrong address. Well, there he was, surprised to see me, his face brown from his stomach ailment, surprised to know he actually had a son who had finished college and had a place in the society. I tried not to feel sorry for him! I visited him only for my mother's sake, but I am glad I went.''

"Man's life is puzzling, isn't it!" Sunhee commented.

"You know what he said? 'If your mother wishes to be buried in the Yoon graveyard, her place will be next to me.' I mean he said it as if he were doing her a great favor, as if it would make up for all her hardships. Does he think my mother would crawl back to be buried in the same place with him after all these years? I was amazed. And you know what amazed me more? I told my mother what he had said. She listened in tears. I asked her 'You mean you actually want to be buried next to him, Mother?' Then she turned to me as if I were the one who was in the wrong and said 'Why not?'''

"I don't know. We can never understand mothers, can we!"

They crossed the little arched foot-bridge and came to a pavilion. After the elementary children chattered off, the garden of the palace was left to Sunhee and Hyonsup. They stepped down on the turf. Walking to the far end of the pond, they enjoyed the stillness of centuries embracing this ancient place.

"Now, coming back to us. How do you feel about me? Sunhee, do you suppose I would make a good husband?" Slowing down, Hyonsup looked into her face. Sunhee turned away trying to cover her excitement. His calling her by her first name caused a strange tingle throughout her body.

"I am sure you would. I will make you so," Sunhee replied.

"I will try—my best."

Sunhee felt her hand being squeezed hard. It was a solid grip as if signaling a solemn promise.

"May we stop over there at the pavilion, Mr. Yoon?" She had to catch her breath. They went back. Sunhee walked a few steps ahead and stood in front of the little steps. Hyonsup caught up to her, wrapped her in his arms.

"I want you to be my wife!" he whispered.

* * *

"Look at Sunhee!" said Choi's wife. "I still remember when she was still about this high. And now just look at her! A lovely young lady about to get both a college degree and a fine husband. She looks like a young princess who has nothing but a bright life ahead. She should remember, though, how her ma brought up all of her girls.

"Listen, Sunhee's ma. Nothing is worth giving up your own happiness for. You see, you've given up your youth and worked your head off to make your daughters what they are now, and do you think they'd have any appreciation in their hearts? Believe me, you have to think of yourself. Once they are gone, that's that! You think they'll even remember your birthdays? Think it over, Sunhee's ma. You think of the life you will have when the last one is gone!"

Choi's wife had dinner with Chinjoo and, after her wordy speech, left.

"Mom, what is she talking about?"

"Oh, that silly old woman! She is trying to do some matchmaking for me, and make me a laughing stock of the whole neighborhood. See?

280

Even Sookee is laughing."

Sookee, the maid, now nineteen years old, giggled with her hand over her mouth.

"Now, save this salad. I just love it. Eat a lot, Sookee. You need to have strength to do the housekeeping." She piled up the empty dishes on the table for her. After the maid left with the table, Sunhee examined her mother. She still looked attractive for her age. Her hair was combed back nicely. She had put on some weight, but her forehead was unlined.

"Mom," called Sunhee.

"Yes?"

"Why don't you?"

"Do what?"

"Get married."

"You must be out of your mind!"

"Mom, honest! It's not like the old days. There's nothing wrong with a widow getting remarried." Sunhee, who until a few years ago would have rejected any such suggestion, was surprised to find herself reacting differently. Finding her own happiness had made her more considerate of others.

"It would be all over town, even in the newspapers. I wouldn't be able to go out with my head up."

Chinjoo's reaction was a mild one. Lately she had been left alone at supper time a great many days. And there were solitary evenings when Sunhee was dating. She had little to do. Business moved along as usual and the tailor shop was staffed by trusted employees. And even the accounting work had been turned over to a young man who had worked in the tailor shop ever since it had started. Much of the day she spent in the tailor shop servicing the old customers who seemed more satisfied if they dealt directly with the owner. But on evenings, she read newspapers, everything from politics to the advertisements. After that, she usually retired early.

"Oh, Mom, so I can have somebody to give me away at my wedding."

"You really want me to?" Chinjoo asked half jokingly on one of those rare occasions when all her daughters were together.

"'We do! We do!" They chorused their approval.

* * *

Finally they were left alone. Chinjoo pushed the mushroom dish closer

281

to the man the Choi couple had brought along.

"Try some more of this, sir. It's delicious."

The man, his sideburns and some of his front hair gray, had arrived at the restaurant in a rumpled Western suit, his tie askew. He was considerably different from the man Choi's wife had described. He seemed to have a very poor appetite. With his chopstick in each hand, he separated every bean sprout from bean part and ate only the sprout, munching with his front teeth. Every so often he cleared his throat and coughed with a grimace.

"Try some more of this. Why, today it tastes better than usual."

"Ah, leave it there, Lady. I will get it myself when I want to." He took out a pipe smudged with burned ash, filled it with tobacco, took time in tamping it down with his stained thumb, and slowly lit it up. Then he puffed at it several times. "That meat in there is so tough!" he said.

"Then why don't you try this. This sea-cucumber dish is very good. It's soft."

"I don't eat sea-cucumber. Those things are nothing, and cost like anything. I would rather have gone to some other restaurant, but they insisted I come—" He cleared his throat and coughed into his soiled handkerchief.

Chinjoo quit pleading. The man puffed at his pipe again, but had to stop when he started to cough. When it was over, he switched his pipe to his left hand, reached into his pocket with his right and took out the soiled handkerchief again.

"Ah, this pestering phlegm. It's not too bad, but it's a nuisance."

"Have you gone to see a doctor?"

"Ah, it's just a phlegm. I don't think they can do much about it. And doctors charging such fees, it's just plain outrageous." Then the man stopped to clear his throat. Still red from his prolonged coughing he continued. "They say stewed bear's gall is good for this. But I can't afford bear's gall."

His cough had quieted down. He leaned forward putting his arm to her.

"Say, what shall I call you—come closer. There's nothing to be shy about at our age, right? All those formalities. We don't need them. I will just move into your house and we will be a man and a wife in no time. My house—it's messy. My daughter-in-law comes once in a while to clean up, but that's not enough. Ah, it's not easy being a widower, I will tell you." He coughed again, mumbling and wrinkling his forehead. "Now, a woman needs a husband too. You must have had a very hard time, raising children all by yourself. You don't have young children living with you now, do you?"

"I have my youngest daughter who is not yet married."

"Ah, I don't mind her staying with us for a while. I am sure she will soon be married and gone, am I not right?" The man grimaced again, "Now, when shall I move in with you?"

Chinjoo had been staring at the man in disgust. Now she became revolted altogether. She opened her purse and grabbed a handful of money.

"Here! Here's the money to pay for dinner. Take your time. Finish it. You will need to eat a lot of these before you start going after a bear!" Chinjoo got up closing her purse. The man looked up, astonished.

"When shall I see you again!"

"You won't see me again. Consider we've never met!" Chinjoo walked toward the door, stopped, and turned to him. "It's getting pretty bad. You must do something quick about that sickness of yours, otherwise it will get you before your time!" She hurried out of the back room of the Chinese restaurant.

* * *

In the middle of the day, Jungsoon and her sons were called to Yoon Daeyoung's deathbed. The old man did not recognize his sons or his former wife. It was too late. His face a deep brown, he was breathing his last. But his eyes were fixed on her as if he had something to say to her. It could have been 'I am sorry. I didn't mean to put you through all that trouble.' Or, it could have been 'Tell Hyonsup to take care of Taisup, will you?'

The little boy was at his bedside wondering and dejected. When the end finally came, he cried with the rest of the family.

Jungsoon helped the frightened widow arrange the funeral with Hyonsup in charge.

The road to the familiar Yoon graveyard was long and bumpy. In the funeral procession Jungsoon walked beside the present widow. She recognized weathering gravestones: the grandmother-in-law, the grandfather-in-law, the father-in-law and the mother-in-law who had been reintered there. Legally she was not a part of the family now, but her heart had always been with them. She patted the mounds and brushed off the

283

decaying leaves from the mounds.

* * *

Aid had come a little late. Once she had been desperate to get hold of the money for registration fees. But Wonsup had paid his last registration fee in the fall. The money Hyonsup put into her hand after visiting his father's insurance company would have covered more than three semesters' registration. He had divided his inheritance equally among the brothers including Taisup in the other house, disregarding the tradition that the eldest should receive the largest portion. The two brothers had discussed and divided theirs into three equal parts, and had put one into her hand.

"Mother, buy some silks and sew yourself a chima and chogori!"

"Me, too?" Jungsoon's heart was warmed. She held her money and contemplated. Buy silk fabric for herself? She wasn't used to that kind of luxury.

In the evening she called Hyonsup to her room.

"I am not in a hurry to make my clothes. Taisup—Do you think this will help Taisup have his teeth fixed?"

"Mother! This is for you!"

"I know. But Taisup needs it more urgently. Go, find a good dentist, and take Taisup to him, won't you?"

XXIV. Farewell

Spade too is an edged tool;
But in sharpness sickle certainly wins.
Father is father of man;
But in love the mother surely surpasses.
Yes, his indeed cannot be more than hers.

Anonymous

Spring 1962.

Two dragons, their colorful scaly bodies, entwined with bits of fluffy clouds, puffed fire at each other from a brilliant wall hanging. Against an embroidered screen, a rectangular table inlaid with mother-of-pearl waited for the couple to be seated. The reserved banquet hall was elaborately decorated. Sunhee, radiant in a light green silk chogori, its collar and tie imprinted with gold, gathered and tied snugly on her bosom, wore a pleated red silk chima embroidered with a slender peacock design which flowed from under the chogori.

"You look gorgeous!" Her friends and sisters surrounded her touching here, smoothing there, trying to make her look even lovelier.

"Here they come!" someone called excitedly.

Chinjoo, in a costume of rich opalescent yangdan, hurried out of the room to greet the late arrivals. She saw a woman in her late fifties, her hair partly gray and her tall body stooped, enter accompanied by two sons. Hyonsup was dressed in the traditional four piece outfit. He stepped forward with a smile.

"Please, meet my mother. Mother, this is Sunhee's mother."

At Hyonsup's introduction, Chinjoo took Jungsoon's hands in her own.

"Oh, how do you do? Pleased to meet you!"

"How do you do? I am sorry we are late."

"Ah, no need to hurry. We've rented the hall for the rest of the day. Come in." Chinjoo ushered the older lady in.

"Couple to be engaged, please be seated!" announced Teacher Song from Pyongyang, who was performing the ceremony. He was now Elder Song.

As the couple walked to the front and sat rather far apart, everybody clapped.

"Sit closer, still closer!" Hyonsup's friends cried playfully.

"Oh, this is almost like a wedding party," said one of Sunhee's friends.

Elder Song talked about the groom-to-be and the bride-to-be as much as he knew. He called for recognition of parents on both sides.

"Throughout the years of war, through bloodshed, hardships, and crises, these mothers have sacrificed themselves and have brought up their youngsters to the joyous celebration of this day."

Amid the applause and vocal response, Jungsoon bent her head, overcome by joy and sadness. Chinjoo clapped her hands too, saying,

"Oh, those youngsters are the ones who brought this happy day!"

Presents were exchanged. The gold necktie pin was presented to Hyonsup from the bride-to-be's family. Sunhee pinned it on his chogori tie. The groom-to-be's family passed a little box to the presiding Elder who took the ring from the box and gave it to Hyonsup to put on Sunhee's finger. Jungsoon was ashamed because the gold ring was only three dons. It seemed so little compared to the tie pin her son had just received. Brides nowadays expected a diamond ring. How she wished she could present a more precious present to that lovely young lady!

The Elder, his eyes closed, bent his head as he gave his blessing prayer. Finally, he announced with pride,

"I hereby declare that Yoon Hyonsup and Kim Sunhee are engaged to be married!"

The guests applauded. Smiling, the young couple sat quietly.

"Now, you may sit closer and hold hands!"

Hyonsup extended his and Sunhee shyly gave him hers.

The pretty young lady would soon be her son's wife, an addition to her family. Jungsoon lifted the handkerchief to her eyes.

"Come, come, don't cry. This is a happy day!" Chinjoo comforted Jungsoon. Instinctively, Chinjoo knew Jungsoon's life had been more difficult than hers.

Food was served. Hyonsup's friend, a tenor, sang "When the Spring Comes," with piano accompaniment:

When the spring comes,

Azaleas are abloom,

In the mountain and in the field.

Where the azaleas bloom,

Blooms my heart, too.

O, a young maiden

From the village yonder!

When you come to pick flowers,

Pick not only the flowers,

But my heart, too.

Sunhee's high-school friend performed a traditional dance, and the two mothers watched with fascination.

"This is your first son?"

"This is the second. The first one died years ago."

"I am so sorry. Must have been during the war."

"Yes. He was sick for a while."

"So, this will be your first daughter-in-law!"

"Yes, I have one younger son."

"You've done a good job. Sunhee is my last one. Now, she has been a good student and engaged in other activities. She isn't quite familiar with the things that a housewife should know. So when she fails to come up to your expectation, teach her how, and be understanding. Consider her your own daughter, won't you?"

"Oh, I will," smiled Jungsoon. Mother-in-law! She would be a mother-in-law. She couldn't get over the thought of it. Times had changed. Now no young lady would go through what she had. Even if times hadn't changed, she knew she would be a mother-in-law different from the one she had had. Not that the old lady had been bad—but just different.

* * *

It had been an eventful year for Chinjoo. The first birthdays of her grandsons, Sunhee's graduation, and her wedding planned for the fall. At forty-eight, she was as robust as she had been twenty years ago, her business skill more tempered, and her ambition at its highest. Chinjoo needed ready funds. It would be the last wedding for which she was responsible. She would make it so big even a princess would be envious. If lucky, she would be able to buy a house for Sunhee. The house of the in-law-to-be, she had heard, was small. Heavens! Sunhee deserved a lot better than that. Most of her money was tied up in her business. The rest was invested in mortgaged land. But she would take care of those finances very soon. The stock market was on the rise.

Her head spinning with plans, Chinjoo hurried to her tailor shop. She had made investments since the beginning of the year and was proud of her intuition. Her holdings had tripled in three months. It had started with Kim's advice. But borrowing the money from the bank with the land across the Han River bridge as security was her own idea. Five days ago she had bought 10,000 shares of strong companies.

"Lee, give me that pencil!" She picked up the phone and dialed the stock broker. "How much is Dai Security today?"

"Fifteen hwan and twelve chuns, and will go higher in the afternoon."

Fifteen! That meant she had made another 10,000 hwan. It had gone up daily by one hwan. Oh, she should have bought more then.

"Can you buy 10,000 more today?"

"I can't promise you that. It's hard."

"Get hold of as many shares as you can. How about Bank Securities? Yes, yes, Is that right! Buy 4,000 each. Now how about Dong Shipbuilding? You think so? Buy 100,000 hwan. Right!"

"I will try, Auntie. But don't count on it. Everybody seems to have the same idea."

"Do all you can. I will be there in the afternoon with a promissory note. Cash? I've got cash. Don't worry, I am coming to settle that, too, this afternoon."

Chinjoo waited on a few old customers, took inventories, and balanced her checkbook. She stopped by the bank and then rushed to the stock broker. People crowded the narrow streets of Seoul's financial district. Animated as Chinjoo herself, listening and speculating, they craned their necks into the stock exchange for more information. Her broker was at work in his small, messy office, gesturing as usual.

"Now, the transactions you called about this morning—the prices have gone up since then."

"What's going on? How can it go up that much while I went to the bank?"

His face was flushed.

"Don't ask me. This is crazy. This is the craziest thing I've ever seen in my life."

"Sell Hanyang Electric. I've got to make a payment."

"You don't understand. Auntie, why sell? It will double again by the end of the month. You were fortunate just to have gotten hold of that number of shares. Tell you what, Auntie. If you don't have the money, buy only what you can afford, and let me handle the rest. I will do my best in your interest.''

His telephone rang and he answered gesturing with his hand. He put the receiver back and the telephone rang again.

"1,000 Dong Shipbuilding. All right, 1,000. Banks Securities, 5,000." He jotted them down fast, then assuring the other party, he put down the receiver. He got up and felt through his jacket and trouser pockets looking for something. "Now, where was I? No, you still don't understand the situation, Auntie. People out there want to make money, too. The price just keeps on going up as if it has no ceiling. People who bought in January quadrupled their money in March. They put 100,000 hwan yesterday and made 20,000 overnight just sleeping. So why not? But if you don't have the money, buy a little and make a little.''

The telephone kept ringing in the stuffy room. Investors and brokerage men clattered up and down the stairs of the narrow building.

"Who said I don't have money?" Chinjoo stared at the flat nosed broker. "Buy all you can. Yes, I can book it.''

"Auntie, it's close to two million. Can you get that kind of money? The end of the month is just around the corner.''

Yes, two million, now, but it could bring her eight million in another three months. After all, she might easily buy Sunhee a house, a decent one like her customer Chung's. A week ago Lee declared her assets were worth 500 million hwan. But with inflation, everybody's got 500 million. She should make more. Oh, she should have invested in January. It was only a hwan and some chuns back then. She had hesitated even a week ago. This time she wouldn't hesitate. All her life she had worked hard. Everything came with hard toil. Finally luck seemed to be with her. She deserved it. She would see her assets reach a billion. Who knows? She might end up owning that tall department building being constructed in the middle of the block. She had admired it. Envisioning a brilliant future, she rushed to the bank. She didn't feel the early spring wind prickling her cheek.

Chinjoo mortgaged her tailor shop and borrowed a million, but where could she get the other million?

"Lee, how much do we have?"

"200,000. Why? I was about to pay for the materials, ma'am.''

"You've made the collection from E-high, haven't you?"

"Yes, ma'am. I have just finished computing salaries for this month."

"Give it all to me."

Her tailor-shop manager stared at Chinjoo.

"Can you hold off the salaries a couple of weeks? We will have some collections due by then. Tell them they will be paid in exactly fifteen days. You know, I've always been punctual. I've never failed them. Tell them I will pay them their salaries plus ten percent. And about the materials, buy on credit."

Chinjoo hurried to the Cosmos Building Co., which Kim owned. Chinjoo had known the young man from the days in Pusan. He was from the same home town. His name was also Kim, but of different origin. It was his suggestion that gave Chinjoo the courage to come to Seoul before the war had ended. In the beginning years in Seoul, he had operated a store in the same mall as Chinjoo. He had sold it, and now was engaged in the construction business. He was the builder when she developed her land into housing subdivisions. It was also he who had advised her early in the year to buy the very first stocks. He was now married to a young woman and had a son. They called Chinjoo "our baby's grandma" and considered her as a family member.

"Auntie, we were just talking about you. 'Tiger appears at his name mentioned,' still holds." The young man chuckled with his wife, enjoying the child that had come late in his life. "I couldn't get hold of you at the tailor shop. I was going to discuss with you about another business opportunity. Where have you been? Relax. What keeps you so busy lately?"

"Kim, you don't understand what's happening. People should be busy. You should take advantage of the stock market. Now, I've got to have money to buy stocks."

"But, Auntie, in the first place, you don't have the money to play the market."

"That's why I am here. Lend me some money. I will give you interest."

"Why don't you sell some of your stocks. Sell while they are up."

"You don't understand. Sell now? It keeps going up every day. Even this very minute. I don't have time. Let's discuss it later, but I need money now."

"I have only 100,000 and can scrape up another 100 by five o'clock.

That's all the cash I have. I need it returned by the 15th though.''

"The 15th is plenty of time. I am just going to use it for two weeks.''

Chinjoo rushed to Choi's wife, who she knew, had been lending money with high interest.

"Are you sure? You think you are doing the right thing?''

"Sure, I will repay it in a month.''

"You know what they say, if you lend money to a friend, you lose both your money and your friend.'' Choi's wife dubiously searched Chinjoo's flushed face and counted out the money.

Finally she made it. Chinjoo struggled through the crowds to the broker's office. She dumped a certified check together with the cash on the broker's littered desk.

"Here! Two million! What the heck! If you lose money, you lose money!''

The broker was right. She had made the right decision. The steadily rising stocks were sold out. Chinjoo frequented the market daily, staring breathlessly at the figures posted on the paper on the wall in India ink. The prices continued to rise. In the evening, she rushed home excited and exhausted, clutching newspapers.

"Sunhee, look. I've done the right thing. Everyday when I wake up I am 100,000 hwan richer.''

"Mom, you said we became millionaires long ago.''

"Yes, but with the value of a hwan now, soon there will be more millionaires than beggars in the street. I've got to make more.''

"But, Mom, why do you need so much money?''

"You don't know what's going on. Do you think money rolls into your lap just because your ma runs businesses? We've had many celebrations these last three months, and your wedding is just around the corner. And you need to buy a house of your own, too. The way it is now, it will be a long long time before that Yoon of yours can afford a decent house of his own.''

"Oh, don't worry, Mom. I will get a job and we can both pull through on our own.''

"You plan to work? Heavens! No daughter of mine will work to earn money. A woman's place is in the home. No woman in her right mind would want to work outside her home once she gets married unless she becomes a widow like your ma. Now, Yoon is a bright young man, but he needs help in the beginning. I can provide that help.''

"You need not worry about me. Anyway, he is too proud to accept help from anybody."

"Just wait a while. You will see it double, triple, soon, I will make more than I did running ten businesses for ten years."

"Mom, what do you think? About five hundred boxes of cakes would be enough for the guests?"

"Five hundred boxes of cakes! Why, you can't just let them go home with a meager box of cakes. We'll have a big dinner reception at the restaurant. Then we'll have a huge party at home. Your Sariwon aunt will come and help, and also Bokye's mom and Teacher Song's wife. But let's discuss this later. We've got the whole summer ahead. By the time I come home tomorrow, I may have another million."

Two weeks passed. Chinjoo managed to pay the interest on her employees' salaries and put them off for another month. The monthly collection paid the interest on the borrowed money.

"Auntie, you have to do something," her tailor shop manager wailed. "They can't go on without their salary for two months. Now I am more worried about supplies. 'No more credit!' the supliers say. We've got to pay cash for our materials. Otherwise, no materials, and this business will have to be shut down."

"Don't worry, Lee. I will pay them at the end of the month. Give me a little more time. It's not a year or anything, you know."

The interest that had seemed so small at the beginning amassed rapidly. It became increasingly difficult to make the payments.

"What's the outlook?"

"Still hot," the flat nosed broker answered.

"I want to sell."

"Hold on, Auntie. Stretch it some more. Your profit is much higher than the interest you're worrying about. So, hang on."

She had to find money. But where? She took the deed of her house to the bank. It helped her survive another month. The stocks continued upward.

But she would pay the salaries. That was important.

A graduate now, Sunhee, window-shopped along the street with a friend.

"Mom, where are you scurrying off to like that?"

"Uh? Oh, it's you! I am on my way to the bank."

"Again?"

"What do you mean 'again?'? A businesswoman should always work with banks."

"Here, Mom—for you." Sunhee stuck a tiny bunch of cherry blossoms under her nose. "I visited my alma mater this afternoon and one of the teachers gave this to me. Pretty, right?"

"Uh? Oh, yes, yes. Now, I've got to hurry before the bank closes. Go on. Have dinner with Sookee if I am late. Don't wait for me."

The usually civil manager of the bank became a little impatient.

"Ma'am, your loan exceeds the mortgage value. I am sorry but you will have to seek a loan elsewhere."

Chinjoo rushed to the mall and asked Choi's wife.

"Can you lend me some more money? Here, here's the last month's interest."

Choi's wife took the interest but said she had no more money.

"Can you find anybody who would lend me money? Ten percent a month. I am just going to use it for a week."

The moneylender Choi's wife referred her to had just given her last money to someone else.

Chinjoo returned home with tired feet and withered cherry blossoms.

A week passed. Now she couldn't hold any more. She called the broker.

"This time I really have to sell it."

"Auntie, it has come down. I don't know. Yesterday and today too. Wait a few more days. It will go back up again."

Then suddenly it happened.

Stocks plummeted.

"What's the matter? What's happened?"

Waves of people surged into the market, blocking the street.

"It can't be!" Chinjoo struggled into her agent's office beside herself.

The broker was as unkempt as his office, his eyes red from lack of sleep.

"What's the matter? What's happening?"

The man didn't answer. He couldn't.

"What's the matter?" she screamed.

"I don't know. I don't know. It's crazy."

"Don't you dare say that to me again!"

The broker got up.

"No, you aren't going anywhere. Tell me what has really happened."

"Everybody is selling. They just sell. So, Auntie, if you want, sell."

"Sell? At half price? What you talking about?"

He ran out to the stock exchange. Chinjoo followed, demanding an explanation. Cars jammed. People screamed. An ambulance wailed, parting the crowd. A broker had collapsed inside.

Prices nosedived faster than they had gone up.

Total chaos. Huge fortunes of industrialists were wiped out and the meager savings of widows. Chinjoo was destroyed. Rumor spread that a newly formed political party had manipulated the market to raise funds quickly.

The stock exchange shut down.

Chinjoo stood alone in the empty stock exchange—her mind too stunned for anger, her lips too dry to curse, her eyes too empty to cry. She saw Sunhee. As if waking from a dream she stumbled forward.

"Sunhee, dear, I've lost it all—my money, your money. I've lost it all. Can you believe it!" Chinjoo sobbed uncontrollably, her face buried between her fists.

"Come, come, Mom!" Sunhee wrapped her arm around the quaking shoulders.

"I lost the money for your marriage, the money for your house. Even our house. We are beggars now. Can you believe it!" Chinjoo trudged past the people standing in line before the bank. "I don't even have any money to exchange into the new currency."

"Mom. It's only money. Money—comes and goes, you said, remember?"

Chinjoo spent the rest of the summer trying to rescue whatever the frenzy had left behind. She declared bankruptcy. The statement of liquidation included a stupendous sum. She had no idea how much her possessions had totaled.

It was heartbreaking to let the tailor shop go. The loyal young accountant manager, Lee, the hard-working seamstresses, and the faithful old customers that had been coming there for years.

"Oh, what have I done!" She didn't even own a house of her own.

The bank seized the house and the distraint-papers were pasted on her furniture.

"Ma, you can't let it go!"

Tongja met with her sisters. She and her doctor husband put up the two thirds of the money necessary to save the house. Kwangja and Steve contributed what they could, and Sunhee made up the deficit with her savings.

In the master room where Chinjoo had enjoyed her prosperity for the last decade, she sat like an invalid. When the daughters returned the deed of the house to her, and placed it into their mother's hand, Chinjoo smiled bitterly.

"It's your house until I pay you all back." She stared at the familiar paper. "I guess you should know when to quit, uh?"

A sigh, rooted in the unforgotten misery of the road for refuge and the misery of shattered hope, gurgled in her throat and died behind her teeth. Then a light returned to her dead eyes.

"Well, what the heck! We only had a strip of dried fish and one magoja button when we crossed the 38th parallel. Remember?" Chinjoo's laugh bordered on hysteria.

* * *

Fall, they said, was the season of high firmament and fat horses. It was also the season of marriages, and one was to take place in the Yoon household. The bride-to-be's family decided to go ahead as planned.

Lovingly Oh Jungsoon prepared a haam, the chest of presents, to be delivered to the bride's home. Her hair had become gray, her face more lined than the year before. With memory she wrapped the silks: the red silk in the blue paper and the blue silk in red. She tied them together with a tasseled cord and carefully placed it in the lacquered chest. She wanted to do more. During the past weeks she had made a wardrobe of silk ensembles for her daughter-in-law-to-be. She would be a mother-in-law! Her heart swelled with joyful expectation. It would be a thrill to have a young lady in her house. She never had a daughter. She would treat her as she would her own daughter. Jungsoon looked for thread in the chest drawer, and came across the little gem box saved for the bride for the wedding day. A set of gold rings. She hoped the bride would understand. Someday, Hyonsup would be able to afford a diamond ring if that's what his wife wanted. She didn't want her future daughter-in-law to feel behind today's fashion. Now all she had to do was to sew some underchimas and posuns.

Jungsoon cut the material for an underchima and started to pleat by hand. She remembered her childhood, the time of the preparation for her own wedding, the Yoon household in Myongyoon-dong, the time of liberation, and moving into the house in Donam-dong. Funny, they say when one is close to the end of life, one becomes dispirited, depressed, and hazy. That's what she seemed to have become lately. She should be happy and she was happy, yet somehow she was sad. It must be that she would be throwing the jujubes all by herself. The time she got jujubes thrown by the father-in-law seemed only yesterday. Some fell on her lap, a lot scattered on the floor. Looking back, her life had been interwoven with sadness and grief. If she had had a suitor other than Yoon Daeyoung, would she have led a different life? She had seen many happy couples whose marriages had been arranged by the parents. Although they had never seen each other until the day of their wedding, they lived together happily. It must have been her fate. The whole thing was bound to happen to her, anyway. Born into the Oh family in a home of the chestnut rich land, she had married into the Yoon family, suffered the household's decline. Those trains she used to ride to and from her brother's home. And—the man—on that special trip when he offered her a seat in the crowded compartment. She could never fathom how he had obtained her rice sack back and brought it to her. He seemed so gallant. If she had married a man like him—"Oh, what am I thinking!" Jungsoon shook her head to clear her thoughts. In the middle of the pleating she halted. She hadn't felt well all morning. Perhaps it was indigestion. Something seemed to stick in her chest. She paused a while and resumed her pleating.

The two brothers had been talking. Wonsup was home on leave from the army for his brother's wedding. They discussed each other's responsibility for the wedding. Suddenly, a thud sounded in the master room.

"What's that?" They rushed to the room.

"Mother!"

Jungsoon lay among the sewing materials. Hyonsup knelt beside her and examined her eyes.

"Quick! Help put her on my back!"

Hyonsup, carrying his mother, rushed into a taxi and sped to a hospital, accompanied by his brother.

A dignified elderly doctor received them, his thick eyebrows turning gray, his large thoughtful eyes softened with age. Carefully, he examined the patient. The woman had been working too hard and suffered from malnutrition and fatigue. But his professional term for the sickness was cerebral anemia. He and his assistant tried to revive her with oxygen. He fixed his stethoscope and stooped closer to Jungsoon's heart. Then he lifted his head. Gently, he held Jungsoon's rough hand. He could only guess at the tortuous road the woman had walked. He stared down at the lifeless face. She was not the type he would have gone to for pleasure. But he would have cherished and loved her as wife and mother of his children. Somehow he felt he and this gentle soul had met before.

Once, long, long time ago, he had met a lady and a child on a train. He was returning from a visit with his parents in the countryside. A young doctor then, in his second year of practice, he carried the burden of a broken heart. Somehow the lady's quiet manner attracted him. Then standing behind the line in the incoming gate of the Seoul station, he saw her taken away by a Japanese policeman. He went after them and watched at a distance. He was amazed when the pregnancy turned into a sack of rice, and realized the shame she was bearing. He followed her all the way to her home. After he had removed the appendix of the police chief, Tanakawa, he had asked for the sack of rice for his fee.

The aged physician was still a bachelor.

"Your mother—" finally, the doctor looked about and spoke quietly, "she is gone." He lifted his hand and closed her eyelids as if she had been his own.

The woman with graying hair and wrinkled forehead, her knuckles deformed from hard work, lay on the hospital bed, a great deal older than her fifty-two years.

"Mother!" Hyonsup's mind whirled. "Oh, Mother!" The sons wept.

It was a sunny day and the procession moved toward the Yoon family graveyard in Suwon. The sons watched the coffin being lowered into the grave next to the tombstone marked 'Yoon Daeyoung'.

"I will take care of you," Wonsup had always promised. But here he was, home from the army, attending his mother's funeral when he came home for his brother's wedding.

Chinjoo and her three daughters were there too, as she had urged, "I want you all come to the lady's funeral. She doesn't have many relatives."

Late in the afternoon the new mound was finished.

Sunhee quietly placed her hand on Hyonsup's arm.

All other daughters and their husbands were waiting for Chinjoo to speak. She shook herself out of deep reverie. As if for the first time, she saw her youngest daughter standing side by side with a young man. As a sign of mourning, he wore a simple strip of hemp cloth around his arm instead of the traditional hemp cap and robe. They were the dignified descendants of a fine family. Chinjoo walked to the young couple standing side by side, and said to them,

"Well, you are the last ones. Take good care of each other. I wish you two the best of fortune. And I pray your children and your children's children, and their children never see war, misery, and destruction. I will tell you, a happy family is the best thing any human being can wish for." Looking at her other daughters, Chinjoo continued. "I can't tell you how proud I am of all your families. I might not have been the greatest and the wisest mother in the world, but I will tell you this. I've raised you and provided for you to the best of my knowledge and with the best of what I could."

"Oh, Mom, you couldn't have done better. We are all so proud of you!" exclaimed all the daughters, almost in unison, with heartfelt meaning.

Chinjoo waved her hand.

"You were all good girls. I know that too. Now, go on."

"Aren't you coming with us?" asked Sunhee as Chinjoo turned from them.

"I will leave you young people alone."

"Where are you going?"

"Ah, I am going to join the Chois and tour the city a bit. They say they have many historic pavilions and gates here. And then after I marry off Sunhee? Well, then, I will think of something else. Who knows? I might go down as far as Cheju Island. I will buy a big chunk of land there and start making a green pasture out of that barren soil, and build myself a huge ranch. When it becomes a land of beautiful pastures and cattle, won't you all come visit me? You don't believe it, do you? Well, I will think of something. Go on! Enjoy yourselves!"

Her purse tucked under her arm, Chinjoo walked down the hill, the bottom of her turumagi fluttering in the wind.

Somewhere far away in the northern land, Kim Insoo lay under the layers of dirt at the foot of a mountain beyond the demarcation line.

"What therefore God has joined together, let not man put asunder."

The union with Kim Insoo hadn't taken place under that admonition. It was the result of the wishes of the parents and carried out with downcast eyes and curtsies before relatives, but it was meant to hold as good as any union ever joined. Sometimes it seemed so remote, a time obliterated—the years with Kim Insoo—yet, again, it felt like only yesterday or the day before. She remembered him as young and unfaltering. She knew she couldn't quite embrace the God he had worshiped. Still, she remembered, on the road for refuge among the flying shrapnel, she called His name fervently. That was all. But Chinjoo felt her husband's God had been protecting her all those years and had helped her bring up the children. And when she had become so greedy, He punished her and made her lose all her money. Would the country's unification be realized during her lifetime? When the hatred wears away and the two minds become one, would warm blood run through one whole body as before? Would she be able to visit her home then? Wherever Kim Insoo was, she wished there would be at least a mound she could visit, pull out the weeds and say,

"Here are your children, Yobo, all grown and with their own families. I don't know whether they've grown to be what you want them to be. But I've done my best. You know that, don't you?"

From the graveyard the young people watched Chinjoo as she reached the roadside and stooped into one of the waiting taxi cabs.

The sisters left with their husbands. Wonsup moved away with his friends. A little boy walked up to Hyonsup. Hyonsup beamed down on him.

"Let me look at your teeth."

Taisup opened his mouth wide. Rows of fillings shone brightly under the setting sun. Hyonsup gave him a gentle tap on his shoulder.

"Now, you have to watch real careful. No more candies!"

The little boy nodded and followed his brother, Wonsup.

Hyonsup turned around once again and silently bid a farewell, his swollen eyes caressing his mother's newly finished mound next to his father's.

"I will come back in a few days to see the tombstone is properly carved."

"I will come with you." Sunhee followed Hyonsup toward the road where the last hired taxi was waiting.

"Poor lady! You will never guess what she had to go through," sighed Hyonsup. "Ah, the worst things—I remember the time she tried to smuggle rice for us and was caught. I remember the night when my father divorced

299

her. Can you believe it? She just left, without even raising her voice."
Hyonsup walked with his hands in his pockets, his eyes fixed on the ground,
kicking rocks. "Now, it's all over. She's gone. But there's got to be more.
There's got to be!"

Sunhee cautiously slipped her hand into his.

"There are horrible times some of us have to live through. I guess
our mothers had the worst time of all. Those hard days during the Japanese
rule. I was very little then, but I remember the dark cotton chima and
the soiled chogori as she carried me on her back from place to place after
my father left for Manchuria. Not to mention the time we crossed the
38th parallel, the refugee life, her tireless efforts to provide for us.
Sometimes doing the lowest sort of work. But I don't want to think about
it now. I don't want to think about it at all. All I want to remember is
that my mother is the one who brought us all up and made me meet a
person like you." Sunhee showed him a bright smile. Hyonsup smiled
back at her, the first smile since his mother's death. He turned to take
a last glimpse of the graveyard falling far behind.

"Funny though," said Hyonsup. "No matter what kind of road
they've taken, in the end they all arrive to the same place like that, occupying only that much earth. Do you think things will be different in the
other world, if such a place exists?"

Sunhee didn't answer. Shivering from the chill air, she snuggled closer
to him and slipped her hand into his in the pocket of his trench coat.

"I don't want to talk about it, not just yet. Let's talk about this world.
Have you decided who is to be your best man? I went to the florist with
my friend. Oh, those mums are gorgeous. But I doubt they'd last until
our wedding. I like carnations and roses but I don't think I can wait that
long. I guess I will have to settle with forsythias and azaleas. People will
think they are too vulgar for a bridal bouquet. What do you say?"

Hyonsup looked down on her, his tired eyes beginning to glow with
deep love.

"You know, Sunhee? I always thought of women from the north
as being rough and tough. You are not."

"Oh, I wouldn't count on that. I wouldn't count on that at all."

With the young couple inside, the last taxi moved off and soon picked
up speed making its way through the lonely autumn countryside.

300

Epilogue

Jungsoon had longed for but two things in life: to be reunited with her husband's family, and to see her sons well on the road to productive lives.

She would rest throughout eternity within inches of Yoon Daeyoung and the other family members she had served and loved.

Her sons took their place in the vanguard of the new Korea—educated men with quiet regard and affection for the traditions of their ancient homeland—men, and their wives, who helped the war-ravaged nation heal and earn a proud place in the computerized world.

Ishikawa's son got off the taxi and stood in the heart of the capital city that houses 10 million people and their accessories. Since the re-establishment of diplomatic relations between Japan and Korea, he had frequently visited this country. Each time he came here, he got lost. The wood and brick house and the narrow alley where he used to play as a child were gone. So was the trust company his father used to work for. The gray-haired Japanese gentleman turned his head from side to side. "Aha!" He spotted the ornate architecture of the South Gate amid the high-rise buildings and looped thoroughfares. His mouth was curved into a smile of satisfaction as he mingled with the crowd that flowed toward the hotel where his wife, Yukiko, was waiting. "Arirang, arirang," he hummed a Korean folk song. It felt good to be walking in a friendly country.

Chinjoo, moved to Cheju Island and started a new life. She built a new ranch by an ancient evergreen. For twenty years her cattle grazed and multiplied in her green pasture. When she finally decided it was time for her to quit, she sold her lands to an ambitious young man from Kyongsang Province. Now seventy, she enjoys her new business in Seoul—tending her great granddaughter.

THE END

Glossary

bed. The bed is a thick quilted mat used by one person, and is folded away during the day.

bulgogi. A Korean meat dish (thinnly sliced, seasoned and barbecued).

changgi. An oriental chess game, with round wooden pieces and a board. Each piece has its own name with a Chinese character printed on it.

chigeh. A wooden A-frame for carrying loads, worn on a man's back with straps around the shoulders.

chima. A pleated skirt, extending to the feet and worn by women.

chinjoo. A pearl.

chogori. A shirt, crescent-sleeved with a tie attached on each front gore and worn by men and women. Women's chogori extends to the chest and men's chogori covers the waist.

dining room. Every room except kitchen and storage is multi-purpose: dining, living, studying and sleeping.

don. A unit of weight ($=0.1325$ ounce, or 3.7565 grams).

fuel hole. A little fireplace on the ground level attached to the outside wall of a room, in which fire is made to heat the room. Fuel holes in the kitchen serve a dual purpose: cooking, and heating the master room attached to the kitchen.

fulling. An old-fashioned ironing process by pounding the cloths on a stone block with a pair of small bats.

garden balsam. Annual plant. Girls in rural area used the flower and leaves to color their fingernails.

go. An oriental chess game utilizing black and white stones and a checkered board.

haam. A chest of silk sent to the bride's home by the groom's family on the eve of their wedding.

hall room. A large room size hall between the master room and the opposite room with or without doors, facing the courtyard. The floor is laid with wood, varnished or waxed, about two feet above the ground and on the same level as the other rooms.

jangkoo. A Korean drum.

kayakum. A Korean harp. Twelve strings set on a piece of board and plucked with the fingers.

kisaeng. A singing girl who entertains men.

kimchee. Pickled cabbages or radish, seasoned with spices such as garlic and ground hot pepper.

kimono. A wide-sleeved Japanese robe worn with a sash.

magoja. A traditional two-button jacket for men.

majigi. A field wide enough for planting about four gallons of seeds.

mandoo. A dumpling filled with seasoned chopped meat and vegetables. A wonton.

Meiji. Emperor of Japan (1867-1912) who opened his country to Western civilization.

mompei. Trousers worn by Japanese and Korean women during World War II.

nengmyun. Cold noodles in iced soup.

ondol. A heating system of traditional Korean homes. The level of a room is raised so the fire in the fuel hole heats the large stone block under the floor. The floor, covered with baked clay, is laid with shiny glazed paper.

paji. Men's loose trousers, tied at the waist and ankles.

posun. A traditional sock, pointed up at the toe, lined and stuffed with cotton.

premises. A separate courtyard and a building before going into the main courtyard and house.

soojungkwa. A dessert of persimmon, sugar, ginger root and water.

sool. Wine of rice.

table. A table is shaped like a large tray with four short legs like those of a coffee table, and high enough to accommodate a person sitting crosslegged. Made of wood, it is lacquered or varnished.

Taewonkun. Prince Regent and father of King Kojong. He ruled the country when the king was very young. Emperor Kojong was virtually the last king of Korea before he was forced to abdicate in favor of his son in 1907.

tatami. A floor covering in a Japanese house.

tubu. A soybean cake. Tofu in Japanese.

turumagi. A robe-like overcoat. (Upper part is made like a chogori but the length extends to the ankles.)

yangban. Originally meant two classes (civil and military) of nobility which ruled throughout the Yi dynasty. Refers to any of those and their descendants.

yangdan. A thickly woven silk for cool weather.

yobo. A term of address used between husband and wife.

younggam. A term of address used by an elderly wife to her elderly husband.

yumjoo. A string of beads, usually wooden.

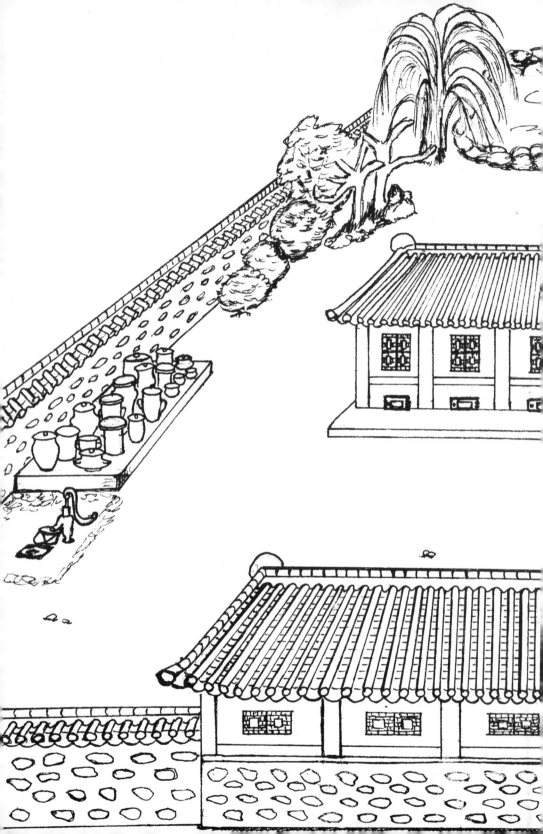